AN HONORABLE GERMAN

Charles McCain

GRAND CENTRAL
PUBLISHING

NEW YORK   BOSTON

Copyright © 2009 by Charles McCain

Grand Central Publishing
Hachette Book Group
237 Park Avenue
New York, NY 10017

Visit our Web site at www.HachetteBookGroup.com.

Printed in the United States of America

First Edition: May 2009
10 9 8 7 6 5 4 3 2 1

Grand Central Publishing is a division of Hachette Book Group, Inc. The Grand Central Publishing name and logo is a trademark of Hachette Book Group, Inc.

Library of Congress Cataloging-in-Publication Data
McCain, Charles L.
    An honorable German / Charles L. McCain. — 1st ed.
        p. cm.
    ISBN 978-0-446-53898-5
    1. Germany. Kriegsmarine — Officers — Fiction. 2. World War, 1939-1945 — Naval Operations, German — Fiction. 3. War stories. gsafd 4. Suspense fiction. Gsfad. I. Title.
    PS3613.C344 H66 2009
    813'.6—dc22

                                                                          2008033187

Book design by Charles Sutherland

With love to my older sister Mimi,
who many times in her life has given me the courage to go on.

And in respectful memory of my friend and mentor Al Rose,
who encouraged me to write.

AN
HONORABLE
GERMAN

CHAPTER ONE

THE SOUTH ATLANTIC
ABOARD THE GERMAN POCKET BATTLESHIP *ADMIRAL GRAF SPEE*
30 SEPTEMBER 1939
0830 HOURS

"Bridge!"

"Bridge, aye."

"One ship, fine on the starboard bow."

Max focused his binoculars on the starboard horizon and saw a thin tower of smoke. He stiffened. A warship? No. Must be a freighter. A warship would never make that amount of smoke— gave you away to the enemy too quickly.

"Bridge to gun director, train rangefinder on smoke," he ordered, his command passed by the telephone talker. The officers in the gunnery directing post, high above the bridge, could see much farther through their optical range-finding device.

In a few moments the telephone talker, receiving information over his headset, relayed the word to Max. "Herr Oberleutnant, gunnery says the ship is a freighter, three to four thousand tons. Range is ten kilometers."

"Acknowledged. Continue tracking."

Max took up the metal phone that connected him to the captain's sea cabin.

"Ja?"

"Oberleutnant Brekendorf reporting from the bridge, Herr Kapitän. We've sighted a small freighter about ten kilometers off the starboard bow."

"Coming."

Max's pulse quickened. They'd been wandering around out here for three weeks, searching the empty ocean, waiting for this. Max again put the binoculars to his eyes and swept the sea; the blue water shimmered in the morning sun, the symmetry of the view spoiled only by the smudge on the horizon. Around him, the South Atlantic stretched away seemingly to the ends of the earth.

"Good morning, Oberleutnant."

Max turned to see Dieter step onto the bridge with his usual wry smile. A dark smear of grease cut diagonally across his forehead. They had been friends since their cadet days at the Marineschule Mürwik. An engineering officer on *Graf Spee,* Dieter stood sweating in his leather coat and pants—standard issue for the engineers, designed to protect them from the engine room machinery. Comfort had not been taken into account. When *Spee* went to full speed with all eight of her diesels on line, the temperature in the engine room went to one hundred twenty degrees. Dieter paused to let the fresh salt breeze wash over him.

"What brings you up from the bowels of hell?" Max asked.

"Fuel consumption report for the Kommandant."

"I hope we have enough for a chase."

Dieter lifted his eyebrows. "Are we having one?"

"We may. Just sighted a freighter off the starboard bow."

"Well, don't worry, we're not down to the paint thinner yet." They laughed.

"Attention on deck!" a starched bridge messenger called.

Everyone came to rigid attention as Captain Langsdorff made his way to the center of the bridge. Langsdorff removed the cigar from his mouth. "Stand easy," he said, and the men resumed their positions.

The captain raised his binoculars, scanned the sea around them, then fixed his gaze on the distant smoke. He dropped the binoculars to his chest and lit a fresh cigar from the stinking butt of the old one. Langsdorff was the only man Max knew who chain-smoked cigars. Taking up his binoculars again, the captain peered once more at the unknown ship, balancing the binoculars on his fingertips, his body swaying to the easy motion of *Graf Spee*. "What do you make of her, Oberleutnant?"

Max answered carefully. There was a great difference between identifying silhouettes and pictures of British ships in your cabin and saying for sure that a smudge on the horizon was a British freighter. "Appears to be British built, Herr Kapitän."

Langsdorff let his gaze linger on Max, and Max felt the captain's disapproval. Langsdorff stood silent for a moment, then looked again at the ship. Taking the binoculars away from his eyes, he noticed Dieter, who came to attention under the captain's stare. "Yes?"

"Fuel consumption report, Herr Kapitän."

"Thank you but not now, Falkenheyn. Muster your boarding party and stand by."

"Jawohl, Herr Kapitän." Dieter executed a sharp salute, raised an eyebrow at Max, and hurried off the bridge. Langsdorff returned his attention to the unknown ship.

"Range?"

"Nine kilometers now, Herr Kapitän."

Langsdorff took the cigar from his mouth and studied the ash. Max knew the captain had to be careful: orders prohibited him from interfering with neutral shipping. Three weeks into the war would not be the time to start protests burning the wires to Berlin from neutral powers whose ships were being sunk by a German commerce raider. That was exactly what the Oberkommando der Kriegsmarine wanted to avoid. *Graf Spee*'s mission was to sink

British merchant ships and draw off units of the Royal Navy from other duties. It did not include engaging enemy warships, and definitely did not include blowing some Swedish or American freighter out of the water by mistake. The Naval War Staff in Berlin had been very clear on these points in their operational orders—in fact, they regarded the matter with such concern that, on this cruise, *Graf Spee* reported to Berlin directly, bypassing the admiral commanding Marinegruppenkommando West in Wilhelmshaven altogether. This had caused quite a row—Marinegruppenkommando West was supposed to control all German warships in the Atlantic—but *Graf Spee* and her two sister pocket battleships were the pride of the German fleet; Admiral Raeder himself, commander in chief of the German navy, wanted to keep close tabs on their performance. "I believe *Ajax* was on mercantile patrol in these waters before the war, yes?" Langsdorff asked Max.

"She was, Herr Kapitän."

Langsdorff pursed his lips for a moment. "Have turret Anton's center barrel depressed to the deck."

"Jawohl, Herr Kapitän."

Max addressed himself to the telephone talker, who passed the order over the system to the captain of the forward turret. A hydraulic whine sounded through the bridge as Anton's center barrel was lowered. From a distance, the turret would appear to have only two barrels, like the forward turret of H.M.S. *Ajax*, a Royal Navy cruiser familiar to merchant ships in the area.

"Range?"

"Seven kilometers now, Herr Kapitän."

"Sound action stations."

Max nodded to the signalman, who jerked the red-handled battle alarm upward. Gongs sounded throughout the ship while loudspeakers blared: "Achtung! Action stations! Achtung! Action stations!"

The sailors dashed for their battle posts, hundreds of shoes pounding steel decks throughout the ship. Guns revolved outward from the center line. Stewards snatched crockery from tables in the mess, as watertight doors were slammed shut and dogged home up and down *Graf Spee*. All eight of the massive diesel engines were fired off and connected to the propeller shafts.

In the gun turrets, hydraulic loaders rammed the six-hundred-seventy-pound shells into the breeches of the main batteries. Orange ready lights for each of the batteries flickered on in the gun directing tower, where the gunnery officer and his staff took the range of the small ship in the distance. The big guns would be ready to aim and fire as soon as the captain gave the order.

On the bridge, several more messengers and officers appeared. Max looked at his watch. "Cleared for action, Herr Kapitän. Two minutes, forty-one seconds."

Langsdorff nodded. "Excellent, excellent."

With the sailors buttoned up in their action stations, a strange quiet descended over the ship, broken only by the swish of water as it flowed down the steel flanks of *Graf Spee* and the creak of the ship as she rolled in the seaway. Max cupped his trembling hands against the breeze and lit a cigarette. Captain Langsdorff lit another cigar.

Max drew on his cigarette, looked through his binoculars, then began to repeat the motion but stopped abruptly. He must not appear nervous. He was nervous, it was true—but not from fear. He was sure of that.

"Range?"

"Six kilometers, Herr Kapitän."

"She's signaling," the lookout yelled.

"Read it out!" Langsdorff ordered.

"Glad to . . . see . . . you . . . big brother," Max read, translating the Morse code, binoculars at his eyes. Like all German navy officers, he'd studied English at the Marineschule Mürwik and, at the urging of his father, had continued his studies since leaving the Academy—mainly by reading the American movie magazines his fiancée, Mareth, gave him. Max knew a lot more about Tallulah

Bankhead's love life than he wanted to, but he now spoke fluent English, as did the captain and many other officers aboard the ship.

"Signal, signal . . . 'None shall make them afraid,'" the captain said.

The clattering of the Morse lamp sounded through the bridge. Max kept his eyes fixed on the small ship.

"Range?"

"Five kilometers, Herr Kapitän."

The freighter's Morse lamp blinked to life again. "But . . . beat your . . . ploughshares into . . . swords," Max translated.

Langsdorff smiled. "A sense of humor, that one. Signal, 'Heave to, I have Admiralty dispatches for you.'"

The bridge signalman began to work his lamp.

Max lowered the binoculars and squinted at the horizon. All traces of mist from the dawn had burned away in the sun, bright now in the morning sky. Through the open bridge windows, the breeze continued to blow. He wiped the salt mist from the lenses of the binoculars, then, balancing the glasses on the tips of his fingers to cushion them from the gyration of the ship, peered again at the freighter. Suddenly the ship veered hard to the left, away from *Graf Spee*.

"She's turning to port!"

Langsdorff rapped out his orders. "Run up the colors! All ahead full!" The signalmen hoisted the blood red ensign of the Kriegsmarine—international maritime law required a belligerent warship to identify itself before firing, and Langsdorff was a stickler for the rules. As the ensign rose up the halyard, bridge messengers reached for the engine telegraphs and rang for full speed. Below, in the engine room, duplicate telegraphs and blinking lights alerted the engineers that new orders had been given. They responded instantly. Max watched the revolution counter move swiftly upward. "Making turns for twenty-eight knots," he said, his voice strained from excitement.

The pocket battleship shuddered as she went to full speed, her huge propellers foaming the sea beneath her stern. The steel deck vibrated heavily under Max's shoes.

"Signalman!"

"Ja, Herr Kapitän." The chief signalman snapped to attention.

"Signal, 'Heave to, no wireless transmitting.'"

Bright signal flags soared up Spee's signal halyards now that she was close enough to dispense with the Morse lamp, but the small ship continued turning away, soon presenting her stern to Graf Spee. A square of brilliant red cloth broke over the stern—the Red Duster of the British Merchant Navy. What fools! Spee could blow the freighter out of the water at eighteen kilometers. By God the English were always stubborn in their pride; Max had never met an Englishman who wasn't arrogant as a Prussian general.

"She's transmitting a distress signal!" one of the young telephone talkers screeched, repeating what the codebreaking squad down below was telling him.

"No need to shout," Langsdorff said quietly. "What's she saying?"

"She's, she's . . . transmitting, 'Immediate to admiral commanding South Atlantic, RRR S.S. Clement gunned.'" RRR was British Admiralty code for attack by a surface raider. Max already had his hand on the gunnery phone when Langsdorff delivered his next order: "A shot over her bow, quickly!"

They could not afford to have the freighter disclose their location and bring down the wrath of the British fleet.

"Bridge here," Max barked to the gunnery officer on the other end of the phone. "Order from captain: the target is the merchant ship. A shot over her bow."

Immediately the firing gongs sounded, warning the ship's company that the main battery was about to fire.

Turret Anton revolved under electric orders from the gun director. Max bent his knees and gripped the metal handhold just below the bridge windows to avoid being thrown to the deck. The forward battery fired with a deafening report, the recoil blasting throughout the ship. As the shock waves passed through him Max instantly smelled the cordite propellant. A tower of white water shot into the air a hundred meters forward of the freighter's bow.

But the ship continued her flight, oily smoke pouring from her stack, and *Graf Spee* kept up her charge, spray breaking over her as she beat through the swells. *Spee*'s Morse lamp rattled back to life, continually repeating the order to cease transmitting, seconded by the whipping signal flags.

"Still transmitting, Herr Kapitän," the telephone talker said.

"Range?"

"One and a half kilometers, Herr Kapitän."

"Rake her bridge—quickly, quickly!"

Max snatched up the gunnery phone again. "Order from captain. Target is the bridge of the merchantman. Forward machine guns, fire!"

The staccato rap of the machine guns rang out, bullets punching holes in the freighter's superstructure and smashing her bridge windows. But still the propellers of the British ship churned up an angry wake as she tried to make her best speed. Max's heart thumped in his chest. Every minute she kept up her distress call increased the danger for *Graf Spee*. Still, the British captain displayed courage, he gave him that; probably an old sea dog, haughty as a lord, stubborn as pig iron, knowledge of half the world's oceans tucked into his mind. Max wondered if the captain would be stubborn enough to get his crew killed.

Suddenly the British ship began to yaw. A crewman dashed to the stern and struck the Red Duster.

"Transmission ceased, Herr Kapitän."

"Cease firing," Langsdorff ordered, "reduce speed to dead slow."

The machine guns fell silent, spent brass cartridges tinkling as they rolled around on the deck. Max could feel the ship slow beneath him as her way fell off.

"Oberleutnant."

"Ja, Herr Kapitän?"

"See the boarding party away. I want the captain, the chief engineer, and any of the ship's papers they can find. Remind them. And Oberleutnant?"

"Herr Kapitän?"

"Of course, there is to be no bloodshed."

"Jawohl, Herr Kapitän."

Max saluted and ducked out of the bridge. He grasped the metal side rails of the outboard stairway with both hands, then lifted his feet and slid to the boat deck where he found the boarding party formed up, Dieter at their side, trying his best to look stern. In front of the sailors, both he and Max were very serious. Langsdorff always told them, "If you don't take yourselves seriously, you cannot expect the men to do so." Since Max outranked him by a grade, Dieter came to attention first and gave Max a parade-ground salute. Max returned the salute with equal formality.

"Orders from the bridge," Max said.

"Boarding party standing by, sir."

Max repeated the captain's orders. Dieter saluted again, then faced his crew and ordered them into the sixty-foot motor launch. Once they'd settled in, one of *Graf Spee*'s two cranes plucked the boat from the deck and lowered it into the sea.

Max returned to the bridge and watched the launch speed toward the British ship, its sharp bow throwing up spray. The Brits weren't waiting. They clambered into their own boats, lowered them, and began to row frantically away, oars thrashing the water—a useless gesture since Dieter quickly overtook them. He seized the British officers wanted by the captain and brought them to the deck of *Graf Spee*. They left the remaining British crew to sail for shore—maybe fifty kilometers. *Spee* would have rescued the men if they'd been another fifty kilometers out from land. That evening, Langsdorff would report the position of the British life-boats to the marine station at Pernambuco on the six-hundred-meter emergency band.

Max met the British officers with a rigid salute, nearby German sailors also coming to attention. Langsdorff insisted all prisoners be treated with proper military courtesy, and his men needed little prodding to respect this order. Such courtesy was part of the brotherhood of the sea. Max led the three British officers from the deck to the captain's formal day cabin. Outside the door stood two sentries, arms crossed, each with a drawn dagger in his right hand, the blade held across his chest. Max ushered the British officers into the well-appointed cabin, its stuffed sofas looking incongruous in a warship, and motioned for them to sit. A bookshelf along the far wall held leather-bound titles in both German and English, including Winston Churchill's *World Crisis* in two volumes, prominently displayed. "Gentlemen, if I may," Max said, "I am Senior Lieutenant Brekendorf, second watch officer of *Admiral Graf Spee*."

"I am Captain Harris and this is First Officer Gill and Chief Engineer Bryant," said the oldest of the three men, his thick Scottish accent hard for Max to understand. His uniform coat had four gold rings on each sleeve, but the other two men were in shirt-sleeves and bore no insignia of rank. They'd left their ship in a hurry; none of them even had their caps.

Max ordered Langsdorff's steward to bring coffee, then offered each prisoner a cigarette. Lighting one himself, he considered Harris briefly through a haze of smoke. The man had taken a pointless risk—the war would be over in a year. Everyone knew it—the British could never hold out against Germany. And this wasn't even Britain's fight: the Germans had gone into Poland only to reclaim what had been stolen from them at Versailles after the First War. But the conceited Brits couldn't stand to see Germany regain her rightful place in the world; Chamberlain had foolishly signed a treaty with Warsaw committing Great Britain to war should the Poles be attacked. Well, now the Germans had Poland and the British had their war. "Why did you run, Captain? You placed your crew in unnecessary danger."

Harris stared at him for a moment. "I was a prisoner in the first lot and didn't fancy spending the second go-round that way as well."

"You were captured by Germany in the First War?"

The captain nodded and puffed his cigarette a few times before speaking. "By the bloody raider *Wolf* in 1915, on an Argyle and Dundee steamer bound for Calcutta. Bastard caught us at dawn and there was nothing to be done for it but haul down the colors and go over in our boats. I was a prisoner on that damned cow for months."

The steward interrupted with coffee, serving the men in china cups. It was good coffee too, bitter and strong, the kind one needed at sea.

"Of course, we will want your codebooks and cargo manifests," Max said.

Harris smiled pleasantly. "Of course, I put them over the side as soon as I saw you weren't *Ajax*. We keep them in a canvas bag weighted with a firebrick, just like in the First War. They're at the bottom of the drink if you want them. I thought you bloody Germans were supposed to be so bloody smart."

The other two officers looked away. Blood came up in Max's face. Arrogant, these British—even as prisoners, sipping coffee in their captor's ship. He wanted to hit the British captain but squared his shoulders and nodded curtly instead. "Naturally, that is the usual thing," he said. "What cargo were you carrying?"

"Oh, for God's sake, man," Harris snapped. "I'm not obliged to tell you that."

The firing gong sounded, cutting the discussion short. The British officers looked quizzically at Max. "The firing gong, gentlemen. I'm afraid we're going to sink your ship. Kindly place your cups down and brace yourselves." Max held on to the captain's desk—bolted to the deck, like all the furniture on the ship.

A great roar sounded, like dynamite going off in a well. *Graf Spee* heeled from the recoil, tossing all their coffee cups onto the carpet, the report sharp in Max's ears, even belowdecks. First Officer Gill leapt to the porthole, followed by the chief engineer. Harris, white-faced, kept his seat, staring at the bulkhead. Max glanced through the porthole but saw no smoke or flame rising from *Clement*. The abandoned freighter bobbed placidly on the swell.

"Missed her," Gill said, almost to himself.

Max said nothing. Presently the gong sounded and the big guns fired again. This time Max watched the shells fall into the sea, sending up geysers of seawater well short of the British ship. He felt the heat rising in his face again. No one spoke. When the third volley missed, Harris turned and looked at Max.

"Hard to find the range in this chop," Max said, feeling foolish as soon as he spoke. Harris raised an eyebrow. The sea was hardly raging. *Graf Spee* was heavily armed for a ship her size—too heavily armed—and the main batteries made her top-heavy, which had a poor effect on her seakeeping and, in turn, on the accuracy of her guns. The gunnery officer had managed a perfect warning shot over *Clement*'s bow during the chase, but Max wondered now if it had been nothing more than luck.

"Perhaps we should wait until this storm passes," Harris offered, blinking in the bright sunlight pouring into the cabin.

"Of course our guns are also not designed to engage a ship at such close range," Max said. This excuse also sounded foolish, though it was true. Another loud volley missed its mark, sending up more towers of water. At this rate it would be easier to row a boat over to *Clement* and shoot holes in the merchantman's hull with a pistol. Max resolved to provide no further comment and the four men fell silent as *Spee*'s big guns banged away, shaking the cabin, knocking several books from the shelves. Captain Langsdorff became so frustrated that he ordered a pair of torpedoes fired at the merchantman. Both missed. Finally the gunnery officer found the mark and managed to set *Clement* afire; Max watched the flames spread across her deck. Suddenly the freighter exploded, sending a bright orange fireball high into the air.

"Gasoline?" Max asked in surprise.

"Kerosene, sir," said Gill. "Packed in cases."

Max shook his head. Harris had braved *Graf Spee*'s fire with a hold full of kerosene.

"Steward, a beer for each of these officers." Max looked at each one of the three in turn. "I must ask each of you for your word of honor that you will not interfere in any way with the operation of the ship, else I will have to order an armed guard over you at all times."

Captain Harris answered without meeting Max's eyes again. "You have it, laddie."

"Then, gentlemen, I must return to my duties. Our captain will be along shortly to speak with you. Please make yourselves comfortable. If you need anything, kindly make your request to the captain's steward or to one of the sentries outside the bulkhead. Our barbershop and canteen are both available to you and our medical and dental staff shall attend upon your request." He bowed slightly to the men as he'd learned to do at the Naval Academy, and the two junior officers nodded back. The captain just sat in silence.

Graf Spee had stood down from action stations; the men had returned to their regular duties. Everywhere Max looked, the crew repaired the damage caused by the repeated firing of the big guns. Doors had been lifted from their hinges, flooring cracked, paint stripped off bulkheads, and light bulbs shattered everywhere by the concussions.

When Max reached the administrative office, he opened the door to find two clerks wiping ink from the desks and floor.

"What is this?"

"Inkwells not secured, Herr Oberleutnant," the senior rating said. Max frowned. What a mess. He helped the men clean up. By the time they finished his uniform was stained with black ink.

His bridge watch was over and he'd been on duty since 0200, but before he slept Max sat in the office and read through the radio intercepts of the past hours. *Graf Spee* had a special staff of B-Service cipher experts whose only task was to intercept and decode as many British radio signals as possible. They spent their time in front of special radio receivers that automatically combed all frequencies and stopped on one when it detected a message being transmitted. And the B-Service men were damned good. They had picked up and decoded the signal from the British Admiralty declaring war on Germany three hours before *Spee* received official notice from Seekriegsleitung—the Naval War Staff—in Berlin. Most of the codebreakers had been mathematicians before the war, others wireless operators aboard merchant ships. Often they could immediately decrypt the ciphers used by the British Merchant Navy. Any code they couldn't break in thirty minutes was sent on to their parent unit back in the Reich.

The B-Service men could also put their mathematical skills to more mundane use. They'd recently relieved Max of two weeks' pay playing cards in the officers' mess. Max's father had warned him about gambling away all his money in the service, but the money was gone and there was nothing to be done for it. Still, the B-Service men were good comrades, even though they seemed to do nothing but smoke, play skat, and listen intently to the wireless.

Max read carefully through the new messages but none of the ships broadcasting were anywhere near *Graf Spee*. Damn. Finding a transmission from a ship close enough to intercept would be a lot quicker than this endless patrolling, roaming back and forth across the empty South Atlantic like *Flying Dutchman*. Traffic was sparse now in this, the third week of the war. British merchantmen were under strict Admiralty orders to maintain radio silence. Except for occasional lapses, they did so. Max wondered if *Spee*'s sister ship, *Deutschland*, was having better luck on her assignments farther north, along the trade routes that crossed to England from Canada and the United States.

He replaced the messages in their notebook and returned to his cabin, stripping off his ink-stained uniform and stuffing it into the laundry bag at the foot of his closet. Tian, head of the six Chinese laundrymen on board, would retrieve the bag in the morning and return the uniform, starched and pressed, by midafternoon. All German naval ships employed Chinese laundrymen, though Max could hardly imagine where on earth they came from. Probably the old German concession at Tsingtao—another piece of German territory stolen by the Allies after the First War, along with the Germania Brewery that made Tsingtao beer.

Max massaged his neck, muscles still knotted from the tension of the morning, then reached for the picture on his small desk. The frame had been cracked by the gun blasts. Mareth stared out from under the spiderwebbed glass. Max had taken the photo himself on a dock in Kiel two summers ago. Mareth's face was tilted slightly downward and she looked askance at the camera with a close-mouthed smile, shy but crafty. A breeze off the water rippled her long blond hair. One of the navy's new destroyers crossed the harbor behind her. What time would it be in Berlin now? Night. She would be getting ready for bed—letting her hair down from its ponytail, slipping on her silk pajamas. Or maybe one of his old cotton jerseys. Max smiled to himself. Was he homesick after only three weeks at sea? Get a hold of yourself. Still, how he wished he could tell Mareth in person about the excitement of finally sighting a ship, about the capture and even the embarrassment he'd felt with the British officers as he constantly made excuses about *Graf Spee*'s lack of accuracy. She would laugh at that, and then Max would be able to laugh at it himself. He put the picture back on his desk and climbed into his bunk.

Enough sleep was hard to come by on combat assignment. He

tried to get some after his morning watch and then a little more late in the evening. Like the crew of any warship at sea, the men of *Graf Spee* moved in the strict routine required for keeping a third of them on duty at all times, but this routine was frequently disrupted by the call to action stations, drills, and other essential tasks. So Max had learned to take sleep when he could get it. Porthole covered, lights out, the droning of the ship's massive engines soon lulled him to sleep.

CHAPTER TWO

THE SOUTH ATLANTIC
DAY 102 OF THE WAR CRUISE OF *ADMIRAL GRAF SPEE*
2 DECEMBER 1939

MAX WOKE TO THE FOUR SHARP BELLS OF THE FLIEGERALARM: SHORT, short, long, short. He jerked open the door of his closet, snatched a uniform from its wooden hanger, and had a leg into his pants before he stopped. He felt no increase in the deck's vibration beneath his bare feet; the ship was not working up to her full speed, as she would immediately begin to do if a plane really attacked. Then he remembered the orders of the day: *Anti-aircraft guns will be exercised at 1400.* Damn. He folded his pants and climbed back into his bunk.

Odd that the launching of the floatplane had not wakened him. Usually the steam catapult made hell's own racket when it shot the Arado into the air. Max didn't envy the pilot—Spiering, a Luftwaffe man. He had to stream a target three hundred meters aft of the plane, then fly around and around the ship for hours so the anti-aircraft gun crews could practice their spotting and tracking skills. Max knew the endless circling would make him sick; Spiering didn't seem to mind, but pilots were daft. They'd do anything to be up in an aeroplane—even one like the Arado, which looked to Max like nothing more than a pile of aluminum and wood cobbled together with glue in someone's cellar. Sailors called it "the ship's parrot"; they loved to tell youngsters fresh from boot camp to go and find the ship's parrot. The new sailors would search for hours while the older men watched and had a laugh. Captain Langsdorff enjoyed the joke as well, though he would often be the one to finally let the youngsters off the hook by telling them where the ship's parrot was: on the catapult.

Max slept again, but it seemed only minutes before the action station alarm sounded, the bells shrill and demanding. Conditioned by countless drills, Max's body moved before his brain began to operate.

Dressing quickly, he stepped into the companionway, the river of sailors dashing for their battle posts parting to let him through. Some ran barefoot, shoes hanging around their necks by the laces. Others carried shirts or pants they hadn't had time to struggle into. Petty officers hurried the few laggards. "Schnell! Schnell!" Men of the gun crews wore black anti-flash overalls and looked like running bears as they barreled their way through the ship. The five short bells of the action station continued to sound: "Action stations! All hands to action stations!" the loudspeakers blared.

Lights flickered on and off as the electricians tested the circuits. Pictures were snatched from walls, deck rails removed, scuttles screwed tight over portholes, ready boxes of ammunition broken open at the anti-aircraft posts. One of the gunnery officers walked quickly past, face lathered with shaving cream. As soon as the engineers below saw the action station alarm begin to blink, they cut all unnecessary ship's water to give more pressure to the firefighting mains.

As Max hurried up the ladder to the bridge, two burly gunner's mates pushed him aside. "Warschau! Warschau!" Gangway! Gangway!

Max reached the bridge two minutes and ten seconds after the alarm sounded. Unlike the barely controlled bedlam on the decks, the bridge was calm and quiet. Captain Langsdorff insisted on it. No shouting, no idle talk. Several other officers had just arrived, breathing hard. Max pulled his binoculars from their bracket and took up his post in the middle of the bridge with a telephone talker and a bridge messenger on either side of him. As second watch officer, he passed the captain's orders to the rest of the ship during battle. The first watch officer, the senior navigation officer, and others took their positions toward the stern of the ship in the aft controlling station. From there, the first watch officer would assume command of *Graf Spee* if the captain was killed.

The hollow drone of the ventilating fans sounded as they sucked air into *Spee*'s mighty engines. Beneath Max, the ship began to vibrate terrifically as she went to her full speed. "Making turns for twenty-eight knots," Max told the captain, his voice rising over the fans.

On either side of him, the telephone talkers reported the ready status of the ship as it was relayed to them.

"Fore and aft engine rooms manned and ready."

"Main gunnery command manned and ready."

"Aft damage control station manned and ready."

"Aft controlling station manned and ready."

"B-Service standing by."

Max heard the reports out, mentally checking off the departments, and then looked at his watch. "Ship cleared for action, two minutes, fifty-three seconds, Herr Kapitän."

More than a thousand officers and men had taken up their action stations in that brief time. It was as if an anthill had been kicked over, then perfectly reestablished in three minutes. This efficiency came from incessant training. Max could not count the days, the weeks, they had steamed back and forth in the Baltic running to action stations, to firefighting stations, to anti-aircraft stations, day and night, under the gaze of Captain Langsdorff and his stopwatch; ship starting and stopping, slow ahead, all ahead full, all back full, all ahead emergency. Man overboard. Swing boats out! Fore engine room shut down. Steam on two engines, on one, on eight. Maneuver with engines, no rudder orders allowed. Steer from aft controlling. Junior officers taking charge while their seniors ground their teeth. Lights put out. Damage control parties finding their way in the dark. And always, always, the alarm bells with their different sounds for different emergencies: five short bells for action stations; short, short, long, short for anti-aircraft; two long bells for man overboard. Eventually he had wanted to smash every damned bell on the ship.

"Leutnant Spiering believes he has sighted a merchantman to the east of us," Langsdorff said. "Come hard starboard thirty degrees to a new course of zero eight five. Let's see what he's found."

Max leaned forward to the voice tube. "Helm!"

"Helm, aye."

"At right full rudder, come thirty degrees to new course of zero eight five degrees."

A moment passed and then the answering hail: "At right full rudder, coming thirty degrees to new course of zero eight five, Herr Oberleutnant."

At that rudder deflection, *Spee* heeled sharply to starboard as the helmsman brought the ship around to a course of almost due east. He had no bulky wheel to contend with; *Graf Spee*'s rudder was operated by push-button control. Because enemy ships aimed for the bridge in a sea battle, the helmsman sat in the heavily armored wheelhouse below the navigating bridge itself. If he were hit and killed, the standby helmsman in the aft controlling station took over.

Max reported the course change to Langsdorff.

"Acknowledged," the captain said, keeping the binoculars at his eyes.

Langsdorff made no secret of his dislike for Spiering. Like many of Göring's Luftwaffe boys, the pilot was arrogant, undisciplined, contemptuous of the navy. He had drawn the captain's wrath not three weeks before by continuing to machine-gun a stopped freighter for several minutes after *Graf Spee* had ceased fire. Afterward, brought before the captain in his formal day cabin with Max and Commander Kay present, Langsdorff asked, "You will please explain to me why you fired your weapon on a defenseless cargo vessel."

The pilot hesitated. "I—I was attacking an enemy, sir."

"Did you see *Graf Spee* firing?"

"No, sir."

"Why do you think *Graf Spee* was not firing at the freighter?"

"Because she was stopped and under our orders, sir."

"That is correct, Leutnant. She was stopped and under *my* orders, like you and everyone else aboard this vessel. You were not under attack but you fired your guns on innocent civilians. Such behavior is an affront to the honor of our country and my ship. You should be most thankful no one was seriously hurt."

"Yes, sir."

Before dismissing, Langsdorff had spent long moments with his blue eyes fixed on Leutnant Spiering, staring for a minute or more without so much as a blink. Now the captain's stern blue eyes continued to peer ahead through his binoculars as brief reports were given to him by the chief navigation officer, whose men were following Spiering's position on their chart. Around Max, the officers and men adjusted their hastily donned clothing without taking their eyes from their respective tasks. Langsdorff insisted on a neat appearance from his men at all times. Conducive to military discipline, he said. Max straightened his tie. He had learned to dress on the fly at the Marineschule Mürwik, where everything was double time and spit shine. No excuses.

Graf Spee, now worked up to her full twenty-eight knots, shuddered as she pushed her way through the waves.

"Oberleutnant?"

"Ja, Herr Kapitän?"

"The French flag, if you please."

"Jawohl, Herr Kapitän."

Max passed Langsdorff's order to the chief signalman, who took all of ten seconds to produce the tricolor of France from the ordered shelves of his flag locker. He rolled the flag into a ball, ran it up the signal mast abaft the bridge, and with a twist of the halyard, the French colors broke over *Graf Spee*. As long as the flag was hauled down before an attack commenced, international law would not be violated. To the untrained observer, looking from a distance, *Spee* resembled the French battleship *Dunkurque*; the flag would add to this illusion—and because the French had foolishly joined the British in their war against Germany, *Dunkurque* was a friendly ship to a British merchantman. If the hoax could fool the freighter's crew until they were under *Graf Spee*'s guns, the dispatch of a radio warning to the British Admiralty might be prevented.

Tricolor whipping from the signal mast, *Spee* charged toward the freighter, her prow breaking the waves, sending towers of spray into the air. Aft, the churning propellers left a two-kilometer wake. Swells advanced at a perpendicular angle and smacked against *Spee*, heeling her over back and forth. Max swayed like a metronome.

"Range?"

"Three kilometers now, Herr Kapitän."

"Can you identify her?"

This time Max had brought his heavy artillery—*Lloyd's Register of Merchant Shipping*—which provided the silhouette and essential details of every merchant ship in the world. He leafed through the book, found the page he was looking for, then peered again through his binoculars. "Appears to be a refrigerated ship of the Blue Star Line. *Doric Star*, I would say, Herr Kapitän. Ten thousand tons, built 1921 in the Lithgow yard in Glasgow. Speed is sixteen knots. Probably running home with a load of Argentine beef."

Langsdorff nodded. "Very good." The bridge fell quiet as they closed in. Apparently their ruse worked; *Doric Star* showed no signs of being alarmed.

Two kilometers from the merchant ship, Langsdorff broke the silence. "Come starboard two points and keep us bows on. Run up our flag. Signalman!"

"Ja, Herr Kapitän?"

"Signal, 'Heave to, no wireless transmitting.'"

The metallic clatter of the signal light sounded through the bridge. "Uncover notice," Langsdorff said, and Max passed this by megaphone to the sailors on each of the bridge wings, who unfurled the large canvas sign that hung just under the bridge windows: NO WIRELESS OR I WILL OPEN FIRE.

A half kilometer from the British ship Langsdorff came hard starboard. As her giant rudder bit the sea, *Graf Spee* turned broadside to the British ship. The electric motors whined as the main gun turrets revolved on their ball-bearing rollers to face the merchantman.

"Dead slow!"

The bridge messengers rang the brass engine telegraphs and set the needles to dead slow. Max watched the revolution indicator to see if the propeller shafts were slowing down. "Making turns for two knots," he reported to Langsdorff. "B-Service reports no wireless transmissions."

"Very well, Oberleutnant. Take the boarding party across yourself and personally search for the ship's papers, logbooks, anything."

This was their ninth capture, but so far they hadn't been able to capture any British naval codes. The B Service men were able to break a number of Royal Navy and British Merchant Navy codes, but these changed periodically and capturing a codebook would ease the strain of constant decoding.

Max quickly made his way to the boat deck, where Dieter had already mustered the boarding party. The older men had grown beards, now bushy and full in their third month at sea. Some of the younger sailors didn't have enough whiskers for a beard and they looked all the younger for it. Max empathized with them; he couldn't get the blond hair on his face to grow beyond a few pale strands. So he kept himself clean-shaven but wished he could grow a full beard and mustache like Dieter, who now looked more like a Wagnerian hero than an engineer.

Max returned Dieter's salute. "I will command this boarding party, Leutnant. All is in order?"

"All is in order, Oberleutnant."

Each sailor in the party carried a pistol and several potato-masher hand grenades. A piratical-looking lot, Max decided—a crew of Viking raiders. Carls, the senior petty officer in the group, handed Max a Luger. Max jammed the gun down the front of his belt and instantly felt ridiculous. If he removed the Luger, it would look bad to the men. Besides, Carls hadn't given him a holster. Max knew that as an officer there were times when one had to go along with what the men wanted you to do.

He ordered his crew into the launch.

After the crane had deposited them in the water, Viktor, the coxswain, gunned the engine and they moved swiftly toward the ship. Spray flew into the boat and Max could taste the salt on his lips.

Viktor maneuvered them underneath the rope ladder the Brits had trailed over the side. Tendrils of rust streaked the hull of the ship, belying the neat appearance she had presented from a distance. Many British freighters looked this way. Owners had scrimped on maintenance during the Depression years. Max stood up in the launch and managed only with difficulty to keep his footing as the boat bucked up and down in the swell. As the officer in charge, he went first. On the upswing he jumped for the ladder, caught it, then banged painfully into the side of the ship. The pistol felt cold and greasy against his stomach as he struggled up the rungs. Below, Dieter grabbed hold of the ladder and began to climb, the rest of the crew following after him.

Three more pulls and Max came level with the gangway, blood pounding in his temples from the exertion and excitement. On his face he fixed his fiercest look, came to attention, and gave a curt salute to the British captain and his officers, who were assembled at the gangway. Max's crew formed up behind him, pistols drawn.

"Gentlemen, I am Senior Lieutenant Brekendorf. You are now prisoners of the German navy," Max said. "Captain, please assemble your men on the aft deck for transport to our ship."

The captain, red-faced, glared at Max, then saluted in return. "Captain Stubbs, *Doric Star*." He gave the first officer a grudging nod. "Assemble the crew."

Under his prodding, the English crew—more than forty men, rumpled and mostly unshaven—formed themselves up aft of the bridge. Max instructed them to lower the lifeboats. "The first officer will remain aboard to conduct me through the ship," he told the captain. "You will accompany your men to *Graf Spee*."

"It's *Spee* that's got us then," Stubbs muttered. "Thought you were *Deutschland*." The captain and first officer looked at each other for a moment. "Carry on, Number One," the captain said, then he turned away and loaded his men into the lifeboats.

Max turned to Dieter and Carls, both of them with their pirate beards. To this image of fierceness, Carls added a tattoo of the Kaiser's Imperial Crest on one arm and the crest of the Kronprinz on the other. "Got them in China, sir," he'd once told Max. "The Chinks do tattoos good." Carls also had a windjammer tattooed on his chest—a living picture of the first ship he had sailed on. He carried a submachine gun slung across his shoulder with three potato-masher hand grenades in his belt.

"Have them search the ship, as usual. I'll take the radio room. Stay alert." Max turned to the British officer. "You'll show me the radio room, yes?"

"This way, sir," the first officer said.

He led Max below. When they got to the radio room the wooden door was locked. "Key?"

"I don't have it."

Max scowled at the Englishman. They never admitted defeat,

these people. He drew back and gave the door his best soccer kick, bursting it open. The room was in a shambles. Drawers had been pulled out and overturned on the floor, cabinets ransacked, charts and notices ripped from the metal walls, papers strewn everywhere. Pencils rolled to and fro across the deck as the ship wallowed in the swell. The wireless set itself was still on, warm to the touch. Max turned it off and looked at the British officer. "Codebooks?"

"O-o-overboard, sir."

"Cargo manifest?"

"Overboard."

Max frowned. Dammit. The scene in the radio room suggested that the Brits had been looking for something—possibly something they hadn't found. He sat down in the radio operator's chair and sifted through the various papers covering the counter and desk at his side. A muffled sound came from belowdecks, but Max ignored it.

The next explosion threw him to the deck.

"You bloody English swine!" he yelled at the first officer.

Another blast from below. The first officer cringed in the corner, breathing rapidly. Steel plates creaked as the ship began to list. From the shelves above, books cascaded to the desk. Max drew the Luger from his pants and lunged at the Englishman. "What's happening, damn you!"

The first officer's eyes were wide. His mouth opened and closed but no words came out. Max jammed his pistol into the officer's mouth and the acrid smell of urine filled the cabin. "What's happening?" He withdrew the gun to the Britisher's lips.

"Scuttling charges, sir. In the engine room. Cap—Captain planted them."

Max shoved the Luger's barrel back into the first officer's mouth. "If any of my men die, I will kill you." He jerked the muzzle out and ran from the room.

Almost losing his balance on the listing deck, he flung his free hand out to steady himself. The explosives must have blown open the seacocks, allowing tons of water to pour into the ship. Max smelled burning meat. The cargo had caught fire. He burst out onto the main deck. Dieter was assembling the men by the gangway. Max counted them. Only ten. Shit. Damn these English. "Who's missing?" he shouted.

"Carls," Dieter answered. "He was going to the engine room."

"Into the boat, now!" Max ordered. Three long blasts sounded from *Graf Spee*'s whistle—the recall signal. Except for hand grenades, the boarding party had carried no explosives with them to the British ship, so Langsdorff knew something was wrong. Max dashed to the companionway leading to the interior. "Carls! Carls!" he called down. No answer. He descended to the next deck. "Carls!"

"I'm down here, Herr Oberleutnant."

Max dropped down the ladder. Carls lay in the corridor propped on his elbows, one leg splayed at an unnatural angle. Smoke blew up from below and set Max to coughing.

"Explosion threw me against the bulkhead, Herr Oberleutnant," Carls said. "Leg looks to be broke." His face was ashen, but his voice remained calm. Carls was older than most of the men, a prewar petty officer who had enlisted in the navy in 1915, during the First War. Skillful, reliable, steady in a crisis, good with a knife; killed three mutinous sailors who attacked his captain during the Kiel mutiny in 1918, so the story went. But he was a big man, well over two hundred pounds, most of it muscle. Max wasn't sure he could move Carls. No time to summon the others.

"Carls, can you sit up?"

"I will try, Herr Oberleutnant."

The smoke thickened. Max labored for oxygen.

He knelt between Carls's legs with his back to the larger man. "Carls, wrap your arms around my neck." He grasped Carls by the thighs. The petty officer gasped in pain. Max grimaced with the strain. He leaned forward, putting all his strength into his legs, and got halfway to his feet before pitching forward. Carls let out another sharp gasp as the two of them toppled together. Max's face slammed into the deck beneath Carls's weight and he tasted blood. He was not strong enough to do this.

"Go, Herr Oberleutnant," Carls said, rolling off sideways to let Max up.

Smoke billowed around them, thick and black. Max hesitated. How would he get Carls to the upper deck? Then he heard the pounding of feet, and suddenly Dieter appeared through the smoke.

"His leg," Max said, nodding toward Carls.

Dieter understood at once. They each draped one of the big man's arms around their shoulders and got him up. Moving sideways down the passageway, they reached the ladder to the upper decks and Carls, with help, pulled himself up the ladder with his burly arms. In two minutes they emerged, gasping for air, onto the main deck, faces black as coal. Clouds of oily smoke billowed out behind them as Max and Dieter dragged Carls to the rail. Max glanced around. A length of manila rope lay on the deck. Max snatched it and tied a bowline around Carls's waist. "Viktor," Max shouted over the roar of the fire, "bring the launch close abeam. We have to lower Carls over the side."

"At once, Herr Oberleutnant," Viktor shouted back.

As they lowered Carls, Max felt the heat of the burning ship baking his skin. The charred meat in the hold sent an acrid odor down his throat. In the distance, the insistent whistle of the recall signal sounded again, deep and loud. Below them, Viktor worked to maneuver the launch under Carls. Swells tossed the launch up and down, the crew fighting to keep from being dashed against the freighter's hull. Carls made no sound as he hovered above the water, lips compressed to whiteness so as not to cry out from the pain. Max's arms burned. Cords of muscle stood out on Dieter's neck. Slowly they lowered Carls until his torso reached the outstretched arms of the crewmen in the launch.

"Untie him!"

They quickly released the rope and Max hauled it back up, tied a double half hitch to the rail, and handed the line to Dieter.

"After you," Dieter said, handing it back.

Coughing from the smoke, Max slipped over the side and down. Dieter followed, tumbling into the boat.

Without waiting for the order, Viktor put the wheel hard over and turned the launch toward *Graf Spee*, Langsdorff still sounding the ship's whistle. The British lifeboats had reached *Spee*, and the crew had been fetched up on deck, where they stood under armed guard. In Max's own boat, the British first officer cowered in the bow.

Spray thrown up by the speeding launch again washed over Max, but this time the salt burned his lips, chapped from the heat of the fire. He turned to Dieter, who sat beside him in the stern. Black streaks covered his face like greasepaint, but Dieter smiled broadly, as if they were on some kind of pleasure cruise. "After you?" Max asked him, raising his voice above the engine.

Dieter laughed. "Age before beauty." They were both twenty-five, but Max was older by all of ten days.

Max shook his head. He would thank Dieter later, when they weren't in front of the men. Behind them, the merchant-man blazed, flames now engulfing the rail where they had stood only minutes before. The fire threw an eerie reflection across the choppy gray waves, casting a dull yellow light on the face of the British officer, who watched his ship burn with a pathetic expression of grief.

Max wanted badly to draw his pistol and kill the first officer — though he had never felt such an urge before. When *Graf Spee* fired her guns, he didn't make a personal connection with the shells. Being a naval officer involved shooting big guns at other ships from time to time, but the combat was detached. They hadn't even been in a battle yet; the ships they'd sunk had all been unarmed merchantmen. And firing the guns was actually just a small part of their job. They spent most of their time simply moving *Graf Spee* from one location to another. Firing at another ship was a relatively rare occurrence.

Like all German naval officers, Max was forbidden to join any political party, including the Nazi Party, so he wasn't swayed by fiery speeches about blood and iron, but now he felt a blood-lust, that breath of rage the Führer called for, the Teutonic fury. These treacherous British swine—you didn't have to be a Nazi to hate them. Everyone knew how the Royal Navy had maintained its blockade of Germany during peace negotiations after the Armistice that ended the First War. Food and medicine were allowed through only if the Germans could pay in cash, of which they had none, and carried in German merchant ships, which had all been seized. All over Germany, people who had survived the brutal war years starved in the streets in 1919; they died in droves from Spanish flu. Max's mother fell sick that May, and they took her off to a quarantine hospital in Kiel. She never came back. His father was no Nazi, he cared nothing for Hitler's rhetoric, but Johann Brekendorf knew how to despise the British. It would be the easiest thing in the world, Max realized: pull the gun from his belt, point it, squeeze the trigger. Instantly, the trembling Englishman in the bow would cease to exist. It frightened him, the ease.

The coxswain steered the launch under the sling coupling that dangled from *Graf Spee*'s starboard crane. "Hook on," Max ordered.

The sailors nearest the couplings hooked them to the launch. "Hooked on, Herr Oberleutnant."

Max tilted his head back and cupped his hands around his mouth. "Give way!" he shouted.

Gears ground, then caught, and the crane jerked the launch from the water, depositing the boat in its chocks on the deck.

The British captain stood at the head of his men, ten paces off. Max, enraged, climbed out of the launch and made straight for Stubbs, who turned to meet him, throwing his shoulders back and raising his bearded chin. "You filthy swine," Max said, pushing his face in very close to the Englishman's. Max's hands twitched at his sides; the captain's sour breath smelled of pipe tobacco. Max balled his right hand into a fist. "You shit! Goddamn you!"

"Achtung!" a sailor cried. Everyone within earshot came to quivering attention as Captain Langsdorff strode across the deck.

"Oberleutnant Brekendorf!"

Max had come to attention and stared silently ahead.

"You are dismissed," Langsdorff said.

"This man almost killed . . ."

"Dismissed, Oberleutnant."

The discipline of the Kriegsmarine asserted itself. "Jawohl, Herr Kapitän."

Max executed a parade-ground about-face and marched to the companionway. Behind him, Langsdorff greeted the British officers with his unshakable calm, his impeccable English, and his drawing room manners.

Once in his cabin, Max pulled off his uniform, blackened with soot, wadded it into a ball, and threw it against the closet door. He lit a cigarette, filling the cabin with gray fumes much lighter than the ones that had almost choked him on the freighter. Damn that Englishman and damn the dirty English bastards. Damn them all. He burned quickly through his cigarette, stubbed the butt, and walked down to the officers' lavatory for a warm shower. His heart still beat fast, anger mixed with leftover fear. He breathed deeply, closing his eyes and summoning a picture of Mareth. In August, in Berlin, just two days before Max sailed, the two of them had taken a hotel room with its own private bath for the weekend, and they had put that shower to excellent, creative use. Already it seemed like years ago, but the hot water on his skin helped recall the memory.

He returned to his cabin and slept, waking at 1800 hours to put on a clean uniform for the evening meal. Other officers had just come off duty and the atmosphere in the officers' mess was like a slightly raucous gentlemen's club. Langsdorff dined in his sea cabin, as he often did when the ship was under way. His presence in the mess put his officers on their most correct and formal behavior, not allowing them to relax. Max looked around for Dieter. Some officers were drinking at the bar, others played skat in the back, but he couldn't see his friend. He found a seat instead with Reinhold, one of the gunnery officers, and Hollendorf, second navigation officer.

"Gentlemen, gentlemen, guten Abend," Max said, dropping into a chair. Reinhold was an older man, but Hollendorf—a squat Bavarian—was, like Max and Dieter, a member of Crew 33, the small group of young officer cadets who had come to the Marineschule Mürwik in 1933.

One of the civilian mess stewards poured Max a cup of coffee. Nigger sweat, the men called it. All the coffee they were drinking and all the fresh food they were eating had come from captured British ships. Fresh eggs from S.S. *Trevanion*; coffee and tea from S.S. *Huntsman*; beef, mutton, and chicken from S.S. *Newton Beach*; potatoes and sugar from S.S. *Ashlea*. The British fed them well. They had captured nine ships now and sank them all, save one used to house overflow prisoners. Still, with today's capture, more than a hundred prisoners bunked aboard *Graf Spee* herself, and a damned lot of complainers they were, too.

One of the English captains insisted that he had to have Brill's patent medicine for seasickness, as if such a ridiculous item could even be found on a German man-o'-war. Another, Captain Dove of the tanker *Africa Shell*, captured off Mozambique, refused to leave his ship without his new set of golfing clubs. "Cost me twenty quid custom made in Mombasa and I'll be damned if I leave them for you, Fritz," he said to Max, who threw his hands in the air and let the man bring the bloody clubs across to *Graf Spee* along with half a dozen bottles of Gordon's gin. "I'll not leave good gin for Davy Jones's locker."

Despite their constant grumbling, Captain Langsdorff extended every courtesy to his British prisoners. He fed them the same rations allotted to *Spee*'s own crew, supplied them with beer and cigarettes, with English books and magazines seized from captured merchant-men, with copies of newscasts from the BBC, an occasional bottle of whiskey—and for Captain Dove, champagne on his birthday. Langsdorff had even given one of his own pipes and a packet of tobacco to a British captain who had lost his. They even buried one British officer—dead from a heart attack—with full military hon-ors: the body covered with the Red Duster of the British Merchant Navy; a British merchant captain reading the Church of England service; Langsdorff, Max, and other officers attending, each in full dress uniform, backed up by a starched honor guard of German sailors. Max had been required to wear his sword, which he could not abide because it was so easy to trip over. He had tripped over it, in fact, in his cabin as he dressed for the funeral, and banged his skull against the bulkhead. Still, it occurred to him then, and not for the first time, that *Graf Spee* might be acting with unreasonable generosity toward its prisoners. Military courtesy and the brother-hood of the sea only went so far—the Brits remained the enemy. Standing with Langsdorff on deck after the burial, Max ventured to ask the captain why he felt compelled to be so kind.

Langsdorff smiled patiently. "International law, Oberleutnant."

"I understand, Herr Kapitän, but we go far beyond those re-quirements. We don't owe this to the English, sir. You know what they did to us after the First War. They meant to destroy us then and they mean to destroy us now."

The captain looked at Max. His smile faded at the edges. Qui-etly he said, "Who meant to destroy us, Maximilian? The bosun's mate from *Huntsman*? The crew of *Ashlea*? These men are sailors, as are we. They follow their orders, as do we. They love their coun-try, as do we. And they are honorable men, as I hope that we are, too. Do they not deserve our respect?"

Max looked away for a moment to master his anger, then turned again to Langsdorff. "Proper military etiquette is owed to them, Herr Kapitän, but not our respect. Sir, you *commended* the wireless operator of S.S. *Tairoa* for his bravery in continuing to broadcast a distress signal while we machine-gunned her!"

"Was he not brave, Maximilian?"

"Herr Kapitän, that doesn't matter. He's English!"

Captain Langsdorff looked calmly at Max for a few moments. "And you are a German naval officer, Oberleutnant Brekendorf, and our country and our navy will be judged by your conduct, which is why you must always uphold the honor of our flag and our navy. Always."

The mess waiter set a large steak topped with fried eggs in front of Max. They spoke little as they bolted the meal. The sea gave a man an appetite, and who knew when he would eat again? Future mealtimes might find you at your action station with nothing save Pervitin and the emergency ration of chocolate bars to keep you going. Crockery and silverware clattered, glasses clinked, a laugh sounded at the card table. They ate substantially better on the war cruise than they had back home, where even men of the Wehrmacht were subject to the hardships of strict rationing. The program had been in place for years, and one had to look high and low throughout the Reich to find a fat man, except for Reichsmarshall Göring—"der dickie," the Fat One, everyone called him. "Guns will make us strong. Butter will only make us fat," he said. "That's because we received the guns and he got all the butter," so the joke went. The Führer had ordered that, in this war, Germany not be caught short of food, as it had been in the last. The nation had spent most of the previous decade building up its food stores in preparation for war—an end to the rationing would be one more reward for defeating the Allies quickly.

After finishing his meal, Max pushed his plate away and lit a cigarette. Steak, eggs, coffee, tobacco; he felt expansive. He clapped Hollendorf on the back. "And so, young Hollendorf, where to next?"

Hollendorf looked at Max through horn-rimmed glasses. "Sorry, old boy, that's on a need-to-know basis."

"My good man, don't you think as a deck officer responsible for steering the ship I need to know?"

Hollendorf laughed. "All right, El Maximo, but only because of all those times you polished my shoes before inspection. We are to rendezvous with *Altmark* in three days to take on fuel and stores, and then we're bound for the estuary of the Rio Plata to pick up merchant traffic outbound from Uruguay and Argentina."

Altmark belonged to the Secret Naval Supply Service. Disguised under neutral colors, she served as a supply ship to U-boats and surface raiders like *Graf Spee*.

"And then?"

"To London, where we bombard Buckingham Palace, of course."

"If you can find it."

"I have a Michelin guide," the navigator said.

They laughed. It was a running joke—the deck officers claimed the navigators never knew where they were going, and the navigators said the deck officers were always steering off course, doing such things as turning the ship to avoid hitting a porpoise.

Lempke, one of the supply officers, came and sat in a vacant chair. "Anyone for bridge with your brandy and cigars?"

"I can't," Max said. "Paperwork."

"And these other young officers?"

"I fear the complexities of the game are beyond these simpletons."

His friends laughed and tossed their napkins at Max. He smiled and rose from the table. "I bid you fine gentlemen good evening. Some of us have important work to do." He bowed low to his colleagues and made for the administrative quarters.

The passageways of the ship were deserted, the men either

on watch or still eating. A sad blue gleam illuminated the passageways—the interior of the ship lighted this way after sundown to protect the crew's night vision. Max returned the salute of the armed sentry on duty and entered the administrative office. The sentry stood guard over the ship's payroll. Inside, Fest, the chief paymaster, labored over his accounts. He nodded at Max, his bald head gleaming in the light from the lamp above his metal desk. Odd that in the middle of a war such details as calculating men's pay went on. Max had almost been killed today, and here sat Fest, doing sums and consulting wage tables. And he would have been doing it just the same even if Max had died.

Sailors were paid monthly in accordance with the number of specialties they'd mastered. The calculations necessary to determine the wages for everyone on a ship the size of *Graf Spee* were incredibly complex. Every man in the Wehrmacht carried a paybook in which his wage calculations were entered, along with a detailed catalog of additional information: what equipment he had been issued, what decorations he was entitled to wear, the units he had served in, how many wounds he had sustained. The list went on and on. The paybooks doubled as identity papers. "Produce your paybook" was the only phrase those blockheads in the Feldgendarmerie seemed to know; Max had seen them drag soldiers off trains all over Germany for not having their paybooks in order. Even an officer could be arrested for a discrepancy in his paybook. Rank mattered little to the Feldgendarmerie because they reported outside the chain of command. Even at sea, the men checked their monthly pay carefully, scrutinizing the calculations, and delighted in finding errors that could be called to the paymaster's attention.

Max sat at the desk he shared with some of the other officers and read through the intercepts. B-Service had not yet cracked the most secret codes of the Royal Navy, many of which were employed only once and then discarded, but they had broken the one used for giving orders to convoys. From this they had learned the call signs of a number of British men-o'-war. Urgent messages had been flashed that day to *Ajax*, *Achilles*, *Exeter*, and dozens more British warships. These messages, like many others sent by the British Admiralty in the last ten weeks, contained a single order: sink *Graf Spee*. And so the Royal Navy stalked them, scouring the ocean south of the equator for any sign of *Spee*. How close were these ships? Max had no way of knowing.

Here, sitting behind a desk in the quiet of the evening, the soft drone of the engines in the background, the sea hissing gently alongside the hull, it seemed possible to imagine that the war was very far away, or even that there was no war on at all. Yet he could just as easily have gone down with the British merchant-man; he probably would have if not for Dieter. But he would be back in Germany soon enough, hopefully by Christmastime. He and Mareth had let their engagement continue for years, hoping her family would eventually accept Max, which they had no intention of doing. But somehow since the war began, their displeasure seemed to matter less. Christmas would make a wonderful time to get married—and it was only three weeks away.

CHAPTER THREE

ABOARD *ADMIRAL GRAF SPEE*
FOUR DAYS LATER
6 DECEMBER 1939

WITH THE SWELLING OF THE STORM, MAX HAD MANAGED NO MORE than ten minutes of rest in the last four hours. The largest waves heeled *Graf Spee* over thirty-five degrees from the center line, giving the sensation that she was about to capsize. Max would defend his ship to anyone, be they army, navy, or air force, but truth be told, *Spee* rolled like a pig in a barnyard. Most of the young crew had never been through a Force Ten gale. Max knew many younger sailors were puking their guts out, convinced *Spee* would capsize at any moment.

To hold himself in his narrow bunk, Max sat cross-legged, knees braced against the special storm railing, hands grasping the railing as well. In this position he tried to sleep. While the ship rolled from side to side, she also plunged up and down, sometimes in a violent corkscrew motion. Several times during the night, Max lost his grip and slammed against the bulkhead.

His entire body felt black and blue from two days of pounding by the storm. He had been in rough weather before, especially in his sailing ship days as a Seekadett, but nothing this bad. *Graf*

Spee, big as she was, shipped green water over the bow, burying her foredeck repeatedly into the sea, spray reaching over the fore turret and striking the ports of the navigating bridge. One of the lifeboats had been carried away, smashed to matchwood by the force of the waves. Sleeping, relaxing, having a shit—all were impossible. Eating was out of the question. There had been no hot food since the storm set in, only sandwiches and the emergency rations of chocolate bars.

Belowdecks in the large compartments where the sailors lived—bedlam. Gear had come loose and flung itself in all directions. Pea jackets, socks, underwear, playing cards, movie magazines, letters from home, strewn everywhere. Water leaked in from the ventilator shafts topside and sloshed around the decks, the tossing of the ship so brutal that the petty officers had been unable to organize cleanup crews. But at least the sailors—the Lords, as they were known in the Kriegsmarine—could get some rest, except for those who were violently seasick. Unlike the officers, the men slept in canvas hammocks that simply swayed back and forth to the motion of the ship. Max envied them, snoring away like so many fat sausages hung from the ceiling.

The officers' steward rapped on his door. "Herr Oberleutnant, zero three thirty." Max had the watch at 0400.

Spee heeled over again and plunged into a wave, the vibration strong even this far back in the ship. Max gritted his teeth and held on. He waited for *Spee* to right herself, removed the storm railing, and slid to the deck. Around him the ship creaked like an old coach and four. From time to time, the turbines raced as the screws came temporarily out of the water, the powerful sea lifting the stern of *Graf Spee* clear of the surface. From his porthole Max could see nothing, but he felt the waves pounding against the ship's hull.

He pulled himself up and wedged his body between the small desk and closet. His closet door was secured with special fasteners to prevent it from swinging loose and banging against the desk. He reached up and jerked it open. Max didn't dare report to the bridge in the wrinkled clothes he'd worn to bed. Pulling on a pressed uniform was half wrestling match and half gymnastics. The worst part was tying his shoes. Sitting on the deck, feet against the bed, he flexed his legs to keep his back fast against the closet door, freeing both hands to knot the shoelaces. Damn it all. He winced, feeling his bruises.

A sailor's life. Clean air, brilliant sunshine, dolphins leaping clean from the water as they raced you kilometer after kilometer; starched uniforms, brass buttons, gilded dirk at your side, bands playing, men saluting, girls throwing kisses — what the recruiting posters did not show was the ship wallowing like a North Sea trawler in a Force Ten gale, heeling over, whipping back, now plunging down, a wall of white water breaking against the base of the bridge tower. Max shook his head. To hell with it. No hot food, no word from home, the bloody Tommies scouting for them everywhere, endless work, no sleep, no hot water for shaving. Which reminded him that he'd forgotten to shave. It was a good way to cut your throat in weather like this, and Max barely had any growth to begin with, but Langsdorff would disapprove if he noticed the blond fuzz on Max's chin and upper lip. On *Graf Spee* you either had a proper beard or mustache, or else nothing.

He massaged his temples. Could there be a lonelier time than four in the morning? Maybe three in the morning. Why had he joined the navy? If they made it back to Germany he would never set foot on a ship again, never go farther than ten meters from land; give up swimming. He pulled himself upright. To hell with the navy. To hell with the storm. To hell with everything. The officers' steward rapped again. "Ten minutes, Herr Oberleutnant."

"Ja, ja." No choice in the matter, must make the legs move. It was a courtesy to relieve the watch ten minutes early.

Max stepped into the passageway that ran through the officers' quarters, quiet at this time of night, pale blue in the gleam of the nightlights. Fumbling for a moment, he buttoned his heavy bridge coat and made his way toward the main companionway, staggering like a drunk. Going out on deck would be suicide in a storm like this; he climbed the interior ladder to the bridge, clinging tightly to the handrail as the ship bucked beneath him.

The wind howled around the navigating bridge, and even here, in the enclosed section, Max could barely hear. Gerhard gave him a weary smile. A four-hour watch exhausted a man in these conditions. The constant giving at the knees tired your legs and made you feel like you had been mountain climbing. This high in the ship the motion was even more pronounced. Just keeping your feet was hard enough; paying attention to your duties, almost impossible.

Max lurched to the starboard binnacle, grabbed hold. He saluted Gerhard. "Sir," he said, almost shouting, "Wachoffizier Brekendorf reporting."

Gerhard returned the salute. "We are proceeding northwest by north, steering a compass heading of three three zero. Wind is out of the northeast by east coming from zero six zero degrees at fifty knots. Making turns for twelve knots. Engines two, three, four, and six are on line."

Langsdorff had them heading perpendicular to the wind, the force of the gale striking the ship all along her starboard side. This explained why they were shipping so much green water to starboard and constantly rolling thirty-five degrees to port, then whipping back on an even keel for a moment, only to do it again. And again. Even Max began to feel queasy. Normally a captain would position his ship bows on into the wind with just enough power to maintain steerageway and ride it out. Since the bow was the strongest part of the ship, this method had been used by mariners for centuries. Instead, Langsdorff proceeded at his best speed with the storm abeam, which exposed the starboard side of *Graf Spee* to the full fury of the gale, creating the harshest conditions for the men—the ship rolling and plunging like a porpoise. It would have been easier on the men to ride the storm out hove to, but *Spee* could not afford that luxury. They had to proceed northwest by north to make their rendezvous with *Altmark*.

"Ship is battened down," Gerhard continued. "Main batteries only are manned. Captain is on the bridge."

Max turned. Langsdorff was wedged in the back corner, buttoned tightly into his bridge coat, a glowing cigar jutting from his mouth.

Max came to attention and saluted. "Sir, I relieve you." Gerhard saluted in return. The relief crew assembled behind Max. Max and Gerhard initialed the logbook. Formalities completed, the men moved to their posts, replacing the exhausted bridge messengers and telephone talkers.

The only light on the bridge came from the illuminated instrument dials—the two chest-high compasses and the smaller gauges giving speed, wind direction, engine revolutions, depth of the water. Max clung to one of the compasses, squinting in the pale green glow. He waited for the right moment, then moved to the center of the bridge, grasping the handrail that ran underneath the wide, square portholes, which showed nothing but black outside. Rain drummed loudly against the heavy glass. Beneath him, the deck shuddered as the ship pounded into the waves.

"Weather officer believes we are on the edge of a vast storm but should be through by tomorrow."

Max turned. The captain had come up beside him. "I hope so, sir," Max said. "But this will delay our rendezvous with *Altmark*, yes?"

Langsdorff nodded, then leaned in close. "By a day, but it cannot be helped. The sea has other plans, as you can feel."

"And where do we meet *Altmark*, sir?"

"Off the estuary of the Rio Plata. We will try to pick up an outbound British convoy after we resupply. Then home by Christmas," Langsdorff said, smiling at the last remark.

Max turned to the captain. "Home by Christmas, Herr Kapitän, would be the best present we could have."

"I'm certain all aboard agree with you, Maximilian, myself most of all."

Langsdorff said nothing else, only stared into the darkness. Max scanned the instrument dials. He had little to do with the captain exercising direct command on the bridge, especially with a crew so well trained as that of *Graf Spee*. The men knew their jobs and performed them with little prodding from the officers.

The last two hours of night were a vigil, weary and long, Max's body constantly tensed against the motion of the ship. To let go of the handrail was to be flung to the deck, which happened twice to one of the bridge messengers. Dawn broke, revealing vast mountains of water heaving around them. Wind caught the wave tops and blew the spray against the ship, rattling the vessel as if striking the hull with chains. *Graf Spee* would rise to the top of one gray-green mountain, then down, down, Max holding fast, till the ship buried her prow into the sea, shipping water in a torrent to the foot of the bridge. Just when it seemed as if she might not rise again, *Spee* would drag herself out of the trough and climb to the top of another wave, her sides streaming water like a hunting dog coming out of a pond.

Sun hit the waves, and the sea laid bare the insignificance of the ship. In the months since he had come aboard, Max had always thought of her as a fortress—stout and strong, armored against her enemies by the finest Krupp steel—so large that young sailors often lost their way when first aboard. But one could hardly maintain that illusion now—a fortress wasn't thrown about like a woodchip in a stream. So *Graf Spee* labored through the storm, the marching waves pounding her to starboard in a relentless parade, at one point rolling her so violently to port that even Captain Langsdorff lost his footing and went sprawling across the bridge.

Still, *Spee* could not turn bows on into the wind and ride out the storm, for even now the British would be plowing into the gale, drinking endless cups of tea, cursing the weather and the Germans. *Graf Spee* was the most wanted ship in the South Atlantic, and they would not be able to outfox the British forever. The Royal Navy knew every ocean and every sea, every wind and every current. They had charted every coastline, every harbor. They knew every merchant shipping lane. And they knew how to chase down and destroy a commerce raider. They had been doing it for three hundred years.

Around 0700, Max fastened his oilskin and left the enclosed bridge for one of the exposed wings. Wind knocked the breath from his chest. He clung to the handrail and inched his way around to the signal post, a small platform directly behind the enclosed bridge from which the signalmen ran their flags up and down the signal mast. The wind dropped off as *Spee's* superstructure formed a sort of lee.

Max pulled his binoculars from under his coat and scanned the sea astern of the ship. A clean ozone smell, the smell of storm air, filled his nostrils. Windblown rain quickly splotched the binoculars. He licked water off the lenses, took another look, then put away the binoculars. Looking down to button the coat, he paused. Three sailors struggled with the floatplane. The plane threatened to break loose from its moorings; young, inexperienced men tried to add restraining wires to hold it fast to the catapult. Exposed to these waves, they worked without lifelines. They had not yet learned that the sea was a hard master, deadly and remorseless, unforgiving of mistakes. One of the rules drilled into every Seekadett—never go on deck in a storm without a lifeline. In a tropical storm off Florida, while on the training cruiser *Emden*, two cadets had ignored that advice. They were the first of Max's crewkameraden to die.

Max yelled at the men to get below. The wind snatched his words and they didn't hear.

Max shouted again. Then his eyes widened. A giant wave bore down on them. Cupping his hands against his mouth, he bellowed with everything he had. The men, only ten meters away, did not hear.

The wave arced. One of the sailors looked up and screamed at his shipmates. Too late. A wall of angry water hit the ship, heeled her over thirty degrees, and broke over the floatplane in a shower of spray and foam. Water ran from the deck as *Spee* righted herself. Two men were gone. The third hit a stanchion of the deck railing on his way overboard. He clung to it in desperation.

"Hold on! Hold on!" Max yelled. The man did not move—no doubt injured. The next wave would take him. Max spun around, jerked open the flag locker, seized a length of manila rope. He dropped his binoculars into the locker and slammed it shut.

Coil of rope in hand, he grasped the outer rails of the metal stairs, slid to the next landing, then vaulted the railing and dropped three meters to the teak deck. He heard the rush of water, the freight train sound of the big waves racing toward them, and dashed to the sailor—Keppler, a deckhand, all of eighteen.

Graf Spee began to heel.

Three times around the stanchion for a running half hitch, then Max whipped the rope around both himself and Keppler, then around the stanchion again. He looped the end around his wrists, the weight of their bodies drawing it tight. The water broke over them. Max's breath blew from his body. His mouth opened and filled with brine. Water invaded his ears, ran up his nose. The ocean sucked at them. A shoe went but the line held taut, biting deeply into Max's flesh. He thrashed, shaking his head violently, the water clawing at them. And then it was gone, over the side, but he and Keppler remained.

Max retched, coughing and spitting, then drew a lungful of air. He unfastened the line and dragged Keppler, unconscious, to the foot of the bridge housing. Popping the toggles on the heavy metal door, he strained against the weight until the door swung open. He pulled Keppler inside and started puking again, acid burning in his throat. That was how the senior bridge messenger found him.

"Herr Oberleutnant!"

"Fetch the doctor, now!"

Max lay in his soggy uniform on the hard steel deck, fighting to regain his breath. With the adrenaline gone, he began to tremble. Death taunted—over the side, a last scream, mouth filling with water, arms thrashing, the ship now a gray shadow, now gone. Alone in the tossing waves. He shivered at the thought.

"Oberleutnant," said the doctor, crouching over him.

"See to Keppler, please, Doktor."

Summoned by the doctor, orderlies appeared, bundled Keppler onto a stretcher, and carried him away to the infirmary. Max wanted to tell the doctor to carry on, that he was fine and had his watch to finish, but he didn't feel that brave. His wrists, scored by the bite of the rope, bled into little red puddles on the deck. A knot on his head ached—the wave had pounded his skull against the stanchion.

Max leaned against the doctor—like a damned old woman, he thought—as they made their way to the ship's hospital, tottering like drunks to the motion of the ship. *Spee* had a twenty-bed infirmary complete with two operating theaters as well as dental and X-ray units. As good as the Charité Hospital in Berlin, they said. With over a thousand men, thousands of kilometers from land, she had to be so equipped. Several sailors were lying in the starched white beds when Max entered, a normal complement during storms, which always brought broken bones and sprains and gashes.

Max lay down and the doctor put a needle in his arm. A warm feeling spread through his body as the morphine took effect. He fought it for a moment, tried to concentrate, to tell the doctor that it wasn't necessary. But it felt wonderful. He let go and allowed the drug to embrace him.

He woke some hours later, coming slowly out of his stupor. It took him a moment to realize where he was and what had happened. The pain reminded him. The morphine had worn off and his wrists burned. Thick gauze bandages kept him from surveying the damage.

"Guten Abend, Herr Oberleutnant," said the orderly, coming forward.

Max propped himself up. "What time is it?"

"Just coming on twenty-four hundred hours, Herr Ober-leutnant."

"My God, I slept that long?"

"It's the morphine, sir. It does that to everyone."

Max grimaced as he moved to sit up. "Keppler?"

"Broke both legs and three ribs, Herr Oberleutnant. We gave him twice the morphine dose you received, so he'll be out for a while. But he's doing fine—thanks to you, sir."

Max shrugged.

Dieter entered the infirmary, both arms raised in the air like a prophet. "Already your bravery is legend among the lower orders, who have begun to worship you as a god." Max grinned. Dieter punched him lightly on the shoulder. "You are well, Max?"

"Well enough for someone who just woke up from an opium dream."

"Was it good?"

"So good I can't remember it."

"Ha! Like many of my finest nights," Dieter said. "Stitches?" he said, looking at Max's wrists.

"Just abrasions from the rope."

"That can hurt, too. You remember the time I had to hang from a rope off the balcony of that hospital room in Danzig, so the matron wouldn't find me with Olga?"

Max nodded. "I do remember, but I think her name was Helga."

"Attention on deck!" an orderly called.

Dieter went rigid and Max sat up straight. Langsdorff entered, smiling around the cigar in the corner of his mouth. "Young Brek-endorf is always trying to get himself killed," he said.

Max felt the color come up in his face.

"Well done, Brekendorf. Very well done." Langsdorff reached into his coat pocket, produced a second cigar, and offered it to Max.

"Thank you, Herr Kapitän."

"Save it for a quiet moment, Oberleutnant. As you know

from the radio message we received yesterday, Grand Admiral Raeder has authorized me to award one hundred Iron Crosses Second Class to members of the ship's company who have shown a special devotion to duty. It is my pleasure to award one to you, Oberleutnant, for your actions in rescuing Seaman Keppler, and for your exemplary conduct during this war cruise."

"I'm honored, Herr Kapitän."

"It's only what such an act deserves. The highest duty of any officer is to watch over the well-being of his men." Langsdorff turned to Dieter. "Keeping our young friend company, Falkenheyn?"

"I am, Herr Kapitän."

"I understand he might not be with us had you not helped him with Oberbootsmann Carls."

"Ja, Herr Kapitän. But this time he waited till I wasn't there, so he could keep all the credit for himself."

Langsdorff smiled again. "Well, I bid you young gentlemen a good evening."

Dieter again came to attention.

"Herr Kapitän?" Max said.

"Ja?"

"I wish to report for duty at my regular hour."

Langsdorff studied Max, taking in the bandages on his wrists and white gauze around his forehead. "If you can secure the surgeon's permission, then you may."

"Thank you, Herr Kapitän."

"But Oberleutnant."

"Ja?"

"Shave before you come on duty."

Max tried not to smile. "Jawohl, Herr Kapitän."

Langsdorff exited and Dieter produced a package of cigarettes, Murattis at that, hard to come by these days and not something Dieter shared readily. He took one for himself and then offered the rest of the package to Max.

"He's right, you know," Max said. "I don't think Carls and I would have made it off that freighter if you hadn't come back for us."

Now it was Dieter's turn to shrug. "I'm sure you would have managed."

"Well, thanks anyway. I've been meaning to say that."

Dieter nodded through the blue haze of his cigarette. "You're welcome, El Maximo."

They smoked in silence for a while.

"Captain says we'll find a convoy off the Rio Plata," Max said. "Then home by Christmas."

Dieter smiled. "A Christmas goose. Sleigh rides with the girls. Carols around the fire. Sleigh rides with the girls. Mulled cider, maybe a sleigh ride or two with the girls. A man could get used to such a life. Naturally I'd miss being awakened in the dead of night by alarm bells—perhaps I could employ someone to do that for me while I'm home."

Max laughed. "I'm going to get married while we're on leave," he said.

Dieter raised an eyebrow. "The brave groom schedules his wedding. Again."

Max ignored the cut. "You'll be the best man, of course. We'll have the ceremony at the Lutheran church in Bad Wilhelm, then a wedding feast—perhaps at Herr von Woller's country house."

"Ah, a feast. You know I do love a feast, Max, especially at a venue as auspicious as Castle von Woller. Very high-toned and sure to be covered by the *Berliner Morgenpost*. But, El Maximo, a question: has Herr von Woller agreed to speak to you yet?"

"No."

"I would not wish to present myself as an expert on social etiquette among the aristocracy, my own distinguished antecedents notwithstanding," Dieter said, putting his right hand to his chest and making a slight bow, "but might that be something you should address before the wedding? Especially if you're planning to have the reception at his estate?"

Max looked away. In his mind formed a double line of starched naval officers, swords held high to create an arch for him and Mareth to walk through as they left the church, his father following behind, beaming with pride. Mareth's parents, too. If they even attended. The von Wollers were Prussian aristocrats, long associated with the Prussian Court—old family and old money, much of it from the exclusive coaling supply contract they had enjoyed with the Imperial Navy until the years before the First War. The von Wollers had not been pleased when their only daughter had announced her intention to marry the local grocer's son. Dieter would have been a more acceptable choice, his wild behavior aside, since he was officially Dieter Freiherr von Falkenheyn, with his own listing in the *Almanac de Gotha*, and his mother listed as well, since she was a countess and a former lady-in-waiting to the Crown Princess of Bavaria.

"Well, I'm happy for you anyway," Dieter said, "and I hope you go through with it this time. The poets tell us that love is blind, and marriage is a venerable institution. Personally, I'd rather not be blind and living in an institution, but if anyone is worth being married to, it's Mareth—no matter what her parents think of you."

Max grinned. Dieter would know. He'd spent a lot of time with them when the two had just begun seeing each other. Dieter was the perfect friend to bring along with a new girlfriend because he was funny and entertaining, but enough of a scoundrel to make Max look a prince by comparison. And Dieter not only understood his role but loved an audience. He kept everybody laughing when the three of them went to the Gnomenkeller, the cadet hangout in Flensburg, also frequented by young women eager to meet a Seekadett. On occasion, Mareth would approach girls on Dieter's behalf, pretending to be his sister.

One night, she had introduced him to a set of vacationing Bavarian twins, big-hipped mountain girls of the kind Dieter most adored. Mareth told them that her brother had been captain of

Germany's Olympic juggling team at the '36 games in Berlin, and, of course, Dieter obliged with an impromptu demonstration— using two shot glasses, then three, then four. Max had surreptitiously caught the fourth one when Dieter dropped it, and the girls were none the wiser. The Bavarian fräuleins had been very impressed and shortly thereafter both left with Dieter. Next day, Max had asked, "And what happened with the girls?"

"No one should ask a gentleman a question such as that," Dieter said.

"Of course not, but then again I'm not asking a gentleman, I'm asking you."

"I won't say a thing."

Max had laughed. "That means you didn't."

Now Dieter reached out and shook Max's hand. "Congratulations," he said, "again. Sadly, I must leave your heroic presence and return to my duties."

"You engineering officers actually have something to do?"

"Only keeping the engines running. A modest contribution compared to the mighty deeds of the sea officers."

Max lay back when Dieter had gone. An Iron Cross. True, only an Iron Cross Second Class—just a small ribbon worn in the middle buttonhole of your tunic—but still, an award for bravery. Mareth's father could not look down his nose at that. He certainly didn't have one. Helmuth von Woller had spent the First War sitting on his duff in various diplomatic postings, playing bridge with the other brave diplomats. Helmuth's brother, Oberstleutnant Ernst von Woller, had fought shoulder to shoulder with Max's father in the village Landwehr battalion at Verdun—a yearlong siege that was meant to destroy the French but ended up destroying the Germans. In one of those terrible battles, Johann Brekendorf had carried a horribly wounded Ernst von Woller through an artillery barrage to the battalion aid station. Yet when he laid his commander on the ground outside the aid post, Ernst was dead. Instead it was Johann, bleeding from dozens of small shrapnel wounds, whom the medics had bandaged and carried to the hospital train. For this, Johann had been awarded the Prussian Military Cross, the highest award for bravery an enlisted man could receive in the Prussian army. While he did not possess the decoration his father had, Max felt he had proved his bravery to his father and to himself.

By the time Max returned to the bridge, *Spee* had been out of the storm for some hours. The wind and rain had gone, but heavy swells remained and continued to rock the ship. Max's wrists ached as he stood at his post, gripping the handrail for balance. The rest of his body ached, too. When he had changed his uniform before coming on duty, the mirror showed black-and-blue flesh in many places. He had refused the surgeon's offer of aspirin. That was foolish. Now he would have to go back for it, and going back would make him feel sheepish.

An hour after daybreak, they sighted *Altmark*, squat in the water like any tanker, her crew sporting white American sailor caps, the Stars and Stripes flying from her stern and painted on her sides. "A real Yankee Doodle," Langsdorff said, "full of good Texas oil." The two ships closed in to exchange the recognition signals and formally establish each other's identity. Naval etiquette satisfied, they stood off; the heavy swell made it impossible for *Altmark* to trail out her fuel hoses or for either ship to launch boats.

"Take station on me," Langsdorff signaled.

The ships steamed in a wide circle all day—a bothersome delay but one welcomed by the crew of *Graf Spee*. A warm, bright sun shone upon the ship and most off-duty sailors rigged their hammocks on deck and had their first good sleep in days. Others put on their swimming trunks and sprawled over the teakwood deck, using their towels as pillows, and took the sun. Even Captain Langsdorff indulged in sun worship, although in uniform. His steward set up two deck chairs by the aft torpedo tubes where Captain Langsdorff and one of his prisoners, Captain Dove of *Africa Shell*, took the sun and had one of their many private talks. Curiously, they had become friends of a sort and often talked for hours.

Max found it hard to understand. Did they just avoid the obvious? Perhaps the captain enjoyed Dove's bold personality. If the meek shall inherit the earth, then Captain Dove was certainly not going to get anything.

When he had first come aboard, Captain Dove insisted that his ship had been in the territorial waters of neutral Portuguese Mozambique and that Langsdorff violated international law by seizing his ship. Langsdorff insisted that Dove was still in international waters and thus liable to be sunk. Then occurred what Max had thought of as the "Battle of the Charts" because each man produced his own nautical chart and they dueled for two hours, their weapons being dividers and compasses and finally cigars and scotch. They never did agree about the exact position of their ships at the time *Graf Spee* took *Africa Shell* as a prize of war. The battle ended when Langsdorff suggested Dove write up a document of protest, which both Dove and Langsdorff later signed, although Captain Langsdorff's signature simply affirmed that he had officially received the protest, not that he agreed.

But that had been three weeks ago, and now, safely out of the storm, Max, too, welcomed the short break from the ship's routine that gave him extra time to rest. He slept like a dead man between his watches, despite *Spee*'s constant rocking, and felt close to his usual strength again by the next morning when the swell began to die away. Two hours after dawn, the waves had settled, and the men went to work.

Max supervised a loading party. With another day of bright sunshine, his men again took off their shirts to feel the warmth on their pale skin, while they worked to strike a mound of 105-millimeter shells belowdecks. *Altmark* had sent the load of shells over in *Graf Spee*'s launch, and, using a block and tackle, Max's crew hoisted the shells one at a time and lowered them into the refrigerated magazine. Cordite, the propellant used to blow the shells from the guns, deteriorated and became unstable at high temperatures.

"Easy, easy!" Max shouted as one of the shells swayed over the access hatch. "It's slipping!" The words had barely left his mouth when the shell slid free of the harness and dropped six decks to the hold. Max shut his eyes and jammed his fingers into his ears. Nothing. The sailors grinned at him—everyone, from the assistant cook on up, knew the shells could not explode without their detonators, which were not inserted until the shells were about to be fired. Without the detonators you could drop the shells from an aeroplane and they wouldn't explode. Max had to laugh, too, even if he was embarrassed.

A series of curses drifted up through the hatch from the deck below. "Back to work," Max ordered, "and be more careful!"

Three boats from *Altmark* and two launches from *Graf Spee* hauled a warehouse of provisions to the big ship. Canned food, boxes of macaroni, crates of apples, tins of pickled cabbage, dried fruit, coffee, cigarettes, cases of Beck's beer, slabs of frozen beef, all piled up on the teak deck boards. Along with the food came supplies to run the ship: jerry cans of lubricating oil, cylinders of carbolic acid for the refrigeration plant, replacements for burnt-out engine parts. In turn, the men filled the unloaded boats with most of their British prisoners. They looked bedraggled and moved slowly into the launches, gripping their small suitcases and kit-bags. Max wondered what being a prisoner of war would be like. No action, no job, no responsibility. Crushing boredom.

Sweat streamed from his men as they wrestled the stores below. Officers ran around yelling orders, sailors muttered under their breath, winches screeched, cargo nets rose into the air, swayed over the deck, then down into the holds. Commander Kay, *Graf Spee*'s executive officer—a thin, fussy martinet of a man—darted among the stacks of supplies urging everyone on. "Keep those men working," he said to Max, whose bare-chested sailors already pushed and hauled cargo with all their strength.

When Kay saw something he didn't like, he blew a silver whistle that dangled from a string around his thin neck. By late morning, Max wanted to grab the whistle and throw it overboard along with the commander.

Still the supplies kept coming to fill *Graf Spee*'s empty storerooms. A thousand men consumed enormous amounts of food. Even with the provisions captured from the British ships, *Spee* was running low on almost everything. Sacks of dried beans, of flour, cases of tinned milk, boxes of dried eggs, all came aboard in massive quantities. Freshwater was one of the few items they did not need from *Altmark*. *Graf Spee*'s desalinization equipment produced the fifty tons of water required every day by the crew and the huge diesel engines, which could not be cooled with salt water because salt corroded their inner parts.

At 1200 Langsdorff passed the word for everyone to put their shirts back on. Several of Max's men were already a bright shade of pink, and Max's own face felt burnt from the morning sun. November was summer in the Southern Hemisphere but it was easy to be fooled by the wind. A strong southerly breeze kept the air cool, masking the strength of the sun's rays.

Half the working parties were sent below for lunch but the other half remained on deck. Everyone had been rousted out to load supplies, even the paymaster's assistants and pipefitters and dental assistants. Only the band members were exempt, entertaining the sailors instead. Every hour, the band left its perch aft of turret Bruno and marched twice around the deck, picking its way through the mounds of supplies. Max pushed his men, now working to unload a net filled with tins of jam. The sun had heated the teakwood deck planks, and Max shifted from foot to foot—though it was still better than standing on steel. Wood gave the men better footing, and teak didn't splinter when hit by a shell. Wooden splinters could be deadly; in the days before ships were made of steel, the majority of casualties in sea battles had come from flying splinters.

By 1630 hours the sailors were exhausted, their beards dripping with sweat—many bent over, hands on their knees, gulping air. At 1700 a silence not heard for months came over the ship—the diesels had been stopped, Langsdorff had brought *Graf Spee* to a complete halt. Max and the other men on deck paused and looked to the bridge. The order came over the loudspeaker: "By divisions, on the starboard side, swimming until dinner is piped." A cheer went up among the men.

Oberbootsmann Carls and his men dragged cargo nets to the starboard side and hung them down to the water. Max went quickly to his cabin, put on his swim trunks, returned to the deck, and climbed down one of the nets. The ocean water was cold on his skin, and the salt stung the bandaged cuts on his wrists, but it felt good. He dived, went under, came up and shook the water from his head. Damn it felt good. Men poured down the nets, spreading out before the ship's towering hull. Wagner, one of the bridge messengers, swam over laughing and dunked Max. Soon all the officers were being dunked by the men. Max laughed too and splashed the sailors around him. Two days ago going over the side meant certain death. Now they played in the ocean, surrounded by comrades, a brilliant red sun sinking behind them. The war seemed a rumor from a place far away.

CHAPTER FOUR

ABOARD *ADMIRAL GRAF SPEE*
13 DECEMBER 1939
EARLY MORNING

MAX SIPPED COFFEE AND LISTENED TO DIETER EXPLAIN ANOTHER one of his get-rich-quick schemes. They sat in the officers' mess, preparing to go on duty.

"After the war is over, there will be a big demand for glass eyes, you see, tens of thousands will be needed, maybe even more. And how many glass-eye factories do you think there are in the Grossdeutsches Reich?"

"I don't know," Max said, "how many?

Dieter furrowed his brow. "I don't know either, but there couldn't be many or you would've heard about them. So I propose to set up this venture and all I need is a few farsighted investors, if you'll excuse the expression, to come up with twenty thousand reichsmarks."

"Perhaps your friends will help you."

"Exactly. Now I know why you're an officer—such perception."

Max laughed. He was tightfisted; his father had drummed that into him. It pained him to waste money as he had with the B-Service cardsharps. Save two, spend one, his father always said.

But Dieter spent two, then spent two more, then borrowed a few and spent those as well.

An officers' steward interrupted them. "Zero three forty-five, Herr Oberleutnant."

"I have to go relieve the watch," Max said, "and so I must take my leave from the future founder of Germany's great glass-eye empire."

Dieter grinned behind his dark beard. "They laughed at Krupp when he said he could build a better cannon." Of course Krupp, the great arms dealer, was now the biggest supplier of cannons to the Wehrmacht. His name could be found on every one of the huge naval guns on the deck of *Graf Spee*.

"When you are rich, mein Herr, remember me."

"I will, I will. What was your name again?"

Max grinned and shook his head as he left the officers' mess. Dieter was a reckless schemer, but he came by it honestly. He was third-generation navy—his father, too, had been an engineer, and the lone heir of an old and prominent family in Kiel. But the mutiny of the High Seas Fleet at the end of the First War had destroyed Lothar Freiherr von Falkenheyn emotionally, and post-war inflation had wiped out his fortune. His circumstances much reduced, the Kaiser in exile, the aristocracy abolished, the navy he loved now nothing more than a glorified coast guard, he hanged himself from a crossbeam in his dining room in 1922.

Max knew that Dieter's bravado was a front, and that his dreams of easy money carried with them a bitter edge. With her husband gone, her jewelry pawned, Dieter's mother had been forced to turn their home into a boarding house for retired naval officers trying to survive on military pensions, pensions rendered almost worthless as the terrible inflation of the early Weimar years destroyed the finances of all but the wealthiest. Not Dieter's father, nor his mother, nor anyone they knew could ever have imagined that the First World War would bring such catastrophe and that every single pillar of their stable lives would collapse. And the fall had been precipitous. To Dieter and his mother and to so many others this bitterness became the dominant emotion of their lives.

Coming out onto the deck, Max paused and breathed in the clean night air. This war would be different; it would end in no such disgrace, but rather in triumph and pride, and Germany would take back all that had been wrenched away from her two decades before. Above him, a blanket of stars spread across the blue-black sky. He picked out the Southern Cross, shining bright in the Southern Hemisphere. Like every sailor for a millennium, Max knew the night sky by heart; the unchanging position of the stars was still a crucial guide in the navigation of any ship, be it merchantman, man-o'-war, clipper under sail, or even one of the new cruise liners that sailed to exotic tropical locales. Maybe he and Mareth would take a cruise someday, if he could ever bring himself to step off a dock again once the war was over. On a calm, clear night like this, it seemed a pleasant idea. Mareth had been on several cruises with her father around the Mediterranean, but Max had only heard her stories. Together they could do the Hamburg-to-Rio run on the Hamburg-America Line. Tea at four on the deck. Dining at seven—gentlemen in dinner jackets, please. Dancing at nine. Cigars and brandy. Reading in a deck chair, legs wrapped in a blanket, and then a brisk turn around the deck, nodding to the officers.

Sailors brushed past Max in the dark on the way to their posts. He climbed quickly up the three flights of exterior stairs to the navigating bridge.

Gerhard stood on the starboard bridge wing, leaning against the metal plating with the vast sky stretched out above him and a gentle breeze in his face. Max went over and saluted. "Sir, I am ready to relieve you."

Gerhard returned the salute. "Seas are calm. Wind is three knots coming due south from one eight zero degrees. Barometer is steady. We are steaming south-southeast on a compass heading of one five five. We are two hundred forty-five kilometers off the mouth of the Rio Plata. Making turns for twelve knots. Engines one, three, five, and seven are on line. Shafts are revolving at one hundred twelve revolutions per minute. All equipment is functioning. The captain is to be called for anything not strictly routine."

Max stood at attention. "Sir, I relieve you."

Gerhard saluted and they ducked inside to sign the log. This done, Max went back out to the open wing alone. He licked his lips and tasted the salt. A breeze cooled his face, the wind clammy with moisture. *Graf Spee*'s wake glowed wide and bright at her stern as her propellers stirred up the phosphorus in the water. The diesel fumes wafted strong from the funnel abaft the bridge.

Graf Spee was darkened, no lights to give her away to her enemies—of which she had many, especially in the estuary of the Rio Plata. The wealth of South America flowed from the Plata—wealth measured in tons of frozen meat, hundredweights of creamy butter, cargo holds filled with grain, ingots of steel, all bound for England. The river's very name gave notice of the riches that flowed down its waters to the broad Atlantic: Rio de la Plata— the River of Silver. Of course, the Tommies knew all this as well as Max did. Indeed, they probably knew it better since British investors owned everything worth owning in Uruguay and Argentina. The Royal Navy constantly patrolled the estuary of the Rio Plata; they would be on high alert for *Graf Spee*. She would have to slip in like a fox, take some fat merchantmen, and be quickly on her way.

At 0551 Hollendorf, the second navigator, came out of the chartroom at the rear of the bridge. "Sunrise in five minutes, Oberleutnant."

Max nodded and stretched his arms. Like most men at sea, dawn was his favorite time of day. He watched the line of the horizon until the sun came burning up slowly from the water. It was easy enough to understand how so many pagan tribes had come to be sun worshippers. Even now, Tian, the head laundryman, knelt on the prow of the ship in submission to one of his gods.

Max lit a cigarette and inhaled, drawing the bite of tobacco deep into his lungs. You couldn't smoke on deck at night for fear of giving the ship away. In Berlin, it was midmorning— Mareth would be living her normal life, twelve thousand kilometers away, not knowing where Max was. Maybe she would be meeting friends at one of the cafés she loved along the Unter den Linden. She couldn't stand the brew of chicory roots and acorns that passed for coffee in the Reich, so she would drink one of those American Coca-Colas. She loved all things American— movies, magazines, Lucky Strikes, Coca-Cola. Or she might be walking alone in the Tiergarten, the evergreens laden with snow, or perhaps taking a quick walk through the zoo. He imagined her rising late from bed—she kept cabaret hours—and paging through a copy of the *Berliner Morgenpost* while still in her pajamas, blond hair tousled from sleep. Maybe she was sipping real coffee supplied by the Sergeant Major, her name for Max's father. Where he obtained the coffee was a mystery he would not reveal even to Max.

A polite cough brought Max back to the present—Rolf, the bridge steward, had appeared with coffee in thick china mugs for the watch and first offered the tray to Max.

Coffee. Strong and hot. Max drank it down. He yawned, rubbed his belly. God, he couldn't be hungry already.

"Bridge! Two masts in sight, twenty kilometers off the starboard bow," said the young telephone talker, the one who always screeched, his voice high with excitement.

Max jerked the binoculars to his eyes. Nothing. The lookouts, perched high above the bridge and peering through the rangefinder, could see farther. He picked up the metal phone to call the captain, but the telephone talker shrieked again. "Bridge, six masts in sight, twenty kilometers off the starboard bow."

A convoy! At last—it had to be. Langsdorff answered the phone. "Ja?"

"Captain to the bridge!" Max yelled, too energized to

observe formalities. He replaced the phone, seized the red-handled battle station lever, and yanked it upward. The piercing alarm sounded through the ship, the five long bells jolting the crew from their sleep.

"Action stations," Max ordered the telephone talker, who spoke into his rubber mouthpiece, his words now blaring over the loudspeaker. "Achtung! Achtung! Action stations! All hands to action stations!"

Max picked up the engine room phone.

"Engine room, aye."

"Ships in sight. Prepare for emergency full ahead."

"Aye-aye!"

Belowdecks, sailors rolled from their hammocks and ran for their battle posts, struggling into lifejackets and balancing helmets as they went. Engineers cut all unnecessary power and water. Emergency lighting flickered on and off. Petty officers hurried the men to their positions. "Schnell! Schnell!"

The surgeon lieutenant and his medics set up a makeshift operating theater in the officers' mess, to supplement the ship's hospital and take over if it were put out of action. Damage control parties stood by, ready to carry lumber and mattresses for plugging shot holes below the waterline. Firefighting parties tested pressure in the water mains. Fire posed a special danger with all the ammunition piled on the top deck to serve the smaller guns. Shells for the larger guns came up directly from the main magazine by automatic hoists. These magazines could be flooded from the bridge at the touch of a button if they were threatened by fire. No ship could survive the explosion of its magazine, so the powder and the heavy shells were hidden in the safest and most heavily armored part of the hold.

As the noise of the battle alarm died away, Captain Langsdorff, cigar in hand, appeared on the bridge. "Report."

"Six masts in sight, twenty kilometers off the starboard bow," Max said. "Ship is cleared for action."

"Make revolutions for full speed."

Max passed the order and soon the ship's vibration increased. Had he secured everything in his cabin? He couldn't remember. Anything left sitting on a flat surface vibrated to the deck when *Graf Spee* went to full speed.

Langsdorff flipped his cigar ash and smiled. "A convoy, Brekendorf, a convoy—a nice Christmas present for us all. Perhaps we'll capture some tea. A chest of fine English tea for your young lady." He grinned and puffed. "Chests of tea all around, Oberleutnant."

Max grinned, too. Chests of tea and home by Christmas. Nine ships captured plus whatever they sank today. A brass band at Kiel, a hero's welcome, a spread of color photographs in *Signal*. No doubt a promotion as well. A promotion and an Iron Cross.

"Left standard rudder," Langsdorff ordered.

Max leaned over the speaking tube to the wheelhouse. "Helmsman, left standard rudder."

"Rudder is left standard, sir."

Standard rudder was the degree of turn needed to take the ship in a circle. Left full rudder put the rudder over by thirty degrees. Emergency left rudder put it over thirty-five degrees, the farthest it would go. *Spee* heeled to port as the rudder bit. Langsdorff let her swing. "Rudder amidships," he ordered. "Steady on a new course of two three six degrees, southwest by west."

Max relayed this to the helmsman, who checked *Spee*'s turn and brought her steady on course two three six degrees. At full speed, there was no keeping the smoke under control, and it poured thick and black from the funnel. Max smelled the diesel fumes and knew dark particles were staining the scrubbed deckboards. But it didn't matter: the fight was on. Langsdorff wasn't going to skulk around anymore, masquerading as a French battleship. He headed straight for the convoy—a wolf going in among the sheep, Max thought, and to hell with the Royal Navy.

The bridge phone buzzed. Max picked it up, listened, turned

to Langsdorff. "Herr Kapitän, gunnery says leading ship is H.M.S. *Exeter*, heavy cruiser. Six eight-inch guns, fires one-hundred-twelve-pound shells, turret armor two inches—"

"I am aware of *Exeter*'s defenses. What about the other ships?"

"They can't make them out, sir."

Gunnery called again. Max listened. "Herr Kapitän, gunnery officer says there are three ships. Leading ship is H.M.S. *Exeter*, the other two are destroyers."

They had to be screening a convoy—a heavy cruiser certainly did not require two destroyers as escorts. Convoy must still be below the horizon. They would sight it at any moment, and those destroyers were nothing to worry about. They couldn't hold their own in a battle. When heavy shells began to fly, a destroyer could do little except run away or get sunk. *Exeter* was another matter, but still no match for *Graf Spee*. Perhaps they would add a Royal Navy warship to their list of ships sunk. It would make their victory even sweeter.

Spee raced in for the kill, leaving a trail of foaming white water in her path. The morning sun warmed Max's face. He peered through his binoculars at the three British warships, straining for a glimpse of the convoy beyond.

"Convoy must still be below the horizon," he said to Langsdorff.

"We shall see," the captain replied. "They may put up a good fight but we shall swallow them."

For the first six months of the year, they had done nothing except steam up and down the Baltic, performing fire drills, anti-aircraft drills, shooting off so many rounds of ammunition that they had to play the fire hoses onto the barrels of the guns to cool them down. Lowering boats, then hoisting them back up. Stopping ship, then lurching forward at emergency speed. All in preparation for this—to prove the German navy capable of something more than surrendering to the British, as they had at the end of the First War. The handing over of the Imperial High Seas Fleet to the English still shamed Germany. No one could forget the image of their proud ships steaming from Germany to internment in Great Britain under the guns of the victorious Royal Navy. They had salvaged only what little remained of the navy's honor by scuttling their ships all at once in the British fleet anchorage of Scapa Flow eight months later.

The phone gave an insistent ring, startling Max. He picked it up and took the gunnery officer's report. "Gunnery says the two ships in company with *Exeter* are not destroyers as previously thought, Herr Kapitän. They are light cruisers."

"Is there a convoy behind them?"

Max spoke into the phone. "Can you see . . ." He turned to Langsdorff. "Nein, Herr Kapitän."

The captain made no reply. Max lit a cigarette and drew in the smoke. Shit. Three British cruisers. Three British cruisers out here off the Rio de la Plata, hanging about like street-corner idlers, just waiting for them. Damn the English. Not one of the cruisers could damage *Spee*, but, taken together, and fighting as one unit, which they would, they had enough firepower to cripple her, perhaps render her unfit for traversing the winter North Atlantic on her run home to Germany. But they had to fight, they had to and damn the odds. Only by sending ships of the Royal Navy to the bottom could they win the war.

Langsdorff peered through his binoculars for a long time before speaking. At last he said, "We're not to engage."

"Herr Kapitän? Not engage?"

"We are a commerce raider, Oberleutnant. Our operational orders are to avoid engagement with enemy warships unless we are caught without recourse."

"I am aware of our orders from the briefing you gave us, Herr Kapitän, but Seekriegsleitung couldn't have meant us to run away."

Langsdorff lowered the binoculars and removed the cigar

from his mouth, working his jaw slowly back and forth. Orders from Berlin were not to be lightly brushed aside, but the captain did not want to turn around. The ship's motto—*Faithful unto death*—was the personal motto of Admiral Graf von Spee.

Count von Spee had been one of the Imperial Navy's greatest heroes, commander of the German squadron that handed the Royal Navy a stunning defeat at the Battle of Coronel in the First War, sinking two British warships—the first to be sunk in a sea battle in over a century. The British took their revenge a month later, destroying most of the German squadron at the Battle of the Falkland Islands, a thousand kilometers south of *Graf Spee*'s current position. Admiral Graf von Spee went down with his flagship, *Scharnhorst*, as did his two sons, both aboard as young officers. He fought to the end with flags flying, firing his guns till the water closed over them. Not a single hand survived. Max had a postcard that showed a defiant German sailor at the Battle of the Falklands waving the imperial ensign as his ship sank out from under him, into the green waters of the South Atlantic. At long last this was their chance to avenge Admiral von Spee's defeat. "I saw him several times," Langsdorff, who had grown up in Düsseldorf, Count von Spee's hometown, once told Max, "walking in the park with his children. I always wished I had spoken to him, but it was long before the First War and I was still a youngster and much too afraid."

Langsdorff continued his silence. Many of the officers, including Max, urged him to seek battle with a Royal Navy ship before heading home. How could they think of themselves as truly brave when the only ships they had attacked were ships that couldn't shoot back?

The captain hesitated, binoculars still focused ahead. Langsdorff put the cigar back between his teeth. "We have not yet been fully tested," Langsdorff said, taking the binoculars from his eyes. "The enemy is here, and we must fight for our honor and the honor of our flag."

Max snapped off a sharp salute. "Jawohl, Herr Kapitän."

Max and Langsdorff turned again to face the three warships strung out along the horizon.

"Bridge," screeched the telephone talker, "B-Service reports transmission in the clear."

"Read it out."

"Signal from *Exeter*: 'Immediate to Admiralty. One pocket battleship zero three four degrees south, zero four nine degrees west. Course two seven five degrees.'"

And so the Royal Navy had found them at last. Max's stomach muscles tightened.

"Signaling again in the clear: 'From *Exeter*, general broadcast merchant ships. One pocket battleship, thirty-four degrees south, forty-nine degrees west, steering two three six. Am engaging forthwith. Stand off.'"

Big brother shooing the flock out of harm's way. Langsdorff nodded. His face was calm. "Have gunnery begin calling down the range," he said to Max.

"Jawohl, Herr Kapitän."

"And Oberleutnant."

"Herr Kapitän?"

"Run up the battle flag."

"Yes, sir!" Max said, grinning as he passed the captain's order. Quickly the signalman broke out the red, white, and black naval ensign of the Kriegsmarine and hoisted it above the ship. Atlantic wind caught the banner and it streamed out over *Graf Spee*.

On the navigating bridge stood Langsdorff, Max, a deputy watch officer, and Hollendorf. As second navigator, Hollendorf tracked *Graf Spee*'s exact position as she began to twist and turn in the coming battle. Also on the bridge stood the four signalmen who would pass Langsdorff's fighting orders through the ship by phone and voice tube. Four additional messengers stood by to run orders manually if the phones were knocked out. Two sailors manned each of the engine telegraphs. Rolf, the bridge steward, was on hand to provide sandwiches and coffee.

While the enlisted men waited silently at their posts, Max and the other officers trained their binoculars on the charging British cruisers. It seemed unreal to Max, like a practice shoot in the Baltic. In their two and a half months of commerce raiding, nobody had actually fired on them.

One of the bridge signalmen chanted the range as it came in over his earphones. "Twelve kilometers, eleven and three-quarters, eleven and a half . . ."

The British had the curious habit, left over from the days when all wooden warships looked alike, of flying gigantic battle ensigns. As *Exeter* drove toward *Spee*, Max watched the huge red-and-white flags break over the cruiser—two up the radio aerials, two more up the signal masts. If they were hauled down before the end of the battle, it could have but one meaning: H.M.S. *Exeter* had surrendered. Unlikely, Max knew. A Royal Navy warship had not surrendered in a sea battle for a hundred and fifty years.

Above one of the ensigns flew a yellow signal flag—the classic signal of the Royal Navy: *Enemy in sight*.

At ten kilometers, *Exeter* changed course ninety degrees to her left and ran perpendicular to *Graf Spee*. Now all of *Exeter*'s guns bore on *Spee*, while only *Spee*'s forward guns bore on *Exeter*.

Alarmed, Langsdorff bypassed Max and stepped directly to the voicepipe. "Helmsman, hard port. Come to new course of one two zero!" *Spee* heeled sharply to port and began running parallel to *Exeter*. *Exeter*'s two comrades then altered course so they, too, steamed parallel to *Graf Spee*, but in the opposite direction. Max knew the light cruisers would steer a wide arc, cross *Spee*'s stern, and come up on the other side. They would try to compel *Spee* to divide the punishing fire of her eleven-inch guns.

Silence again on the bridge. Max felt a tremor in his legs. Only the enclosed portion of the navigating bridge had any protection at all—an inch of steel plate to stop shell splinters. They could pull steel scuttles down over the large portholes, but then they wouldn't be able to see anything. The open bridge wings had no protection of any kind against incoming fire, just salt air and a flawless view of the British guns taking dead aim.

"Range of *Exeter*?"

"Nine and a half kilometers now, Herr Kapitän."

"Commence against *Exeter*," Langsdorff ordered, his voice as soft and pleasant as if he were ordering coffee.

Max came to attention. "Jawohl, Herr Kapitän." He seized the gunnery phone.

"Gunnery, aye."

"Order from captain: target is *Exeter*. Repeat, target is *Exeter*. Commence main battery fire."

The firing gong sounded through the ship. The main batteries fired. Max was nearly thrown off balance by the force of the recoil. Black gun smoke lingered briefly over *Spee*, to be snatched away by the wind. Close to *Exeter*, geysers of white water shot into the air. "Note to log," Langsdorff said to Hollendorf, "*Graf Spee* commenced firing against *Exeter* at zero six eighteen."

"Over!" Max shouted.

Orange halos blossomed from *Exeter*'s guns.

"He's fired!" yelped the young telephone talker.

"Steady," Langsdorff said, hands clasped behind his back like a squire looking over his acres.

A half kilometer from *Graf Spee* the incoming shells struck the ocean and sent up towers of water.

High above the bridge in their directing tower, the gunnery control team peered through their optical instruments, calculating *Exeter*'s range, course, and speed, sending this data to a mechanical tabulator deep in the armored bowels of the ship. This tabulator computed the trajectory of the shells and automatically trained *Graf Spee*'s main batteries. The recoil of the naval cannon comprising the main battery also had to be computed since a full broadside by both turrets heeled the ship over by five degrees or more.

In *Spee's* armored turrets, the deafened sailors, bundled up in their anti-flash overalls, frantically worked the huge naval cannons, ramming a six-hundred-seventy-pound shell hydraulically into the barrel, followed by a silk-wrapped powder charge. When the gun captain slammed home the breechblock, the ready light blinked on in the gun directing tower. The gunnery officer pressed the orange firing button and an electric current ignited the cordite, blowing the shell from the barrel. The gun crew flung open the breech, blasted the inside of the cannon with compressed air to clear any burning residue, thrust in a long-handled mop and swabbed out the barrel. In with a new shell and cordite charge and they were ready to fire.

The wind picked up and ruffled the sea. *Exeter* and *Graf Spee* plowed through the waves, spitting shells back and forth, disfiguring the water with angry spouts as the shots fell off the mark. Max kept his binoculars fixed on the British ship. His body shook each time *Spee's* forward battery fired. Black smoke drifted up from its barrels and eddied through the bridge. Finally, a hole opened in *Exeter's* midships.

"We hit her!" Max shouted.

But *Exeter's* broadside flamed out again, its report audible across the water. This time *Graf Spee* shook. Max saw nothing. Must be aft of the bridge. The main batteries were unharmed. They had to fire faster.

Max lost all sense of time as the Krupp-built cannons fired again and again, every twenty seconds, their muzzle blasts shaking the ship. Smoke draped *Spee*, spray from near misses washing over her sides. Langsdorff shouted helm and engine orders over the roar of the guns. Both ships steamed at emergency full ahead, smoke pouring from their stacks. The engine room would be unbearably hot and loud, dark and claustrophobic. Below the waterline, hatches battened down, they knew little of what was going on above. The ship's loudspeaker provided updates for many of the crew belowdecks, but these announcements could not be heard in the engine room over the terrific roar of the diesels. During battle, Dieter and his mates were the safest men aboard, but if *Spee* sank they would never get out.

The captain continually swung his binoculars from *Exeter* to the two light cruisers now crossing his wake, many kilometers astern. Max had nearly lost his hearing. Acrid cordite smoke burned his throat and brought tears to his eyes.

Again *Exeter* fired. Seawater thrown up by the near miss sprayed onto the main deck and drenched the sailors out in the open, sluicing across the teakwood boards. The ship rocked and Max almost lost his footing. As he grabbed the handrail, a shell struck with a violent explosion, ripping metal with a terrible screech. The force threw Langsdorff down. Max jumped to the captain's side and knelt over him. "Herr Kapitän! Herr Kapitän!" Gun smoke billowed across the trembling bridge. Max seized the captain by the lapels of his uniform coat. "Herr Kapitän Langsdorff!"

Above the roar of the guns, Hollendorf bellowed helm orders as he temporarily guided the racing ship, shifting her a few degrees off their base course every thirty seconds and then back so *Spee* would never steam in a straight line. Langsdorff opened his eyes, shook himself, and let Max help him up. "I'm fine, I'm fine," the captain said. "The others?"

"No casualties, Herr Kapitän."

"Very well."

The shell had struck the deck below them; the bridge only received the secondary shock wave. The ship rocked again as another shell found home. Flames shot up from the port bow. Damage reports streamed in, and Max tried to make sense of them. *Spee* was riddled with holes, but all her guns still fired.

Once again he focused his binoculars on *Exeter*. The British heavy cruiser was also on fire in several places and down by the bow. One of her forward turrets was out of action, its steel case split by a direct hit, the gun crew certainly killed. The two light cruisers had almost completed their arc. They readied to fire on *Graf Spee* from the opposite side, but *Spee*'s main guns ignored them. Another explosion and *Exeter*'s second forward turret split open, too. Smoke engulfed the ship's front half, and only her single stern turret continued to fire. They battered her; the British ship wouldn't be able to take much more.

But *Exeter* fought on. Above her flaming decks, the white battle ensigns waved defiantly. Below one of the ensigns flew the time-honored signal of the Royal Navy since Nelson's day: *Engage the enemy more closely*.

Suddenly, one of *Graf Spee*'s shells split open the steel cocoon of *Exeter*'s rear turret. Smoke poured now from her stern as well; she was out of guns. Max watched in disbelief as the huge burning ship slowly turned her course to converge with *Graf Spee*. "She's turning into us," he shouted to the captain.

Langsdorff ignored the warning. The two light cruisers now closed the range and began to fire. With *Exeter* no longer shooting, Langsdorff could not spare the shells to finally sink her. "Train main batteries to starboard!" he ordered. "Commence against light cruisers!"

Max spoke into the gunnery phone. "Order from captain: main batteries, commence against light cruisers. Repeat, main batteries to commence against light cruisers."

Momentarily the great cannons fell silent as they rotated to starboard on their ball-bearing rollers to meet the new threat. The two smaller cruisers, now eight kilometers out, charged bows on at *Graf Spee*, their prows pointed at the center of *Spee*'s right flank. *Spee*'s main turrets opened fire as soon as they bore. Geysers of seawater ringed all three vessels.

At a range of five kilometers, the British ships heeled over and began running parallel to *Graf Spee*, communicating with each other in hoists of brilliantly colored signal flags. This turn brought all their guns to bear. The cruisers opened a furious barrage. An English shell hit the fore part of the ship, carrying away a piece of the anchor chain. Another smashed one of the launches. A moment later the starboard side of the low steel bridge wall blew open, spraying the bridge with steel splinters. Max slammed to the deck beside Hollendorf and the deputy watch officer. Two signalmen fell, blood spraying everywhere, running into the scuppers and fouling the deckboards. Langsdorff went down, too.

"Torpedoes!" a telephone talker yelled hoarsely, repeating what the lookouts were telling him. "Torpedoes fired to the starboard!"

Max scrambled to his feet. The captain was sprawled out cold, covered in blood. To the ship's starboard side, a pair of torpedoes plowed through the water, trailing white tracks from the compressed air that powered them. Max lunged for the speaking tube. "Helmsman! Emergency right rudder!" He picked up the engine room phone and shouted, "Achtung! Full astern starboard, emergency ahead port!"

The bow of *Graf Spee* turned ponderously into the torpedoes. Max braced himself against the jagged steel of the bridge, heart pounding, watching the white arrows speed toward his ship. Sailors tumbled from their perches all over *Spee* as she heeled. Steel plates creaked in the turn, equipment crashing to the deck. Smoke billowed from the ship's lone stack and her bronze propellers thrashed the sea—the starboard prop full astern to drag them to the right, the port propeller pushing them to starboard at emergency ahead. Max struck his leg with his fist in a determined rhythm as he watched the bow turn. Faster. Faster. It seemed to be coming around in slow motion.

But they were in time.

Spee combed the tracks, the torpedoes speeding harmlessly down her sides. But now only her forward turret bore on the British ships. The light cruisers hounded her with all sixteen of their combined guns. On the other side, the burning *Exeter* continued to press on, bidding desperately to close the range—and what? Ram? Fire her torpedoes?

"Emergency left rudder," Max shouted to the helmsman. The rudder bit and *Graf Spee* swung slowly back to parallel with the light cruisers. "Ring for full ahead all engines," he ordered the men at the engine telegraphs.

"Report, Brekendorf." It was Langsdorff, back on his feet with blood spattered across his uniform.

"*Exeter* closing to port, sir. Two light cruisers engaged to starboard. Main batteries trained to starboard and firing."

"All batteries to fire on the light cruisers."

Max went to the gunnery phone, wiping blood from its receiver. "Order from captain: all batteries commence against light cruisers. Repeat, all batteries to commence against light cruisers."

Immediately, all *Graf Spee*'s guns that would bear—main and secondary batteries, anti-aircraft guns, machine guns—opened fire on the two British ships. *Spee* bucked with the recoil, metallic reports ringing loud in Max's ears.

The fusillade riddled the light cruisers. A hoist of bright signal flags broke over the two ships and they immediately turned away and bore off toward the horizon, engaging their smoke generators till they both disappeared into clouds of oily smoke.

Max could hear the sailors cheering.

"All batteries train on *Exeter*," Langsdorff ordered.

Again the main batteries fell silent as they turned on their rollers and trained onto H.M.S. *Exeter*. The crippled heavy cruiser was still five kilometers from *Graf Spee*, still too distant to fire her torpedoes. With a tremendous roar the big guns opened back up. *Exeter* cut a zigzag through the pockmarked sea, always steering for the most recent splashes—a standard tactic for throwing off enemy gunners. But *Spee*'s gunnery team found *Exeter*'s range, pounding her again and again. Suddenly she came hard a port and turned away. Dark smoke billowed from the fires up and down her length as the British ship struck out hard for the horizon.

"She's turning away!" Max shouted.

Langsdorff did not react. The bridge crew watched in silence, grinning at one another. "Train main batteries on the light cruisers," Langsdorff ordered.

But gunnery could not find them in the black clouds into which they had disappeared. Max reported this to the captain.

Langsdorff nodded. "Cease firing."

The sudden quiet unnerved Max. The tinkling of brass shells as they rolled on the deck, the swish of the sea as it flowed past the hull, the whine of the ventilators as they drew air into the engines, the tramp of feet—all these sounds, unheard during the battle, filled the stillness. Pain throbbed in Max's battered eardrums, spiking with each thump of his heart.

The concussions had stopped his watch. He put his head into the navigator's cubby to check the clock. Thirty-three minutes. The entire engagement had lasted only thirty-three minutes. Max's arms and legs quivered from the tension. Blood washed the bridge, obscuring some of the instruments. If the shell had been bigger, the ship slower, if he'd been standing on the other side—the fear now pressed in on him, catching in his throat. But he had survived.

Far in the distance, the light cruisers were still marked by their smoke clouds. They would now shadow *Graf Spee* from afar, outside the range of her big guns, afraid to come any closer and baying incessantly to the Admiralty for help. Royal Navy battleships from Rio de Janeiro to Cape Town would already be recalling their crews from bars and whorehouses, building up steam to slip their moorings, sailing to intercept the wounded *Spee*.

Langsdorff turned to Max, who came to attention and saluted. The captain nodded in return. Max picked up a small scrap of the metal plating that had been sheared from the bridge. He turned the fragment over in his hands, then slipped it into the pocket of his tunic. Medics were on the bridge now, hauling the casualties away. They loaded one of the signalmen onto a stretcher, his left arm hanging by tendons from the shoulder, torn from the joint and flopping at his side. Two deckhands stood by, under the watch of a bosun's mate, ready to sluice away the bits of flesh and rivulets of blood on the deck. Max turned away, vomit catching in his throat.

"Oberleutnant."

"Ja, Herr Kapitän?"

"Reduce speed to eighteen knots. Train turret Bruno on light cruisers."

"Jawohl, Herr Kapitän."

Max passed the captain's orders. In a minute, the vibration of the steel deck eased as *Graf Spee*'s speed fell off. Surgeon Commander Kertzendorff appeared, his coat smeared with blood from emergency operations. The doctor advanced on Langsdorff.

"Not now, Doktor."

"Herr Kapitän, I insist."

"A moment then, Doktor, a moment. Oberleutnant, are you able to carry on?"

"Jawohl, Herr Kapitän."

"Very well. Come hard starboard and resume our base course on a compass heading of one five five south-southeast. Maintain speed. As you come hard starboard we will have a chance to give them a broadside. Instruct the gunnery officer to fire on the light cruisers whenever they come in range and he can make them out. I'm going below to let the doctor examine me, and then I must inspect the ship. Carry on."

"Jawohl, Herr Kapitän."

Langsdorff took a last slow look around the blood-soaked bridge and went below.

Max notified gunnery, then came hard starboard and swung the ship around by almost one hundred eighty degrees.

A few minutes later, one of the signalmen spoke. "Herr Oberleutnant, damage control requests you to reduce speed. They are taking too much water in the bow compartments."

Max took the phone from the signalman. "Wachoffizier," he said.

"Ah, what a pleasure to know that Your Braveness lives."

"Dieter! What are you doing?"

"Groener's dead. I've been posted to damage control."

"What's the damage?"

"Well, we'll stay afloat but we've got more holes than a Swiss cheese. We're taking a lot of water up in the bow compartments. There's a hole in the port bow about three by six meters, and it won't be easy to fix. You have to slow us down so we can plug it."

"I can't. Captain's orders are to maintain course and speed."

"Max, there's a damn hole the size of a picture window in the port bow."

"Above or below the waterline?"

"Above, but just barely. Wind is picking up now and forcing water in."

"Dieter, you'll just have to rig more pumps. We can't slow down.

"Dieter . . ." Max paused on hearing the firing gong and braced himself as the aft turret fired at the shadowing British ships.

"Dieter, are you still there?"

"I am, but I won't be soon."

"You have to find a way to carry on. We can't reduce speed because those light cruisers keep darting out of their smoke to fire at us. We have to shake them."

"I'll do my best."

Max hung up and went to the starboard wing of the bridge. He fixed his binoculars on the smokescreen being thrown up by the distant British ships. From time to time one of the cruisers would charge out of the smoke, let loose a broadside at *Graf Spee*, then retire into the smoke again. *Spee*'s rear turret fired back.

They'd have the devil's own time shaking the cruisers, but they could do it, especially if they hit some heavy weather. In a storm, a larger ship could go faster than a smaller one. On their present course, *Graf Spee* headed east away from land into the deep ocean, the way home, to Germany. Max knew the raiding cruise was over. The most dangerous part of their journey had now begun. But if they made it through, and they would make it, he'd be home in two weeks, perhaps three. Home. Mareth. His father. His wedding.

Exhaustion filled him as the tension of the battle drained away. Still, he kept the bridge all morning, forcing himself to listen to the damage reports as they came in. More than twenty British shells had struck *Graf Spee*. Many had simply bounced off the ship's four-inch armor belt, but one had exploded in the galley; another smashed part of the internal communications system; others had carved up the launches, shattered lenses in the rangefinder, and punched numerous small holes in the deck and hull. Thirty-six men had been killed, many more wounded.

Fortunately, neither the engine room nor the main gun turrets had sustained any damage, although they'd shot away half their main battery ammunition. Apart from the hole in the bow, the ship appeared to Max to have sustained no crippling damage.

But when Langsdorff returned to the bridge at midday, he stood silent for a long moment, gazing out at the sea in front of them. Then he took his binoculars and looked aft, seeing in the far distance the two small towers of smoke that marked the shadowing British cruisers. "Oberleutnant," he said at last.

Max came to attention. "Herr Kapitän."

"Come hard port and steer new course of three one zero."

Without thinking, Max stepped to the voice tube. Then he stopped. That course would turn them right around and head them west, toward land, toward the mouth of the Rio Plata and Montevideo. "Herr Kapitän, there must be some mistake."

"Oberleutnant, steer three one zero."

"Sir, they will trap us in the Rio Plata. We'll never get home." He stared at Langsdorff. The estuary of the Plata was difficult enough to navigate, and after passing through the river's mouth, they would still have to steam fifty kilometers upriver to reach Montevideo. And when they chose to leave, they would have to conduct a fifty-kilometer running battle to get out into the South Atlantic again. The British would have them trapped like rats.

Langsdorff looked at Max. His voice when he spoke was slow and quiet. "The British cruisers would never have attacked us so aggressively on their own. They *must* be supported by larger British warships nearby. We cannot take the risk of encountering a Royal Navy battleship."

"Herr Kapitän, better to find our graves here at sea than run and hide!"

"Oberleutnant, steer three one zero."

Max hesitated, then came to attention again. "Jawohl, Herr Kapitän." He leaned over the voicepipe. "Helm."

"Helm, aye."

"Come hard port to new course of three one zero."

Graf Spee heeled hard to port as the rudder turned and came a port in a half circle, before steadying up on three one zero, northwest by west, the direction of land, the deep ocean left behind. Max knew they had been bluffed. Of course the British cruisers had come at them aggressively. That's what the Royal Navy did: attacked their enemies whenever and wherever they found them no matter what the odds. The British Admiralty expected no less, would accept no less. In the 1700s the Royal Navy court-martialed and shot an admiral who had not fought aggressively enough. That was their tradition.

But the German navy had no such traditions. After the only major engagement they ever fought with the Royal Navy—the Battle of the Skagerrak, off the Jutland peninsula—the German fleet turned around and went home. And there they stayed, safe and sound, the best men transferring to the U-boat force, until surrendering to the Royal Navy at the end of the First War. Max realized this was the only tradition Langsdorff knew: to run for safe harbor after a battle. But in his soul Max knew that a Royal Navy captain would never do as they were doing: turning away from battle with the enemy in sight. And standing next to him, Max saw that a weary and dispirited Captain Langsdorff knew it as well.

CHAPTER FIVE

MONTEVIDEO HARBOR, URUGUAY
FOUR DAYS LATER
17 DECEMBER 1939

MAX STOOD AT THE GANGWAY, EYES ON THE APPROACHING LAUNCH carrying Dr. Alberto Guani, the Uruguayan foreign minister, and his deputy. Just that morning the Uruguayan technical commission had finished their inspection and returned ashore to inform the foreign minister how much time would be required to render *Spee* seaworthy again. Langsdorff had asked for fourteen days. The chief engineer and two German civilian contractors from Argentina believed it would take that long to fully repair the ship, but Max doubted they would get so much time. The British government was strongly pressuring the Uruguayans to force *Graf Spee* out of Montevideo harbor and into the arms of the British fleet, now assembling like a pack of hyenas off the mouth of the Rio Plata.

Article XI of the Hague Convention of 1907, to which Uruguay—like Germany and Great Britain—was a signatory, forbade belligerent warships from staying more than twenty-four hours in the territorial waters of a neutral power. However, Article XIV of the same treaty stipulated that the stay could be extended only if the ship in question was badly damaged—but it was the right of the neutral government to decide how long the necessary repairs should take, and under the treaty, the only permissible repairs were the minimum required to make the vessel seaworthy; any repairs to damaged guns or any other equipment affecting the combat capabilities of the ship were not allowed. No doubt the British were arguing that *Graf Spee* was seaworthy already, having already steamed more than three hundred kilometers to reach Montevideo after her battle with the Royal Navy squadron.

But seaworthy was hardly the same as battleworthy. To escape into the broad Atlantic, *Spee* would have to fight her way through a mighty squadron of Royal Navy ships now standing off the mouth of the Rio Plata. To have any chance, they must have at least seven or eight days to prepare. And it wasn't one major repair—that would be easier—but a laundry list of damages large and small. Radio aerials had been shot away; water mains shattered; electrical wires severed by enemy shell splinters that had cut power in key areas of the ship; several anti-aircraft guns were out of commission, along with the forward AA command post, which had suffered a direct hit; ammunition hoists were out; searchlights smashed; voice tubes cut; telephones broken; hatches jammed; plating bent; the lenses in the main rangefinder damaged beyond repair. Even the galley had been blown up—a significant problem with so many men to feed—and the ship's entire store of flour contaminated by seawater. Worst of all, Max knew, as if it wasn't bad enough already, the high-pressure steam system that purified the diesel fuel had also been destroyed, and all the diesel engines had cracked motor mounts; the diesels might actually shear off their beds if heavy strain were put on them. Langsdorff had concealed that damage from the inspectors by barring them from the engine room, knowing the Uruguayan inspectors would gossip like old women at a tea party the moment they stepped ashore and tell all to the British.

All around Max, the many skilled craftsmen among the crew

caulked and hammered, welded and rewired. If only the work could be done in the builder's yard in Wilhelmshaven, instead of in this South American backwater sweating the starch out of their uniforms, swatting flies and waiting to find out if they would be thrown like scraps of meat to the waiting British dogs.

At length the launch drew up to the gangway. The foreign minister and his deputy came up the side to the twitter of the bosun's pipe. Both men wore black swallow-tailed coats and striped cravats, sartorial code for a formal diplomatic call. Only if they we wearing spats would they look more ridiculous, Max thought. But he came to stiff attention and saluted them all the same.

"Bienvenido a *Graf Spee*," he said, botching the pronunciation, feeling very foolish. He'd taken an introductory Spanish course at the Marineschule Mürwik years ago but hadn't spoken it since then. Fortunately, the foreign minister and his man spoke fluent English, the only language they had in common with the Germans. They conducted all of their meetings with Captain Langsdorff in English, an irony they all remarked on.

Guani seemed nonetheless to appreciate the gesture. He smiled and said, "Gracias, mein Herr."

Max ushered the Uruguayans quickly through the ship, past the busy sailors and into the captain's formal day cabin. Langsdorff stood as they entered, rigid in his white dress uniform, sword buckled around him, two of the ship's other senior officers at his back. Max had been ordered to remain as the captain's adjutant, so he shut the door and stood at the back of the room as the diplomats advanced.

"Captain Langsdorff," Dr. Guani said, bowing deeply.

Langsdorff bowed in return.

"My deputy, Señor Diaz."

"Señor."

Langsdorff exchanged bows with the deputy as well, then turned to indicate the men behind him. "My second in command, . Commander Kay, and my senior gunnery officer, Commander

Ascher." He gestured toward a leather settee. "Gentlemen, please sit." The captain took a seat himself, as did Kay and Ascher. *Graf Spee* had no air-conditioning and the cabin was very hot. The temperature hovered somewhere over a hundred degrees throughout the ship's interior; in the engine room it was closer to a hundred and forty. Max could feel the sweat running down his back, soaking his uniform.

Langsdorff's steward, Jak, appeared with a silver tray and served each man coffee. Then Max offered around a cigar box filled with Havanas. All five of the seated men took a cigar and the cabin filled with the scent of rich tobacco.

"I trust you gentlemen had a pleasant ride across the harbor?" Langsdorff said.

"Most pleasant, Captain, most pleasant," replied the foreign minister. "The weather is particularly fine this time of year for a boat ride."

"I have found it so," the captain said.

"Your wounded are ashore?" Señor Diaz asked.

"Yes, yes they are. Receiving excellent care from your countrymen, I am told. I am most grateful for your kind attention to them and for your assistance in the burial of our comrades killed in battle."

This had taken place the previous morning, when thirty-six coffins, each draped in the German naval ensign, a blood red flag with black stripes and a swastika in the center, had been lowered from *Graf Spee* to the deck of a tugboat for transfer to the cemetery. Langsdorff mustered what sailors he could spare for the funeral ceremony, with Max detailed as one of the officers. They were joined by Langmann, the German ambassador, and even two of the British merchant captains who had been captives on *Spee* until she reached Montevideo. The British captains—Dove and Captain Brown of *Huntsman*—contributed a wreath inscribed: "To the memory of brave men of the sea from their comrades of the British merchant service." They had not forgotten the deference shown to them by Langsdorff and his crew during their time of imprisonment on *Graf Spee*.

Now a charged silence settled onto the captain's cabin. Langsdorff smoked while Guani examined the bulkheads with utmost care, like a detective looking for a clue. When his eyes had completed a full circuit of the room, he straightened his gray cravat and spoke. "The technical experts from our navy have, have, ah, how do you say, examined your ship, Captain, and it is my job to present you with their findings. I am here to perform that service con permisso . . . with your permission."

Langsdorff stared.

"Captain Langsdorff, as you know, we sent several of our best naval officers, several of our most industrious and intelligent officers, to look upon your gallant ship, and they have made a report which I assure you is very factual and sound because they are, as I've said, our most experienced experts on matters such as this."

Max gritted his teeth. He doubted the Uruguayan navy had even one warship, let alone one so complex as *Graf Spee*. Probably their "experts" had never worked on anything more complex than the beat-up patrol boats he had seen in the harbor.

Langsdorff removed the cigar from his mouth. "I look forward to Your Excellency's report."

Guani looked straight at the captain. "We grant you seventy-two hours."

Max felt his heart plunge.

Langsdorff stood from his chair, straightened his coat, and adjusted his sword. "That is not enough time, Herr Minister. It's impossible. International law stipulates that a man-of-war may remain in neutral harbor for as long as necessary to effect repairs. This is our right under the Hague Convention."

"As you know, Captain, the Hague Convention stipulates that a neutral power must allow a man-of-war to remain in port only as long as required to make the vessel seaworthy. We are not obligated under the treaty to do more, and indeed, Captain, we are specifically abjured by the Hague Convention from allowing you any time to restore the fighting power of your ship in any way."

Langsdorff fixed his blue eyes on the men as if he could change their minds with his will. Yet Max knew Dr. Guani was right, and so did the captain. Langsdorff had even understated his case by not disclosing the damage to the fuel purification system or the cracked engine mounts.

"Our naval experts have examined your ship most thoroughly, Captain Langsdorff. They are unanimous in their agreement that she can be rendered seaworthy in seventy-two hours. It is our right under the Hague Convention to determine the length of time required to make repairs and we have done so with our most talented men. I give you my firmest assurance on that point, Captain. Two of the inspecting officers are graduates of the Annapolis Naval Academy in the United States."

Max shifted his feet. He would never get home. He would be stuck in this godforsaken hinterland forever—or else killed in a sea battle in a few days.

"I must protest, Herr Minister," Langsdorff said, "I must protest most strongly. With all due respect to the Uruguayan navy, I must submit, Your Excellency, that the men who inspected our ship do not understand the complexities involved in repairing a sophisticated warship like *Graf Spee*. One cannot simply hammer and weld as if one were repairing a motorcar. One must cut plates and weld them perfectly. Men of great skill are required to do this work—men who are presently being summoned from German communities all over South America."

The foreign minister recoiled and stayed silent for long moments. Finally he said, "You will find excellent riveters here in Montevideo, Captain."

Langsdorff flushed bright red in the face. "Riveters! Riveters! Mein Gott, there isn't a single rivet in this entire ship! Herr Minister, I must say again that *Graf Spee* is a very, very complex vessel. She is welded together, and only expert craftsmen can repair her.

She is like a fine Swiss watch, not a cheap alarm clock. Your Excellency must understand this. Anyone of competence who visits the ship will know she cannot be made seaworthy in seventy-two hours."

"I am truly sorry, Captain Langsdorff—grievously sorry to be the one required to impart these facts. I was loath to come and do so, was I not, Señor Diaz?"

Diaz nodded solemnly.

Guani held his hand up. "This is a most delicate moment in the history of our nation, Captain Langsdorff. Most delicate. I beg you to understand our dilemma. We are a very small country and very far from Europe, but even here world tensions have an effect. I feel most unfortunate to be the bearer of this news which is so distressing to you."

Langsdorff turned away from the Uruguayans, then wheeled back around, left hand tight around his sword hilt. "I shall instruct our ambassador to protest."

Guani puffed his cigar till he was almost hidden in a cloud of smoke, like an escaping battleship. "Your ambassador has already presented us with a most eloquent protest, Captain. He is a personal friend of mine, a man of intelligence and charm, and his letter has received careful attention at the very highest levels of my government, I can assure you. But I fear we are under instructions from the president and the cabinet to answer it in the negative."

Langsdorff stepped toward the diplomats. Max thought he might draw his sword and strike them. "Have you no pride that you must succumb to the British like dogs?" he said, seething beneath his spotless white coat.

That brought the foreign minister to his feet. "You are one German ship! At this moment three Royal Navy battleships are steaming for the Rio Plata. An aircraft carrier and three cruisers are at the river's mouth as we speak. We did not ask you to come here, and I can only say to you now, Captain Langsdorff, that your presence in Montevideo harbor is a grave embarrassment to the

Uruguayan government. We are acting fully within our rights under the Hague Convention. Every nation in the Americas supports our position, Captain, including the United States of America and their illustrious president, His Excellency Señor Franklin Delano Roosevelt, with whom our president had the honor of speaking yesterday. The Royal Navy will not be deterred by diplomacy. I can only tell you, sir, and I'm sure you will understand, that a naval battle in Montevideo harbor would be a catastrophe for Uruguay. Seventy-two hours. Good day, Captain Langsdorff."

Dr. Guani turned and strode from the cabin, followed by Señor Diaz. Max stayed at attention; one of the sentries outside the door would escort the Uruguayans to their launch. Langsdorff, silent with rage, stood stock still in the center of the room. Kay and Ascher remained uneasily in their chairs. Max stood rigid for a full five minutes before Langsdorff noticed and told him to stand easy. "Ask the senior officers to assemble here at noon," the captain ordered. "Dismissed."

Max saluted and withdrew.

At noon precisely Langsdorff entered his day cabin to face the senior officers of his ship, all of them crisp and ramrod straight in their starched summer uniforms.

Kay and Ascher were there again, along with two of Ascher's gunnery officers; Max and the other two watch officers; Klepp, the chief engineer, and his two top men, including Dieter; Wattenberg, the senior navigation officer; the surgeon commander; the supply officer, the communications officer, and several others.

Hot coffee, which few wanted in this weather, had been served by Jak, who brewed it with water heated in the engine room.

Everyone stood to attention the moment Captain Langsdorff entered and remained standing until he seated himself, his ever-present cigar trailing its hazy blue cloud. Jak fetched him an ashtray and withdrew.

"Be seated, please, gentlemen," the captain said.

Max could see the gloom on the faces of the other officers. Nothing evaporated faster than morale on a man-o'-war. These were the same men who had wreaked havoc on the British Merchant Navy for nearly three months, yet now they had become despondent.

Langsdorff rapped the table for attention, even though everyone was looking at him already. The captain's eyes were bloodshot and puffy from lack of sleep, Max noticed.

"We must decide whether to fight or scuttle the ship," the captain said. "I would like your opinions."

Max's mouth fell open. Scuttle the ship? Scuttle their own ship?

"Herr Kapitän," Ascher said. He was a heavyset man near Langsdorff's age, also a veteran of the Imperial Navy. "Herr Kapitän, to scuttle the ship . . . Sir, I, I was aboard *Frederick the Great* when we scuttled her in Scapa Flow after the First War. We had no choice then. The men would not fight and what else could we do? But I will never forget the sight of her going to the bottom, Herr Kapitän, and the whole fleet around her—all of them at our own hands. It haunts me still, sir. They called us heroes afterwards, some people did, but I never felt like a hero. It was the worst day of my life." He spoke the words slowly, shaking his head back and forth, looking down at the table.

The High Seas Fleet had spent much of the First War behind a screen of protective mines in its harbors at Kiel and Wilhelmshaven, keeping a safe distance from the superior forces of the Royal Navy, allowing the British blockade to strangle Germany by methodically starving her out. In the waning days of the war the admiral commanding the fleet had ordered the ships to sea in a suicide mission to break the blockade, but their crews mutinied. They refused orders. Killed a number of officers. The Kiel mutiny spread like a fever to other naval bases and led directly to the collapse of the imperial government, the abdication of the Kaiser, and Germany's capitulation to the Allies. Once in captivity in the Royal Navy anchorage at Scapa Flow, the officers of the Imperial Navy schemed to save their honor by sinking the fleet.

Eight months after surrender, on a signal from the flagship, they opened the seacocks and scuttled their seventy-four ships, ending the darkest chapter in German naval history.

Max looked down at the table now, too, as did others. When Ascher spoke again, his voice trembled. He said, "It would be better to die than repeat this act, Herr Kapitän."

Langsdorff sat silently, face slightly flushed. The cigar burned forgotten in his hand. Finally he said, "It will mean death, I can assure you of that. In our present condition, with the Royal Navy amassed to meet us, we will have no chance. You may choose this for yourself, Ascher, and I believe a captain's fate cannot be separated from that of his ship, but we have given our lives to this navy already and we are no longer young men. What shall we tell this lot of boys under our command? When they ask why they are dying, what shall we say? I have already buried thirty-six of them half a world from home. I'll be quite sure of my purpose before I bury a thousand more."

Max glanced up at Dieter, whose face was drawn, eyes burning. It was not a characteristic expression. Dieter's father had known the shame of the Kiel mutiny, had watched the ships go down at Scapa Flow; no doubt that terrible moment had been in his mind when he hanged himself. Dieter had entered the navy to avenge his father, not to suffer his plight all over again. Max could not hold his tongue.

"We have to at least try and fight," he blurted out. "The men of this crew may be young, but they are navy men all the same. They have sworn to protect the honor of the Kriegsmarine and they will fight if you will lead them, sir." He stood and slapped the table with the flat of his hand. "I, too, have devoted my life to becoming a naval officer, and I did not spend all those years studying and training just to blow up my own ship. Has the Royal Navy ever done such a thing? In five hundred years? Herr Kapitän, you know how the British will gloat if we scuttle her. Then who will be the ones submitting like dogs?"

Langsdorff fixed his stare on Max. "Yes, I know, Brekendorf, and you are so eager to die for valor. Perhaps they will bury you with a Knight's Cross around your neck, but I have been charged with the care of more than a thousand sailors, so I cannot think only of myself. I know our young crew is brave and I know they will follow me. The question is whether my conscience will allow me to lead them to slaughter for no good reason. Getting us all killed in a pheasant shoot will not help Germany win the war."

Langsdorff's face seemed to have aged ten years in a week; the bones seemed closer underneath his skin. Max did not respond, but neither did he turn his eyes away from the captain's. He did not want to die—that much was certain—but he was prepared to, as every fighting man must be.

Ascher said, "You have already made your decision, then, Herr Kapitän?"

Langsdorff nodded again. A faint, bitter expression—almost a smile—passed like a shadow over his features. He went on nodding, saying nothing, for what seemed like a very long time.

———

Max spent the next two days working in the officers' mess, assisted by Dieter and two other officers. Gone were the solicitous mess stewards. Around them, *Graf Spee* had grown silent save for the gentle hum of the engine that supplied electrical current to the ship. No tramp of feet, no chisel against the deck, no cursing petty officers. Only a skeleton crew remained aboard. The ship was not quiet like a tomb, Max thought, but like a museum toward the end of the day when the last group of youngsters has been ushered out and only the charwomen remain to tidy up.

Dieter rose from his schematic drawing of the ship's magazine and switched on the large wall-mounted radio. It was their last evening in Montevideo. Above the radio, a faded square showed where the portrait of Admiral Graf von Spee had hung. It could not be allowed to go down with the ship, and so had been sent ashore along with the ship's bell, its war diary, and most of the men.

The voice of an American announcer crackled from the radio speaker. Max and Dieter had been listening to the man's reports off and on for the last two days—listening as his voice alternated between shrillness and ponderous gravity. Tonight it was shrill. "This is Mike Fowler reporting to you live. The scene here in Montevideo is unbelievable, ladies and gentlemen, simply unbelievable. Tensions are at the boiling point here in Uruguay. Thousands—no, it must be tens of thousands—of people are lining the harbor here in Montevideo, waiting to see how this drama will play out. It's as if all of Brooklyn had gone to Coney Island at once. People are jammed everywhere—on top of cars, hanging from lampposts, leaning out of buildings. Just an incredible spectacle. Below me I can see the entire harbor, a huge circle ringed with docks and hotels and white sand beaches, a lovely sight, ladies and gentlemen. Vendors are doing a land office business in ice cream and soda pop here today. The heat is better than ninety degrees, but everyone is scrambling to get a look at the wounded Nazi battleship moored in the middle of the harbor, and still no one knows what the Germans will do. Many in the crowd are eager to see a real naval battle right here in the harbor. Blood will spill into the South Atlantic . . ."

Max got up to switch the radio off, but Dieter stopped him. "I want to listen."

"Dieter, please. I can't work with this racket."

"Yessir, ladies and gentlemen, there will be blood in the water as a suicide squad of Nazi fanatics prepares . . ."

Max turned it off. "I cannot work with that idiot yelling in the background."

Dieter held his hands up in surrender—a fitting gesture. For once he was without a response. Even Dieter's swagger had dropped away. He wasn't bothering to hide his depression, his thin face pale from the strain.

"We have to finish these plans tonight," Max said, dropping back into his chair.

Dieter sighed. He lit a cigarette and ran a hand up through his hair. "I don't remember much about my father. It's curious, our mind, our memories—often I'm not sure whether things I remember about my father happened or whether I only wish they had happened. But what I truly remember, and remember so clearly, are the old naval officers my mother boarded in our home. They were bitter men, Max, mein Gott." He laughed, a bitter sound in itself. "No victory, no glory, and after the war, barely enough money to keep themselves fed. Every dignity stripped away. When I looked at them, I could see why my father had done what he did. At first I was so angry with him. Killing himself—it seemed a terrible mystery to me. Later, I understood."

Max lit a cigarette of his own. He didn't know what to say. "This war will be different," he offered, "no matter what happens tomorrow. We're not going to end up like those men."

Dieter smiled.

The two friends sat for a moment looking at each other, Dieter puffing out perfect little rings of smoke. It was a trick Max had never mastered.

In the morning, they began preparations to weigh anchor

It took thirty minutes to unbolt the warheads from a half dozen sleek torpedoes. Max knew the torpedo mechanics could have done the job in a fraction of the time, but they had all been sent ashore. Emil, one of the Dieselobermaschinists, did it instead, whistling tunelessly as he went about his work. Each warhead was set gently onto a small trolley, and Max then led the way to one of the ship's elevators, his six-man crew following behind in a row with the yellow trolleys.

They rode the elevator all the way down to the refrigerated magazines on the lowest deck. One magazine, toward the bow, supplied shot and powder to the forward guns, while another, toward the stern, supplied the after guns. Max left three of the warheads in the corridor, then had his men push the other three to the forward magazine.

He produced the brass key—given to him by Ascher—and unlocked the magazine's heavy metal door. A blast of cold air hit his face. It felt wonderful amid the heat of the roasting ship. Max stepped through and held open the magazine's double-sealed door. Still whistling, Emil led the crew inside.

In the main powder room, wooden shelves—so made to prevent sparks—were bolted to the wall and piled high with silk powder bags. The bags looked harmless, like so many sacks of flour. Max stroked one of them—it felt like lingerie—then jerked his hand away. Each contained enough force to blow a six-hundred-seventy-pound shell twenty kilometers through the air. The sailors looked about the magazine with keen interest. It was a secret, sacred space, strictly off-limits—none had ever seen it before. Yet it was this powder, mixed in just the right way, measured in just the right amounts, that elevated *Graf Spee* from being merely a ship to a man-o'-war.

A hand signal set the sailors to work pushing and pulling the torpedo warheads through the double steel doors. Max felt the chill air drying the sweat on his face and back. It was the first time he'd been cool since they arrived in this cursed place, where it was so damned hot that a man could get third-degree burns if he touched the armor plating at midday. Only the giant ventilating fans going full out and blowing fresh air into the ship made it remotely bearable. Hard to imagine what a thousand men locked in a steel ship without ventilation would smell like—not pleasant.

His sailors manhandled the three warheads into the middle of the magazine. Still whistling, Emil piled powder bags atop the warheads. Then he snapped to attention. "Completed, Herr Oberleutnant."

Max nodded. The sailors were in no hurry to leave and neither was he. Oddly, the magazine did not seem like a forbidding place. It was dark and cool, like a root cellar on a summer's day. As in the officers' mess, there was no sound this far down in the ship except the faintly throbbing diesels. The bloodthirsty crowds on shore were a world away. Max felt an insane desire to smoke and laughed at the thought. "Let's get out of here before someone lights a cigarette," he said, smiling. His men laughed with him and filed out the double doors. Max paused and extracted the timer with the detonator from his pocket. All his desire for glory and it had come to this—sinking his own ship. He set the timer, placed it atop the sacks of powder piled on the warheads, and with that, he turned and left, locking the magazine door behind him and putting the brass key in his pocket.

They repeated this procedure in the second magazine and Max emerged on deck afterward, blinded by the brilliance of the sun. He blinked like a lizard. The sea of people along the harbor shore seemed to still be swelling, as if nothing this interesting had ever happened in Uruguay before. They would get their damned show soon enough and to hell with them. Beneath his feet the teakwood planking had become so hot that the varnish began to peel. Damn this forsaken place.

He motioned for his men to follow him to the stern of the ship, where one of the main fueling ports was located. Dieter's engineering crew, stripped to the waist and running with sweat, had wrestled the cover off the port and attached a coupling that connected to a set of emergency fueling hoses.

Max set his men to work pulling the hoses along the deck to the aft companionway. There he stationed Emil and Krancke, a deckhand—son of "the best-known taxi driver in all of Leipzig," he liked to claim. They pulled each hose hand over hand and let the forepiece with its brass cap play out down the metal stairs behind them. Two more sailors waited at the bottom to pull the hoses through to the next stairway, at the bottom of which Dieter had posted two additional men. In this way each hose made its way down, deck by deck, until it reached the top of the staircase descending to the lowest deck, where the magazines were located.

Only the morning before *Graf Spee*'s decks had been scrubbed and mopped, as they had been every morning during their war patrol. This was a German warship—no dirt allowed—but soon the gleaming decks would run black with stinking fuel oil. The very thought provoked Max and made his temples burn with anger.

Once the hoses were in place he assembled his men on the main deck and turned them over to Dieter. They came to attention and saluted, sweat glistening like mineral oil on their bodies. Max was soaked and bedraggled, too. Sweat had leached all the starch out of his white uniform. Unlike the men, orders forbade him from removing his shirt or tunic. Even his shoes were damp, so much that they squeaked when he walked.

He climbed the narrow outboard staircase to the bridge and found it still and hot, even with the windows open. There was no breeze in the harbor. The men in the engine room must be close to fainting.

Langsdorff stood alone on the bridge wing, smoking his cigar, watching the thousands of people on shore. The crowd's buzz drifted over the water, distant and indistinct, like the roar from a soccer stadium blocks away. Max came to attention and saluted when the captain turned to face him.

"Completed, Herr Kapitän."

Langsdorff touched his gold-braided cap in acknowledgment. "Prepare to get under way."

Max saluted again, then picked up the engine room phone. "Order from captain: prepare to get under way."

"Jawohl, Herr Oberleutnant."

A deep hum sounded through *Graf Spee* as four of the mammoth diesel engines were fired off and hooked to the propeller shafts. Max, hand on the bridge rail, felt the vibration pick up. Aft of the bridge, black diesel smoke began to waft from the funnel. Normally Oberbootsmann Carls would have his men swab the diesel particles from the deck, but *Graf Spee* was through with all that now. Max supposed he could actually spit on the deck if he wanted to, though it was a serious offense. In the British navy, he knew, sailors used to be flogged for spitting on the deck since it was held to be the same as spitting against the King.

"Up anchors," Langsdorff ordered.

Because the telephone talkers had already left the ship, Max lifted the megaphone against his lips and shouted through the open window, "Up anchors."

On the bow, Carls saluted, then, drawing on his gauntlets, he threw the lever on the anchor motor, which began to grind away as it pulled the wet black chains from the harbor's muddy water. A loud thump sounded as the anchors were drawn flush to the bow. The aft anchors had been raised before the crew had gone ashore.

"Anchors secured, Herr Kapitän."

"Hoist the battle ensign."

"Jawohl, Herr Kapitän."

Max made his way to the bridge wing, then across the metal catwalk to the signal deck. The signalmen had left the ship too, but the chief signalman had attached the battle ensign to the halyard before he went. Max gripped the rough hemp in his fingers and hauled the flag up. It hung limp in the heat but he came to attention and saluted. He could barely look at the captain when he returned to the bridge.

Langsdorff said nothing, only continued vacantly puffing on his cigar. A slight breeze ruffled the harbor waters, and that along with the lazy current of the harbor caused the huge ship to begin a slow drift. Max glanced at the captain but stayed quiet. The almost imperceptible movement of the ship finally seemed to shake Langsdorff from his reverie. "Ahead dead slow," he ordered.

"Jawohl, Herr Kapitän." There were no sailors on the bridge so Max rang the engine telegraph himself.

Her bronze propellers bit the water and *Graf Spee* moved slowly toward the harbor entrance. Max peered through his

binoculars at the people on the shore. Many waved white hand-
kerchiefs and many, members of Uruguay's German community,
gave the stiff-armed Nazi salute. They'd been standing out there
in the sun all day. More than a few must have fainted. Seventeen
hundred hours now and the air had cooled by a few degrees but
the bridge plating was still too hot to touch.

The sound of one of the phones startled Max, so quiet and
gentle was the ship's motion. He picked it up. "Bridge."

"B-Service here, sir. Observers report two British cruisers have
moved into the Rio Plata and are steaming upstream at flank
speed."

Max repeated this to the captain. "Acknowledged," he said. It
was only what they had expected—the little barking dogs sent in to
nip at their heels while the capital ships waited over the horizon,
shells loaded in the breech of every cannon, ready to discharge an
immense broadside against *Graf Spee*. Langsdorff withdrew the cigar from his mouth and gave an order so quietly that Max had to
have him repeat it. "Left standard rudder," the captain said again.

Max bent over the speaking tube and passed the order to the
helmsman. Langsdorff let her swing until her raked bow almost
pointed toward the channel that led out of the harbor, into the
river beyond. "Rudder amidships," he ordered.

Max passed this order, too. The ship steadied up on the new
course and headed into the channel followed by a long motorized
barge. Max turned aft and gazed at Montevideo. So many people
had turned out to see their final voyage. Most of them just wanted
to watch death on the water, as if warships were bulls in a ring. He
turned his back on the harbor and cursed them.

Slowly *Graf Spee* moved through the channel and into the Rio
Plata, fifty kilometers wide at this point, the water stained khaki by
the silt carried down from the mountains. The sun moved lower
now, the breeze picking up. How long before the British cruisers
arrived? Two hours? Maybe three? Because ships of one belligerent nation were not allowed to sail from harbor within twenty-four

hours of a ship from another belligerent nation, the cruisers had been forced to wait beyond the river's mouth—outside the territorial waters of Uruguay. But they were coming hell for leather at *Graf Spee* now that she was under way, and they would let the diplomats sort it out later.

Langsdorff stood on the bridge wing and took careful bearings from the land with the mounted compass. When he was satisfied that the ship had come far enough, he said, "Stand by to disembark."

"Jawohl, Herr Kapitän." Max took up the P.A. system microphone. "Achtung! Achtung! All personnel not on the special detail, report to boarding ladders on the port side."

Spee continued to glide slowly through the river, followed obediently by the barge. By now the two vessels were five kilometers out from the crowded harbor.

"All stop," Langsdorff said.

Max passed the order and the vibration died away as the engines went to standby. *Graf Spee* drifted to a halt in the muddy river.

Langsdorff stood for several minutes without speaking, then turned to Max. "Commence."

Max again picked up the microphone for the loudspeaker. "Commence disembarkation."

Almost everyone still aboard would leave the ship now. They gathered quietly by the boarding ladders and climbed down into the barge, which had come up alongside. Langsdorff watched his men go, each sailor giving the captain a respectful salute. The barge was loaded in ten minutes. It cast off and moved away, leaving only a tiny detail of officers and men behind. Langsdorff came inside and ordered the ship to proceed ahead, dead slow.

The diesel smoke began to trickle again from *Spee*'s lone funnel as she started to move, her propellers churning the brown water under her stern into a froth. Aft of them, the barge had anchored itself in the middle of the river. Max followed Langsdorff back out onto the bridge wing, wrinkling his nose at the muddy stench of the Plata. He could see the lights of Montevideo beginning to flicker on in the blue twilight. Sailors on the barge had come to attention to salute their receding ship.

Max took his binoculars and peered out ahead of the bow. They were alone on the wide river, which stretched away to the horizon. He hadn't really expected to see any British ships, but you never knew about the British. If they came upon *Graf Spee* now, Langsdorff's plan would be ruined.

The captain smoked in silence, peering at the horizon through his binoculars from time to time. Langsdorff's shoulders were hunched from the stress of the last few days. Well, Max thought bitterly, they would soon have plenty of time to rest. A check of their bearing off Montevideo's tallest building confirmed their position on the chart. "International waters now, Herr Kapitän."

Langsdorff looked at him quizzically, as if he'd forgotten Max was there. "What?"

"We're in international waters now, Herr Kapitän."

"Very well."

"Helmsman is standing by, sir."

"Very well."

Now they were out where the British could hit them with no warning and no repercussions, yet Langsdorff did nothing, only continued to stare absently ahead. The two British cruisers were probably no more than an hour's steaming time from them. This was no time for melancholia.

Suddenly Langsdorff left the bridge and ducked into the small chartroom behind. He returned wearing his dress sword.

For God's sake, Max thought.

Ahead of them the sun touched the horizon, its dying rays coloring the ship a deep pink. River wind blew through the bridge, wet and cool, stinking of fish and mud. Max felt it play across his face as he silently watched the captain.

"We'll miss the deep-water channel if we don't turn, Herr Kapitän."

Langsdorff made no reply. Should Max order the helm changes himself? He understood the captain's feelings—his own stomach was clenched tight with anger. Beneath his hand, Max felt the warm pitted steel of the ship—a ship that had given him so much. You couldn't love a ship like a woman, but you could feel a gratitude for her, and *Graf Spee* had certainly earned that from him and the others. Old sailors said ships had a soul, and perhaps it was true, for it seemed to Max that *Spee* sensed her destiny and went to it slowly, haltingly, like the men who gave the orders.

"Herr Kapitän, we must turn. We must."

Langsdorff drew the sword from its gilded scabbard, the silver blade gleaming in the last light of the sun. He said, "The All Highest himself gave me this sword when I was commissioned in 1912. I accepted it from his own hands. 'I swear by God's holy name that I will wear this sword with honor and courage, Your Imperial Highness.' That is what I said to him."

Max nodded. The wind blew over them both. "Herr Kapitän, we . . ."

Langsdorff thrust the shining sword back into the scabbard with a clang. "I know, Oberleutnant, I know. Right standard rudder. All ahead one-quarter speed."

Max passed the order, then looked again at the captain, who seemed to have regained some of his composure. *Graf Spee* swung to starboard and the vibration picked up as the men in the engine room stepped up their revolutions.

Langsdorff watched carefully now, eyes darting from the compass to the channel markers. When the bow pointed directly upriver, the captain checked her turn and now the huge ship moved up the muddy river toward Buenos Aires.

They steamed in this direction for five minutes. A dazzling red sun, now just an orb on the horizon, seemed to float behind them. Langsdorff puffed his cigar and surveyed the water through his binoculars. "Any more information on the British warships?"

"B-Service reports that our observers have them about one

hour south of our present position, maybe less, and closing at full speed, sir."

The captain frowned. "Left standard rudder."

Max repeated this order down the voicepipe to the helmsman. When the rudder bit, *Graf Spee* cut to the left and moved out of the ship channel.

"Stop engines."

Max rang the engine telegraph and moved the needle to *Stop Engines.*

The gentle hum of the engines died away as they were disconnected from the propeller shafts. *Spee* glided softly as her way fell off. On the bow, Oberbootsmann Carls stood ready at the anchor controls.

"Let go fore," Langsdorff ordered, now more in control of himself.

Max took up the megaphone and bellowed into it with his best quarterdeck voice: "Let go the bow anchors!" A loud splash echoed through the twilight, followed by the roar of the long black anchor chains playing out.

"Let go aft," Langsdorff ordered.

Already Oberbootsmann Carls was running down the wooden deck to the ship's stern. In a few seconds, Max heard the stern anchors splash into the Plata.

Calm descended over the ship. Captain Langsdorff glanced slowly around the deserted bridge, passing his eyes across the shining brass of the compass mountings, the soft green glow of the instrument lights, the river chart tacked to the chart table. Through the bridge windows, the sharp prow of *Spee* was still visible in the murky evening. "Finished with engines," he whispered hoarsely, reluctant to say it.

Max picked up the engine room phone and gripped it tight, closing his eyes for a moment to master himself.

"Engine room, aye." It was Dieter's voice.

Max stared out into the gathering dark.

"Engine room, aye," Dieter said again.

"Finished with engines," Max said.

Dieter was silent for a moment and then replied quietly. "Finished with engines, aye-aye."

It was the traditional order given at the end of every voyage. Max slammed the phone down.

The captain said, "Execute your orders, Oberleutnant."

Max came to attention and saluted but didn't speak, not trusting his voice to be steady. He descended to the main deck and found Dieter among the deckhands.

"All crew accounted for," Dieter said, saluting.

Max saluted his friend, then turned and made for the main companionway. He began descending into the bowels of the ship as Dieter and the crewmen prepared the launch.

He moved quickly, like the others. If the British caught them in the launch in international waters, they could be taken prisoner. In the darkened interior of *Graf Spee*, the blue nightlights had come on, casting a lonely glow over the deserted corridors. Max followed the hoses down through the ship, making sure they were still in place. Satisfied, he lingered for a moment, looking around the abandoned interior. A lifejacket lay on the deck, dropped there by a careless sailor on his way out. Worse, a cigarette butt had been crushed out beside it. A cigarette butt. On the deck of his ship. By the Lord God and all the Holy Saints in heaven if he ever found the swine who had done that he would see the man got a month in the brig. He picked up the cigarette butt and put it in his pocket. Turning about, Max made his way up the flights of metal stairs to the top deck, his footsteps echoing through the emptiness of *Graf Spee*.

Back on the main deck, he signaled Emil to start the pump. The hoses plumped as they began to fill with the stinking diesel oil from the ship's fuel bunkers. Oil ran through the hoses into the depths of the ship, where it would spill out in a viscous black puddle, spreading out like ink from an overturned inkwell. The noxious oil would splash down the narrow stairways, spill into cabins, into the crew spaces, and foul the once spotless decks of the pocket battleship *Admiral Graf Spee*.

When all the remaining crewmen had taken their places in the launch, Max heaved himself in, leaving on board only Dieter, who had to operate the crane, and Captain Langsdorff, who stood in lonely splendor on the deck in his sparkling white uniform, sword buckled at his side. Without speaking, the captain climbed into the launch, ignoring the outstretched hands of the men who offered to help him. He sat quietly in the rear, knuckles white on the hilt of his sword.

Max cupped his hands around his mouth. "Give way!" he shouted. Dieter put the crane in motion, gears grinding loudly in the peaceful evening. Without a bump, the launch came out of its chocks. Dieter maneuvered it over the river and gently lowered the boat till its bottom smacked the water. Two of the sailors started the motor but didn't engage because they were still hooked to *Spee* by the rope from the crane. Dieter shimmied like a monkey down the heavy manila rope and dropped into the launch.

"Unhook," Max ordered. A flip of the release gear and they were free, drifting with the tide away from the ship. "Give way," Max said, and the motor was engaged. One of the sailors took the rudder, swung the boat around, and headed downstream from *Graf Spee*.

Max looked intently at his watch, then at the sun almost below the horizon. After five minutes he ordered the launch halted, and when the motor was cut a terrible stillness came over them. Only the soft gurgling of the river could be heard. Max felt shame as he looked back at the ship, now a half kilometer away. She had been worthy of them but they had not been worthy of her and so she lay at lonely anchor, a defeated hulk of steel.

Langsdorff stood in the launch. Max and the others also came to their feet. Nineteen hundred and fifteen hours, Max could see from his watch. Sunset. A huge explosion rent *Graf Spee* as the torpedo warheads detonated in the magazines. The blast literally lifted the ship from the water. A series of smaller explosions then rippled through her hull, twisting and ripping her metal skin. The huge diesel tanks aft went up; first tongues of flame shot over the ship, then came the compressed force of a giant explosion that tossed the aft eleven-inch turret into the air like a child's toy.

Max clenched his jaw. Langsdorff stood rigid beside him, hand to the visor of his cap in a naval salute. Max, too, saluted, as did the others. Several of the youngest crewmen began to raise their right arms in the Nazi salute. Max stared daggers at them and they quickly brought their palms to their foreheads in the navy salute.

Black smoke eddied around *Graf Spee* as the proud vessel settled into the water. The warheads in the magazines must have blown her bottom out. Fires on board heated the steel skin of the ship until it glowed orange. As the superheated hull sank into the muddy water of the Plata, clouds of steam rose hissing from the river. A vast tower of smoke and flame arched high over the sinking ship into the night sky.

The reflection of the fire danced red across the faces of the men in the launch. Max dropped his salute. Enough of this charade. Langsdorff had led them into a trap, and now the British had scared them into blowing up their own ship. Slowly *Graf Spee* listed to starboard and sank into the river. Steam and black smoke rose from the great warship until she disappeared, then nothing but the lingering smoke remained.

CHAPTER SIX

THE INDIAN OCEAN
DAY 390 OF THE CRUISE OF THE AUXILIARY MERCHANT
   RAIDER *METEOR*
FOUTTEEN MONTHS LATER
FEBRUARY 1941

MAX SLIPPED THE WHITE COAT OVER HIS DARK BLUE NAVAL TUNIC.
The coat came to his knees. Two turns around his waist with the
sash fastened it in place. Next came the round sunglasses, and
finally the conical straw hat. From a distance—a great distance—
Max hoped he would look Japanese. "You certainly have the buck
teeth for it," Dieter had told him.

The action alarm had died away by the time Max left his cabin.
Unlike his spartan quarters on *Graf Spee*, officers on *Meteor* had
spacious cabins with chintz curtains, large bathtubs, and deep carpet. All her passageways were carpeted, a remnant of prewar days,
when *Meteor* had carried passengers and freight to South America
for Norddeutscher Lloyd. The Kriegsmarine had converted her for
commerce raiding in the shipyards at Bremen, but the work had
been done on a tight schedule and many peacetime amenities—
the soda fountain, the swimming pool, the reading room—had
been left in place. The reading room with its hundreds of books,

including a collection of Karl May's western novels, Max's favorite, became his sanctuary. Mareth had once given him a beautiful set of leather-bound Karl May novels, which he had taken with him on *Graf Spee* but had been forced to sell in Argentina because he needed money. He spent many of his off-duty hours alone in a club chair in the corner of the reading room, lost in the American frontier adventures of Old Shatterhand and his faithful Indian pal, Winnetou.

When Max reached the bridge, Captain Hauer looked him over but said nothing. Hauer was all navy—a regular like Max, but a man who adhered strictly to the conventions of the Imperial Navy, where captains did not speak to Oberleutnants and certainly not to Oberleutnants dressed in Japanese costume. In retrospect, Captain Langsdorff seemed a kindly uncle compared to Hauer, who suffered from both migraines and a nervous stomach, conditions that reflected themselves in his disposition.

Fregattenkapitän Breslau, the second in command, smiled when he saw Max. "Ah, the Mikado," he said, making a slight bow.

Max grinned.

"We are gentlemen from Japan," Breslau sang, quoting Gilbert and Sullivan.

"Well, I hope that through a pair of British binoculars I'll look that way, sir."

"I'm quite sure you will, Oberleutnant. Now be a good fellow and stroll around the deck with Felix."

Breslau, a reservist, had been captain of a small passenger liner before the war and treated all his sailors like guests aboard his ship. "Be a good fellow," he would say, or, "If you please," or, "Would you be so kind." When he spoke, however, he spoke with authority because his voice was as strong and deep as a foghorn. He could hail the masthead from the quarterdeck and be heard in a Force Ten gale, several of which he'd been through while commanding a sailing ship carrying wool from Australia in the twenties.

Breslau and Hauer made an odd pair, but there were many

odd things about *Meteor*—grumbling, cliques, harsh looks, slack petty officers. Worse, she'd been more than a year at sea, her crew never setting foot on land in all that time. Small grievances became major conflicts among three hundred men, crowded together for more than a year in a ship half the size of *Graf Spee*, always alert for the enemy, always on short rations, with a captain whose severity would make a Prussian general proud. All the films aboard had been screened and rescreened till the men could parrot every line; the books that mentioned sex read till they fell apart; the swimming pool used until no one could bear the thought of swimming. Max had tried to organize a shuffleboard tournament like the one they'd had aboard *Graf Spee*, but the men, despite their boredom, had shown little interest. In the end, only he and Dieter had played. Max won.

"You cheated."

"You need glasses."

Perhaps Max and Dieter should not have been so excited when the chance to go aboard *Meteor* presented itself, but they weren't about to sit out the entire war interned in Buenos Aires. Not that Dieter had been crushed by the months of idleness—he seemed to be on good terms with the madam of every private gentlemen's club in the city and passed long nights in the finest of their establishments, cavorting with the girls, drinking champagne, and winning money from British expatriates at the card table. Because Argentina was a neutral country, the British and the Germans often encountered one another, interacting with icy politeness. Dieter found poker his best means of revenge against the Tommies; his mathematical mind made him a menace at cards. True to his nature, he spent the money as he won it: champagne and a generous tip for the tango band, champagne and gifts for the young ladies of the establishment, champagne and cigars for any German gentlemen who happened to be in the club that evening. He must have bought a thousand bottles of champagne for his friends and compatriots during their stay in Buenos Aires.

Max was less adventurous, but he enjoyed his freedom in the city as well. The Argentines made little effort to control the movements of the crew of *Graf Spee*, so Max spent long mornings wandering through Buenos Aires followed by long afternoons of reading on the Plaza de Mayo. But no amount of wandering could set his mind at ease; and for all his debauched exploits, Max knew that Dieter felt the same. It maddened them both to sit on their backsides in Argentina with their painful memories of *Graf Spee*'s scuttling while other Germans won the war. News of their victories never let up; everyone but Max and Dieter was off winning medals. France had fallen in June of 1940, after just six weeks of blitzkrieg—no surprise, Max's father wrote, since the French preferred to eat cheese rather than wage war. The Wehrmacht defeated the Netherlands in a matter of days, then stopped off in Belgium long enough to accept surrender from the King, then on to Paris; the only bad news—the British army had gotten clean away from France, evacuated from the beaches at Dunkirk by the damned Royal Navy, the Kriegsmarine too weak to interfere. But while the surface navy wrung its hands, the U-boat men were off sinking ships, receiving medals, getting promoted. Max felt ill with frustration when he heard that Wolfgang Lüth, one of his crew-kameraden, had received command of a U-boat and had already won the Knight's Cross for all the tonnage he had sent to the bottom. Fortunately, Seekriegsleitung needed its officers. They hadn't enough to begin with, and as the fighting grew more intense, casualties worsened the problem. Well-trained regular officers were a precious asset, so the Naval War Staff and the German embassy began making the complex arrangements necessary to smuggle *Graf Spee*'s officers out of South America. Wattenberg, the senior navigation officer, went first, three months after their internment began, smuggled out on a fishing boat. Ascher went next. Carrying perfectly forged papers that identified him as a Portuguese businessman, he simply boarded a plane to Rio, took a ship to Lisbon, and then bought a seat on the regular Swedish Air flight to Berlin.

Six weeks after Ascher went, Diggins had his turn. The embassy procured false papers identifying him as an Argentine language professor scheduled to visit Japan to learn more about their language. Unfortunately, the Argentines caught him and he had to try three more times before he finally got away, smuggled aboard a Japanese freighter. Others had to do it the hard way: cross the Andes into Chile and dodge the Chilean police, who apparently had much better eyesight than the Argentine police. With so many officers spirited away, Max and Dieter were desperate to escape, so they jumped at the chance to go, even if the assignment was to an auxiliary surface raider skulking about in the Indian Ocean. At the end of September they left Buenos Aires in the trunk of the naval attaché's automobile, spent a comfortable weekend at his country home memorizing the names of their contacts, then slipped away. They spent the next three months stealing from one German community to another across the pampas and over the border into Brazil, dodging local officials, sleeping in barns, straining to comprehend the dialect of the second-generation German immigrants who sheltered them. By the time the two friends reached Porto Alegre in late December and boarded *Dresden*, a freighter from the Secret Naval Supply Service, which would transport them to *Meteor*, they strained at the bit to get back into the war. But now they found themselves alone in a vast sea on a ship marked by tedium and discontent, Max dressed up like a vacationer from Osaka.

Exiting to the deck, he saw that Felix, one of the young deckhands, stood ready for his part in the play. A slight lad, he wore a kimono and a black wig, as well as the standard conical hat. His delicate hands steered a pink baby carriage, and in the carriage lay a doll from Karstadt's in Berlin. Max wondered who on the Naval War Staff had been ordered down to the department store to purchase the doll. "Expect the unexpected in war," Admiral Tirpitz had said, although he hardly could have imagined that assignment.

"Ready, Felix?"

"Ja, Herr Oberleutnant." His deep voice brought a smile to Max's face.

"Off we go, then."

They began to stroll around the deck, which had been scrubbed to a dazzling whiteness that morning as every morning. Captain Hauer insisted on it. The importance of proper appearances was a rule upon which he and Langsdorff would certainly have agreed. Max had come to understand their preoccupation. Scrubbed decks and polished buttons, caps worn per regulations, and hammocks lashed up and stowed each morning in the proper manner reminded the men that they were members of a proud service, and that discipline was the hallmark of that service. But today Max and Felix had left the navy behind: they were just an innocent couple giving their infant some sea air. Other sailors, also in costume—white headbands and shirts worn outside their trousers in the Japanese fashion—worked topside, swabbing the decks, chipping paint, doing the kind of routine maintenance performed on any merchantman, especially one as efficiently run as *Osaka Maru*, the Japanese freighter *Meteor* had been disguised to resemble. Unfortunately, Breslau had told Max, the characters on the stern had been copied from a Kodak advertisement in a Japanese magazine; for all he knew the characters might spell out: "Want better pictures? Buy Kodak film!"

Max clasped his hands behind his back in the relaxed posture of a strolling father. "Talk to me, Felix. We're supposed to be the proud parents of a wonderful baby."

"Why do I have to be the woman, Herr Oberleutnant?"

"Because you're slight like a woman."

Felix said nothing. He set his mouth and stared down at their wooden baby, swaddled in a pink blanket.

That was the problem with these sailors on *Meteor*. Seekriegsleitung had expected the raider to have a short life, so they manned her with the sweepings of the Kriegsmarine. But their assumption had proven wrong; the ship had already survived for thirteen long months. Thirteen months at sea was a difficult achievement for a crew that possessed the dash and polish of *Graf Spee*'s men, but it was impossible to expect a second-rate crew to be out so long, never sighting land, never being with a woman, never getting drunk. Their only pleasure came once a week when the bosun issued each man two bottles of Japanese beer brought along with their other supplies by *Dresden*; the original store of Beck's was drunk long ago. Only Captain Hauer's iron discipline had kept the men under control.

"Look, Felix, a porpoise."

Felix didn't bother to look. "I've seen enough porpoises to last me a lifetime, Herr Oberleutnant."

What could he talk to this surly youngster about? They had to keep their lips moving so that from a distance they would genuinely appear to be a Japanese couple on a stroll. Max knew that on the other ship, in this case a British merchantman five kilometers off their bow, several pairs of binoculars would be on them. Hauer nudged *Meteor* on a slowly converging course with the freighter. If they could get within two kilometers before their ruse was discovered, the Brits would be under their guns and have no choice but to heave to with no wireless transmitting.

But two kilometers was a very close range, so everything about *Meteor*'s disguise had to be perfect. A whiff of suspicion, the smallest detail out of place, the glint of sun off a brass button, and the British ship would flee at flank speed, filling the air with the dreaded RRR signal, "Under attack by surface raider." They had to get that close because *Meteor*'s guns were old, built before the First War. They lacked the range and the accuracy of modern naval cannons. Her guns were concealed by hinged sections of the hull that operated on a counterweight system. One pull and the metal flaps collapsed to reveal the weapons.

Everyone had worked long hours to transform *Meteor* into *Osaka Maru*. Breslau had pored over Lloyd's shipping register for weeks before they sailed, searching through the names and descriptions of several thousand merchant ships, looking for a vessel of roughly eight thousand tons from a neutral country with a silhouette similar to that of *Meteor*. As part of the hoax, the masts and ventilators were painted yellow, the funnel painted black with a bright red top. When Max first saw her a month ago from the deck of *Dresden*, he had been convinced. So far two British merchant ships had fallen for the ruse. Max hoped they were closing in on a third victim.

"Now Felix, tell me about yourself. Where are you from?"

"I'm from Danzig, Herr Oberleutnant."

"Danzig. I see—a Prussian like me."

"Yes, sir. A Prussian." Certainly the boy didn't have the discipline of a Prussian. He seemed more like a Bavarian.

"And you had a job in Prussia before you came into the Kriegsmarine?"

"Group leader in the Reich Labor Service, Herr Oberleutnant."

Not a lad with all his cups in the cupboard, Max thought. The Labor Service managed the flow of teenagers putting in their obligatory six months of work for the benefit of the Reich. They marched in parades wearing storm trooper uniforms and carrying polished shovels at right shoulder arms. The shovel was the proper symbol since they spent most of their time digging ditches. Felix had obviously stayed on after his six-month service to serve as head ditch digger, but he didn't seem to have much respect for authority now. Probably heard too many Nazi Party slogans about equality. Max could think of nothing else to say, so the two fell into a tense silence. They made a full lap of the deck that way before *Meteor* suddenly went to full speed.

With a loud boom, the hinged portion of the hull gave way and exposed the guns, which fired immediately. Because *Meteor* had no firing gong, the loud report of the batteries surprised him. Max dashed for the bridge. The six-inch guns barked again, the sound sharp in his ears. He smelled cordite mixed in with the salt air. Just as he came onto the bridge, the signalman reported, "Wireless transmitting stopped, Herr Kapitän. She only got one signal off."

"Cease firing."

The gunnery officer spoke into the circuit that connected him with the gun captains and the shooting stopped. Because *Meteor* had no system of centralized fire control, the gun captains aimed and fired their individual batteries as in the days of sail.

"She's struck her colors," Max said, peering at the Britisher through his binoculars now.

Hauer rapped out his orders: "Boarding party away. Engines all stop. Guards on deck. Oberleutnant Brekendorf."

Max came to attention. "Ja, Herr Kapitän?"

"You will escort the prisoners below and see that they are settled."

"Jawohl, Herr Kapitän."

"Signalman."

"Ja, Herr Kapitän."

"Ask the radio officer to cancel the distress signal."

"At once, Herr Kapitän."

A difficult maneuver, Max knew. *Meteor* carried several reservists who had been telegraphers aboard merchant ships and tapped the Morse key with a merchantman's feel. Sometimes they could cancel a British distress signal by tapping out that it had been a mistake, but British operators could usually tell the way a German signaled, even if the German had a civilian touch. Rarely could the Brits be fooled.

Max left the bridge, went to his cabin, and removed the Japanese disguise. Damned if he would confront the enemy in a straw hat. The British lifeboats were in the water and rowing toward *Meteor* by the time he came up on the main deck. He watched the small boats bobbing on the light swell. The sea was calm and deep blue in the bright afternoon sun. They were twelve hundred kilometers southwest of Java with weather warm and fair. Pray it stayed that way. The Brits reached *Meteor* in short order, and the first man up the ladder was the captain, binoculars still at his neck.

Max saluted. "Captain, I am Senior Lieutenant Brekendorf, second watch officer of the auxiliary merchant raider *Meteor.*"

"I can bloody well see that, young man. If I had been on the bridge instead of my fool of a second officer, you'd never have gotten within five miles of me, laddie."

"I'm sure of it, Herr Kapitän," Max said. Even on the verge of losing the war, the arrogance of these Englishmen never stopped.

The rest of the British officers came up the ladder, followed by their crew—thirty Africans, each one dark as chocolate. Lascars, the English called them—natives they used to crew ships because they worked cheaper than English sailors. Max had encountered Lascars before, on a small freighter captured by *Graf Spee*, but the sight of so many still surprised him. He'd seen an African only once in his entire life before going to sea. That was with his father, in Berlin in 1925. Negroes from the former German Cameroons sold fruit on the streets in those days, and Max's father had bought him a banana from one of the men. But Max was so frightened that he just cried. Finally his father ate the banana himself. On *Spee*, Max had learned that Lascars came mainly from British colonies in Africa and India. They seemed to feel that one group of white men was the same as the next, and they were just as happy to work for the Germans as the British. Langsdorff had assigned them to cleaning the interior of the ship, and the Lascars fell upon the task with great vigor.

When everyone from the British ship had assembled on deck, Max addressed them: "Gentlemen, you are now prisoners of the German navy. You will be treated in accordance with the rules and regulations governing the treatment of prisoners of war under the Geneva Convention. There are already seventy-four prisoners on board and you will be confined with them. You are free to roam the deck during daylight hours and make use of the

swimming pool and library as long as you stay out of the way of
the crew and do not interfere with their work. All sailors remain
under the authority of their officers and our orders to you will be
given through them." The British captain raised his hand. "Yes,
Captain?"

"We won't be expected to bunk in with these chaps, will we?"
He inclined his head toward the Lascars.

"No, Captain. Officers all bunk together and are attended by
their stewards."

This pleased the captain and he nodded. "But you're not going
to bunk these niggers in with the English crews? I mean . . ."

Max thought for a moment. Putting the Lascars in with British
crewmen they had previously captured would cause problems. He
hardly wanted to be called to task by Captain Hauer for not fore-
seeing this. "No, Captain. We will not mix the men together. This
way, if you please, gentlemen."

Max led them down the main deck, past the ship's crane to
the aft companionway. The prisoners followed him down the
narrow metal stairs to the lowest deck of the ship, which was
below the waterline. Max gave a curt nod to the sentry on duty,
who casually produced the key to the officers' brig and offered
it over. Did no one on this ship move with the snap of a real
German navy man? Max refused the key. He pointed to the
door and barked, "Open it!" That was the only way to deal with
these loafers.

Max stepped into the large cabin, which was lined with bunks
on both walls. The eleven British officers already in residence were
enjoying their first drink of the afternoon. "Hello, old boy," the senior man said. "Steward, chota peg for these officers. More guests,
lads. Do come in, chaps, come in. Damned sorry to see you." He
stuck out his hand to the new captain. "Carruthers, *Duchess of
Connaught*."

"Philbrick," said the new captain. "*Durmitor*."

Once the introductions had been made, Carruthers assigned

bunks to the new prisoners and helped them stow their meager personal effects.

"You'll be let out once we're under way," Max said. He returned to the corridor and led the colored crewmen to the mine room. There were no mines anymore—they'd all been laid months ago off the South African coast, back when Max was still languishing in Buenos Aires. "In you go," he ordered. The men filed in one by one and seated themselves disconsolately on the floor. "Who's the senior man among you?"

"Nkhomo," said a tall, older man, indicating himself.

"We will send in bedding for you. Crews mess together, officers served first. That is all. I expect you to keep order in here. Do you understand?"

"Yes, sahib." Nkhomo inclined his head in a bow.

Max had never been addressed this way before, but he liked it. Sahib. No wonder the British were so fond of their colonies. Moments after he left the Lascars, he realized he'd forgotten to ask Captain Philbrick for his binoculars. Prisoners were not allowed to keep seafaring instruments of any kind—in fact, Max should have searched everyone's baggage. Damn. It wasn't like him to be so neglectful of his duty. Was the lackadaisical atmosphere of the ship beginning to affect him as well? He had to be better than that. He must be better than that.

He had almost reached the officers' brig when the loudspeaker blared: "Oberleutnant Brekendorf to the bridge."

Max hesitated, then made for the bridge. Hauer and Breslau were waiting for him when he got there, looking over the British cargo manifest. "Ah, our Japanese gentleman," Breslau said. "Be a good fellow and have a glance at this for us, Oberleutnant."

Max spoke better English than any of the other officers, something Hauer seemed to resent. He took the document from Breslau. Across the top in bold letters: *Official Cargo Manifest.* Below that: *If the responsible officer feels that this manifest may fall into the hands of forces hostile to H.M. Government, he may dispose of it in accordance with Admiralty instructions issued 20 September 1939 in Notices to Mariners Vol. III/p12/ParagraphE.*

"Cotton," Max said, continuing to read. "She's loaded with cotton from Bombay in transit to a convoy forming up off Cape Town."

The explosion surprised Max so much that he dropped the manifest.

"She's going," Breslau said.

"The boat's still standing off," the watch officer cautioned.

Max collected the papers from the deck, then removed his binoculars from their bracket and peered at the burning ship. *Meteor's* launch was standing off about ten meters from the Britisher.

"The recall signal, now!" Hauer ordered. A deep-throated whistle split the air, then split it again.

Another explosion. Through his glasses Max saw a figure come on deck—grinning, of all things. Dieter. Max knew his friend loved being the engineer on the demolition party. "I can't decide which I like better," he'd once said, "working with dynamite or cavorting with fräuleins." He certainly had a will to mayhem that fit nicely with the work of blowing things up.

Dieter ran down the tilting deck of the British ship, climbed the rail, threw his cap toward the boat, and dived overboard. His grinning sailors hauled him and his cap into the launch and came full speed for *Meteor.*

Binoculars still to his eyes, Hauer said, "One day Falkenheyn is going to cut it too damn close." He frowned disapprovingly, but Max felt certain that strict as he was, the captain enjoyed Dieter's irrepressible behavior as much as everyone else did.

Max stayed on the bridge till they were under way, then took leave to return to the brig and search the belongings of the British. He found the officers standing in a loose group when he came out onto the main deck. Approaching Philbrick, he said, "I'm afraid, Captain, that I shall have to trouble you for your binoculars."

Philbrick gave him a bitter look. "Afraid you're too bloody late.

One of your souvenir-hunting Nazi chums already beat you to them."

"I'm sorry, Captain, I have no idea what you mean."

"Well, too bloody bad for you," Philbrick said, turning away.

Carruthers came forward, smiling weakly, and took Max's arm. "It's like this, old boy. Seems that after you brought along the new fellows, two of your chaps came into our cabin and searched their luggage. Looking for contraband, that sort of thing, they said. Captain's orders, they said. Seems they found some whiskey, which they pinched. Then they noticed the binoculars around Philbrick's neck and pinched those as well. Spoils of war and that sort of thing, eh? But the whole business smelled rotten and I'm afraid Philbrick is rather browned off. Can't say as I blame him, either."

Max struggled to compose his features. "They said, 'Captain's orders'?"

"That's right, old boy."

"Please come with me, Captain," Max said. He led Carruthers below. A theft so brazen could not go unpunished. For a crewman to steal anything from a prisoner of war was against the regulations of the Kriegsmarine and a violation of the Geneva Convention. Such theft was a serious breach of discipline. To engage in such thievery while pretending to be under orders from the captain was an even more serious breach of discipline. They made their way through the ship to Hauer's cabin, whereupon Max rapped on the door and stated their names. Immediately the captain admitted them and Max handled the translation as Carruthers repeated his story.

Hauer sat speechless for a moment when it was over, his face red with anger. Whether his headaches and stomach trouble were the product or the cause of his quick temper, Max had been unable to tell, but this incident drove him to fury. "Captain, I must apologize most deeply to you and your comrades. Only Oberleutnant Brekendorf has the authority to search prisoners.

He would have given you a receipt for anything he was obliged to confiscate so your belongings could be returned to you when we made port. The sailor responsible for this outrage will be found and punished." He slammed his fist on the desk. "Punished most severely." Max repeated all of this in English for Carruthers, then Hauer gave a slight bow of his head, signifying the interview was over. "Return after escorting Captain Carruthers to the deck, Oberleutnant."

"Jawohl, Herr Kapitän."

Max returned as slowly as he could to Hauer's cabin, knowing that he was about to receive the worst dressing-down of his career. He rapped, slipped into the cabin, and found Hauer standing with his back to the door, hands clasped behind him. The captain's uniform was immaculate, his steward saw to that. Like Felix, the captain was a Prussian—but a real Prussian, like Max. His cabin reflected it. A set of books on navigation and seamanship stood on a shelf, neat as a line of grenadiers. There were no unruly papers on his desktop; all were filed away. A water glass scrubbed clean as an angel stood near the edge of the desk on a perfectly starched napkin, along with three tablets of bicarbonate of soda, a small pitcher of water, and a silver spoon polished into gleaming submission. There were two pictures on the bulkhead—one of the Kaiser, one of Admiral Tirpitz—and neither dared to be off center. Max was sure he could have bounced a five-mark coin off the bunk, so tightly were the sheets folded.

Until this moment, Max had not attracted the captain's fury, though once he had come close. One morning, no more than a week after coming aboard *Meteor*, Max had sat in a deck chair during his off-duty hours, rereading *The Treasure of Silver Lake*, his favorite Karl May novel. He had just reached the end of a chapter when Hauer happened by. He caught Max folding down the right corner of the page instead of using a bookmark and stopped short. "Oberleutnant!" the captain shouted.

Max bolted out from his chair and stood at wooden attention.

Hauer stepped up to face him at less than half a meter. "Books should never be treated with such disrespect, Oberleutnant. Never crease a page or put a mark in a book—not on my ship, not anywhere. Books are all that separate us from the apes. Do you understand? I should never wish to see such behavior again."

"Jawohl, Herr Kapitän," Max barked obediently, thinking then, as he would later do on many occasions, that Captain Hauer was truly a bastard.

Now Max stood quietly at attention, knowing Hauer would eventually take notice of him. At length the captain turned and stared at him for a very long moment. "Oberleutnant Brekendorf, you are a disgrace to the service and I shall have no choice but to bring your appalling dereliction of duty to the attention of the Naval War Staff when I submit my final report. That *you*, a trained and experienced regular officer, should so fail in your duty by forgetting, *forgetting*, your explicit standing orders to search prisoners is so shocking to me I am speechless!" Hauer banged the table with his fist. "I am speechless! Speechless!" Then be quiet, Max thought. "But the situation aboard this ship, which you made infinitely worse by your reprehensible dereliction of duty, the situation is so delicate that I have no choice but to continue to rely on you and I will pray to Almighty God that you remember your duty in the brief period of time you have left in the navy. Consider yourself fortunate that I am not going to confine you to the brig."

Hauer looked away from Max and said nothing for a few minutes, letting the curtain fall on act one. Then he began to speak, acting as if nothing had been said heretofore. "There are three regular naval officers on this ship. Three. Only three. Before you and Leutnant Falkenheyn came aboard, there was only me. That's why the two of you were sent here at such great risk—the navy didn't smuggle you out of Buenos Aires for a holiday. I require officers I can rely on implicitly."

Hauer stared at him. Max didn't flinch. He feared one word

from him would push the captain over the edge. It wasn't only the crew who were in need of leave. Max wanted to suggest that Hauer go ahead and drink the bicarbonate of soda.

"Would you shoot someone if I ordered you to?"

"Jawohl, Herr Kapitän."

"A German?"

Max hesitated.

"A simple question, Oberleutnant Brekendorf! Answer. Would you shoot a German sailor engaged in mutiny aboard a German man-o'-war in a time of war?"

"Jawohl, Herr Kapitän."

Around them the ship rolled slightly in the seaway. With all of her wooden paneling and wooden doors from her days in the passenger trade, she creaked like an old house as she steamed. The captain said, "I will announce to the crew that the defaulters have twenty-four hours to turn themselves in. If they do not—and I do not expect they shall—I will order you and Leutnant Falkenheyn to search the crew quarters. Some of the troublemakers on board may resist this. You will have me and a party of armed officers with you . . ." Hauer paused. "I asked for the best crew they could give me and they cleaned out the brig, thinking I'd be sunk in a fortnight." He glanced around his cabin. "I will not have a mutiny on my ship, do you understand? I will not!"

Max continued to stand at rigid attention.

"At ease, Oberleutnant," the captain said, fatigue in his voice. He pulled a key from his pocket and opened a cabinet next to his desk, from which he withdrew two pistols in polished leather holsters. "One for you and one for Leutnant Falkenheyn. I will have one as well. The guard contingent will have truncheons. Questions?"

Max spoke with caution. To question the captain's orders directly could be taken as mutiny itself. "Must it come to this, Herr Kapitän?"

Hauer stared him down. "Thirteen months at sea. No women.

No leave. Short rations. Not enough alcohol. The crew becomes a tinderbox. One spark and they will ignite. I saw it at Kiel in 1918. One spark and a whole damn crew became Bolsheviks, Red Bolsheviks—actually killed the first officer. They spat on me—spat on me! But not on my ship. There will not be mutiny on my ship!"

Max came to attention. "At your command, Herr Kapitän."

"I will not have prisoners mistreated under my watch. Just as there are rules in peacetime, there are rules in war. The men who have violated those rules will be found and discipline will be restored." Hauer emphasized the last word by striking the desk again. "You are dismissed."

Max saluted and took his leave.

Over dinner, he spoke to Dieter about this very unpleasant encounter with the captain. As usual, Dieter was unfazed. "First, El Maximo, don't worry about what Hauer will say about you. Do you think the Naval War Staff is going to give any credence to what the man says? He's mad as a March hare. As to the thieves who took the binoculars, a show of force and the shits will give way," he said. They were eating blood sausage and bread—a heavy meal to stomach in the heat of the Indian Ocean—and drinking Sapporo beer, which they couldn't abide. Watered-down horse piss mixed with medicinal alcohol would taste better, but they didn't have any of that. All they had was the Sapporo. Dieter upended his bottle, then sat back. "I've seen this sort of thing before. Nothing to it."

Max had known Dieter since April of 1933, when they had begun their first year as Seekadetten. They were crewkameraden, had drilled together, furled sails together, been aboard the training cruiser *Emden* together, exploring together the various American cities *Emden* visited from New York to New Orleans to San Diego. They had learned navigation together, gotten drunk together, served aboard *Graf Spee* together, gotten stuck in Argentina together, and finally come here. Max looked at his friend.

"Now exactly when and where have you seen this kind of thing before?"

"Well, I haven't, El Maximo, but I can't worry about it. Cigarette?"

That night, in his bunk, Max worried about it. Just shoot whomever the captain pointed out? Mutiny was a serious crime — a capital offense in any navy, and rightly so — but a sailor pinching a pair of binoculars did not constitute a Bolshevik revolt. A certain tension was evident throughout the ship: furtive looks, muttered curses, a hand slow to salute. But there was hardly an open rebellion. *Meteor* did have more than her share of brig rats, but to shoot a German sailor in cold blood?

By the twenty-four-hour mark, an air of expectation hung over the ship. Crewmen stopped working and even the helmsman became inattentive and had to be reprimanded by the watch officer. Captain Hauer, in full dress uniform, pistol holstered, stood on the main deck at parade rest, waiting for the binoculars and whiskey to be returned. The deadline expired. Five minutes went by. Then ten. Time moved slowly as it always did when one wanted it to move faster. Thirty minutes past the deadline, he called for the guard. Max and Dieter, also with holstered pistols, led four reliable men onto the deck. Each of the four had a truncheon. Max wanted to say something, anything, that might head off this confrontation, but the look on Hauer's face did not suggest an openness to compromise.

Hauer led the way belowdecks, striding into the crew quarters. Sailors crowded around, some menacing, many fearful. But they presented themselves in solidarity as a group. Crowded together in this heat, sweat dripped from the men. Max felt himself sweating through his uniform.

Hauer pushed through the men to a row of lockers. "Open it," he said, pointing to the first locker.

No one moved.

The captain turned to one of the junior petty officers. "What kind of German sailor are you? Call these men to attention."

The petty officer hesitated, then stepped forward and bellowed, "Achtung!"

The response varied; a handful snapped to, but without conviction. The rest stood as they were.

"You." Hauer jabbed his finger at one of the older seamen— Harslager, who sported a pale knife scar across his left cheek.

"Which is your locker?"

"Nine."

Max could see the captain's nostrils flare at the omission of "Herr Kapitän." Harslager's own face was tight and defiant, though his hands nervously grasped and ungrasped the seams of his trousers.

"Open it!"

Harslager stood his ground. Max wondered what had happened to the man who gave him that scar.

"Open it now!" the captain shouted.

Nothing.

"Oberleutnant."

"Ja, Herr Kapitän?"

"Cover this man with your pistol."

Max pulled the pistol from its holster and pointed it at Harslager's belly. The wooden grip was damp in his hand from sweat.

"I will count to five," Hauer said, speaking slowly to Harslager. "If you do not open the locker, I will order the Oberleutnant to shoot you. He is a regular naval officer and understands what it means to obey orders."

Max could see the sailors staring at him. Most had gone white in the face. Harslager looked down at the deck.

"One."

No one moved. No one even seemed to breathe—as if the air itself had been sucked from the room.

"Two!"

Max pulled the Luger's slide back, forcing a shell into the breech, the sound loud and metallic.

"Three."

Harslager looked up and stared Max straight in the eye.

"Four."

Sweat beaded on Max's forehead and ran down his chin.

"Five!"

Harslager stayed motionless. Max's finger curled around the trigger.

"Fire!" Hauer yelled.

Slowly Max lowered the pistol. He might be court-martialed, but he wasn't going to shoot a German sailor in cold blood. Seeing them killed in battle was bad enough; he still had nightmares about the dead signalmen he had stepped over during the battle off the Rio Plata. Captain Hauer stared at him with rage, face twitching, looking as if he might use his fists to strike Max. He opened his mouth to speak, but the loudspeaker interrupted: "Feindlicher Kreuzer in sicht!" Enemy cruiser in sight!

Everyone was moving before the alarm bells rang. Max holstered the Luger, dashed for the main companionway, and reached the bridge in seconds, followed closely by the captain. Hauer stared daggers at him, then began giving crisp orders that sent *Meteor* to full speed just as the first British shells exploded in the water fifty meters off the port beam. Everyone jumped to Hauer's commands—no question of insubordination now; they must all work together or be killed together. The ship's disguise had not fooled anyone this time. Yet Max felt relief flooding his body, unwinding the muscles in his gut. He was almost glad to be under attack. Another volley of shells exploded into the water off their starboard bow, closer this time, sending up towers of water taller than the ship. A straddle. The British cruiser, running at speed eight kilometers off their port bow, had their range.

"Prepare to fire," Hauer ordered.

The hull flaps dropped, exposing the batteries.

A moment as the gun captains double-checked their range—

"Fire!"

With a sharp report the batteries fired, their smoke drifted over the ship. Did the captain mean to fight? Max looked on in astonishment but said nothing. Instead he stood impassively, hands behind him, exactly as Langsdorff had done under fire.

Meteor had been built as a passenger liner—she wasn't protected with heavy plates of Krupp steel like a warship. One or two hits would turn her into an inferno. They must turn away *now* and run with every bit of speed they could muster from the engines.

Another blast from their guns sent smoke eddying into the bridge. A third set of British shells bracketed *Meteor*, spraying the ship with water and shell splinters—shattering the bridge windows. The helmsman went to his knees, blood pouring from his face. Max stepped to the wheel and steadied them on course, the helmsman's blood staining his hands and his uniform. *Meteor* shook violently as Dieter and the engineering crew below pushed her engines to their very limit.

"Make smoke," Hauer ordered, "hard starboard, take us into the smokescreen."

Max put the wheel hard over. "Rudder is hard starboard, Herr Kapitän." Thank God the man had given up the idea of fighting it out with the British cruiser. In moments, a cloud of oily smoke boiled from the special generators on the stern, creating an impenetrable cloud that hovered over the water. Just as *Meteor* began to turn, a volley of British shells hit her hard.

Max felt the raider shudder beneath him and then the bridge exploded, the force wrenching the wheel from his hands and tossing him across the deck. The navigator screamed in agony, covering his eyes. Blood seeped out between his fingers. A slick of blood now covered the bridge deck, most of it coming from Captain Hauer's body, shredded by the blast. Smoke poured through the shattered windows. Men screamed from below.

Choking on the smoke, Max retched, rose to all fours, slipped on the blood, felt the ship listing beneath him. He pulled himself up again just as another shell struck *Meteor*, and another, throwing him back down. One of his front teeth broke against the deck.

He scrambled up and saw flames covering the stern. *Meteor's* guns stopped firing, their crews torn apart by the shell splinters. All Max could hear was the roaring fire, punctuated by the cries of sailors—some wounded, some dying, some thrown into the water.

He lurched to the engine room voice tube. "Engine room!" he shouted. No reply. Max wiped the blood from his eyes and found the radio room voice tube. "Radio!"

Kurtz, the radio operator, answered as if nothing were out of the ordinary. "Radio, aye."

"Kurtz, make to Seekriegsleitung: 'Most Immediate. *Meteor* sunk by British cruiser. Need assistance.' Give our position. Do it now!"

"Understood, Herr Oberleutnant. And whose name do I sign the message?"

"Mine, dammit. Send it! Then get the hell off the ship."

Habits of bureaucracy died hard. *Meteor* lurched to starboard, the funnel coming down in a shower of sparks and soot. Max crawled to the loudspeaker microphone, seized it, but it didn't work. Where were the bell signals? Shit! Still on his knees, he looked frantically around through the smoke. An explosion below rocked the ship again and she listed even more to starboard—almost forty degrees now. She would turn turtle in a moment. Get out, now! There it was, the panel for the bell signals. He slid across the deck on the slick of blood and banged the "abandon ship" button. Pray God the emergency power circuit still worked. It did. The continuous trill of the distress bell sounded through the ship.

He scrambled off the bridge to the starboard rail of the listing ship and made the short jump into the sea. The cold of the water shocked him. Salt stung the little cuts on his face and hands. *Meteor's* fuel tanks ruptured, tons of oil spilling into the sea, creating a large black slick upon which the ship appeared to float. He turned onto his back and kicked away from the ship, swimming through a pool of oil that covered him like a foul-smelling blanket. It soaked his hair, forced its way into his ears, trickled from his head into his mouth—Max puked and puked again. *Meteor* loomed above him. He feared that she would fall on him, and he thrashed in panic against the water. Screams filled the air—men dying aboard or men dying in the water. He couldn't tell. Probably both. The alarm continued to trill. The ship settled by the bow, listing violently to starboard, spilling men over the side.

Max cleared the oil slick, turned onto his stomach, and struck out for a lifeboat maybe forty meters away. He thought for a moment that he might not make it—his limbs seemed weighted down by the oil—but at last he felt the wooden hull and the men leaned over and pulled him in by his gun belt, the only place they could get a grip.

Once in the lifeboat, he turned to see the ship afire. Flames engulfed most of the top deck, save for a gap amidships. Here Dieter appeared, along with a group of the Lascars. He must have stopped to let them out on his way up from the engine room. He limped from the companionway and stumbled onto the slanting deck. One of the Lascars helped him to the starboard rail and they tumbled overboard together. Both were struggling hard in the oily water when the burning deckhouse fell into the sea.

"Dieter!" Max leapt to the gunwale of the boat as the oil ignited. "Dieter!" he yelled.

Dieter heard him, he thought, looked up.

Max tore open his tunic, brass buttons flying everywhere, put one foot on the gunwale and moved to dive back into the water, but a burly sailor held him back—Harslager. He said nothing, only wrestled Max away from the side of the lifeboat and held him in an iron grip. Max watched as flames tore across the oil-slicked water, shooting out from the deckhouse to burn a wide circle around the ship. The blaze overtook Dieter quickly. A wall of orange fire shot up and Max lost sight of him. The screams of the burning men were so loud, they pierced the terrible roar of the inferno. Max stared openmouthed into the spreading flames. His body shook, then lost all sensation. Harslager let him go and Max collapsed in the bottom of the boat.

How long did he lie there? Three hours? Four? It made no difference. Darkness had fallen by the time his senses returned. The wind had picked up and waves lapped against the wooden sides of the lifeboat in a rhythmic, staccato slap. It was cold now and he shivered in his oil-soaked uniform.

The lifeboat itself was one of the larger ones. It could hold up to sixty men, but as Max looked around in the semidarkness he saw no more than fifteen, perhaps twenty. He tried to speak but the oil had dried his tongue. He spat, the spittle black and viscous.

"The Oberleutnant is awake," one of the sailors announced, helping Max sit up. His entire body felt bruised; pain stabbed his right side with every breath. Must be broken ribs.

"Here, sir." The sailor offered him a cup of water. He drank some water, swished it around in his mouth and spit it out. The rest he drank slowly, the liquid cool on the raw tissues of his mouth.

"The ship?" Max asked in a whisper.

"Sunk, just on four hours, Herr Oberleutnant."

Max hung his head. The image of Dieter in the burning oil came back to him, and he knew that it would keep coming back. "The British cruiser?"

"Picked up the boats and tore away, sir."

"Not us?"

"We was on the opposite side, drifted inside the smokescreen, Herr Oberleutnant. Couldn't see us till it blew off and by then they was too far away."

Max nodded. Silence came over the boat. The war had been a strange and bitter trip. First came the scuttling of *Graf Spee*, now *Meteor* had gone to the bottom, Dieter had been incinerated, and Max found himself adrift in a lifeboat, twelve hundred kilometers from land. He hadn't seen Mareth in two years and would never see her again; they would never be married. He would die here, in the middle of the Indian Ocean, twenty-six years old, and no one would ever know what became of him. The telegrams Mareth and his father received would say only that Max was "missing." That was how Oberkommando der Wehrmacht—Armed Forces High Command—listed you if your body was never found.

Hundreds of thousands of men from the First War were still listed this way, but these men hadn't deserted and run off with French girls. They were missing because they'd been blown to bits by an artillery shell, or torn to pieces by machine-gun bullets. Some had been dragged to the ocean floor aboard a sinking ship, others had gotten a sniper's bullet in the face and fallen into an old shell hole filled with stagnant water and covered with algae. But the telegrams never made this explicit. Mothers all over Germany had gone on for years after the Armistice in 1918, hoping that somehow their precious Fritz had not been ground into the blood-soaked mud of Verdun. They went to church every morning, praying that their wonderful boy, a gentle soul who loved his mother, a handsome boy with a smile bright as sunshine, was suffering from amnesia. Perhaps he had wandered over the Pyrenees into Spain and had been taken in by nuns. At this very moment, he could be sitting on a hillside in Catalonia, herding goats for the good sisters who looked after him.

Max wanted his telegram to tell the truth: *With great regret the Oberkommando der Kriegsmarine must inform you that your husband/son/father/brother/lover*—then a blank to be filled in with the appropriate name and rank, must get the rank correct—*is missing in action at sea. Though his body has not been recovered, we have reason to believe that he was incinerated/drowned/ripped apart by a British shell/trapped in the engine room and suffocated/hit by the collapsing funnel of his ship/choked on viscous fuel oil/starved in a lifeboat/eaten by sharks. He gave his life for Greater Germany. The Führer and the Oberkommando der Kriegsmarine extend their deepest sympathies. Heil Hitler.*

Max shut his eyes, swallowed. If he went missing, would the navy send his father and Mareth a copy of the *Consolation Book for All Who Mourn for the Fallen,* written especially for the bereaved by a navy chaplain? Or did loved ones get a copy only if you were officially dead?

He was the lone officer in a boat filled with mutinous sailors, but none of that mattered. Besides, he was the only one among them who could navigate. Like most lifeboats, this one was equipped with a sextant and a set of charts. He supposed they could make landfall somewhere—if the mast and sail were undamaged; if they didn't die of hunger or thirst or sunstroke; if they didn't capsize in a storm or get killed in any of the other numberless ways the sea had of taking men.

It was Harslager who finally spoke up, respect in his voice. "What are your orders, Herr Oberleutnant?"

Max thought. Give them hope? Be harsh? He remembered advice from somewhere: minimize the difficulties at hand. Not so easy in this case. "We sent off a signal to Seekriegsleitung before we sank," he said.

"You did?"

"Yes, I ordered it from the bridge."

"Did it go off before the antenna fell?" one of the young sailors asked.

"You will address me as Herr Oberleutnant," Max reminded him firmly. "I will not overlook this again."

The sailor stiffened, squaring his shoulders in a gesture of attention. "May I ask the Oberleutnant if the signal went off before the antenna fell?"

"Yes, it did," Max said, with a certainty he did not feel.

"Are you sure, sir?"

Harslager said, "If the Oberleutnant says it was done, then it was done. Don't question the officer. So we should stay here, sir?"

"Yes, I believe we should, but I don't know for how long."

"Do we have U-boats in the Indian Ocean, sir?"

"Yes, of course we do," Max said, hoping they believed him.

He spent the next hour overseeing the inventory of their supplies. They didn't have a full complement of rations because sailors had been filching them to supplement the short rations they received on *Meteor*. Max would happily shoot the thief who had stolen provisions from the lifeboat. Stealing emergency supplies was a far more serious crime than lifting a pair of binoculars and a few bottles of whiskey. They had enough water for six days at two pints a man, which wouldn't be enough to ward off dehydration after the third day. There should have been more water, too. Their food supply—dried biscuits, powdered soup, and chocolate—would last seven days, Max calculated. Maybe eight. He put Harslager in charge of the rations.

When the morning sun came up it baked the greasy oil into his skin, which tightened and even split in some places, but oddly, the oil served as a kind of protective coating. Without it, the others blistered more severely. During the day they huddled under the sail for shade, but it wasn't big enough to cover every part of them. It barely helped anyway. The canvas was thin and the sun burned them through it. Their skin peeled. Lips cracked. Pus oozed from burst blisters

Oskar, a cook's helper with a broken leg, was the first to die—not from the infected leg, Max thought. He simply gave up. They rolled Oskar into the sea, and though all the men were sitting or kneeling in the boat, Max ordered them to salute, something one normally did only while standing. It was late afternoon, the sunlight had softened, and with Max leading, they began to quietly sing "Ich hatt' einen Kameraden":

> I had a comrade
> None better have I had
> The drum called us to fight,
> He always on my right,
> In step, through good and bad.

A bullet it flew toward us,
For him or meant for me?
His life from mine it tore,
At my feet a piece of him,
As if a part of me.

Max dropped his head and put his hands over his eyes so his men would not see the tears that rolled down his face, though he could not hide the trembling of his body. In his mind's eye he could still see Dieter being incinerated by the burning oil.

His hand reached up to hold mine.
I must reload my gun.
"My friend, I cannot ease your pain,
In life eternal we'll meet again,
And walk once more as one."

Max thought back to his first week in the navy when he had met Dieter and how he disliked him in the beginning, thinking him a braggart and a blowhard. But over time Dieter proved to be a true comrade — Max never had a better one. Dieter was also the most audacious person Max ever knew. If there were a prank, Dieter was behind it — in the middle of a January night at the Marineschule Mürwik, they had driven a cow up sixteen flights of stairs to the very top floor of the main building. The cow would go up the stairs, but not down, so it had to be butchered right there, an act that earned the entire crew a fifteen-minute cursing out from the commandant. They glued the boots of the riding instructor to the floor, short-sheeted beds, put salt water in the water pitchers in the officers' mess.

In song he was my comrade,
None better you could find,
His voice he dedicated

To our choir and elated
Our hearts with song and kind.

Max remembered the times Dicter spoke to him of the father he never knew; of how it felt to be the one who found his father's body hanging from the noose, a picture he was never able to drive from his constant nightmares.

Now rest your bones, my singer,
All woe and pain is past.
Sing with the angels up above
In praise of God and His love,
My friend, at peace at last.

Soon we will also follow
You through that heavenly door,
It's there that we shall meet again
To harmonize our old refrain,
With you, my friend, once more.

Max continued to weep quietly until exhaustion overtook him and he slept.

For those who died in the following days, there was no song, no salute—just the grunts of exhausted men as they rolled the bodies into the sea. If no breeze came up, the corpses would float beside the lifeboat far too long, the living staring into the bilge to avoid looking into the eyes of the dead. By the fifth day they were down to twelve, the youngest among them proving the most vulnerable. They'd never faced a crisis before. They gave up and they died.

Max hung on, clinging to life with a part of himself that had been a stranger but now came to the fore with a strength he had never known. If anyone survived, he knew it would be him. There was so much he still wanted: to put his hands on Mareth again, to feel her body against him, to have his life with her; to take revenge on the English for Dieter, to protect his country; and he wanted to see his father at least once more. "You would understand if you had been at Verdun," was something his father had often said to him. And now he did understand. It wasn't anger, or love or desire or even fear that kept him alive. It was simply his primal will to survive; an independent force within him, bound neither by logic nor by reason; a force few ever discovered in themselves. He wished it would go away.

By the ninth day his limbs were bloated, his joints ached, his skin blistered. He lay in the bottom of the boat, lips parched, tongue swollen to twice its normal size, his breath short and ragged against his broken ribs. How many alive now? Eight? Nine? Each day for the last seven he had taken a sun sight at noon and then made the men row the boat to their original position, but Max understood now that it was hopeless. The sun beat down till he wanted to scream from the pain. He desperately wanted to immerse himself in the cool sea but knew if he went into the water he would die there; he'd never have the strength to pull himself back into the boat. Then night came and, with it, cold so piercing that his teeth chattered and he curled up with the other men for warmth, all of them piled together in the bilge like dogs.

In a half-sleep, barely conscious, Max often dreamed of home, of his father, of his mother, of waltzing with Mareth on top of the Brandenburg Gate; of playing poker with the English and winning one of their ships; of Dieter burning alive in the sea; of things that had happened and things that had not. And now most of his life seemed this way: unfathomable, dreamlike, an indistinct line between what was real and what was not. But as he lay in the bottom of the lifeboat, he knew from the terrible pain of his burning skin that this travail was not a dream but a reality from a world beyond the worst nightmares he had ever known.

Two more lay dead in the lifeboat on the tenth morning, staring up with sightless eyes. One of them was Harslager. Max wondered if he should have shot him after all. It would have turned out to be merciful. Their food and water were three days gone; another two died that night.

Four men were alive the next day when U-329 found them.

CHAPTER SEVEN

PARIS
GERMAN-OCCUPIED FRANCE
TEN MONTHS LATER
4 NOVEMBER 1941

ON A BRILLIANTLY SUNNY DAY IN EARLY JUNE OF 1929, WHEN MAX
was fourteen, his father took him aboard the warship *Emden* during the annual Kiel Week celebration, a maritime festival that attracted ships and visitors from around the world. Everything Max
saw that day fascinated him: the clipper ships still being used to
haul wool from Australia; the modern freighters going into service
for Norddeutscher Lloyd; the new high-speed patrol boats built
for the navy. But it was his tour of the warship that stayed with
him, etched into his memory as sharply as the clean lines of *Emden* herself. He remembered everything: the outline of the cruiser
sharp against the blue sky as she towered above the dock, the pride
of the men in their starched uniforms, the order and precision of
their movements, the power of the ship, the size of its guns, the
coils of thick rope, the smell of the sea. On that day Max decided
to become a naval officer. His desire was so strong that his father
enrolled him in the Marine Bund, an organization devoted to in-
stilling in young men the virtues necessary to make them good

citizens and future officers. The closest branch was in Kiel, twenty kilometers from Bad Wilhelm, but Max's father drove him to every meeting. The Marine Bund taught Max many of the skills he would need to win a coveted place at the Marineschule Mürwik: Morse code, signal lamp, marching, semaphore, nautical science, sailing. He mastered them as fast as anyone in the group.

Yet to become a Reichsmarine Seekadett was a difficult process—less than three percent of applicants were accepted. Candidates had to pass a series of rigorous tests, some written, some physical, some psychological. The most important was the Mutprobe, the Courage Test, which involved grasping two metal bars through which a steadily increasing electrical current was run.

When the day came for him to take the Mutprobe, Max's will to succeed was overwhelming. Having made the commitment to become a naval officer, he dared not disappoint himself or, worse, disappoint his father. He had pledged to himself that no force on earth would be enough to make him let go of the bars; he'd repeated this fact to himself over and over as he practiced holding on to a pair of bicycle handlebars in his room, imagining the force of the current. He stood in line on the morning of the test, watching as other boys wilted in the face of their pain, whispering to himself that he would not let go, he would not let go. He did let go, but only after blacking out.

But with his life in the balance, Max would not let go at all. He remembered nothing of his three weeks aboard the U-boat, save a few hazy moments of the doctor's care. He was fortunate U-329 even carried a doctor. Most U-boats didn't—their loss rate was too high, the supply of doctors too limited. But U-329 had a naval physician aboard because she was on the backside of an extraordinarily long voyage—to Japan to exchange one thousand flasks of mercury for crude rubber, a material Germany needed desperately. The doctor tended the wounded men with the greatest of care, but only Max and a seaman first class named Klaus survived.

"I'm not sure how you managed it," the chief physician at the base hospital in La Rochelle told Max. "Three broken ribs, dehydration, punctured lung, fracture of the upper right humerus, infected scalp, sun poisoning, exposure, starvation. You should be dead."

Max shrugged his shoulders. Well he wasn't dead, now was he?

But it had been a race closely won. For many weeks after his admittance to the base hospital in Lorient, his survival had been in doubt. Only after two months had passed did the doctors even allow Max to be taken by ambulance to the main Kriegsmarine hospital in Paris where the navy's top specialists could look after him.

Mareth came as soon as she got his telegram. She arrived on his third afternoon in Paris, wearing a simple blue dress with white lilacs printed on the fabric. The fedora on her head might have been a man's; she wore it with a feather in the band, like Marlene Dietrich.

"Max," she whispered from the doorway. He opened his eyes and they each simply looked upon the other. Late afternoon sun poured through the window, cut by the blinds into strips of gold. Her hair was a little shorter; she smiled with her small, perfect teeth. She looked the same yet took his breath away. But he could tell from her expression that he still must look a fright, pale as death and thin as a pikestaff.

"Come here," he tried to say, but his voice wouldn't work. He motioned her closer with his hand.

She came to the edge of the bed, glanced down at his bony legs beneath the sheet, then back up to his face, pale and rough as the new skin grew in. "Max," she whispered again. He reached out and she took his hand. Feeling her touch, tears came to his eyes and ran down his face.

She took his hand in both of hers and kissed his fingers. "I'm going to be fine," he said, voice cracking. "If you help me, I'll be fine." He smiled as best he could and Mareth began to cry as well, but she was smiling, too. She took her hands and put them on his face, cradled his head lightly, and brushed her lips across his forehead.

"I missed you," she said. "You can't imagine the way I missed you."

"I can," Max said in a hoarse whisper. "I can."

He fought night and day to regain his strength, and toward the end of the seventh week he woke one morning with a violent erection. Mareth had fallen asleep beside him in a chair, as she did from time to time. He gently shook her awake, pointing to where the bedsheet was tented. She laughed and pounced onto the bed, slipping under the sheet and straddling him, leaning forward to kiss his mouth.

"Maybe we should take this one step at a time," Max whispered.

She covered his mouth with her hand. "Maybe you should be quiet and follow orders, sailor."

Max hadn't been with a woman for more than two years, except for three drunken trips to a private gentlemen's club in Buenos Aires, where Dieter was welcomed like a conquering hero by the madam and her girls, a welcome they extended to Max as Dieter's friend. He still felt guilty about those three evenings. He had actually gone to confession in Buenos Aires, but the priest took a broad view of these matters.

"It is wartime and you are a young man. Say one Hail Mary and God forgives you."

"That is all, Father? For three trips to a house of prostitution?"

"Then say the Hail Mary three times," the priest said sternly, not partial to negotiating with penitents. "Ego te absolvo a peccatis tuis in nomine Patris et Filii et Spiritus Sancti Amen." Catholicism in Argentina was different than in Germany.

Max was inside Mareth for all of thirty seconds before

exploding with a groan. She kissed him again as the tension drained from his body, her tongue polishing his teeth. Then she laughed and nestled down beside him on the narrow bed. "Now I believe you're getting well," she said.

The nursing sister found them that way when she entered with Max's breakfast tray. She immediately fetched the matron. "Do you think this is a brothel?" the matron scolded when she came into the room. "Out, out with you, before I call the Feldgendarmerie," she said to Mareth. "Mon Dieu, there is nothing these fallen women would not do for a few francs."

The nursing sisters were Ursuline nuns and partial to Max since he was a Catholic, but he had to laugh at the matron's prudish alarm. Mareth did not laugh. She returned that afternoon with an official pass allowing her to stay in Max's room, signed by General von Stülpnagel, the military governor of France. And she did stay, every night, until Max was discharged three weeks later with ninety days of leave.

Mareth's father, who had arranged for the pass, also arranged for Max and his daughter to remain in Paris for two extra weeks, living "like gods in France," as the men said, at the Hotel George V. This generosity surprised Max. Perhaps Herr von Woller was just relieved they weren't getting married. Marriage seemed out of the question to Max. The horror of his ordeal in the lifeboat—of watching Dieter burn, of seeing *Meteor* go down, the uncertainty of the war—made running off on a lark to get married feel like an emotional impossibility. "It's not the right time," he told Mareth. It hardly seemed right to her either, though people all over the Reich were jumping into marriage precisely because of the war—since its promised end was always close but never arrived. You could even marry your sweetheart by proxy over the radio or telephone, although the honeymoon wasn't much fun—especially if the bride went back to her ammunition factory and the groom went back to his muddy trench somewhere in Russia. Her dearest friend, Loremarie, had finally married her artillery major by proxy over the radio, she in Berlin, he with his division outside of Lenin-grad. Three other friends had done the same.

The months when Max had been sick had been difficult ones for the Reich. First was the inexplicable journey of Deputy Füh-rer Rudolph Hess, who had stolen a twin-engine Messerschmitt fighter and flown to Scotland alone for reasons no one could say. Hess was a skilled pilot, but how had he managed to elude the radar and night fighters of the air defense of the Reich, then slip unnoticed through the British radar and fighter net? Could that have been good luck? Max didn't think so. The Führer had been caught completely unawares, claimed that "Party Comrade Hess" had gone mad, as evidenced by his frequent consultation with as-trologers. But how could the number two man in the party have been a lunatic and the number one man not have known? Ma-reth had whispered the latest joke to Max: Hess is brought before Churchill and Churchill says, "So you're the madman." Hess re-plies, "No, I'm his deputy."

While Max had been so ill, the Kriegsmarine won its greatest victory and suffered its worst defeat. *Bismarck*, the most powerful battleship in the world, attended by the heavy cruiser *Prinz Eugen*, had broken out into the North Atlantic and in a fierce battle with the Royal Navy had sunk the most famous British warship afloat: H.M.S. *Hood*, which exploded and went down in two minutes, the result of a hit in her magazine. But the Tommies took their revenge not three days later by pounding *Bismarck* into a flam-ing wreck. She fought bravely, went down with her battle ensign flying, but Max now realized that the men of Germany's surface fleet could do little to affect the war save die gallantly. Ascher of *Graf Spee*, so eager for glory, had been assigned to *Bismarck* after he slipped out of Argentina. He found his glory and a sailor's grave when the battleship went down, killed along with two thousand other German sailors. Their deaths accomplished nothing. Valor alone could do little against the overwhelming might of the Royal Navy.

Yet being with Mareth again, spending two weeks with her in the Hotel George V in Paris, helped Max shut out the terror of the war if only for a few weeks. He couldn't get enough of Mareth, didn't want to let her out of his sight. She modeled her clothes for him; let him watch as she applied her makeup, bought on the black market for her by the ever-cooperative hall porter—as long as she paid him in Swiss francs. Max was fascinated by the skill with which Mareth handled the pencils and brushes. She seemed to do it recklessly, smearing her lipstick on with quick swipes, but the effect was always precise. Sometimes they would put the radio on and dance naked around the suite. Every day she massaged coconut oil into his skin, which was still coarse and irritated from the sunburn and fuel oil.

On the first morning of their second week at the George V, Max awoke on his stomach to the pressure of Mareth sitting on his back. He felt her warm breath in his ear. "Herr Oberleutnant," she whispered.

Max reached back and ran his hand along her silky calf. "The Oberleutnant wishes to sleep awhile longer."

He heard her uncrumpling a piece of paper. "But Herr Oberleutnant, already this morning a telegram has arrived from the Oberkommando der Kriegsmarine asking if you planned to take your lover to Printemps to buy a pair of shoes." Max groaned. She slapped his naked rump. "Naturally I had to reply immediately to such an important telegram on your behalf. I told them to rest easy; the Oberleutnant will take me to Printemps promptly at zero nine thirty." She rubbed his shoulders softly, then a little less softly. "Max."

"Fräulein," he said, "obedience to orders is the hallmark of the German naval officer."

"Very good, Herr Oberleutnant. Now achtung!"

Max, still on his stomach, stiffened in mock attention. Mareth rose to her knees. "About face!" she ordered. He rolled over, his morning erection pulsing. She sank onto him with a wicked smile, bringing her mouth down to meet his.

Max waved the doorman away as they left the hotel. There were no more taxis in Paris; only the Wehrmacht could get gasoline. The cabs had been replaced by bicycles pulling carts like rickshaws, but Mareth preferred to ride the Metro. She had learned to get around the city on the elegant subway before the war, when her father had served for a time as commercial attaché of the German embassy in Paris. She knew the French capital almost as well as Berlin, navigating with the assurance of a native Parisian.

As ever, Max found her confidence and sophistication deeply alluring, but he did not care for the Metro. All the seats were reserved for Germans, but that didn't matter because the seats were always full, the subway cars packed, everyone standing check by jowl, the French staring anywhere to avoid looking at a German. Max nodded to one elderly woman who had glanced his way accidentally, probably confused by his naval uniform, taking him for French till she saw the eagle clutching the swastika on his right breast. She turned away in contempt. Max scowled at the old woman's averted face. If the French had any backbone at all they wouldn't have collapsed like a house of cards when Guderian hit them with his panzer divisions a year and a half before. Sometimes he didn't know who to despise more: the proud ones like her who were so open with their scorn, or the scores of Parisians who seemed to regard their occupation with gutless equanimity, as if they cared nothing for their nation's fate. What was the joke the army officer had told him at the bar last night? "French rifles for sale. Like new. Never been fired. Only dropped once."

Mareth dragged Max off at their stop and he followed her up the stairs to the street, passing a poster of a fat Winston Churchill smoking a cigar and holding a tommy gun with the legend: ENGLAND—CURSE OF ALL EUROPE. How true. A few people in the crowd hissed at them, taking her for a French girl running around with one of the occupiers—a common sight in this defeated city. "There will be many little Germans born in Paris this year," one of the hotel porters had explained to Max, without rancor. "C'est la guerre." Max nodded. "Krieg ist Krieg." Mareth was unfazed by the scattered hisses in any case; Max knew she enjoyed being mistaken for a glamorous Parisian.

Printemps was full of women, few of them French. Most were blitzmädchen—uniformed female auxiliaries in the telecommunications service of the Wehrmacht. "I've never seen so many fat women," Max said. Mareth elbowed him. They were everywhere, filling the store in their drab gray uniforms with their identifying lightning bolt patches on their left sleeves, holding up stockings, pawing at tables of evening purses, gawking over Coco Chanel's latest designs. Parisians referred to the blitzmädchen as "gray mice," and no wonder. Max and Mareth pushed through the crowd to the shoe department. He sat in a chair while she surveyed the selection. Whatever she picked out, the saleswoman would smile approvingly and say, "Oui, Fräulein." Max shook his head in disgust. These people had no character, no pride. Leather had disappeared, all of it consigned to the Wehrmacht, so every pair of shoes in the store had wooden soles with cloth uppers—hardly high fashion, but leave it to the French to make such a thing attractive. They had no character but plenty of style.

The shoe department was packed just as tightly as the rest of the store. The clucking gray-clad women swirled around Max as he sat hunched in his chair, their number multiplied by the mirrors on all sides. The air became close and stale. Max felt his pulse pick up; his palms started sweating. A trembling anxiety came on again—it had come on him before in crowds, in loud places, twice at Café Scheherazade, the unofficial club in Paris for Kriegsmarine officers, and once in the Cathedral of Notre Dame, where he had gone to mass to pray for his dead comrades.

He closed his eyes and tried to will himself to be calm. After escaping a warship as it burned, and surviving two weeks in an open lifeboat, he was now being terrorized by a crowd of blitzmädchen in a Parisian department store. The doctors said the attacks would pass in time, although that seemed their answer for everything: "It will pass in time." Did they say that to amputees? He started to hyperventilate.

"I'll be outside," he gasped to Mareth.

Breathe into a bag, the doctors had told him. One franc bought a copy of *Le Figaro* from a newsstand on the street in front of Printemps. Max twisted the paper into a cone and breathed in and out, the cone filling with air and then collapsing. Slowly his breathing returned to normal and his heartbeat slowed. He leaned against a post and watched the city stroll by. A woman turned the corner and came toward him in green slacks with a cream-colored blouse, striding purposefully on thin heels, chest thrust out in front of her. What was it about these Parisian girls that made them look so good? He stared at the woman so intently that he didn't even notice the black Citroën creeping along the curb behind her until it stopped and two men in dark overcoats jumped out, one of them wearing a gray hat.

They grabbed the woman roughly and she flailed her arms, shouting, kicking one of them in the balls. "Help!" she screamed. "Help!" The other man punched her full in the face, splitting her lip and splashing her clothes with blood.

Max moved by instinct. He brought Gray Hat down with a knee to the gut, then turned and floored the second man with a right hook. The girl darted across the street and was gone. Max froze when he felt the barrel of a pistol against his back.

"You ignorant swine!" Gray Hat hissed in German.

The second man picked himself up from the sidewalk, tenderly rubbing his jaw. "What have we here? A navy hero?" He punched Max in the stomach. Then he opened his palm and displayed the warrant disc of the Geheime Staatspolizei: the Gestapo.

"Into the car," his partner ordered, pushing Max forward with the pistol.

He covered Max in the backseat while the second man drove. As they pulled away from the curb, Mareth ran out of Printemps.

Max caught her eye for a moment through the window of the Citroën and then they were gone.

The driver said, "A navy hero, is that it? We'll make you scream for helping that French whore. Are you a spy, too?"

"I am a German naval officer. You will address me as 'Herr Oberleutnant.'"

"Do loyal German naval officers help French spies escape?" the man with the gun screamed into Max's ear. "The navy is rotten with enemies of the Führer!"

Max turned to face him. "Obviously I had no idea who that woman was, or who you were. How could I have known? I am a German patriot and a combat veteran. I demand that you release me immediately."

The pistol jabbed his ribs. "You will be released in a coffin, my friend."

The car screeched to a halt at 72 Avenue Foch, Paris headquarters of the Gestapo. They pushed Max into the building, the gun still at his back, and led him down a long hallway to a small room furnished with a metal desk and chair. A bare light bulb hung from the ceiling, casting a harsh glare. The two men left, saying nothing, slamming the heavy door behind them. Max heard the bolt slide into place. He examined the walls, running his fingers lightly over the beige plaster that was peeling in spots. There was no window.

The Gestapo had one task: ferret out enemies of the Reich wherever they might hide—in universities, in factories, in unions, even in the Wehrmacht itself. In the Kriegsmarine, rumor had it that people arrested by the Gestapo were never seen again. Max shivered in spite of his thick woolen uniform. A spy? Was that French girl a spy? She didn't look like a spy. Suppose she was one. Still, to see a young woman assaulted on the street right in front of him, hit in the face like that, in broad daylight—how else could he be expected to react? But if she was a member of the Resistance, they were right to arrest her.

Max's confidence in his actions waned with the day. Perhaps an apology was in order. The Gestapo men had acted like a couple of thugs, but he would buy them each a Beck's and admit his mistake, one German to another. Clearly it had been nothing but a misunderstanding. They could hardly shoot him for such a trivial mistake. If he were shot, important people would miss him. Perhaps he should tell them that immediately. Indeed, the very next evening he was to dine with General Admiral Saalwächter, commanding Marinegruppenkommando West. Admirals frowned on having their dinner guests snatched by the Gestapo, Max was sure. Besides, couldn't the admiral get him released? Could the Gestapo arrest you and keep you even if ordered by one of the highest-ranking admirals in the service to release you? Had the Nazis gotten that powerful?

He began to pace the room, sweating again. Sixteen hundred hours by his watch. No German naval officer had ever been shot by his own government over such a trivial and understandable mistake, he told himself. What would the Reich be coming to if such a thing were possible? All he had to do was explain himself, cite his record, clarify the situation. The thugs who brought him in had scoffed at that, but who were they? Max continued pacing for an hour, for two hours, the time seeming to stand still in the hermetic space of the room. By 1900 hours he knew it would be dark outside, but the bulb above him burned brightly as ever, sizzling faintly in the silence. He laid his head on the desk. It was past 2000 hours when the door finally swung open.

Max lifted his head and went cold in the gut. Before him stood a young man dressed in the dazzling black-and-silver uniform of the Security Service of the S.S.—der Schwarz Engel, the black angel. With a loud click of his heels, the S.S. man came to quivering attention and thrust out his right arm. "Heil Hitler!"

Max came quickly out of the chair and even more quickly to attention. "Heil Hitler," he responded, right arm thrust out.

"I am Standartenführer Auerbach." A Standartenführer was a

colonel of the S.S., which used its own table of ranks to heighten its distinction from the Wehrmacht. Auerbach cut the perfect Aryan figure—blond, blue-eyed, lean and strong, wearing the S.S. medal for fitness among others.

"When I heard of what you had done," Auerbach said, "I simply decided to have you shot." He stared at Max to let this sink in. "That French whore you rescued was an enemy of the Reich! A member of the Resistance! A traitor to her country!" He slapped his thigh and paused again, anger in his face. "Then I received a call from a very old and loyal party member. He vouched for you unconditionally and told me of your outstanding war record. So I said to myself that obviously you're just a simple sailor who knows nothing of how dangerous the home front has become."

"Ja, ja, Herr Standartenführer. Everything is so different . . ."

"These French mutts, they seem docile on the surface, but turn your back on them and they'll bite you like mad dogs." He walked closer and poked Max in the chest as he talked. "Bite, bite, bite. Kill our soldiers. Officers just like you, assassinated. Genitals cut off and stuffed in their mouths. Acid poured in their eyes. These people are barbaric pigs!"

Max nodded.

"You front-line officers have it easy," Auerbach said, smiling now. "You're surprised to hear that, yes? But it is true. Yes, you have it easy because you know who the enemy is. Here, we have to search them out everywhere, in every face on every street. And just when you finally relax, a glass of brandy, a cigar, then it comes—the knife in your back. Three officers killed that way just this week."

Now Max shook his head. "I had no idea."

"Of course not. Of course, you have no idea. The war seems like a simple thing to you, and why not? Drive your boat around the ocean till the enemy appears, waving their flag. Fire a torpedo at them and be on your way. Here things are more difficult."

"Yes, I see that now."

Auerbach took Max by the arm and led him out of the room

and down the hallway. "In the end, we're just two men in the service trying to do our duty to the Führer, are we not?"

"We are, Herr Standartenführer."

In the lobby he gripped Max more tightly and pulled him close. "Stay out of police business, Oberleutnant."

"Jawohl, Herr Standartenführer."

Auerbach dropped Max's arm and stepped back, tall, lean as a whippet, immaculate in his pressed tunic and riding boots, the silver runes of the S.S. stark against the black of his uniform. He came to rigid attention and gave the Nazi salute. "Heil Hitler!"

Max clicked his heels together and thrust his own arm out in response. "Heil Hitler," he said. He turned and left the building, descending its front steps to the sidewalk on trembling legs. His underarms were soaked with sweat; the moisture had seeped through his shirt and through his uniform coat. He walked to the corner, breathing in the clean night air. Then he began to run—across the street, up onto the sidewalk again, scattering people in front of him. A uniformed German officer running through occupied Paris meant trouble to them, but Max didn't care. To hell with the Parisians. In his cadet days at the Academy they had run everywhere, for endless kilometers through the forests around Flensburg, and he was always one of the fastest, a champion sprinter from his time at gymnasium. Now he ran till his legs ached, till his body was blown, then stopped and stood gasping in a street near the Eiffel Tower. He could see the long lines of German soldiers waiting for the elevator that would take them to the top to look over the lights of Paris. His whole body was damp now, hair plastered to his forehead by sweat. In the melee with the Gestapo men he had lost his cap. A new one would cost him twenty marks. When his wind returned, he hailed one of the bicycle-drawn carts. "Hotel George the Fifth," he told the driver.

"Oui, monsieur."

He found Mareth waiting anxiously for him in the lobby. She didn't run to him—not in public with the French staring. But when he put his arms around her she kissed him hard on the mouth, clutching his shoulders. "Let's go to the room," she said.

In the elevator she leaned against him, put her blond head on his chest. Max stroked her hair and felt himself stiffening against her. His heartbeat was so loud, he wondered if the elevator operator could hear it. The old man jerked the car to a stop on their floor and opened the metal gate to let them out. "Bon soir, mademoiselle, monsieur."

"Merci, bon soir," Mareth said.

Inside the room she immediately began to cry as much in anger as relief. "How could you do something so foolish?" she said. "You could have been shot. Damn you, Max—you would have been if my father hadn't saved you."

Max sat on the bed and looked down. It had been foolish. "I wondered if it was him."

"Of course it was him," Mareth said. "I had to call him in Berlin and interrupt his meeting with the foreign minister, then threaten to never speak to him again unless he called the Gestapo. He loves me, Max. He's my father and he loves me. But even he hesitated to interfere with the Gestapo. Don't you know how dangerous the S.S. has become? Everyone is terrified of them, Max. They can do whatever they want. They are the real criminals. Worse than the Communists, almost."

"Mareth, I don't even know what to say." He paused. How was this possible? "Mareth, my God, I had no idea . . . I just can't even . . . Has it truly come to that? Surely the navy would have . . ."

"Would have what, Max? Would have what? Do you think the navy is more powerful than the Nazis? Admiral Raeder himself could have come to your defense—do you think anyone would have paid attention? Whatever power he had left went down with *Bismarck*. He just sits in his office and wrings his hands like a helpless old woman. The Führer won't even see him anymore."

"Helpless?" Max stammered. "The commander in chief of the Kriegsmarine is helpless? How can that be?"

"That's what my father says. Damn it, Max, you can be such a fool. Only Dönitz has any power."

"How was it that your father, that he could, he could, make such a call? Is he that high up in the party?"

"He's a golden pheasant," Mareth said. Nazi slang for the oldest party members, a reference to their large Nazi Party badges circled in gold. "He joined in the twenties."

"I didn't think . . . I just never thought that your father . . . I know he is a powerful man but I didn't think many in the nobility supported the Nazis early on. How was it . . . ?"

"Max, you don't understand. You don't know what it was like then. Papa did what he felt he had to do for Germany. In the beginning, Hitler didn't speak like he did later. He only denounced the treaty and spoke about making us respected again in the world. And he promised to crush the Red Bolsheviks who wanted to seize power and kill us all. And they did want to do that, Max, they did. So Papa joined the party because he is a German patriot. He doesn't believe in the rest of it—burning books and banning cabarets or treating the Jews in such a beastly way. But Father puts up with these things because he's a German patriot."

"Aren't we all, Mareth? Aren't we all German patriots? I didn't realize that one had to join the party and wear a swastika to be a patriot."

"You have a swastika on your uniform!"

True enough: on the right breast of his uniform jacket, an eagle clutched a swastika. "That's just part of the uniform. I stay out of politics. I'm a military officer. I have to follow orders."

"And so does my father, Max, and so do I, and so does everyone in Germany because there's nothing else we can do—nothing at all or we'll be shot or, worse, guillotined, because that's what the

Nazis do now. So what should I do? Tell Reich Minister Lammers that he is a dangerous fool? Interfere with the S.S. and get arrested by the Gestapo, like you?"

"And that was my fault? I've been away two years fighting for my country. How was I to know that I was in more danger from the Gestapo than the Royal Navy? How was I to know that I would be in less danger as a prisoner of the British because the Geneva Convention would protect me while I have no protection from the German police except, by the grace of God, from your father, who is one of the few Nazis powerful enough to keep me from being shot."

Max picked up the carafe of wine and a glass from the bed-side table, walked across the room, and sat in one of the two large chairs by the window. He poured himself a glass of wine, then turned and looked at Mareth, who watched him silently. "So your mother and father will entertain Nazis but won't deign to meet me—a decorated navy officer—because my father is a shopkeeper instead of a storm trooper? Because I wear a blue uniform and not a brown one? Is that it? Is that why your mother won't even allow me into her drawing room?"

"How dare you say that, Max. How dare you," Mareth said, her voice rising. "You don't even know my mother! She hates the Nazis and she hates my father for staying with them. They've barely spoken for years."

Max upended his glass of wine. "You're right, Mareth, as always. I don't know your mother. I wonder if I even know you anymore."

Mareth sat on the bed, looked down, pressing her hands to her temples. "You don't know what it is like here now. You don't. Even my mother had trouble with the Gestapo. And it was very embarrassing to my father and it made everything between them even worse."

"What? What happened to your mother?"

"She was collecting ration coupons from friends and we gave them to Jews. Someone reported her—the chauffeur, she thinks— and the Gestapo arrested her."

"They actually arrested her?"

"Yes. I was in Berlin when she was arrested. Someone called my father and he had to call one of Himmler's adjutants and say something, make something up, an excuse, I'm not sure what. They let my mother go and said it was a misunderstanding."

"Why did she do it? Are the Jews starving? I can give you some of my ration coupons."

"Starving? Of course they're starving. They only get half the rations we do, and often not even that. Don't you know this?"

No, he didn't. Mareth continued. "My mother used to go to a jewelry shop in Kiel. It was owned by a Jew, Herr Wertheim. She shopped there even after they published her name in the Kiel newspaper as someone who patronized Jewish businesses. People hissed at her on the street, hissed at her—the lower-class people especially.

"I once went to Herr Wertheim's with her. A bully-boy storm trooper was standing in front of the shop and he heckled any Germans who thought about going inside. When we went to enter he blocked our way and asked why Aryans like us were going into a shop owned by a dirty perverted Jew. 'Because we choose to,' my mother said. 'Now out of the way, you oaf.' And the storm trooper stood aside. But do you know what he did, Max? Do you know what he did?"

Max shook his head no.

"He called us whores who fucked Jews. Dirty Jew whores! He actually said that to us, to her. My mother is a Countess! She was a lady-in-waiting to the Empress! Her great-great-grandfather was court chamberlain to Frederick the Great, and that vulgar boy said that to me, to her, there on the street. Language like that. My mother pushed him aside with her umbrella and we went in, while he continued to call us Jew-fucking whores. And then one day we went back, and the shop was closed and Herr Wertheim was gone."

"Where?"

Mareth looked away from him. "To a resettlement camp in the East, I think. I don't know. That's what someone told us."

Max looked away from her—silence between them now. He didn't want to know more. He had his own problems. Everyone had to take care of themselves in this war. He poured another glass of wine and looked out over Paris, the City of Light, mostly dark now from power cuts—except for buildings commandeered by the Germans.

The water ran in the bathroom sink, then he heard Mareth walk across the room to him. She put a hand on his shoulder but he didn't look up, just continued to stare out the window, so she sat in the other chair, reached across the space between them, and took his hand. After a moment he looked at her. Neither spoke. She gripped his hand very tightly. Max stared silently at her, then flicked his eyes toward the bed. Afterward, they slept the night entwined together.

In the morning he showered and while toweling off he watched her sleeping body moving rhythmically as she breathed. His future, their future, had once been his solace, but he felt less certain of it now. Germany would still win, just not quickly. The stubbornness of the British, along with their vast naval power, allowed a river of food and arms to flow from America, keeping England alive even as the Luftwaffe pounded London. And in the midst of the struggle with England, the Führer had been forced to launch a surprise attack on the Soviet Union in order to forestall their imminent attack on Germany. In the first four months they killed or captured over four million Soviet soldiers, about as many as the Oberkommando der Wehrmacht said they had in their army. Since all of their fighting men had been annihilated, the Soviets had to surrender. Except they didn't surrender because they had more than four million soldiers—many more. OKW had been completely wrong in their estimate. Every time the Wehrmacht shattered a Soviet army, another appeared as if Stalin needed but to sow dragon's teeth after each defeat and another million Russian soldiers appeared. The Führer said they were winning, that the Red Bolsheviks were about to collapse, that brave men of the Wehrmacht had preserved the Reich against the Asiatic hordes of Russia for a thousand years to come. And the Germans were winning. Guderian was one hundred kilometers from Moscow. Two weeks ago the head of the Reich Press Service had even said the war with the Soviets was over and Germany had won. So even though the war against the Soviets was over and they had won, it wasn't and they hadn't. Each day he saw long columns of gray-clad troops moving toward the Gare du Nord to entrain for the East. And as Max watched those columns march by, he could see the life he'd imagined with Mareth receding farther into the distance with each passing battalion.

Tossing his towel aside, he slid into bed beside Mareth and fell into a heavy sleep. The maid awakened them at noon. She smiled at the two of them, apologized, began to slink out of the room. Max told her to come back in two hours.

Mareth grinned. "Why two hours?"

Max worked his hands down her flanks, bent to kiss her stomach, her hip, the inside of her thigh. Glancing up through her blond fleece, he said, "Maybe you'd rather make it three?"

"If you can last that long, Herr Oberleutnant."

"Endurance is the hallmark of a naval officer."

Mareth laughed and put his head in a scissor lock between her soft thighs. "Then we shall have to test this officer."

The maid never did get to clean the room that day.

Toward evening Max dressed in his new uniform, creases pressed to a sharp edge by the hall porter. He had been forced to go to a French military tailor and pay for the uniform with his own money, and it hadn't been cheap. Fortunately, he was able to pay with occupation francs, a currency the Germans printed and forced the French to accept.

A Kriegsmarine staff car called for Max at 1900 hours. The streets of Paris were quiet. The only vehicles Max saw also belonged to the Wehrmacht. Sidewalk cafés were open and filled with German soldiers having drinks, the lucky ones with French girlfriends. Others, weary of drinking or out of money, queued at the Deutsches Soldatenkino, special movie theaters set up for the German military and off-limits to civilians. In some of these theaters, Max had heard, bicyclists from the Tour de France earned extra ration coupons by pedaling stationary bikes to charge the batteries that powered the projectors.

He saw Parisian gendarmes patrolling the city as they normally did, although they were supported by heavily armed contingents of German military police, distinctive with their gorgets hung round their necks, the word *Feldgendarmerie* picked out in luminescent paint.

At every major intersection, wooden supports had been erected to hold the numerous small signs that gave directions to the various German military installations in the city. When the Feldgendarmerie stopped them to allow a small convoy of horse-drawn army wagons to pass, Max saw a mishmash of wooden arrows pointing to, among others, General der Luftwaffe Paris, the Reichsbahn, the Organisation Todt, and the Army Remount Service, which worked to find the several million horses needed each year by the Wehrmacht to pull wagons and guns. They went through the intersection and drove down the Place de l'Opéra, past the Kommandantur, headquarters of the military governor, where armed troops stood a watchful guard.

Max smoked quietly in the backseat. He had never met General Admiral Saalwächter, although his book on naval warfare was required reading for every cadet at the Marineschule Mürwik. The dinner invitation had come as a surprise, and though it was an honor, Max felt nervous, almost lightheaded. He didn't know why the Oberfelshaber der Marinegruppenkommando West would personally wish to see a mere Oberleutnant, no matter what kind of tribulations Max had survived. "Will we be on time?" he asked the driver.

"Time? Seven and fifteen," the driver said in heavily accented German.

"No, are we going to be on time? We have to be there by seven-thirty." Max said the last two words loud and slow—"se-ven-thir-ty"—as if he were speaking to someone completely daft.

"Ja, ja, mein Herr. Not be late."

What was his accent? Russian? How could that be? They were at war with Russia. "Are you Russian?"

The driver smiled in the rearview mirror, showing off a mouthful of steel teeth. "All drivers for Herr Admiral, Russia," he said. "White Russias, hate Communists. Kill Communists." His teeth flashed in the mirror as he drew a finger slowly across his throat.

Max nodded and leaned back. It was a long way from the Bolshevik Revolution to driving a Kriegsmarine staff car in Paris twenty-five years later. At least he still had all his teeth.

Saalwächter's office and the headquarters of Marinegruppen-kommando West occupied the French Ministry of Marine on the Place de la Concorde, commandeered by the navy from the French government. But the admiral had invited Max to his official residence nearby and the car arrived at 1925.

"Time, mein Herr."

"Danke," Max said. He tipped the driver—probably against regulations, but who cared?

He took the salute of the two German sailors in the striped sentry boxes, went up the stairs, and rang the bell. An orderly admitted him. "Oberleutnant zur See Maximilian Brekendorf reporting as ordered to Herr General Admiral Saalwächter."

The orderly led Max to a small dining room. "Herr Admiral Saalwächter will be with you shortly, Herr Oberleutnant."

The table was set for only two. Max hoped he remembered what all the forks and spoons were for. Part of the entrance exam to the Marineschule Mürwik had included a formal dinner for the candidates with naval officers and their wives, this last intended to restrict admittance to proper gentlemen. Fortunately for Max, the headwaiter from one of the large hotels in Kiel had retired to Bad Wilhelm. For the price of one rabbit per week, he gave Max lessons in table manners: which fork to use for fish, which for salad; which glass for white wine and which for red; when to drink brandy and when to drink schnapps; how to eat shellfish; how to serve a cake or pie; how to carve a goose. And that was just the beginning. There were also long hours of instruction in social deportment: when to wear gloves and when to remove them; how and when to bow; to offer your hand; present your calling card; reply to invitations; thank the hostess; talk with your dinner partner; sit while wearing your sword. Later, when he had become a cadet at the Marineschule Mürwik, there were mandatory ballroom dancing lessons for all the Seekadetten—not that he or any of his crewkameraden had been called upon to waltz in the last few years.

Max waited only a few minutes before the admiral came in. Saalwächter was tall and lean, with gray hair receding from the temples. His perfectly tailored blue uniform with his many decorations sparkled in the soft light of the dining room. Max immediately came to attention. "Oberleutnant zur See Brekendorf, reporting as ordered, sir."

Saalwächter looked him over and smiled. "At ease, Oberleutnant." He shook Max's hand. "It is an honor to meet such a brave young man."

Max could feel the blood flushing his cheeks. "Thank you, Herr Admiral."

"You have had many adventures since leaving Germany."

"A great many, sir."

"I hope you will join me in an apéritif?"

"It would be my sincere pleasure, sir."

A white-jacketed steward entered with two glasses of champagne.

Saalwächter raised his glass. "A toast to the young lieutenant, and to his survival."

"Thank you, sir. Thank you."

They drank.

"Come, my young friend, be seated, be seated."

The steward reappeared with a cheese soufflé, followed by baby lobster in champagne sauce, then steak with sauce béarnaise, white wine, red wine, a dessert wine. Strawberries with heavy cream. Espresso. Max felt himself becoming groggy as he made his way from course to course, but each dish was better than the one before; he wondered at the admiral's trim physique. Saalwächter kept the conversation light throughout the meal, asking after Max's home and family, getting all the details about Mareth once the romance had been uncovered. Afterward he showed Max to a study at the rear of the house furnished with overstuffed chairs, a phonograph player, and shelves of leather-bound books.

"Cognac? Cigar?"

Max took both from the steward, who then withdrew.

Saalwächter put a record on the phonograph—an aria from *La Bohème*, he explained. "Opera is the West's highest art form, Oberleutnant. Have you been?"

"No, sir."

"Ah, you must go, young man, you must go. I keep a box but have so little time to use it. If you ever want to attend, just call my adjutant and he will make the arrangements."

Max couldn't imagine anything worse. "The admiral is very kind."

Saalwächter sat and lit his cigar. His mouth drew down at the edges and his manner seemed to change. He said, "When did you leave the Marineschule Mürwik, Oberleutnant?"

"Thirty-seven, sir. I am a member of Crew 33."

Saalwächter shook his head. "So few thoroughly trained men are available now. We've cut training time by half, two-thirds in some cases. Prewar officers like you with combat experience are a tremendous asset to the service."

"Thank you, sir."

Max's cigar had gone out and the admiral offered him another light from the heavy ornamental lighter on the end table. "Were the circumstances of Captain Langsdorff's suicide the same as those reported to the Naval War Staff?"

"I presume so, Herr Admiral. I did not make the report myself, as you must know."

Saalwächter looked away and puffed his cigar. It was a good smoke; Langsdorff would have approved. Quality cigars were becoming rare on the continent because none from the Americas made it through the British blockade, unless they came from Spain via the black market. "Tell me about it, Oberleutnant, if you would. You are the first officer of *Graf Spee* I have had the opportunity to speak with in person."

Max shifted to the edge of his chair. Speaking quietly, he related the events in Montevideo harbor, and the scuttling of *Spee* in the Rio Plata. "We went upriver to Buenos Aires afterwards so we would be interned by the Argentines. Captain Langsdorff regarded it as his duty to see the crew through to safety, and to negotiate the terms of our internment himself. Otherwise, I'm certain he would have gone down with the ship."

Max paused to sip his cognac. The confusion and disappointment of those days still registered in his gut. "They bunked us in the old Naval Arsenal in Buenos Aires when we arrived. I went to my quarters early the next evening because I was tired. The captain's steward woke me around zero six hundred and asked me to come to the captain's room. I thought he was sick, but when we got there, I saw that he'd killed himself."

Saalwächter was gazing intently over the rim of his glass. "And was there anything unusual?"

Max nodded. "Captain Langsdorff had wrapped himself in the ensign of the Imperial Navy before shooting himself." Max knew this had been omitted from the official report; it was a gesture of which the Nazis would not have approved. Certainly Langsdorff intended it as a slight toward Hitler and the party. The captain was not alone in feeling that the interests and advice of the navy were being disregarded by the party leadership. Langsdorff had also been photographed at the funeral of the German sailors killed during the battle, giving the naval salute, hand to forehead, while all the German embassy officials and German civilians around him gave the Deutsche Gruss, the Nazi salute. The photograph had been on the front page of every major newspaper in the world. Berlin was not pleased.

The admiral stood and poured himself another cognac. "Whoever wrote the report was wise to leave that out. Did others know?"

"Only a few of us, Herr Admiral. We unwrapped the body—that is, the doctor and myself—before notifying the Argentine navy of the incident."

"You have much presence of mind, Brekendorf. A valuable trait in a naval officer. Of course we will keep this conversation to ourselves. There is Captain Langsdorff's family to consider. I'm sure you understand."

"More and more, sir."

"We in the navy must be careful, too, Oberleutnant. Old Academy men like you and me do not wield all the power, I'm afraid. Langsdorff wished to express his disapproval of this situation, but his family are not the only ones for whom it might make trouble if word got out."

"Yes, sir."

Saalwächter went to the phonograph. He turned the record over and replaced the needle. "You agreed with his decision about the ship?"

"No, sir, I did not."

"No?"

"No, sir. We had a chance to break out. We should have taken it."

"Fought to the death for Volk and Vaterland?"

"Something like that, Herr Admiral."

Saalwächter gave him a long gaze. Finally he said, "I like your spirit, young man. We will need more officers like you if we are to win this war. Where will you go next, Maximilian? We have lost *Bismarck*, but *Prinz Eugen* fought beside her with great courage at Denmark Strait when they sank *Hood*. Or perhaps *Gneisenau*? Any ship in the fleet would be grateful to have you."

Max paused a moment. He must choose his words carefully. Saalwächter commanded a large percentage of the German navy's surface units, plus the hundreds of minesweepers, patrol boats, and fast attack boats deployed off the French coast. Max did not want to offend him, but he had decided that Germany's surface forces were so small, they could do little more than annoy the British. "With all due respect, Herr Admiral, I would like to volunteer for the U-boat force. I feel that I can best serve my country in that capacity—and best strike at England, sir."

"The English are a damnable people."

"Yes, sir. They caused us to sink our own ship in the Rio Plata, then sank *Meteor* out from under me, killed my friends; they . . ."

The admiral held up his hand. "I understand, Maximilian. Dönitz will be happy to have you, of that I am sure, and you will have my blessing. I shall ring him tomorrow and personally recommend you. With your training and experience, I shouldn't wonder if they give you a boat of your own. We're turning out thirty to forty every month now and experienced seagoing officers are in desperately short supply. It's tough training. Three or four months to work the boat up at the construction yard, then six or seven more in the Baltic to train. You'll be there in winter."

"I survived the Marineschule Mürwik, sir."

"Yes—and much worse than that since, Maximilian. And certainly no one will be shooting at you in the Baltic."

The admiral turned his attention to a small velvet box beside the phonograph. He opened it and displayed the contents for Max, who stood up. "The real highlight of the evening, Oberleutnant. In the name of the Führer, I award you the Iron Cross First Class for bravery under fire at the Battle of the Rio de la Plata and the subsequent action involving the auxiliary raider *Meteor*."

He pinned the Iron Cross to Max's uniform, on the left breast pocket.

Max felt the medal—sharp and cold under his fingers. He looked down and smiled, his pulse quickening. How often in his days at the Marineschule Mürwik had he dreamed of this moment? Yet only now, when the moment had come, did he understand its price—Dieter, Langsdorff, the men who had died around him in the drifting lifeboat, all the others who would never come home. None of that had been part of his cadet fantasies. "I am honored, Herr Admiral."

"You earned it, Maximilian. And now, an even more pleasant task. As of today I appoint you to the rank of KapitänLeutnant." Saalwächter stood back and saluted Max. "Allow me to be the first to salute your new rank, Herr Kaleu."

A promotion and an Iron Cross. The price had been too high, but Max felt his pride welling up nonetheless. "Thank you, sir. I will do my best to bring honor to the rank."

"I know that you will, KapitänLeutnant. Germany will need nothing less from you." Saalwächter saw Max to the door, shook his hand, and sent him off with the traditional U-boat man's farewell. "Good luck, son—and good hunting."

CHAPTER EIGHT

MAX FOLLOWED THE ICEBREAKER OUT OF THE HARBOR, THE GRAY steel of the U-boat's prow pushing aside the slush left in the channel. A violent wind blew across the Bay of Danzig; Max could feel the chill of it on his skin, even though he wore a rubber diver's suit under his heavy sweater, leather jacket, and fleece-lined bridge coat. No one was ever really warm in East Prussia with this damned wind blowing in from Russia all the time. Max wondered how the boys on the Eastern Front withstood it—especially those in Six Armee at Stalingrad, which had been surrounded by the Soviets since mid-November. How much longer could Paulus and his troops hold out? Cut off from their supplies, dying in the thousands from hunger and frostbite. But the Bolsheviks had to be defeated. If not, they would march on Germany eventually, and if the Red Army ever entered the Reich—Max couldn't even allow the thought. It would never happen, must never happen.

The water was black and filled with chunks of ice as they

passed out of the channel and came into the Baltic proper. "Helm, port five degrees rudder, come to new heading zero five zero," he called down the open hatchway.

The helmsman, sitting blind in the conning tower, operated the push buttons that controlled the rudder. "Steady on zero five zero, Herr Kaleu."

"Both engines full ahead," Max called into the voicepipe that led to the control room. Feeling her speed pick up beneath him, he navigated the U-boat into her assigned training area. With so many boats working up, Flotilla Command had divided this part of the Baltic into quadrants. Each boat was limited to a specific quadrant in hopes of preventing collisions. Still, training losses were running high, Max had heard—much higher than officially acknowledged. Bad enough being in a U-boat sunk by the enemy, worse was being in a U-boat accidentally sunk by your own navy. When it happened, Flotilla Command simply removed the name of the missing boat from the roster, removed the crew belongings from the barracks ship, and scrubbed the cabins down. *Gefallen für Volk and Führer*, the telegram would say.

Families printed up small death cards with the name and photograph of the departed that they sent to relatives and friends: *In Proud Sorrow, We Announce the Death of Our Beloved Son, Seaman First Class Otto Muller, 17, fell for Volk and Führer, 5 December 1942, the Baltic Sea. He gave his life for Greater Germany. The Lord is my Shepherd.* Anyone who read the death card would know, as the family did, but would not say for fear of the Gestapo, that the young sailor had died for nothing. In a training accident. In a U-boat. In the Baltic. In the winter. Pray God it was quick. And no doubt it was. There would be no crewmates to assure the parents that their son had not suffered, as much of a lie as that may have been, because they all drowned as well. Not that the Baltic was deep—never more than one hundred fifty meters. But that was still much too deep to use the escape gear since the outside water pressure would prevent the opening of the hatch.

Max had reported to the Deutsche Werke shipyard in Kiel ten months ago to shepherd *U-114* through its final four months of construction and learn everything about this complex machine—a type VII C, the backbone of the German U-boat fleet. Over those four months, he had also moved to recruit his officers and petty officers, gathering the best men he could find, this task made difficult by the demand for men from every corner of the Greater German Reich, especially the Eastern Front, from which no one ever seemed to return. At least he'd been able to get Carls, his Oberbootsmann, from *Graf Spee*, who'd been serving aboard *Scharnhorst* since escaping from Buenos Aires on a fishing boat in the fall of '40. After the U-Boat Acceptance Command had put the boat through trials and officially accepted *U-114* from the builders, the crew had come aboard.

For the last six months, they'd been working the boat up, with the final operational tests scheduled for the next week, including three simulated attacks—the final three of the sixty-six they'd been required to perform over the course of their training. When the operational tests finished, they would finally return to Kiel to load supplies and real torpedoes for their first war patrol.

Beside Max on the bridge, the four men of the watch shivered in the wind. Time to see if anyone was awake. "Alarm!" he bellowed.

The bridge watch jumped through the hatch. An aluminum ladder ran through the conning tower into the control room, but four men couldn't make it down a ladder in fifteen seconds, so they just dropped the three meters and slammed into the deck plates, too bad if anyone got hurt. Most times the control room crew kept a deflated life raft under the hatchway to cushion the fall, but the raft constantly slid out of position. Max secured the main hatch and dropped into the control room, himself missing the raft, as water flooded the bridge above.

On early training runs, they had spent an hour or more checking every wheel and valve before executing the precise movements required to submerge the boat. But in combat you didn't have an hour. You didn't have minutes. You had seconds. Your only real protection was beneath the waves, so you had to learn to submerge at lightning speed—though submerging itself was a dangerous maneuver. The moment Max gave the alarm to dive, seawater began gushing into the ballast tanks, and by the time he closed the main hatch and dogged it home, water nearly engulfed the bridge. If you didn't get the timing just right, tons of water poured into the boat and you sank. Simple. No one knew how often it happened, because no one ever lived to report the mistake.

"All outlet valves open."

"Venting all diving tanks—main tank ready, bow and stern ready . . . port and starboard ready."

"Reporting all air intakes closed."

"Reporting all outboard exhaust valves closed."

"All inlet valves open! Flooding all tanks."

Max watched the controlled panic of an emergency dive. Sailors jackknifed through the hatchways, using their bodies as ballast to increase the forward momentum. "Move, men! Move," Carls yelled. Alarm bells rang throughout the boat. Red lights blinked. Machinists hung from the levers that opened the ballast tanks to the sea. Water flooded into the tanks with a dull roar, a sound like the deluge at the heart of a rainstorm. And then they were under. Thirty-one seconds. Quiet now, the electric motors purring.

In thirty-one seconds, they could submerge to a depth of twenty-five meters, the minimum cushion of water required to absorb the blast of a depth charge dropped by a plane. An Allied aircraft needed close on forty seconds to make a depth charge run, so timing had to be just so. That was the theory. No one knew the exact timing, because the men who got it wrong never came back. But certainly you had to be quick. Aircraft were a U-boat's deadliest foe—half of all U-boat losses came from low-level attack by Allied aeroplanes. Oftentimes, the aircraft was on top of you before you knew it and you had to stay on the surface and fight it out with your anti-aircraft guns. That had its own dangers. Just last month, Max had heard, *U-459*'s crew had been surprised by an RAF Coastal Command patrol bomber coming in just five meters off the water. Recovering their wits, the flak gunners brought it down only to have the plane crash into the conning tower, decapitate the Kommandant, kill the other officers, and mangle the flak crews. The boat limped back to port with its navigator chief petty officer in command and a very nervous RAF tail gunner in the forward mess, having been the only survivor of the plane's crew.

Max grabbed the periscope housing to keep from sliding to the deck as the angle of dive increased. The chief engineer and his two men had just settled in at the hydroplane controls when a thin voice shouted from the stern: "Outboard air induction valve won't close! Boat taking water!"

Shit. "Blow all tanks!" Max ordered. Sailors in the control room spun the wheels on the trim panel and blasted compressed air into the ballast tanks, blowing out the seawater. "Both engines ahead three-quarters. Emergency surface."

At the diving station the two sailors bore down on the push-button hydroplane controls, raising the bow planes and lowering the stern planes. The boat rose to forty meters, then started back down. Fifty meters, sixty meters, seventy meters—this bitch was dropping like an elevator. The boat balanced for a moment on an even keel, then slid backward, the water in her stern too heavy to overcome.

"Pump stern trim tanks forward. Pump out main freshwater tank. Both full ahead," Max ordered. The electric motors went to full speed.

"Can't hold her, Herr Kaleu," the chief said.

A can of ham broke loose from the storage compartment in the forward torpedo room and rolled down the central corridor like a bowling ball till it struck the combing of the control room hatch. More cans now, followed by a suitcase and a pair of pliers. Then a case of potatoes. Men slipped, fell backward, slid down the inclined deck. Max again heard the terrible roar of water spewing into the boat. They hit bottom with such force the light bulbs shattered. Darkness now, water pouring in. The men grew skittish.

"All engines stop," he ordered. Pray the propellers hadn't been damaged. Emergency lighting flickered on. Georg, the control room petty officer, produced a flashlight and illuminated the depth gauge. One hundred and thirty meters. "Silence in the boat," Max called. His men chattered like a bunch of jackdaws. Most of them were just youngsters—seventeen, eighteen, nineteen years old. Only a handful were regular sailors.

Max let go of the periscope and slid down the deck plates to the engine room hatch. Two machinists stood upright, working like demons on the valve, water spraying everywhere, black and freezing. Max felt the frigid Baltic water against his rubber sea boots. He tried to still his anxiety—situations like this would be common on the boat. A depth charge too close, a crack in the hull, a broken valve. Water rushing in. Men screaming before their yells were choked away. "Report!" Max shouted over the noise of the water.

The Dieselobermaschinist had his arm in the valve, straining against something, his face red with the effort as a torrent of frigid seawater sprayed over him. "Something stuck in here, Herr Kaleu," he gasped. He jerked back and fell onto the sloping deck, yanking the obstruction free. His mate spun the wheel that shut the valve. It seated itself and held. The roar died away, leaving the after compartment quiet. The Dieselobermaschinist held up a wrench. Some bloody fool had left a wrench topside and it had jammed the valve.

Max clenched his fists. Jesus Christ Almighty and all the Saints above. He should expect it, not five of his crew out of their teens. Only the senior petty officers were true navy men. Most of his crewmen knew nothing of war; many had yet to discover women. A few weeks back Carls had said to him, "Until I met this lot of pimple-faced boys, Herr Kaleu, the only virgin I knew was the Virgin Mary." The young sailors thought this a grand adventure, their chance to get away from home and avoid conscription to the Russian Front. Even some of the petty officers were retreads like Bekker, the radioman, who had been in the U-boat personnel office before he and other office horses had been put to useful work and sent to the fleet. Because the radioman also served as the medic on a U-boat, Max could only pray that he did not fall ill since nothing Bekker did with his medical kit inspired confidence.

But it was Lehmann, the first watch officer, who should have found the wrench. As first watch officer, it was his responsibility to inspect the boat for any condition that could jeopardize their safety before reporting to Max that they were ready to proceed. And he *had* inspected the boat—which worried Max more—because it meant Lehmann lacked thoroughness. But then he was only twenty, with twelve months of training to master what it had taken Max more than five years to learn. In the old navy, a mistake like Lehmann's would end a sea officer's career. All Max could do now was to speak very sharply to him. If he sent him packing, his replacement would likely be worse.

Admiral Dönitz and UBootwaffe Command had suddenly decided years of training could be replaced by enthusiasm for the party, widespread now among the youngsters coming into the fleet. All these young men had been in the Hitler Youth since they were ten years old—they knew nothing else. Will to Final Victory and Belief in the Führer will get us through, or so Lehmann liked to say. Not an effective way to operate a U-boat. Belief in the Führer had nothing to do with knowing which valve to turn, or knowing that you must thoroughly inspect all intake valves to ensure they were not jammed by a stray wrench.

"All hands to the bow," Max ordered, hoping he sounded as calm as Captain Langsdorff had during battle. He wanted to curse at the top of his voice, but that would accomplish little except to rattle the men. They'd all be finished if he lost his composure now. The crew pulled themselves up the deck plates, now at a fifty-degree angle to the bow. "Faster! Faster!" Max shouted. "Bosun, move these men along, now!"

Carls growled at the young sailors. "Move, move, move! Raus, raus!" Max thanked God he had been able to steal him from *Scharnhorst*.

Several young sailors sniffled in fear as they went. "Quiet in the boat," Max ordered again. If they sniffled now, what would they do when British depth charges exploded overhead? Carls drove everyone into the bow, taking two youngsters who had stumbled and dragging them by the collars of their shirts. Max hoped the weight of the men would be enough to force the boat to an even keel. He worked his way back into the control room.

"Chief, damage report."

"Main lighting circuit out, all fuses blown. All motor relays have tripped. Gyro compass out. Port diesel operable but leaking hydraulic fluid. Fore and aft bilge pumps out. Two motor mounts cracked on starboard diesel and one fastening bolt sheared off. Batteries damaged."

"Gas escaping?" If seawater mixed with the hydrochloric acid from the batteries, deadly chlorine gas would be produced.

"Not yet," the chief said. "I don't think any of the batteries are cracked." He hit the depth gauge with his fist in frustration. "Bloody hell." The chief engineer hated the U-boat even more than he despised the navy. He'd been "volunteered" from the merchant marine, plucked from a comfortable billet on a supply ship in Norway and packed off to the UBootwaffe. He didn't care for Max either, since Max, as a sea officer, stood a long way up the ladder from a mere engineer.

The last man climbed into the bow compartment. Still the U-boat hung, angled up, the tons of water in her stern keeping her rooted to the bottom. The chief unfolded a diagram of the boat's pump circuits and spread it on the small chart table. He and Max examined the drawings in the dim glow of the emergency lanterns. "Bloody hell," the chief muttered again. "Bloody hell." He traced a circuit with the stub of a pencil and looked at Max. "Water to the control room bilge, pump it into the ballast tanks, then blow." Max nodded. There was no other way to get rid of the deadly water that held them down.

"Carls!"

"Herr Kaleu?"

"Bucket chain, now. As much water as possible from the stern compartment to the control room bilge. First watch on duty. Second watch to their bunks." Putting the men to bed would lessen their need for oxygen.

Men tumbled back to the stern, seized pots and pans from the cook, buckets from Carls. The second officer—nicknamed Ferret because he looked like one—joined the line. "C'mon, men," he said, "let's show them what the League of German Girls can do. Put your backs into it, lads, it's a long swim home."

For hours they cursed and passed the water, slopping it all over the boat and themselves. Not a man among them kept dry. The Baltic cold penetrated the hull; the temperature dropped and the cold penetrated their bones. There was no heat on a U-boat, save for a handful of portable heaters that had little effect. Men shivered in the bunks, waiting their turn. Condensation formed on the interior of the hull and ran in slimy rivulets to the deck.

Max knew it might not work. And at this depth they wouldn't be able to open the hatch and use the escape gear. Truth be told, their escape training had been only for psychological solace. Almost no one ever escaped from a submerged U-boat. Only under tightly controlled circumstances could it even be done and certainly never below twenty-five meters. They might be entombed here, with all the other German sailors who had died in these waters. He wanted a cigarette.

Instead he went and lay on his green leather bunk, leaving

the curtain open so men looking up from their work could see him. They might think the situation under control if the captain stepped away for a nap. Not that Max slept, though he kept his eyes closed, shivering in fear, hoping the crew wouldn't notice in the dim light. Imperturbability: a U-boat commander must have it, or else pretend to have it. Forty-six men jammed together in a steel tube no longer than two railway carriages and no wider than a tram—you couldn't hide from them. They could always watch you and watch you they did. If you panicked, they would go crazy. Max found as time went along, he acted more and more like Captain Langsdorff, or even Captain Hauer. He became more formal and distant, a stickler for rules and etiquette. Not a month ago, he had given a sailor three days in the guardhouse for not saluting him. The crew feared him. He wore his blue naval tunic with the gold stripes at every meal, even if it did get filthy, and he forbade the men from wearing the ridiculous checked shirts they'd recently been issued, surplus gear seized from the French navy. His crew loved the garments, but Max wasn't about to let them go to war in checked French shirts. Harsh discipline, spit and polish, or a semblance of it, was the only way. No wonder so many officers cracked.

The watch changed. Sailors of the first watch fell into the vacated bunks as the second watch set to work with the buckets. Max turned on his bunk, faced the black hull, touched it, felt the cold. Twenty millimeters of steel, no thicker than a boot heel, was all that separated them from perdition. And everywhere dampness; permeating everything in the boat with a sodden odor that mingled with other smells—sweat, unwashed men, urine, oil, mold, shit—and produced a heavy fog of stink. That special U-boat odor was recognizable to all who had served in the UBootwaffe. Max didn't want to die with that foul smell on his skin. He didn't want to die on a training mission after surviving the loss of two ships at war. He didn't want to die at all. Were they doing everything they could? Fire the torpedoes to lessen their weight? No, they were too deep for that. Had he failed to think of something? Pump the oil tanks out? A useful trick under heavy depth charge attack, since a heavy oil slick would cause the Brits to think the U-boat had imploded. But it wouldn't help them now. Neither of his outboard oil tanks was even one-eighth full. Lehmann had gotten the second watch to singing Hitler Youth marching songs—one of his favorite maneuvers. "A regular bloody choirmaster, our first watch officer," Carls had said of him. The posturing of the young crew annoyed the chief petty officers. "Lot of bloody good that sort of thing will do when the Tommies are dropping depth charges on your head," they told the sailors. The youngsters sang,

> *We will march on*
> *Until everything lies in ruins,*
> *Because today we own Germany*
> *And tomorrow the whole world.*

Max envied Lehmann his easy way with the crewmen. It came from the camaraderie of the Hitler Youth; Lehmann had been a district leader. Max never joined the Hitler Youth. He took up his appointment in the navy just months after the Führer came to power. He had been a member of the Catholic Youth League as a boy, but they spent most of their time hiking, singing hymns, and secretly discussing how to screw, whatever exactly that was.

Even on *Graf Spee*, Max's relations with the crew had always been professional and correct, less relaxed than some of the other officers. "Officers must never make friends with their men," his father had told him before he entered the Marineschule Mürwik. "They won't respect you for it, Maximilian." Keeping his distance wasn't hard for Max. He did so by nature. But Lehmann was the opposite; he called the men by their forenames, listened to their troubles, joked with them—the new National Socialist officer. The Imperial Navy had been abolished in 1918, after the Kaiser abdicated, but its traditions lived on and were imparted with the greatest vigor to the Seekadetten at the Marineschule Mürwik. Lehmann knew nothing of those traditions. None of the junior officers did. Max despised the English as much as anyone, but the war was a contest between professionals. At least it was supposed to be. To men like Lehmann, the war was a crusade. But why march on until everything lay in ruins? Wasn't that what they were trying to prevent?

Max didn't move from his bunk until the first watch went back on duty. By then the level of black water in the stern compartment had diminished. He wanted more of it hauled to the control room bilge, but he could see there wasn't enough oxygen remaining for the men to continue this kind of exertion. They were breathing like blown horses, though the boat could supposedly remain submerged for twenty-four hours or even longer. Obviously the genius on the Naval War Staff who had come up with that figure had never been aboard a U-boat, and never considered how much oxygen men consumed when they were working hard.

"Halt," he ordered.

The men stopped, too exhausted to even groan.

"Chief?"

The chief gave Max a sour look, his way of saying, "You're the sea officer with the star on your tunic, Herr KapitänLeutnant Brekendorf, so you bloody well decide."

"All hands to the bow, then," Max said. He had to get the boat on an even keel. The men hauled themselves up to the bow compartment and lay there like a pack of whipped dogs. Max nodded at the chief.

A wheel turned, then two. Compressed air hissed like a serpent into the ballast tanks and blew out the water that had been pumped into the tanks from the control room bilge. Then the hissing died away. The boat did not move.

Max had been clenching his fists so hard that his fingernails had drawn blood where they dug in. "All hands to the stern! Quickly, men, quickly!" The sailors tumbled past him, faces pale.

"To the bow, men, to the bow! Faster! Faster now!" They struggled back, Carls pushing them on.

It had to be the mud holding them fast to the bottom. It was the only explanation.

"E-motors both full ahead," Max ordered. In the stern, the Elektriker Obermaschinist pushed his throttles forward. "To the stern men, to the stern. Move, dammit! Move!"

The charging of the sailors back and forth set the boat to rocking. Gently, like a feather floating to the ground, the bow came to rest on the sea floor, putting the boat on an even keel and breaking the suction of the mud. They began to rise. "One hundred twenty meters," the chief called out. "One hundred meters, seventy meters, fifty meters, thirty meters, ten meters. Tower clear and . . . hatch clear."

Max climbed the ladder from the control room to the conning tower and popped the hatch. Baltic air flowed into the boat, so rich and cold that he almost passed out from the rush of oxygen to his brain.

After they limped back to port, the flotilla commander greeted Max. "A good day?"

"Very instructive, sir," Max said. "Very instructive, indeed."

"Excellent, Brekendorf. Carry on then."

———————

Two weeks later, on a frigid Baltic morning, Carls mustered the crew on the foredeck to look them over. There would be a ceremony that afternoon for U-114 and six other boats that had just completed their training. For the final operational tests, Flotilla Command had assembled ten freighters and four escort vessels that they formed into a pretend Allied convoy. The boats then took turns attacking the convoy with dummy torpedoes. The crew of U-114 performed well—Max scored two hits with his dummy torpedoes in their last practice attack. Now an admiral from the

Naval War Staff in Berlin was coming to inspect the crew and Carls wanted to make sure they were dressed strictly according to regulations. "You never know what these youngsters will put on as uniforms, Herr Kaleu," he had told Max. The men stood shivering in their navy blue pea jackets, breath condensing in the frigid air. Carls examined each man, each button, each badge, and adjusted half a dozen caps.

"Achtung!" he ordered, the two lines of sailors coming instantly to attention.

Max and the other officers stood on the bridge, watching the assembly as Carls began to pace.

"Now, if the admiral stops and asks you where you are from, you will just say, Shithole, Bavaria, or whatever no-good rat trap you crawled out of, and you will not go into the details of who is banging your sister because the admiral is a busy man and does not give a shit."

Max looked down to hide his grin. This was the kind of talk he was used to hearing from sailors, not all this bilge about the International Jewish Conspiracy that Lehmann bored him with.

Carls boomed out the answers to other possible questions: "The food is good, you love the navy, and you have complete faith and trust in the captain. Clear?"

"And the Führer," Lehmann called down from the bridge. "Faith and confidence in the Führer and Final Victory, Carls."

Carls looked up. "Of course, Herr Leutnant." He turned back to the sailors. "And you have faith and confidence in the Führer and Final Victory. Satisfactory, Herr Leutnant?"

"Very good," Lehmann said. "You're doing fine."

"I'm very glad to hear you think so, Herr Leutnant. It means a great deal to me."

Max turned away to keep from bursting out in laughter. Carls had been in the navy for twenty-nine years, Lehmann for less than two.

After the ceremony, the men went ashore to pack their

belongings, which would be sent overland to their new home port in Lorient, on the Bay of Biscay. Because of the limited space in the boat, each sailor could bring aboard only a change of clothes and a few personal items—a small toilet kit and some photographs, perhaps a book, or a packet of envelopes and writing paper. Some brought a favorite phonograph record. Men always tried to smuggle extra items on board, but Carls and the other chief petty officers searched them thoroughly at the dock and confiscated everything in excess of the bare allowance. At 1600 hours, crew at stations, diesels rumbling, Max turned to the young signalman of the watch. "Signal to Kommandant of icebreaker: *U-114* ready to proceed."

Using a handheld Morse lamp, the sailor signaled the icebreaker, which quickly blinked a response.

"Signal acknowledged, Herr Kaleu. Their response: 'Signal to Kommandant *U-114*: take station two hundred meters aft of me.'" They followed the stubby ship out of the frozen harbor and into the Baltic proper, which never froze. "Good luck and good hunting," the icebreaker signaled to them.

"Port the helm fourteen degrees to new course two nine five degrees, west by northwest," he ordered. The helmsman in the conning tower repeated the directions, then pushed the metal buttons that controlled the rudder. Max surveyed the Baltic. Chunks of ice bobbed around like apples in a barrel. Wind from the Russian steppe kicked up the water and it sloshed along the submarine's gray flanks, sometimes foaming over the foredeck. The two diesels rumbled behind him in the cold, their exhaust blowing over the bridge in the following wind. Max turned and watched the sun go down. It didn't give much warmth anyway, but the Baltic looked even more desolate once it was gone.

Lehmann had the watch. He stood bundled up with the three sailors and a petty officer who comprised the bridge watch. Each of them was responsible for a quadrant of the compass. No talking allowed and keep your binoculars to your eyes—these were

Max's strictest rules. As Kommandant of the U-boat, he stood no routine watch. He did whatever he thought best, which meant on combat patrol he'd be spending twelve to fourteen hours a day on the bridge, sometimes more. Because he knew this was coming, he decided to rest now and let the officers get used to their responsibilities. "Stay alert, men," he cautioned. "Leutnant, you have the bridge."

With that he dropped into the humid interior of the boat. Georg helped him pull off his heavy bridge coat and leather jacket. "Switch to red," Max ordered. Georg switched the control room's lighting from white to red to preserve the men's night vision in case they had to suddenly go on deck.

Max pulled aside the green curtain and heaved himself onto his bunk. He alone had any privacy. Everyone else slept on bunks arranged in tiers along the central corridor that ran the length of the boat. As soon as one man went on watch, another climbed into his place and slept. Only the officers and the chief petty officers had exclusive bunks, and only the captain's came equipped with a curtain and a small folding desk with a saltwater washbasin underneath. He folded his arms over his chest, reviewed the day, and then let the gentle throb of the diesels lull him to sleep.

They steamed into the Bay of Kiel thirty-six hours later. Max stood on the bridge, guiding the boat into the harbor, breathing morning air rich with the harbor's tang—tar, oil, seaweed, salt—a bouquet compared to the smell inside the U-boat. Several warships rode at anchor, outlines blurred in the mist. Sweeping the harbor with his glasses, Max immediately recognized *Admiral Scheer*, sister ship of *Graf Spee*. He shivered and closed his eyes for a moment; it felt like he'd seen a ghost.

"Dead slow," he ordered.

The helmsman moved the levers on the engine telegraph in the conning tower. Identical repeaters registered the orders in the engine room and activated light signals specific to each command—necessary because the noise in the engine room was too loud for the men to hear the bells that rang when the engine telegraph transmitted a new order. The engineers communicated with one another using hand signals.

Max surveyed the bay, silver in the morning sun, across which he'd first watched the Kiel Week races unfold those dozen years ago. His navy dreams were born that week aboard *Emden*, and he'd come here as a cadet to board the naval training barque *Gorch Fock*, a three-masted sailing ship, named for a sailor-poet who perished in the Battle of the Skagerrak. On the surface, Kiel didn't look so different, but when he looked more closely, the presence of the war became evident. Anti-aircraft batteries covered with camouflaged netting had been set up everywhere, manned by sailors who stamped their feet in the cold of the early morning. Max scanned the shoreline with his binoculars, stopping on the huge covered sheds of the Deutsche Werke shipyards. A year ago the roofs of these sheds had been glass. But Allied bombs dropped in the last months had shattered all the glass. Now camouflaged tarps covered the roofs. U-boats were being built everywhere he looked. He'd watched *U-114* come together in these same yards. The men in the yards were German master craftsmen, the best in the world. The Allies had no one like them.

Dead ahead lay the Tirpitz Pier, named for Admiral von Tirpitz, founder of the German navy. It was a long concrete jetty stretching far into the bay. U-boats were tied up two and three deep on either side, boards laid deck to deck to make gangplanks, armed crewmen stationed on the deck of every boat.

Lehmann had the docking crew ready with the lines. As Max steered for a gap where only one other boat was tied, two of its crewmen straightened up from their tasks and stood ready to catch *U-114*'s mooring rope. Docking this way was a delicate maneuver and Max didn't want to make a hash of it here in the middle of the naval anchorage with God knows how many eyes on him. He approached so carefully that he came to a perfect docking position—except for the three meters of water between him and the other boat. Well, better than ramming the bitch. "Pull us over," he ordered Lehmann.

That would give his men something to shake their heads over while on leave. "He's great at torpedoing ships, our Kommandant, but he can't dock a U-boat." Yet, better that kind of talk than ramming another boat and being called on the carpet by the admiral commanding.

"All secure, Herr Kaleu," Lehmann called from the deck.

"Finished with engines," Max said. The throb of the diesels faded away. After securing the boat, Carls mustered the crew on deck and Max faced them, hands clasped behind him like Captain Langsdorff. "Men, for the next three weeks we will remain in Kiel taking on supplies. Half of you will be on leave for the first ten days, and the other half for the second ten. Quarters have been prepared for you at the base." The men never stayed aboard the U-boat in harbor. Besides being too cramped, it had no bathing facilities and smelled like the devil's outhouse. Hygiene could not be maintained on the boat; the crew grew dirty and foul after just a few days at sea. "Men of *U-114*, remember you are German sailors and members of a proud service. While you are on leave, I expect each of you to conduct yourself with the strictest propriety so as not to bring the navy into disrepute. Leutnant Lehmann has your leave papers. That is all." How many times had he heard that speech from other captains? Thirty times at least. Yet it sounded strange from his own mouth. The speech would have little effect on the sailors. In a few hours most of them would be drunk as lords.

Max reported in aboard the steamer *Lech* before leaving for Bad Wilhelm. The ship served as headquarters for the 5th U-Boat Flotilla in Kiel, which exercised administrative control over all U-boats in the harbor. A nice way to fight a war, Max thought. Never leave the dock, regular meals, white jackets in the officers' mess each evening. Drinks on me, I insist. Toasts all around. Rumor in the UBootwaffe had it that the captain of *Lech* turned the vessel around once a month so everyone aboard would qualify for supplemental sea pay. But this life never would have done for him, Max knew—he would have been disgusted with himself for sitting on his backside in Kiel drinking schnapps. He stayed aboard only long enough to make his supply arrangement and send a telegram to his father, telling him when to be at the station.

The train was packed—every seat occupied, the aisles jammed with young soldiers sitting on their packs, smoking, laughing, most of them just boys, all headed to the Russian Front. They seemed cheerful enough, but tens of thousands just like them had been surrounded in Stalingrad by an overwhelming Soviet force for the last eight weeks—hungry, cold, sick, no way to break out or get food. Surely the Führer had a plan. He wouldn't leave Six Armee to die. Max's father had written that three families in Bad Wilhelm had sons at Stalingrad. How would it end? Not well. Most alarming, a few days after Christmas, in his evening radio address, General Dittmar, the voice of the Oberkommando der Wehrmacht, had begun to speak of "heroic resistance" by Six Armee's brave troops— never an encouraging sign. Everyone in Germany had learned to decipher the High Command's euphemisms: "grim and sanguinary fighting increasing in violence" meant the line had collapsed and troops were being pushed back under murderous fire with terrible casualties; "bitter and prolonged fighting" meant you were hopelessly surrounded; "heroic resistance" meant you were already dead.

Losses on the Eastern Front staggered the mind. The Russians, they could absorb endless casualties. Wipe out one group and the Red commissars simply rounded up another and another and another. If you wouldn't fight, you got shot. Making it incomparably worse for Germany were the Americans coming in a year ago—the Americans with their farm boys and their dollars and all the resources of their vast continent. The odds against every man on the crowded train grew longer by the day. But Max knew he was no better off than the boys around him. Loss rates in the UBootwaffe were beginning to rise and getting worse.

The train drew in and halted in a cloud of steam. His father waited on the platform. "Papa!" Max called as he stepped out of the rail car.

His father marched up to him, smiling like a child, pushed away Max's outstretched hand, and gave him a bear hug. This embarrassed Max—here, like this, in the station, in full view of all the soldiers on the train—but his father paid no mind. "Maximilian, what a surprise to have you here, my boy. A wonderful surprise to see you."

"I would've given you more notice but we're not allowed to contact anyone before going on leave."

The old man grabbed Max's suitcase. "Yes, yes, 'the enemy listens.' I know it from the First War. Come, come." He led Max to the old Ford delivery truck, tossing the suitcase in back. "A beer, yes?"

Max shrugged. Not every shopkeeper had a naval officer son to show off, and certainly not one with an Iron Cross First Class. His father glanced down to examine the medal gleaming on the left pocket of Max's tunic. He quickly unpinned it, polished the medal with his handkerchief, and pinned it back in place. "You were half a centimeter off," he said, smiling at Max, who shook his head. "Always the sergeant major, Papa."

They walked across the town square, past the monument to the dead of the local Landwehr battalion from the First War. Names from every family in the village were engraved on the plaque— among them, Ernst von Woller's, their much-loved and respected commander who was killed at Verdun.

In trying to save his commander's life, Johann had carried Ernst through an artillery barrage to an aid station. But Ernst was dead and Johann nearly so. For these actions, he received the Prussian Military Cross, the highest honor awarded by the Prussian army to an enlisted man. On ceremonial days after the war, Max would finger the medal hung around his father's neck. "There is no glory in it, Maximilian," Johann always said.

A roar of welcome greeted them now as they entered the tavern. It was early evening and most of the regulars were there: Jupp, the butcher; Immelman, the petrol station owner; Zeeger, the apothecary; and Cajus, the town constable ("I saved his fat ass more than once on the Western Front," Max's father always said). Bruno, the tavern keeper, brought over a rank of foaming beer steins. "Comrades, a welcome to our brave warrior of the deep."

Max drank, his beer bitter and slightly cold. God in heaven, he hadn't had one in weeks. His father gave him a cigar and Max wondered where it came from in the midst of the very strict rationing. Probably the same place his father got the real coffee and the real butter and the cream, wherever that was. Max lit the cigar, adding to the smoke in the tavern, some of which came from the dried dandelion cigarettes people rolled now to eke out their tobacco ration.

Bruno kept looking at him expectantly. He didn't want to disappoint anyone, certainly not his father. Max stood and looked around the small taproom at these faces from his youth. What kind of toast did they want to hear? Death to England? Volk and Führer? These were older men; they had been through a war themselves and knew nonsense when they heard it. Max raised his mug. "Let us drink to the memory of Herr Oberstleutnant Ernst von Woller. I hope to defend my country with the same courage he displayed."

Everyone stood and drank. "Prost," Bruno said. Max's father nodded in approval. And it was good, too, for Max to show everyone that he bore no ill will toward the von Woller family. Everybody in Bad Wilhelm knew they opposed his marriage to their daughter.

Buhl, the local Nazi Party functionary, came in a few minutes later. In addition to serving as Kreisleiter, he was the mayor of Bad Wilhelm, a patronage position controlled by the Nazis. Buhl wore a patch over his left eye, which he claimed to have lost in a clash with the Red Bolsheviks during the struggle for power. More likely in a whorehouse brawl, the locals said. Buhl's father had been the village gravedigger, something other children teased him about in school. But Max never teased him; the two of them were even friends of a sort. Buhl had a red face pitted with acne scars, and big ears that pointed outward. He could be full of himself at times but he wasn't a bad man. He smiled as he walked over to Max and gave him a warm handshake. "Another beer for our hero," he called to Bruno. "So they still haven't made you an admiral yet?"

"Well, the war's not over, Buhl."

Buhl smiled but, when he dropped into a chair next to Max, his face became serious—the expression of official party business. "Max, how are things out there? Are we going to stop all those American supplies from getting to the Tommies?"

Max drank, wiped the foam from his mouth with the back of his hand. He answered with care. His comments would end up in a report to the Gauleiter in Kiel. "It's difficult, but we're getting stronger in the North Atlantic every day. My crew is young but they have spirit."

"Can we drive the Tommies back?"

Max nodded. "Certainly we can drive the Tommies back."

Buhl slapped him on the back as if that settled it. "I knew it." He stood, neat in his tan party uniform, the bright red party armband with the black swastika on his left bicep. "And I know, too, that we've sent our best man to defend our Reich and our Führer."

"Thank you, Buhl."

"I mean it." Buhl glanced around the taproom. "A toast to the KapitänLeutnant."

No one would argue with the local party man anyway, but it didn't take any coaxing to get an enthusiastic cheer for Max. After all, he was one of them—not an aristocrat—and the villagers took great pride in him.

He drove the truck home later, the old Ford sputtering along because of the wood burner, which his father had mounted in front of the radiator shell a year back when the petrol shortage had become dire. You saw wood burners all over the Reich now, mounted on cars, trucks, tractors, even buses; it had become impossible for anyone outside the military or the highest levels of the party to acquire petrol, even for a man with as many connections as Johann. Some of the burners were designed to fit discreetly beneath the hood, while others took up space in the backseat or the cab, and some were even pulled along behind on a small trailer. They worked well enough. The burners trapped the wood gas under pressure, and when it was released into the engine, it propelled the vehicle at a moderate pace. But this method supplied much less power than diesel fuel, and the Ford's cylinder heads had to be cleaned every day to prevent the buildup of soot and ash—quite an annoyance, Max's father complained. Fortunately, fuel was easy to come by. If you ran out, you could just chop down a tree. But most drivers kept bundles of wood on the tops of their vehicles since one needed a permit to cut down a tree.

But tonight Johann didn't worry about the truck or the wood or the cylinder heads. He sat beside Max on the bench seat, belting out an old marching song from the First War about the Kaiser and his glory. They were silent when the old man had finished, bouncing through the darkness on the truck's worn suspension. "We believed it back then," Max's father said quietly. "Only two important things in the world then: God and the Kaiser."

"And now, Papa?"

"Only God now, Maximilian."

As Max helped him into the house, straining against his father's bulk, a young woman appeared at the bottom of the stairs. Max came up short.

"Katrina," his father said.

She was thin, a few wisps of dark hair trailing out from under the kerchief she wore around her head. Max could see she was quite lovely, with a fine sharp nose and gray eyes. She said, "To bed, yes?"

"Katrina," Max's father said, "this is my son, Herr Kapitän-Leutnant Brekendorf."

She smiled at Max. "Mein Herr," she said, giving a quick bow of her head. Her German carried a heavy Polish accent. "To bed, yes, Herr Johann?"

"Yes, let's get him to bed," Max said.

"My housekeeper," his father whispered. "Did I not tell you about her in my letters?"

He had not expected to find a Polish forced laborer in his own home. The Reich was overrun with them, but in this house? Katrina shooed Max aside and slipped under his father's arm, guiding him gently to the stairs. "I do," she said. "Is fine, let me."

Max watched them disappear up the staircase. His father murmured in her ear and let his hand linger on her shapely rear. The two of them laughed, then turned at the landing and disappeared. Max shrugged. His father got lonely. Katrina was hardly the first. Max's mother had been dead more than twenty years and no one, least of all Max, cared if his father carried on with Katrina. Still, it was against the racial laws of the Third Reich to be sleeping with her.

In his room, Max removed his boots and lay down on his bed, surrounded by the treasures of his childhood: ribbons won in the Marine Bund, pictures of ships clipped from magazines, a lithograph of Admiral Tirpitz, and his midshipman's sword, still polished each week by his father. When he first brought the sword home, Max had tried to show his father how to polish it properly, but Johann just laughed. He said, "When a naval officer has to instruct a Prussian sergeant major how to polish a sword, then the world truly will be upside down."

A watercolor Mareth had done of *Graf Spee* hung above the desk, and on the desk itself, a brass frame held a photograph of his mother. Max favored her with his fair hair and brilliant blue eyes. She was young in the picture—younger than Max now—not a classic beauty but pretty, with a slender nose and wary eyes, just like Max. Hannah had been her name. She had a proud look with high cheekbones and a strong jaw. Max could understand why his father had been drawn to her. "You are so much like her, Maximilian," Johann often said. "You have her mind; she was so clever at sums and always had a book in her hand."

Two days later, his father drove him back to the village rail station to catch the Berlin train. They said little on the way, or on the platform as they stood waiting for the train. When it finally arrived, his father wrapped him in a hug so fierce Max thought his ribs might break. "I will be fine, Papa," he said, hugging his father back.

The old man smiled, pulling away and holding Max at arm's length. "Ah, you don't know that, Maximilian."

"I believe it, though."

"Do you? I hope so. It does you well to believe it."

Max looked down at the dirty stone of the platform and didn't say anything. He could feel his father's hands trembling slightly where they held him.

"When you were a little boy at the end of the First War, I said to myself, 'At least he will not have to go through what I went through. At least that much is sure.'"

Max looked up again. His father smiled but tears stood in his eyes. "Looks like you were wrong, Papa."

"Hardly a first, Maximilian. Time makes fools of us all."

"But you lived through that war and I'll live through this one."

"Yes, yes. I thought that when your mother went down so ill. I thought, 'I didn't survive Verdun to watch her die of the influenza.' People were starving all around us, but I made sure we had all the food we needed, and if there had been medicine to cure her, I would have found a way to get that, too. But there was no medicine for the Spanish flu, no medicine but God Almighty."

"You're not making me feel much better, Papa."

His father laughed. "Ach, what does it matter what we say? It's just words. You know I love you, Maximilian. I love you more than anything in the world. I pray for you every morning at mass. I haven't missed a day since the war began."

They embraced again, not long this time. Max boarded the train, turned and waved to his father, who stood at attention on the platform, arm cocked in stiff salute, hand at his forehead, palm out—ramrod straight as only a Prussian sergeant major could be— as the whistle blew and the train moved slowly from the station.

CHAPTER NINE

BERLIN
CAPITAL OF THE GREATER GERMAN REICH
THE NEXT DAY

MAX DIDN'T REACH BERLIN UNTIL 0200. EVEN AT THAT HOUR THE
Stettiner Bahnhof was crowded with soldiers from every branch
of the Wehrmacht—changing trains, running for trains, kissing
sweethearts hello or goodbye, Luftwaffe blue standing out against
the field gray of the army, the black of the security police, and the
khaki of the Organisation Todt.

Max left the underground platforms and moved into the larger
station above, feeling the cold wind blowing into the building
through gaps in the canvas roof. Before the war, the superstructure's iron arches had supported a magnificent glass roof, but now
it held up nothing more than a few layers of thin canvas tarps.
Bomb concussions had blasted all the glass out, and the tarps did
little to stop the wind. Max wondered if there would be a pane of
glass left in the Reich when the war was over.

He scanned the crowd for Mareth, but the dim blue light of the
station made it impossible to see for any distance. Leaning against
a lamppost, he lit a cigarette and watched the swirling mass of people, all of them involved in the war somehow. It was everywhere; it

was life. Nothing else happened in Germany now. At mass in Bad Wilhelm yesterday, the priest had quoted Saint Matthew: "And ye shall hear of wars and rumors of wars: see that ye be not troubled: for all these things must come to pass, but the end is not yet." Max had briefly considered this verse on the train but stopped because he didn't want to think about wars or rumors of wars. He was already in a war: if only it were a rumor. And "all these things must come to pass, but the end is not yet"—would God simply allow this madness to go on and on? Would all the suffering continue till He got bored with it? Is that how it worked?

A hand reached out and pinched Max on the bum. He spun around and kissed Mareth before she could speak.

"Why, it could have been anyone," she said when he finally let her go. "Do you automatically kiss any girl who pinches your rump?"

"Just the blond ones." They kissed again. "I love you," he said when they broke.

"I love you, Max."

An elderly woman interrupted them, tapping Max on the shoulder. "Herr Stationmaster, pardon me. When does the express for Stuttgart leave?"

Mareth bit her lip to keep from laughing. Max felt the heat rising in his face. "Madam," he said.

Mareth cut him off. "Madam, unfortunately I have just discovered this young man has only tonight been assigned to this station and knows nothing. But that gentleman over there"—she pointed to a naval captain a few meters away at the newspaper stand—"is the senior stationmaster and will be able to help you."

The old woman flashed a pleasant smile. "Thank you, Fräulein."

Mareth took Max by the hand and the two of them ran laughing from the station into the blacked-out city, so dark that Max almost lost his balance as they emerged onto the street. Not a ray of white light could be seen. Were they even in Berlin? It seemed more like the inside of a coal mine; Max couldn't make out his hand in front of his face. He hefted his suitcase onto his shoulder and bumped Mareth in the darkness.

She laughed. "Watch yourself, sailor."

"It's black as pitch. I can't even see you."

She leaned against him and rubbed a hand across his back. "Welcome to Berlin."

"We'll be lucky if no one robs us out here."

"Oh, no," Mareth said, "there are never any robberies in the blackout."

"There must be."

"No, never. Anyone caught robbing someone in the blackout is shot the next day."

Max nodded. That must cut down on crime. He said, "Let's go to the Rio Rita for a drink."

"It closes at two."

"Johny's?"

"Max! No respectable woman would go to Johny's."

"When Dieter and I used to go there to hear the Negro jazz band, we always saw many respectable women."

"Without their clothes on."

"That's how we knew they were respectable. They couldn't hide anything."

Mareth gave him a light punch on the arm. "Unfortunately for you, Herr KapitänLeutnant, all the cabarets have been closed."

"The Adlon?"

"They close the bar at midnight."

"You Berlin girls certainly know your way around." Max dropped his suitcase and put his arms around her, drawing her close in a gentle embrace. But then she locked her arms about him so fiercely that she almost squeezed the breath from him.

"What's wrong?" he said.

"Nothing. It's nothing."

"Mareth, what is it?"

She had her head on his chest. Without looking at him she

said, "I just hate the war, Max—the war and the bombing and you being gone. Every night I think that I won't be able to stand another day of it, but then I do. It goes on and on and I do stand it."

He rocked her gently, kissing the top of her head as they kept their tight embrace. "We've made it this far," he offered. "We just need to keep going. It's the only choice we have."

"Maybe."

"Trust me."

"I do trust you, Max. I do. You know that."

Max broke their embrace and put his hands on her shoulders and looked her in the eyes. He whispered, "Mareth, I have something very important that I need to tell you."

"What? What is it, Max?"

"I'm freezing."

She couldn't help but laugh. "I have a room for us in a gasthaus at the Alexanderplatz."

"Good," Max said. "That sounds good. We can get warm." She kissed him.

Mareth hung a phosphorescent button around her neck and put one around Max's as well, which annoyed him and made him feel like a child. "Why do I need this? It doesn't help me see."

"It keeps other people from knocking you over. Just follow orders, sailor."

They groped their way along the street, in a constellation of phosphorescent buttons, the true believers wearing ones shaped like swastikas. They found the U-Bahn and rode it to the Alexanderplatz, where Max almost took a header on the stairs as they surfaced once again into the inky dark. They walked the two blocks from there to the hotel; Max came close to getting into a fight with a streetlamp. He signed them in separately at the gasthaus. There was no use pretending to be husband and wife because both of them had to present their identity papers. That was the law. The security police reviewed every hotel register in the country every day.

Once inside the room Max tossed his cigarettes onto the end table, pulling off his heavy overcoat and tunic. He gave Mareth a hungry smile, pulled off her coat, and pitched it into the corner. Then he saw that she was also wearing a uniform.

"Mareth!"

She sat on the bed. "I was going to tell you, write you. It just never . . ."

"What are you doing? Aren't you still working for your father?"

"Yes, yes—this is just two nights a week, a six-hour shift."

"What? Doing what?"

"I . . . I'm in the flak auxiliary."

"The flak auxiliary! What in the name of God . . . Mareth! The flak auxiliary! What are you thinking?" The flak auxiliary manned the anti-aircraft guns that ringed Berlin, most operated by young teenage boys—Kinderflak, the Berliners called them. Many of the gun positions were out in the open, near the massive ammunition dumps that supplied the countless shells pumped into the sky by the quick-firing guns. Dr. Goebbels claimed that a thousand batteries defended Berlin, not that many believed much of anything he said.

Mareth took his hand. "Max, it's not dangerous."

"Not dangerous? How can it not be dangerous? What the hell do you even know about it?"

She stood up and stepped away from him. "What do I know about it? Max, would you have me do nothing? Is that what you want?"

"Yes. I would have you do nothing."

"Have you ever even been through an air raid?"

Max looked away.

"On nights when the British come, they fly over in a cloud with a noise like a thousand steam shovels and the bombs come down like rain—like rain, Max." She spoke loudly, almost shouting. "Am I supposed to just sit back and take it like a dutiful German girl? Just watch my city be destroyed? Max, they're blowing up everything—everything! I can't put it all in my letters—it's too dangerous, you don't know who's reading them. One of the wings of the Bendlerstrasse was blown up a month ago. Father told me twenty general staff officers at the Central Army Office were killed."

"The Bendlerstrasse? That's impossible. It's built out of blocks of stone."

"That doesn't matter! Some of the bombs are two thousand kilos, they can blow up anything. The KaDeWe was practically blown to pieces; Kranzler's was hit two weeks ago and completely destroyed. Remember the Gloria Palast, where we saw *Sons of the Desert*?"

Max did remember. Mareth loved Laurel and Hardy; she had walked around for the next three months saying, "Well, Max, here's another nice mess you've gotten me into!"

"A bomb hit it last week. It's just a pile of bricks and stone. Everything we knew is gone, Max. Everything. Max, people I know are being killed, friends I love buried in the rubble. Loremarie lost her house and her entire studio with all of her paintings last week. You remember my friends Sisi and Kurt? We had dinner with them before you went to *Graf Spee*. They were killed three weeks ago in a raid, with their two children. It was a direct hit on their building. Max, don't you understand? Whole areas of Berlin simply no longer exist. Charlottenburg is gone! It's nothing but rubble. I have to do something." She was yelling now.

Max faltered. It had nearly killed him to be stuck in Argentina for those twelve months while others defended the Reich. But war wasn't for women.

He nodded. "I forbid it."

She let out a brief laugh and shook her head.

"I mean it."

"Fine. Go ahead and mean it."

"What are you saying, that you refuse to quit?"

"That's exactly what I'm saying. You forbid it? Like some Prussian field marshal? You don't even know what you're talking about, Max. I'm not out in the open like the Luftwaffe flak units. It's not dangerous. I worry about you day and night on your U-boat and I'm not even in a dangerous place. I'm working in the Zoo Tower."

"The what?"

Mareth sat on the bed and took a cigarette from his pack on the nightstand. When they were together she always smoked his because a woman's cigarette rations were only half of a man's. "They're building six flak towers around the city. Mine is the first to be finished. It's over by the zoo, so they call it the Zoo Tower. It protects the government buildings around the Tiergarten—Father's office and the High Command headquarters and the other ministries and the Chancellery offices. The tower walls are three meters thick, Max. It's a fortress. And we have everything—a dining hall, a hospital, supplies to last for weeks. Everything is bombproof. The police president tells me it's safer than the Führer bunker."

Max did remember reading something about the Zoo Tower in *Signal*. He took a cigarette for himself and lit it. "What do you do?"

She ruffled his hair. "I don't think you have this job on the U-boat."

"What?"

"I work in the storeroom. I watch over all the paintings and sculptures and everything else emptied from the museums. You cannot imagine the treasures under my care. Kaiser Wilhelm's coin collection, Gobelin tapestries from Sans Souci, paintings by every great master in Europe. We try and protect everything from damage caused by the concussions when the air raids are on. Max, I'm taking care of the treasures of Germany."

He put his cigarette out half smoked. God knows a storeroom in a reinforced concrete tower was less dangerous than a U-boat on war patrol, and everyone had to help the war effort. They were up against the British, the Russians, the Americans, the Canadians, and anybody else the U.S. could bully into joining the Allies. Besides, Mareth would do what she wanted no matter what anyone said. That's what he loved the most about her. He switched off the light and lay down beside her on the bed. "You will show me your Zoo Tower tomorrow, yes?"

———————

Late the next afternoon, arm in arm, they strolled down the Unter den Linden, bundled against the cold, leaning into each other. The lime trees that grew in the median were bare now, sticks against the gray sky, but the crowds on the sidewalks were bright in scarves and hats, the women elegant despite the war. Only the men looked different in their uniforms, and because this was close to the government district many wore the uniform of the Nazi Party. A good way to get out of fighting, shuffling papers in some Berlin ministry. Meanwhile, some men thumped the sidewalks with crutches, an empty pant leg rolled up and pinned into place. Others had empty sleeves hanging limp at their sides. One man was missing an eye and a leg. Please God, he would rather die than end up like that.

They found a small restaurant and had a long dinner, lingering over their food, something Max hadn't done in months. Most of the menu items weren't subject to rationing, so they had to use ration coupons for only the bread and butter, and for the eggs and sugar that would go into a small cake for dessert. Max had been issued extra coupons with his leave papers, so Mareth didn't need to spend any of hers. The waiter took Max's large, multicolored coupon cards—the orange one for rolls, pink for butter and skim milk, green for eggs, white for sugar—and cut off the necessary squares with a pair of scissors. Every waiter in Germany now carried scissors alongside his bottle opener.

The meal might not have cost many coupons, but the price in reichsmarks was steep enough. Max's pay had gone up by half with his promotion, but the already high income tax and war surcharge tax swallowed up most of his raise. Max didn't worry. The money was well spent. Beef, pork, and chicken were impossible to get because all supplies were consigned to the Wehrmacht, so they started with a rabbit stew. This didn't seem so strange to Max— he'd eaten rabbit all the time as a boy—but Mareth had never tried it before and was shocked to learn that he had. Their main course was two boiled lobsters from France. Deep-sea fish were unattainable because the fishing fleet had either been sunk by the British or commandeered by the Kriegsmarine for minesweeping, but French shellfish were still in good supply. French wine, too, was plentiful and cheap, unlike German beer, which had become expensive. So they drank wine and bitter acorn coffee. Mareth screwed her face up as she tasted the acorn brew. "I can't drink this," she said. "I try to, but I can't." Max poured all their skim milk into her cup and she tried it again, shaking her head. "Don't tell me you drank this stuff as a boy." They laughed.

"I'm glad the Sergeant Major brings us real coffee," Mareth said, using her nickname for Max's father. "Where does he get it?"

Max smiled and shrugged his shoulders. "Best not to ask my father questions like that. He knows what he's doing."

Mareth took his arm again when they left the restaurant. "I don't want a simple country lad like yourself getting lost in the blackout," she said. Around them night had fallen and it was almost pitch black, the only illumination coming from a weak moon. A stranger who didn't know his way around would be lost in a moment. You couldn't read the street signs, couldn't see the shop windows or addresses, couldn't see much of anything. You knew where the sidewalks dropped off only because the curbs had been dabbed with thin lines of phosphorous paint at each intersection. You could hear the trams but couldn't see them, their only illumination a thin strip of purple light on the front. Mareth knew two men in the Foreign Ministry who had been run down. And as for motorcars, there were none, save for a handful belonging to the military. These were equipped with cloth covers over each headlamp; small slits in the center of the covers allowed a narrow beam of light to pass through. So this was the capital of the Reich: everything dark, everything rationed, everyone in uniform, everyone fighting. Max could never have envisioned this.

He buried his face in Mareth's hair, moving his hand around to the inside of her thigh until she slapped it away. She always seemed so sophisticated to him. In Paris she could pass for Parisian, in Berlin she seemed like a Berliner to anyone who met her. She'd been raised in the countryside outside Bad Wilhelm, but attended gymnasium in Berlin and spoke German like a Berliner. Berlinerrisch, they called it. Even the cabdrivers thought she was a native so they didn't cheat her. Compared to Mareth, Max *was* just a country boy. Yet the navy had given him confidence beyond his provincial roots from the beginning. Going aloft in a three-masted barque and reefing a topsail forty meters above the deck in a Force Ten gale had a way of improving a young man's self-assurance.

They passed through the Brandenburg Gate and entered the Tiergarten, so green in spring and summer, but covered now with snow, the evergreens trim and clipped. At least the park foresters were still on duty. Everything else in Berlin looked shabby and unkempt; the formerly spotless streets now filthy. When they were some distance into the park he stopped Mareth and kissed her, his nose cold against her cheek.

Reading his mind, she gave him a stern look and said, "No."

Her lips were soft and warm against his. He slipped his hands under her coat.

"Max, no."

The evergreens and the darkness provided plenty of cover. He led her into a thicket off the path and spread his thick naval greatcoat on the snow. She shook her head but a little smile played at the corners of her mouth. "Damn you," she said, lying down on the coat, her fingers already working on his belt buckle.

He collapsed on top of her and the two of them lay giggling in the cold, their hot breath escaping in clouds, when the air raid sirens shattered the brittle winter atmosphere. It was a long, undulating warble so loud it could wake the dead. Mareth pushed him up. "Come on," she said, "that's the red warning." There was a thin edge of panic in her voice.

He pulled up his pants and struggled into his greatcoat. She had him by the arm, dragging him out of the trees. "We have to get to the Zoo Tower. Run!"

In the distance Max could barely see the tall flak tower rising above the trees. How far was it? A half kilometer, three-quarters? Running was difficult in their heavy winter clothes, the snow frozen into rifts impossible to see in the moonlight. They ran without speaking. Mareth stumbled, recovered. Max steadied her, then tripped himself, sprawling on the snow.

"Max!"

He was up again and moving. To the right he saw a brilliant red light in the sky, now two, now more—five or ten at least. They looked like Christmas trees; lighted Christmas trees dropping from the clouds. What in the name of God? He stopped for a moment and stared but Mareth tugged at him, shouting. Max didn't hear what she said. He pointed at the falling lights.

"Marker flares! From the pathfinder squadrons. Run! Run!"

They were thirty meters from the tower when the first bombs hit, somewhere to the left. The sound wasn't very loud, certainly nothing compared to the tremendous banging of the huge anti-aircraft guns on the tower roof. Red and white flashes now illuminated the night sky as the bright green marker flares continued to burn on the ground, showing the bombers where to aim. Another string of bombs fell. Closer now. The warden at the small side door motioned for them to hurry. An explosion flashed behind Max, then the concussion wave. It knocked him over. Rising to his knees, he saw Mareth crumpled in the snow five meters away. "Mareth!" A terrible chill went through him. "Mareth!"

She was breathing. Thank God. And no blood, so it wasn't shrapnel. He hefted her onto his back and sprinted the last fifteen meters to the steel door of the Zoo Tower.

"Hurry!" the guard yelled. With a burly arm he pushed Max through the door, then shut it tight against its rubber seal and dogged it home. That made the shelter airtight; otherwise if a bomb landed on top of them all the oxygen would be sucked out by the explosion and everyone inside would suffocate. "I thought I recognized her," the warden said. "She's Mareth von Woller."

"Ja."

"Get her to the hospital. See the lift?" He pointed down the long corridor.

"Ja."

"Take it to the third floor."

Max carried her limp body through the mass of people in the shelter. Housewives, hair pulled up in scarves, sat atop battered suitcases. Several society women, caught on their way to a reception, held dainty evening shoes in their laps. Another woman cradled a terrified kitten. A younger man, missing an arm, read a book. Children wrestled on the floor. In the corner two old men played chess, one of them with a helmet from the First War on his head. The ceilings of the cavernous rooms were covered with luminescent paint, for illumination if the electric light went out. Faces filled with tension looked up at him, but nobody reacted to the shaking ground or the pounding of the guns above.

A terrible cacophony grew as Max approached the elevator until it pained his ears, louder than anything he had ever heard aboard *Meteor* or *Graf Spee*. Farther down the corridor he saw the source: the automatic shell hoist. It rose thirteen full stories to the platforms holding the eight five-inch guns that fired continuously into the sky—a thirteen-story conveyor belt of shells, clattering and screeching from the basement magazine to the roof.

The young physician on duty knew her immediately. "Mareth von Woller. Stretcher, stretcher here." Max laid her gently on the stretcher and began to follow the bearers as they carried her off. The doctor made as if to stop him. "I'm sorry," he said, "you'll have to wait here."

Max looked down at the doctor's palm against his chest, then looked back up, a warrior's fierceness in his blue eyes.

The doctor blanched. "Come with me. This way, please."

They transferred Mareth to an examining table down the hall and the doctor inspected her at some length, poking and prodding, listening to her heart. He looked at Max. "Do you have some relationship to her?"

"She is my fiancée."

"I see. You are the U-boat captain."

"Yes."

"Well then, not to worry. She just has a slight concussion. I'm certain she'll come to in an hour or so."

Max felt the relief wash over him. His shoulders slumped, falling slack as the tension left them. The stretcher men moved Mareth again, this time to a bed, and Max knelt beside it when they had gone. He stroked Mareth's forehead lightly, pushing back her blond hair; he took her hand and it was limp, almost lifeless. Laying his head down on her chest, he listened to the slow rhythm of her heart as it methodically thumped away.

An hour passed, maybe more. He wasn't sure. Max started to doze and woke only when he felt Mareth ruffling the hair at the back of his head. "Max," she whispered.

"Hey."

"Hey," she said, lifting his chin, pulling him up to kiss her. Max moved his lips from her mouth to her cheeks, her eyelids, the bridge of her nose.

In a few minutes the young Luftwaffe doctor came by, his white coat stained with blood. From the gun crews? People brought in off the street? Max didn't know, though he later learned from a Luftwaffe officer that several of the teenage gunners on the upper platforms had been killed. Bomb splinters. The youngsters were defenseless on the open platforms as they loaded the guns. Unfortunately, a handful were lost in every raid. Nothing to be done for it. Volk und Führer.

The doctor looked Mareth over quickly and told her to stay in bed for two weeks. "A concussion is nothing to take lightly," he said. No doubt they saw plenty of concussions in this place with all the damned bombs being dropped on Berlin, Max thought. The building shook continuously as they exploded all around. Even in the hospital the noise was like muffled thunder.

When the doctor left Mareth put her hand on Max's arm. "Max, you must go tell my father where I am, and that I'm fine. He's working late tonight. I need him to send his car for me in the morning to take me back to our flat."

Max frowned. "I doubt he'll even let me into his office."

"He'll let you in now. I telephone him after every air raid, it's our strictest rule. He'll be frantic for me. I can't ring him from here because only the military can use the telephones. Max, please, do this for me. Please."

Max nodded. He didn't have much of a choice. Besides, von Woller would have to meet him sooner or later, one way or another. "I'll go," he said. "Just tell me the way."

Mareth gave him the directions. Her father's offices were not in the fortresslike Foreign Ministry itself, but in a smaller building several blocks away. Max stayed with her until the siren sounded the long steady blast that signaled all clear and the tower's guns fell quiet. Then he took the elevator downstairs and filed outside with the women and children and frail old men leaving the shelter.

The streets were like a scene from the H. G. Wells novels Max had read as a boy—motorcars on fire, trams overturned, buildings burning everywhere, the heat and roar of flames coming at him from every direction. Broken glass covered the pavement, crunching underneath his boots like thin ice on a winter's morning. Shop windows had been blown out, goods spilled across the sidewalks. Sirens wailed in the distance as units of the Fire

Protection Police made their way through the wreckage. Emergency workers helped panicked families dig through the rubble of demolished apartment blocks. On the sidewalks rows of bodies were lined up with Germanic neatness. The smell of cordite from the bombs hung thick in the air, as it had on the bridge of *Graf Spee* during the Battle of the Rio Plata, but this was madness. Shopkeepers, office workers, housewives, schoolchildren—screaming, digging, laying out bodies.

Noises like gunfire rang out as wood popped in the flames. Water sprayed in fountains from shattered mains. Bricks were scattered everywhere. Books had been blown into the street from flattened buildings. They made an incongruous garnish atop the smoking debris. Max picked up a leather-bound volume at his feet. The Bible. He almost laughed out loud. Farther on he stopped where a crowd had gathered around a ragged bundle on the sidewalk. Looking down, it took Max a moment to realize that the bundle was a body—the body of a small girl. Her head had been blown off. Blood was still spreading in a dark pool from her neck. Nobody in the crowd had moved to cover her.

Where was that shit Göring and his aeroplanes when all this was going on? No wonder sailors in France back from leave in Germany picked fights with Luftwaffe men and beat the tar out of them.

Finally a policeman came along and spread a tarp over the little girl's headless corpse. Max walked on.

Von Woller's office building did not appear to have sustained any damage. Max climbed the steps and entered the lobby. He drew an engraved calling card from his wallet and handed it to the woman on duty. When he was first in the navy, the use of such cards had been standard practice. Calling cards were no longer required with the war on, but Max still abided by all the old traditions of the service. "My compliments to Herr von Woller," he told the front-desk woman. "It is important that I see him."

Usually his uniform and bearing produced immediate compliance, but here in Berlin uniforms and officers were everywhere and the clerk spoke brusquely. "State your business."

"It is personal and urgent," he snapped. "Send in my card immediately!"

The woman nodded and scurried away. Max attempted to compose himself. The clerk returned, scowling at him through narrowed eyes. "Herr von Woller will see you now."

Max straightened his tunic, drew himself up in his best parade-ground posture, and followed her down a hallway to a heavy wooden door. The clerk pushed the door open. Max stepped inside. The door closed behind him and he came to full attention with a click of the heels.

Von Woller stood up from behind his desk, less severe in the flesh than in the pictures Max had seen, but not by much. Winged collar. Striped pants. A ring of steel gray hair surrounded his otherwise bald head, but the baldness gave von Woller a forceful look. His eyes and lips were thin. He advanced on Max. "My daughter?"

Smart old goat. "Slight concussion from the bombing. In the hospital at the Zoo Tower, sir. Doctor prescribes two weeks of bed rest. She asks that your automobile call for her in the morning." It was like giving a damage report to Langsdorff, Max thought, fighting the reflexive urge to salute.

"You have seen her personally?"

"I have."

"And it is not serious?"

"No."

Von Woller rubbed his forehead. Some of the starch left his face. "Thank God," he whispered. He looked up at Max again. "She is my only child. Nothing can be allowed to happen to her."

"I feel the same way."

Von Woller fished a monocle from his breast pocket. Fixing it in place, he examined Max slowly before finally extending his hand. "Yes. A meeting long overdue, Herr KapitänLeutnant. Of course, I have heard a great deal about you."

Max gave a slight bow and they shook hands. "As I have about you, sir. And I must thank you for clarifying my misunderstanding with the Paris Gestapo. Your assistance was most appreciated."

Von Woller waved his hand. "It was nothing. You mean very much to my daughter and she means everything to me. I was pleased to help."

Of course you were. "Nonetheless, I thank you, Herr . . ." What was his title anyway? Ministerialrat? No, it was higher than that. "Herr Ministerialdirektor."

"Of course you know, Herr KapitänLeutnant, that Mareth's mother and I have attempted to dissuade her from seeing you. Only for her own good, you understand. Some might think us old-fashioned, but a correct marriage can do a great deal for a woman—perhaps more than a lad such as yourself would know. Marrying the son of a grocer is unlikely to be so helpful. I trust a young man of your intelligence can see that it's nothing personal. In any event, Mareth has her own ideas and a strong will behind them. I expect you are aware of this already."

"Yes, Herr Ministerialdirektor, I certainly am."

Von Woller seemed almost to smile. "I understand you're in the U-boat force now?"

"That is correct."

"Commanding your own boat?"

"Yes."

"This is most urgent work for our Fatherland, young man, most urgent work. Germany will need men like you to win the war. Quite apart from my daughter, it never would have done for the Gestapo to have you shot. I'm glad I was able to prevent it." He went to the large wooden coat stand and put on his heavy overcoat, leather gloves, and a homburg. A real gentleman. "Will you accompany me to the Zoo Tower?"

"A pleasure, Herr Ministerialdirektor."

"Very well. This way then." Von Woller led Max out of the building. "My brother Ernst always spoke very highly of your father. Said he was one of the finest men he had known."

"I'm honored to hear that, sir. I know my father will be honored to hear it as well. He is proud to have served under your brother."

"I believe he was there when Ernst died."

He believed? "Yes, sir, he was. At Verdun."

Like so many high-ranking Nazis, von Woller favored an open car, in his case an eight-cylinder Horch complete with a starched chauffeur who detoured around the most badly damaged streets and brought them up on the far side of the Tiergarten. Max could see that no bombs had fallen in this area today. The rubble was old, covered with snow pitted black from the soot of the coal fires people used to heat their homes. Rats by the hundreds were everywhere. On the remaining wall of one collapsed building, someone had scrawled in chalk, ALL MEMBERS OF THE SCHLEICHER FAMILY ARE DEAD. Max looked away.

Von Woller said, "We'll pay them back for this, after Final Victory."

Max nodded, drawing his greatcoat around him. It was freezing now and he'd lost his scarf in their dash for the shelter. A ten-mark scarf, real silk. He'd bought it in Paris.

"And you men on the front line, you are keeping faith with the Führer and Final Victory?"

"Of course, sir," Max said, but it was nothing more than a hollow reflex. One of his crewkameraden on the Naval War Staff had told him the war might be over in a year *if* they could shut off the flow of supplies reaching Britain. Oberkommando der Kriegsmarine claimed that loss rates among the British and American merchant fleets were becoming intolerable—though not so intolerable that the Allies stopped sending convoys. Still, everyone spoke of Britain's weakening resolve. Dr. Goebbels said the people of London booed Churchill in the streets, that children in the city were starving, that factory workers all over England had walked off their jobs. The British were finished. But Dr. Goebbels had said the Brits were finished in 1939. And after Dunkirk in the summer of 1940, he said it again: the Tommies are finished, once and for all. And they were finished again in the autumn, when the glorious German Luftwaffe had reportedly shot down the entire Royal Air Force in the Battle of Britain—twice. In 1941 Dr. Goebbels assured the nation that the entire British Empire was a mere house of cards; one small blow and it would collapse. And 1942 was more of the same: the Brits were on their way out of the war, finished. They were used up, ruled by a corrupt Jewish plutocracy, a syphilitic drunk for a prime minister. The Brits were effete, feeble-minded, spineless. Their time in history was up. They were finished. But the Tommies had not yet lain down and surrendered and now it was January 1943, and the Royal Air Force was still bombing Berlin. Worst of all, the British now had their American cousins in the war with them. Max had seen America on his training cruise. He'd spent three weeks in California and had seen half a dozen American port cities from Galveston to New Orleans to New York. He knew the Americans weren't finished. The Americans had barely begun.

"Can the Luftwaffe do nothing to stop the bombers from reaching the city?" Max asked von Woller.

Von Woller looked at him as if he were a fool. "Of course they could, but all our squadrons are needed on the Russian Front. Only a skeleton force has been left here to protect the city. Don't worry, Herr KapitänLeutnant, we can take it. You front-line soldiers are not the only ones privileged to be brave. It's a matter of priorities. The Jewish Bolshevik menace comes first and we'll deal with these terror bombers in our own good time. The Führer and the High Command are laying plans for their destruction even as we speak. See to your own duties, my young friend, and don't fret over Berlin. I'm told these nuisance raids won't go on much longer in any case. The English are near the end of their tether."

Smoke and flame rose to the heavens not three blocks away, and Max could smell the soot of the fires, sewage from the busted pipes, the stink of corpses still buried in the rubble, the tang of the lingering cordite. "I can see that, Herr Ministerialdirektor."

They detoured around another huge pile of bricks and mortar and steel girders and passed a string of vacant lots where mountains of sand had been heaped for putting out incendiary bombs.

"Still, sir, if I may, it seems as if the capital of the Reich is being pounded into rubble. Might it not be advisable to deploy more fighters for the protection of Berlin?"

Von Woller folded his arms across his chest. "I trust in the Führer, Herr KapitänLeutnant, and I should think a young officer like yourself would know to do the same. He is the greatest warlord of all history. I have complete faith in him, and in the decisions of the High Command."

Obviously, Max thought, he had never been on the receiving end of the decisions of the High Command. Faith in the Führer and Final Victory. The Jewish Bolshevik Menace. The Jewish Puppet, Franklin Roosevelt. Complete Confidence in the High Command. The war was its own religion. Max wanted to ask the old man, as he had once asked Lehmann, how it was that the Jews could be controlling Communist Russia and capitalist America at the same time.

The driver pulled to the front of the Zoo Tower's main entrance, Woller's gleaming Horch with its official pendant drawing a sharp salute from the policeman on duty.

Max was surprised at how quickly von Woller's reserve broke when he saw his daughter lying in her hospital bed. "Mareth, my dear girl," he whispered, hurrying to her. Kneeling by the bed, he looked her up and down, as if to make sure she was all still there. "You are feeling well?"

"Father, I'm fine. The doctor says it is not serious. I was just knocked over by a bomb concussion."

Max shook his head at the matter-of-fact way she said it. Just knocked over by a bomb concussion. Apparently that was normal in Berlin now—being knocked over by a bomb concussion or having your windows smashed, your library blown out into the street, your motorcar overturned, your little girl's head blown off. It was less dangerous at the front.

Von Woller pulled up a chair and began talking with Mareth about his work, the goings-on in the Foreign Ministry and other parts of the government. Clearly Mareth had taken the place of her mother where von Woller's professional obligations were concerned. It was Mareth with whom he attended all formal diplomatic functions; his wife rarely traveled to Berlin, preferring to drink away her days in the countryside.

Mareth listened patiently as her father continued. The Hungarians were giving him trouble again—they needed more attention than the Italians. And the Turks, never a straight answer from those people. They would lie to you about what day it was. The Japanese—they promised everything but delivered nothing. Their only contribution to the war effort was the well-stocked bar in their embassy. Finally, after an hour or so, she said, "And so, Father, you have met Max?"

Max had been sitting a few feet away, saying nothing, allowing von Woller to speak freely with his daughter. Now von Woller turned to him and gave him a slight nod, as if he'd forgotten Max was still there. "Yes, I have met the KapitänLeutnant. It was good of him to come and fetch me. A brave officer. He has the Iron Cross First Class, I see."

"Father, Max is on leave for another week and I wish for him to be our guest while I'm recovering."

Von Woller lifted his eyebrows. "I don't know if we have room. I . . ."

"Then I will have to stay in the hotel where Max and I spent last night."

Von Woller looked down at his hands folded neatly in his lap. "Mareth, please."

"Father."

Von Woller gave Max a brief glance. "Of course. It would be a pleasure to have the KapitänLeutnant as our guest."

Max thanked him, nodding curtly. The old Nazi surely knew the life of a U-boat captain was not marked by longevity—a little patience now was worth his while because Max would be at the bottom of the Atlantic before year's end. Nonetheless, Mareth flashed a triumphant grin when he glanced at her and Max couldn't help grinning back.

———————

A week later, Max made a lonesome return to the Stettiner Bahnhof. Mareth had wanted to see him off but the doctors forbade it. Ordinarily this would have meant nothing to her, but Herr von Woller objected strongly, so strongly he became hysterical. Together he and Max prevailed on her to remain in bed.

Before the world had gone to hell, it took no more than twenty minutes on the U-Bahn to reach the station, but he took leave of Mareth three hours before his train's scheduled departure. Though he was in the capital of the Greater German Reich itself, Max could count on little. Trains never came on time. Nothing worked. Everything was broken—the U-Bahn cars themselves dented and scorched, seat cushions torn, windows cracked, floors filthy, no heat. Heating took electricity and electricity required coal and coal was in short supply. There was barely enough electricity available to power the underground trains. After pushing his way aboard, Max pulled his greatcoat closely about him and stamped his feet to fight the cold. That also kept his mind off the odor. Like most enclosed spaces in the Reich, the subway car smelled like a public latrine; bakers used large amounts of bran to stretch the flour supply and the high bran content of the bread ration caused widespread flatulence. As they moved slowly toward the Stettiner Bahnhof, Max watched gangs of Russian POWs working on the rail tracks. They were needed because the German track workers had been drafted into the army and sent to Russia, where they spent their time working on rail tracks. Max wondered if anyone but him saw the absurdity.

After reaching the station, he hurried across the platform toward his train, passing dozens of soldiers huddled with their girls, whispering to them amid the steam and whistles, the sighing air brakes of the trains, the shouts of the NCOs, the loudspeaker announcements of arrivals and departures. He was glad Mareth couldn't see him off. He could not endure another farewell. It seemed as if the whole war was bounded by tearful goodbyes on rail platforms.

He boarded his train, hefted his suitcase into the rack above, then took his seat and stared straight ahead, not speaking to anyone, working to keep his expression steady, to keep the tears from welling up in his eyes. U-boat commanders—recognizable to any serviceman by the white officer caps that traditionally only they wore with their blue uniforms—were not permitted to weep on trains, but the young troops around him were hardly so constrained. Edelweiss patches on their sleeves identified them as mountain troops, perhaps bound for the Norway garrison—or for Russia, God forbid. Most of their faces were drained of blood, pale from the effort of telling mothers and sweethearts goodbye. Many wept openly. Boys, most of them. One of their Feldwebels began to sing very softly, many of his soldiers joining in. Max closed his eyes, giving himself over to the terrible sadness he felt having said goodbye to Mareth. Were he not an officer, not a U-Boat captain, not a man who had led others in battle, he would have wept when the youngsters began to sing "Lilli Marlene," a song of two lovers seperated by war.

As the train gathered speed every man in the car raised his voice: an artillery captain by the front entrance, a group of veterans from the Russian Front, the weeping mountain troops, construction engineers from the Organisation Todt, even a prim major wearing the red stripes of the General Staff. Deep and slow they sang, about a girl they loved named Lilli Marlene, who stood waiting in the lamplight outside the barracks, as did a thousand girls outside a thousand barracks, all longing to see their soldier boy.

Mournful now in the fourth year of the war, men with their eyes to the front like Max's, gazing without seeing into the distance, remembering times before the war, when every parting wasn't thought to be the last, when the Allies and the Soviets and the Feldgendarmerie did not separate them from the girl they loved, when the sound of an aeroplane engine did not send them diving into the nearest ditch.

Full voices now for the last verse, the sadness nothing to feel shame over. Everyone wanted to go home—go home to the girl they loved, a girl like Lilli Marlene, who waited for them under the lamplight, a light slowly dimming as the war continued. How often they dreamed of her warm nearness, but she was a will-o'-the-wisp—for when morning came each soldier found nothing but a rifle in his embrace.

Because of an air raid, they were four hours late arriving in Kiel.

CHAPTER TEN

THE NORTH ATLANTIC
DAY 28 OF THE SECOND WAR PATROL OF *U-114*
20 SEPTEMBER 1943
1500 GERMAN WAR TIME

"KOMMANDANT TO THE BRIDGE!"

Max heard the shout over the dull throb of the diesels, came upright in his bunk, and stepped out onto the deck. No need to worry about getting dressed. Like everyone else on the U-boat, he slept in his clothes.

"Smoke in sight, bearing green one five zero!" the watch officer barked through the open hatchway.

Max felt his pulse pick up. Finally, a ship. The war patrol had been a bust so far, they'd sighted nothing but seagulls. Their first patrol had hardly been any better — all fourteen torpedoes fired and only two small freighters sunk. Max jackknifed through the control room hatch and scaled the ladder to the bridge. Blinking in the bright sunlight, he brought his binoculars to his eyes and followed the lookout's pointed finger to starboard. Smoke in sight? Jesus, Mary, and Joseph, it was a forest fire out there. What were the lookouts doing up here anyway? "If you can piss standing up you can get in the navy now," Carls had told him. Max believed him.

He bent to the voice tube that led to the conning tower, from which the helmsman passed his orders through the boat. "Make to U-Boat Command: 'Convoy sighted grid AK55. U-Max.'"

In radio transmissions, U-boats referred to themselves by their captain's name rather than by their number, hoping to confuse British Naval Intelligence.

"Starboard the helm to zero five zero degrees. Both engines ahead full."

Taking his white cap by the bill, Max fastened it firmly to his head so the stiff wind wouldn't blow it off. The pitch of the diesels increased behind him as they went to full speed.

First he must discern the size of the convoy and send regular reports of its course and speed to U-Boat Command in Berlin, so they could gather the wolfpack. It would take Max several hours to come into attack range, so he didn't order the crew to their battle stations now, though he knew word of the sighting would spread through the ship and the men would take up their action posts anyway.

But damn this wind, sharp and cold even in September and kicking up waves, rolling the boat back and forth like a pendulum in the seaway. The U-boat sat squat in the water, her open, horse-shoe-shaped bridge no more than four meters above the surface. They were constantly sending up leather cloths from the control room for the bridge watch to wipe the spray from their binocular lenses. Max licked his. It was quicker.

Binoculars still balanced on the tips of his fingers, he kept his gaze fixed on the distant smoke. He saw masts now, like match-sticks on the horizon, and as the U-boat drew closer, the hulls of the wallowing merchantmen came into view. God and all the Holy Saints above, there were one hell of a lot of ships out there. Max made a rough count, turned to Ferret, the officer of the watch. "How many do you make out?"

Ferret said nothing, continuing to peer at the distant convoy, lips moving silently as he counted to himself. "Forty merchantmen,

Herr Kaleu. Three men-o'-war this side, corvettes most likely, sir, maybe one frigate. Same on port side, I would guess. One corvette astern. Probably two destroyers ranging ahead."

The Allies were getting stronger by the day. A year ago, no convoy would have had so many escorts. The "happy time" when all the old bulls had run up their scores was over, and the end had come fast. Sinkings of Allied ships had peaked in May, and Max and other U-boat skippers now faced far more effective and more deadly Allied countermeasures. More than half of all U-boats were sunk on their first patrol. Every skipper wanted to be an ace, to sink the kind of tonnage Prien and Schepke and Kretschmer had managed earlier in the war, but that was before the Allies had gotten radar, before they had built enough escort vessels to truly protect each convoy, before they had thousands of planes in the air searching for U-boats. No one would ever match the old records now, and the men who had set them vanished one by one. Prien and his boat had just disappeared one day in the spring of '41. Schepke was killed in action ten days later in the most gruesome way imaginable: the destroyer H.M.S. *Vanoc* rammed his U-boat in the mid-Atlantic, its bow pinning Schepke to the periscope housing and mashing him to a pulp. And "Silent Otto" Kretschmer, the highest-scoring ace of all—forty-six ships sent to the bottom—had been blown to the surface that same day by a Royal Navy destroyer and captured along with his entire crew.

Max bent to the voicepipe. "Make to U-Boat Command: 'Forty merchantmen. Estimate nine escorts. Grid AK55. Base course zero nine zero. Speed seven knots. Attacking at dusk. U-Max.'" A slow convoy. Better shooting for him. No group could move any faster than its slowest ship, so the Allies divided their merchantmen into fast convoys, which traveled at nine knots or more, and slow ones, which proceeded at seven knots and made easier targets by far.

Max ordered the wheel over, setting them on a parallel course to the convoy at a distance of about seven kilometers. Turning to the lookouts, he said, "Stay alert, men, stay alert. Watch for aeroplanes." The Luftwaffe said it was impossible, but after his experience in Berlin he had little faith in anything the Luftwaffe said. Besides, one of his crewkameraden, the first watch officer on another U-boat, told him that new long-range Allied planes flying out of Iceland could stay over the convoys all the way to the western approaches of the British Isles, where patrol bombers from RAF Coastal Command took over. So constant vigilance was his strictest rule, even when contemplating the impossible. He'd ordered a seaman before a court-martial for falling asleep on watch; reduced two others in rank for inattention at their posts, then kicked them off his boat. Those who committed lesser offenses had leave taken from them, or had to do especially dirty cleaning jobs such as scrubbing the bilges. If his men thought him a martinet, Max didn't care—his discipline had gotten them through their first war patrol, no small accomplishment.

He continued to watch the convoy through his Zeiss binoculars. The escort ships swept the flank, the rear escort carving a wide arc. That was the one Max had to worry about. His profile was low in the water and the gray-black U-boat wasn't easy to spot in the dark sea, but its wake, churned up by the sixteen-cylinder diesels, showed white against murky waves. He reduced their speed to two-thirds and came port five degrees to zero four five, north by east. The wake lessened as their speed fell off but still seemed like a white arrow pointing at the boat. The course change swung them away from the convoy, putting some distance between them and the inquisitive rear escort—a corvette by the size of her, as Ferret had said. At least she wasn't a destroyer. A destroyer had twice a corvette's speed, could run down a suspected sighting in a flash and return to the convoy. A corvette could only steam at sixteen knots—no faster than a U-boat—and hesitated to leave the convoy because getting back would take too long.

Dusk. The watch changed, Lehmann coming up to replace Ferret, four new sailors with him to replace the lookouts. Max forbade talking on the bridge because it distracted the lookouts, but the silence also had the added benefit of sparing him Lehmann's pronouncements about Final Victory over the Jewish-Bolshevik Menace—pronouncements that had only become more strident since the massive German surrender at Stalingrad in early February.

"Be alert, men," Max cautioned the new lookouts. This was the worst time of day. It was hard to see anything in the fading light and the sailors had a tendency to believe that darkness would protect them somehow. That was false hope. Darkness no longer protected you. God wouldn't protect you. Only luck could protect you, and there was little of that in this ocean at war.

It came at last light: all four columns of the convoy executed a thirty-degree turn to starboard in perfect unison, tight as Prussian grenadiers on parade, an intricate and difficult task for forty ships. The Tommies intended for this move to throw off shadowing U-boats, and indeed Max had been snookered this way on his first patrol, but it wasn't going to happen again. This time he had gotten in close enough to make out the convoy's new course.

Lowering his binoculars, he bent to the voicepipe. "Action stations! All ahead full. Right standard rudder. Come starboard forty degrees to zero eight five." This put him on a converging course. "Attack sight to the bridge." Max turned to Lehmann. "We'll go in fast. Be ready."

The attack sight—a special pair of binoculars—arrived from below. Lehmann mounted the binoculars on their bracket and watched the convoy. In a surface attack, the first watch officer aimed and fired the torpedoes, while the captain maneuvered the U-boat and selected the targets. Only when the boat attacked from underwater did the captain aim and fire, since only he could see through the attack periscope.

"Stay alert," Max reminded the lookouts again. Escorts could charge out of the darkness, and this convoy had plenty of escorts—nine at least, maybe more. "Are they ready below?" Max asked

Lehmann. Damn, he was chattering like an old woman. Get hold of yourself.

"Jawohl, Herr Kaleu."

"Switch to red," Max ordered the helmsman below, who passed the order to Georg.

Inside the boat, the men tensed as they waited at their battle stations. The engineers waited, too, shut away in the stern behind a watertight hatch, their eyes fixed on the signal lights that indicated engine orders. The electric motor men stood by to bring the e-motors on line the instant Max gave the order to dive. In the control room, Ferret and the navigator waited at the firing calculator, ready to punch in whatever firing data Lehmann relayed. Georg and his men stood with their hands on the levers that would open the ballast tanks and get them under when the time came. Forward, in the torpedo room, Carls along with Heinz, the torpedo chief petty officer, stood ready to push the manual firing levers if the electric firing system failed.

Foam splashed across the tower, rolling across the foredeck and then off the sides. Max felt the wind on his face, colder now. Salt rime covered his leather coat and pants and the salt had worked its way in everywhere—on his hair, on his lips, chafing his arms and ass and thighs, setting off a fierce itch in his crotch.

Max kept his binoculars on the shadow of the rear escort, now falling astern of the convoy to search for U-boats. He pointed a finger to starboard.

"I'm going into that gap," he told Lehmann, shouting over the wind. "Stand by!" Max leaned to the voicepipe. "Helmsman, hard starboard fifteen degrees and come to new course of one zero zero degrees."

The boat heeled into the turn and ran full bore for fifteen minutes, racing through the gap created by the escort dropping back. A large blur, two, then three. They were in. Lehmann peered through the firing sight. "The big one," Max shouted, thumping him on the shoulders.

"Range, fifteen hundred meters!" Lehmann called out, the information repeated to the tracking team below. "Angle on the bow green zero five." They could aim the torpedoes up to ninety degrees off the center line. "Set depth four meters."

Max glanced around. The lookouts urgently swept their quadrants.

"Open forward torpedo doors!" Lehmann ordered. Each tube and its precious torpedo were protected from the sea by a heavy steel door. "Range, twelve hundred meters. Angle on the bow zero seven. Depth, four meters. Number one, fire! Number two, fire!"

With a jolt everyone could feel, the eels shot from their tubes, the chief immediately replacing their weight with three tons of seawater as ballast to keep the boat on an even keel.

"Request course change to one zero five," Lehmann shouted.

Max ordered the helm change, which turned their shark nose to another ship, smaller than the first. Was that the stern escort moving up?

"Hurry!" Max yelled.

A blast, bright orange against the darkness, illuminated the hull of the first ship. A direct hit. Good shooting—damn good shooting. Max swiveled his head, scanning the darkness around them. Where was that God damned escort?

"Range, nine hundred meters! Angle on the bow, green zero one zero. Depth, four meters. Number three, fire! Number four, fire!"

Their last torpedo was in the stern tube. Max didn't know if he had time to swing the boat and fire it, but he had to try. It took two hours to reload the forward tubes and they didn't have two hours, probably not even two minutes. "Stand by stern tube," he ordered. "Helmsman . . ."

A lookout yelled, "Destroyer bearing red two two zero!"

Shit! Through the middle of the convoy. Impossible—but there was no other way. Now the stern escort was moving up.

A white rocket broke over the convoy, the emergency turn

signal. All the ships turned thirty degrees to port, away from the attack. Max had been planning to escape through their ranks to throw the escorts off but they were too close to him now. "Emergency right rudder!" he yelled.

The men-o'-war were converging—must see his wake. "Emergency full ahead," he ordered. That would get the electric motors connected to the propeller shafts and give him another knot in speed. But the warships were gaining—they had spotted him. A tower of water off the starboard bow confirmed it—they were firing at him. There was no more time. He had to get under or get rammed by one of the escorts. "Alarm!" Max bellowed.

Instantly the bridge crew dropped below, their exit lighted by another explosion, then another. The second ship had been hit. Max dropped on top of the bridge watch without even noticing. All he could hear was water roaring into the ballast tanks. "Get us down, Chief, down! Destroyer! All hands forward!" Sailors streamed into the bow compartment. "Both ahead full. Hard starboard. Come to course one four zero."

It was quiet now, the hammering diesels still, the low purr of the e-motors barely audible.

"Thirty meters," the chief sang out, "forty meters, fifty meters."

Bekker, the radioman, listened intently to his hydrophones, trying to make out the bearings of the ships above. "Wasserbomben!" he yelled. Max braced himself against the periscope at the center of the control room.

The explosion was unbelievably loud, like a rifle shot right next to Max's ear. It rolled the boat forty degrees. Light bulbs shattered. A glass dial in front of him burst. Sailors slammed to the deck, some screaming in pain. The dish cabinet in the officers' quarters sprang open and the crockery shattered against the steel plates of the deck. Emergency lighting flickered on in the control room, powered by the auxiliary lighting circuit.

Max clung to the periscope housing, feeling it vibrate in his arms. "Emergency left rudder," he ordered.

Depth charges created such turbulence in the water that it was possible to sneak away by making a radical course change. But the sonar had them now, the sound like pebbles being thrown against the hull.

"Both motors to one-third." Max had to conserve battery power. "Chief, take us to eighty meters."

The chief, standing beside the two hydroplane operators, gave the orders to his men, swearing under his breath. One man controlled the aft hydroplanes, the other controlled the fore. They bore down on the buttons that manipulated the planes, eyes fixed on the depth indicator in front of them.

Another ping hit the boat. It was the second escort, ranging now for the first. Tommy bastards. Max heard the sound of propellers above as the destroyer ran in over him.

"Wasserbomben!" Bekker yelled again.

"Ahead full. Emergency right rudder." Double back on the filthy swine. The explosion of the depth charges often caused escort ships to lose sonar contact. They had to reestablish it after every attack. Sometimes they looked in the wrong place and you could slip away.

Not this time. The next set of depth charges blew out the emergency lighting, leaving the boat black as a cave. A second set exploded over them before Max had a chance to give orders, pushing the boat over and down with such force that his hands were torn away from the periscope and he slid across the deck, banging into the opposite bulkhead. A young sailor wept in the corner.

"Shut up, dammit," Max ordered. "Flashlights. Leutnant Lehmann, take that man's name." Anything could happen if you let the sailors get out of hand—panic, even mutiny. In Danzig he had heard rumors of captains forcing men back to their posts at gunpoint during a depth charge attack.

The control room crew switched on their flashlights, illuminating the critical fighting stations. If the flashlights gave out, the men could still function, since each man could perform his tasks blindfolded. To make this possible, each of the small control wheels had a distinct pattern imprinted on its metal surface.

"One hundred thirty meters," the chief announced—right at their design limit but the boat would have to hold. Around Max she creaked like an old wooden house from the pressure of the depth.

"Both engines stop." He had to spend his battery power like a miser and watch his depth like a hawk—the boat would gradually sink without her propellers turning to keep water flowing over the hydroplanes. It was impossible to establish total equilibrium.

"Engine room taking water through the propeller shafts," Lehmann reported. The point where the propeller shafts left the pressure hull was always a weakness in a depth charge attack.

"Chief!"

"Bloody hell," the chief said, banging the wall of dials and control wheels in front of him. "The devil curse all who built this stinking boat."

"Chief, check the engine room and give me a report on the leak."

"Jawohl, Herr Kaleu."

There was not much the chief could do. At any depth below one hundred meters, the packings around the propeller shafts always leaked.

"Off-duty watch to the bunks," he ordered. That would get them out of the way and conserve air, but Max knew he couldn't have done it: lie in his bunk in the blackness, water dripping in, hull groaning from the pressure, depth charges coming down. Not that standing in the center of the control room and barking orders gave him much solace. If a depth charge exploded within ten meters of the boat, the force would crack the pressure hull and the cold black water would spray in with the power of God Almighty. And they would die: screaming, cursing, praying in their last seconds.

A ping sounded against the hull, now two. The Tommies had found them again. Thank the Virgin Mary and all the Holy Saints that sonar couldn't detect their depth. On his first patrol, Max had learned that if you went deep you could slip away because the Brits underestimated the depth limit of U-boats.

The next set of charges exploded over the stern, sheared the mooring bolts off the port diesel, jumped it two inches from its bed, bent the port propeller shaft, and shattered every glass dial in the engine room and e-motor compartment. Now the outboard intake valve—the opening through which the diesels drew air— began to leak. In minutes they were down five degrees by the stern. Max couldn't run the bilge pumps; that the British would certainly hear.

He sat on the heavy chart chest in the control room, mentally plotting his position relative to the convoy escorts above. Bekker could give him the bearing of the two ships but Max heard them clearly enough with his own ears when they ran in to attack. It was unnerving—a swishing, drumming sound like rain blowing against the side of a house. A destroyer had to make depth charge runs at full speed to keep its stern from being blown off by the four hundred pounds of exploding TNT, so each run was announced by the high-pitched whine of its propellers.

Max listened to these sounds for seven hours as the British ships peppered the U-boat with round after round of depth charges. He lost count of how many. Belongings were strewn everywhere, tools and provisions spilled onto the deck, rolling back and forth as the boat rolled. The leak worsened in the stern, dragging them down to one hundred sixty meters—almost their crush depth. Max had to order a burst of power from the electric motors every ten minutes to keep them from sinking any lower. He clung to the periscope housing, hands clammy, darkness all around him except for the unsteady flashlight beams reflecting off the instrument panels. The crew stood to their posts but some whimpered, some wept, some stood rigid as stone, some puked;

the smell of vomit thickened the stale air. One of the sailors in the control room filled his pants and the stink of it mixed with the other vile odors.

A terrible exhaustion gripped Max. All night he had twisted and turned the boat, never knowing if he was right or wrong until the depth charges exploded, and always the ping of the British sonar, the creaking of his battered boat, the hoarsely shouted damage reports. Sweat drenched him completely. Even his underwear was soaked through. Before they sailed, Lehmann had told the crew, "The Führer expects you men to be quick as greyhounds, tough as leather, hard as Krupp steel." Max liked the sound of that as much as anyone, but after the hours of depth charging it seemed absurd. Half his sailors were terrified and in a handful of moments so was he.

Every time he heard the barrels drop into the water he shouted out a course change and said a Hail Mary to himself. What kind of death would it be? He just hoped it would come quickly—not drowning, not the awful terror of men clawing at one another, fighting desperately for breath as the water poured in. When he was doing his infantry training at Danholm, the training officer had ordered the cadets to put on their gas masks and run repeatedly up and down a hill. With the gas mask both pulled over his head and fastened tightly around his face, Max could breathe only through the filter and taking in enough air that way was almost impossible. He felt like he was choking to death or drowning; Holy Mary, Mother of God, full of grace—if they were going to be hit, let it be a direct hit.

A tap on his shoulder. The chief. "Only fifteen percent battery power left, Herr Kaleu." All of Max's twisting and turning had drained the batteries. He nodded to the chief. Paint flecked off the bulkheads as the pressure of the water compressed the boat. The hull would crack right open if they went much deeper. They were at one hundred eighty meters, a handful of meters from their crush depth. Max could go no lower—this was the absolute limit. The depth gauge didn't even register any deeper. Max drew in a lung-ful of the fetid air. "Leutnant Lehmann."

"Ja?"

"Gun crew stand by."

"Herr Kaleu?"

"Dammit, I said tell the gun crew to stand by."

"Jawohl, Herr Kaleu."

Damned insubordinate Nazi prick. Put him in the guardhouse if they ever got back to Lorient.

The U-boat had a 105mm gun on her foredeck—not a match for a destroyer but it was something. Here, below, they had no hope at all. At least if they fought from the surface until the U-boat sank, the men might have a chance to abandon ship. Or some of them might—the engineers would never make it out, but they never did. Still, Max owed his men whatever chance he could give them; and you could usually count on the Tommies to rescue survivors after they sank a U-boat. So some of them might make it. But pray God the Brits would be so surprised when he surfaced that the U-boat could simply get away in the confusion.

The gun crew assembled in the control room, their faces pinched and drawn, eyes bulging, sweat running down their cheeks. Max looked at them. Several trembled uncontrollably. All of them panted in the thin air, their lungs struggling against the rising CO_2 levels.

"Battle surface. We practiced this in the Baltic. First man out take up the deckboards and open the ammunition boxes. Second man, unscrew the plug in the barrel. Third man, aim at the near-est British ship. Fourth man, load the shell. Understand?"

They nodded.

"You trained for this, remember?"

None of them said anything. They had trained for this in a calm sea with their wits about them and no Royal Navy escorts dropping depth charges.

"Chief!"

"Herr Kaleu?"

"Can you give me full power when we surface?"

"Starboard engine, Herr Kaleu. Port engine is out."

"Then give me whatever you can, but do not leave me lying dead in the water." Max looked again at his sailors, their eyes all seeming to ask the same question. What did they want from him? Was he supposed to reassure them that they weren't going to die?

"Good luck, men. Stand by. Activate all bilge pumps. Blow all tanks!"

A thin whine sounded as compressed air blew into the ballast tanks. Max pulled himself up, clinging once again to the shiny metal tube of the periscope. They weren't moving, still down at the stern.

"All ahead full!" He heard hysteria in his voice.

Sluggishly the boat began to rise, hesitating, then moving faster as she shook off the terrible pressure of the depths and the weight of the water she'd taken on.

"One hundred fifty meters."

Max closed his eyes. They weren't dead yet.

"One hundred ten meters!"

"Gun crew, stand by."

"Seventy meters."

Max began to say the Hail Mary again.

"Thirty meters!"

"Stand by!" Max yelled, his voice hoarse. He climbed into the conning tower.

"Ten meters. Tower clear. Hatch clear!"

Max opened the hatch, the unequal pressure tearing it from his hands. Air—humid and sweet, dense with oxygen—enveloped him. Overcome by the richness of it, he sagged on the ladder for a moment, seeing red. Then, eyes clearing, he hoisted himself onto the bridge.

Behind him the gun crew came up, jumping quickly to the foredeck, followed by the lookouts, who assumed their posts on the bridge. One diesel rumbled to ignition and the boat began to move forward. A light drizzle, wet on Max's face, reduced their visibility. He took up his binoculars. To port, he saw the dim outline of a British corvette perhaps a half kilometer distant. No sight of the destroyer.

A bang and flash from the corvette, then a geyser of white water three hundred meters off the port beam. Even in the darkness and the rain, they had been spotted straight away.

"Fire!" Max yelled at the gun crew. "Fire!"

"Destroyer bearing green zero nine zero!" the starboard lookout screamed. Max turned and saw the ship coming right at them out of the night, her foaming bow wave stark against the dark water. Urine ran hot down his legs. Mother of God. The gun crew abandoned their weapons and jumped overboard.

"Alarm!" Max screeched, his voice gone thin and high. Two of the bridge lookouts dropped down the hatch with him, the other two leapt overboard.

"Get us down!" Max yelled, voice cracking. Men sprinted for the bow as the boat began to dive. "Radio! To U-Boat Command: 'Rammed. Sinking. Grid AK57. U-Max. Collision alarm!'" He gripped the periscope, eyes clenched shut.

The destroyer hit them forward of the bridge with a sound like a locomotive slamming on its brakes, rolling the boat ninety degrees. Metal shrieked against metal. The force slammed men to the deck. The impact on her bow forced the U-boat down at a sharp pitch and she plunged out of control toward the bottom.

Max, on his hands and knees in the control room, vomited onto the deck plates. Around him men screamed, hysterical in the darkness. "Blow tanks amidships!" he ordered. "Blow diving tank forward! Blow forward trim tank! E-motors full astern!"

They had to stop the boat from plunging to the depths, but no one responded to his commands.

"Chief!" Max shouted into the blackness, sliding on the slime of the control room floor. "Chief!" There was a rumble from the forward compartment as one of the spare torpedoes broke loose, followed immediately by a violent wail.

"Chief!" Where in the hell was the man?

"Herr Kaleu." A hand touched him. Flashlights came on, weakly illuminating the control room. Max saw Carls at his side.

"Carls! The bow compartment—we have to get the hatch closed!" That's where the water would be pouring in from the gash opened in the collision. If they could get the hatch closed, maybe they had a chance to surface.

"Herr Kaleu! Herr Kaleu!" one of the hydroplane men shouted. "One hundred fifty meters."

"Planes to hard rise," Max shouted back. "Carls! Close the hatch!"

"Herr Kaleu." Carls pulled him up from the deck. "Herr Kaleu, the pressure hull was not breached."

"One hundred seventy meters, Herr Kaleu!" the young hydroplane operator sang out.

"Blow tanks amidships. Can you do that?" Normally it was the chief who blew the tanks, but all the control wheels were in full view of the boy

"Ja, jawohl, Herr Kaleu."

"And blow the diving tank forward, understand? First amidships, then forward—not at the same time."

"Jawohl, Herr Kaleu."

Blowing the tanks increased their buoyancy and allowed the weight of the U-boat's keel to right them.

"Good lad." Max's breathing slowed and he relaxed his grip on Carls as the boat settled onto an even keel. "No damage to the pressure hull?"

"None, Herr Kaleu."

The U-boat had two hulls. The watertight pressure hull encircled all the vital machinery and living areas. Saddle tanks for ballast, extra fuel, and water were attached outboard and covered by a separate outer hull, which was not watertight. The boat could withstand a tear in the outer hull as long as the pressure hull wasn't breached. The chief must have had them under by just enough for the destroyer to scrape across their foredeck without tearing into the bow compartment.

"One hundred ninety meters!"

A rivet blew with the sound of a gunshot from the pressure, then another and another. Max felt like he was standing on a pistol range. They had to come up on their depth. More flashlights switched on—Lehmann was up and the emergency lights flickered to life. The machinists must still be alive.

"Lehmann, trim the boat."

"Jawohl, Herr Kaleu."

All through the boat Max could hear the crew returning to their stations. He made his way aft, helping men up as he went. The depth charges had not yet begun again, and he wanted to show himself to the crew and inspect the boat during this lull.

"It's the Kommandant! Herr Kaleu!"

"Eh, a little roughhousing from the Tommies," Max said, smiling. The boys smiled back at him, some of them too young to shave, their dirty faces blemished with pimples but all grinning now. "To your posts, men."

He opened the watertight hatch to the engine room and drew back as a thick cloud of steam poured out. Water leaking in had sprayed on the hot diesel engines. Max coughed as he waved the steam away. He stepped through the hatch and into the engine room. Three mechanics were elbow deep in the starboard diesel, furiously checking all the cylinder rods.

"All is in order?" he shouted to the chief Dieselobermaschinist.

"As close to order as we can get, Herr Kaleu."

Max continued through the steam, undogged the hatch to the e-motor room, and stepped through. He snapped a salute to the Elektriker Obermaschinist, a prewar petty officer, still at his post, wearing the protective leather gauntlets that were the badge of e-motor men. "Wittelbach, now you have a war story to tell the folks back home." The man smiled, said nothing. "How much power do we have left?"

"Ten percent, Herr Kaleu."

"Both motors dead slow then."

"Only have the starboard motor, Herr Kaleu. Port propeller shaft is bent."

"Very well." Max had forgotten about that. "Any batteries cracked?"

"Inspecting for that now, Herr Kaleu."

"Carry on."

Wittelbach saluted as best he could, and Max returned to the control room. Lehmann had trimmed the boat and they were on an even keel at one hundred seventy-five meters—way too deep but good enough for the moment. At least until the depth charges started falling again. "Sonar on us yet?"

"Nein, Herr Kaleu."

"Steady on course one zero five then."

"Jawohl, Herr Kaleu."

A moan from the bow drew Max's attention and he made his way forward, stepping over the tools and the cans and the shattered dishes littering the deck. Equipment had been thrown everywhere, smashed and dented from the jolt of the collision. Even the porcelain commode had cracked. Well, they were accustomed to shitting in cans—you couldn't use the toilet below twenty-five meters anyway. Without it the boat would smell even worse, but that would only be a problem if they survived. A twist of his body and Max was through the hatch into the forward torpedo room, which also served as the crew's quarters. Blood covered the starboard bulkhead where the torpedo had come loose and pulped two sailors, breaking the arm of a third. Each torpedo was seven meters long and weighed a ton and a half. When they came loose of their moorings the result was always the same: men died.

Carls had covered the faces of the dead men with towels, but their bodies lay twisted at unnatural angles. The injured lad sat rigid in pain against the bulkhead, holding his broken arm, the white bone sticking out. Heinz, the torpedo chief petty officer, tended to the youngster since Bekker had to stay on the hydrophones. The medical kit lay open, Heinz rummaging through it while the young sailor, desperate not to moan in front of Max, compressed his lips till they went white.

"Heinz will fix you up, lad. He doctored the pigs on his grandfather's farm, didn't you, Heinz?"

"I certainly done plenty of that and there ain't a lot of difference between a pig and a man, Herr Kaleu. Only pigs is smarter. They doesn't go to war with each other."

Max couldn't help but smile and even the youngster seemed to calm down.

He turned to Carls. "Damage?"

"Close on everything, Herr Kaleu."

Max looked around. Bunks had been torn from the bulkheads, lubricating oil had sprayed over part of the compartment, spattering the letters that were strewn about. The winch that hoisted the torpedoes had been pulled loose from the overhead; tins of food, most of them dented, were everywhere. "Clean it up," Max ordered. Best to keep the men busy.

Once back in the control room, he asked Bekker if he'd picked up anything from the escorts on the hydrophones.

"Nein, Herr Kaleu. Nothing moving toward us."

Strange. Very strange. Maybe the ships had hove to while they brought up more depth charges from their magazines—not an easy job under any circumstance, Max knew. But an escort would never stop dead in the water to do that—she would present a perfect target to a U-boat. "Herr Kaleu," Lehmann called.

"Ja?"

"The fuel gauge on the starboard diesel tank, the saddle tank— it's showing empty."

Max shook his head very slowly from side to side, then broke into a smile. Maybe the British ships weren't hove to. Maybe they were gone. The chief had finally woken up and was sitting on the deck by the hydroplane controls, blood matted in his thick beard, but he was smiling, too, when Max looked over at him. "You know what that means?" Max asked him.

The chief nodded. Half his face was swollen, his cheek already turning a deep purple. He said, "It means the bloody Tommies think we're already sunk."

Max laughed out loud. The destroyer had torn open the starboard diesel tank, which left an oil slick on the surface when the boat submerged. That was usually the sign that a U-boat had sunk and its oil tanks had ruptured. Seeing that, the Tommies would have slapped one another on the back and steamed happily away. Looking around at the littered deck, at injured men waiting for medical care, the scene illuminated by the pale emergency lights, Max couldn't stop smiling. He turned his grin back to the chief. "Exactly."

The chief dabbed at an oozing gash on his forehead. "Well, bugger you, Mr. Tommy."

Max surfaced three hours later to an empty sea and the faint smell of petroleum. Maybe the Brits had picked his men up. He hoped so, prayed so. Better a POW camp than drowning in the North Atlantic. The lookouts were wrong to have jumped, but the gun crew had been right—the deck gun was gone, sheared off by the bow of the destroyer. All the wooden deckboards that covered the steel upper deck were splintered or torn away, the starboard diesel tank gouged open, metal plating ripped and bent. Max crossed himself. Had they been just a bit higher in the water, they would have been sunk. Thank you, Holy Mary.

Yet now they faced a new, perhaps more arduous task, one both difficult and not without great danger: their return to Lorient, a voyage of a thousand kilometers. He had lost eight men from a crew of forty-six but was lucky not to have lost them all. He was lucky to be alive himself. Maybe all the good-luck charms the men brought on every patrol had worked: Lehmann's diminutive porcelain gnome, the chief's green sweater, the five-mark coin

Wittelbach had taken from a fountain in Paris, and the aluminum canteen token from *Graf Spee* that Max was never without.

He bent to the voicepipe. "Engage starboard diesel. Blow through." Below, the e-motor chief cut the electric motors, then the Dieselobermaschinist gently started his engine and blew the exhaust through the ballast tanks to expel the remaining seawater. This saved compressed air and helped preserve the tanks from corrosion.

"Control," Max said into the voicepipe.

"Control room, aye."

"Have radio make following message to U-Boat Command: 'Rammed by British destroyer. Eight casualties. Port diesel out. Extensive damage. Two ships sunk. Estimate tonnage 15,000 grt. Returning to base. U-Max.'"

Let the staff figure it out. Ferret had the watch. "Keep on the lookout for aeroplanes," Max told him. "Can you do that? Are these men alert?"

"Jawohl, Herr Kaleu."

Max looked at the men, their faces fish-belly white, sporting whatever kind of beards they could grow. Shaving was forbidden on the boat because freshwater was always in short supply. The eyes of the men were sunken and red. Their condition hardly inspired confidence, but none of the crewmen below looked any better. Besides, Ferret was a good officer and a captain had to trust his officers. He said, "As soon as the batteries are fifty percent recharged I want you to submerge for six hours so the men can rest and take some food. Once you submerge, stay on this heading with the starboard e-motor slow ahead. Understood?"

Ferret nodded and Max patted him on the shoulder, instead of cursing him for not saluting. "The bridge is yours," he said.

Max dropped below, repeated his orders to Lehmann, then withdrew to his cabin, closed the green curtain, and stripped off his clothes. He soaked a towel in the lemon-scented cologne issued to U-boats and wiped the dirt and sweat from his body. Also the dried urine from his legs. That had been shameful but he wasn't going to berate himself about it now. He lay on his bunk after cleaning himself and shook uncontrollably. The spraying water, the screaming men, wanting to scream yourself as your mouth filled with the freezing black sea—they had been no more than a few centimeters away from all of it, and the depth charges would still be raining down if not for the happenstance of the ruptured fuel tank. Eventually, he grew weak from trembling and slept.

A few minutes before dusk they surfaced and Max returned to the bridge. He swept the area with his binoculars and saw nothing at first. Then his eye caught a small white flash in the dying sun—maybe one kilometer off the starboard beam, bobbing on the swell. "Right standard rudder to course one five zero," he ordered.

Lehmann had the watch. Max pointed out the object. "Can you tell what it is?"

Lehmann peered through his heavy binoculars for a long moment. "I believe it is a lifeboat, Herr Kaleu."

Max raised his own binoculars again, but still could hardly make it out. His eyesight was always poor at dusk, while Lehmann had excellent vision at any time. "Is there anyone in it?"

"I believe so, Herr Kaleu."

"Control room."

"Control room, aye."

"Tell Carls to come up with a magazine for the machine gun."

"Jawohl, Herr Kaleu."

The U-boat had a twenty-millimeter anti-aircraft gun mounted on a small platform aft of the bridge—the Wintergarten, the men called it. Max motioned toward the platform when Carls came up and the big man attached the magazine to the gun and swiveled it to point at the lifeboat as they drew closer.

"Stay alert," Max cautioned the bridge watch. "Look to your sectors." Lookouts had a tendency to turn away from their quadrants when something more interesting was happening out of their field of vision. That was an easy way to miss an approaching enemy ship or aeroplane. "Stop engine," Max ordered, and the throb of the diesel died away to a quiet idle, momentum carrying them to within a few meters of the lifeboat.

There were nine men inside—no, ten. One was lying in the bilge, probably wounded. Maybe dead. It was a big lifeboat, too, built for forty or fifty people, the name of its ship sanded off as the Royal Navy had ordered at the start of the war. One of the men stood. He wore no cap, but gold rings looped around the sleeves of his blue jacket. An officer. Max cupped his hands around his mouth. "What ship?" he shouted.

No reply. The officer looked around at the men huddled at his feet against the cold. He was young, no older than Lehmann.

"What ship?" Max said again.

"D-D-*Duchess of Berwick*."

"Bound for?"

"L-Liverpool."

The officer shook. Carls had the machine gun pointed right at him. No doubt the Brits thought they were about to be shot by the bloodthirsty Huns. Turning to Carls, Max ordered him to point the gun aft of the lifeboat and stay ready, but it was just a precaution.

"When were you sunk?"

"Early last evening, sir. Right as we were sitting down to tea."

Tea. At sea during wartime and they were sitting down to tea. But Max had sunk this ship and they weren't so arrogant now. Many times during his training at U-boat school, he'd wondered what he would feel after he sank a ship, and now he could say he was so exhausted he really didn't feel anything. Every motion had been rehearsed and practiced so often that it felt automatic when the time came, and the distance of warfare at sea kept him from having to think too much about the men he might be killing. Besides, he had seen what the British did to *Meteor*, and what they were doing now to Berlin, and he didn't mind the idea of killing

Englishmen. But these men in the lifeboat looked bedraggled, cold, defeated. Their boat was almost the same size as the one in which Max had floated around the Indian Ocean. "Do you need any provisions?" he asked.

The young officer looked at him in confusion, trying to decide whether Max was making a joke. Finally he said, "Water and food, sir. We need both. Provisions locker was almost empty when we launched and some of the water tanks had been stove in." Max knew all about that problem—he supposed it was no surprise that British sailors stole lifeboat provisions, too.

"Stand by then."

Max called down the hatchway. "Tell the cook to come to the conning tower."

"Herr Kaleu," Lehmann said, "I must protest. It is expressly forbidden to give aid to shipwrecked men—expressly forbidden in Admiral Dönitz's standing orders."

Lehmann was right. Max hesitated. What would happen to him if he did this? Lehmann would surely report him. But to the navy or the Gestapo?

"Herr Kaleu," the cook called from below. "Herr Kaleu, you wished to see me?"

"A moment, Cook."

Could he really afford another altercation with the Gestapo? Max looked at the ten British sailors shivering in the evening cold of the North Atlantic, cold that would grow worse before dawn. Much worse. Lehmann stared at him. Beneath his feet, the U-boat rocked in the swell, wavelets lapping rhythmically against the hull. Max had spent many harsh nights shivering in the bilge of a lifeboat, cold, hungry, throat burning with thirst.

"Cook."

"Herr Kaleu?"

"I need ten of the big five-liter cans filled with freshwater. And what do you have extra tins of down there?"

"Ham, sir. And tinned beans. Plenty of tinned beans."

"Good. Get me all of that and be quick about it."

"Jawohl, Herr Kaleu."

Cook was a good man. Before the war he had run a stall selling coffee and buns in the Munich rail station—a busy place in these last years, since the Nazi Party had its headquarters in Munich. "I saw Hitler quite often," he had once told Max, and Max had said something polite about how thrilling that must have been. "No, not really, Herr Kaleu," the cook replied. A true believer.

Now Lehmann said, "I must ask permission to note my protest in the logbook, Herr Kaleu."

"Of course that is your right, Leutnant, but after you go off watch." They both knew that Admiral Dönitz reviewed the logbook of every U-boat after its war patrol, so he would see that Lehmann had not agreed with what Max was doing.

Cook collected the provisions in ten minutes and sent them up to the deck. A number of sailors threw in packs of cigarettes and matches. A good smoke could take a man's mind off his troubles. Max maneuvered the U-boat as close as he could and Carls leaned over to pass the provisions to the Englishmen.

"Do you have a sail in there?" he asked the young British officer. It would be the standard drill. Most of the big lifeboats had sails already attached to masts with the assemblage secured in the bottom of the boat.

"Yes, sir. I believe we do, sir."

"And can you sail?"

"Well, I don't know, sir. I'm an engineering officer myself, Captain."

"You step the mast and raise the sail up, then put the tiller over and—" Max stopped himself. Here he was giving sailing lessons to a jug-eared British engineering officer in the middle of the war. "I'm sure some of your men can help you. You have a sextant and some charts as well, don't you?"

"Yes, sir."

"And a compass?"

"Yes, sir."

"Can you navigate?"

"I—I believe so, sir."

"Very well. Then you want to steer zero twenty-two degrees, north-northeast; that will take you to England. You'll be drinking beer in a pub in less than a fortnight." He had to try to cheer them up, give them some hope to boost morale. Without good morale they would never make it—not in an open boat, in the North Atlantic, a thousand kilometers from England. "I would broadcast your position on the six-hundred-meter band, but then your escorts would be on me in a lightning flash."

"I understand, sir."

"Good luck, then."

The young officer hesitated, then saluted Max. "And good luck to you, too, sir."

Max returned the salute, then set course for Lorient.

CHAPTER ELEVEN

LORIENT
GERMAN-OCCUPIED FRANCE
HEADQUARTERS, 1OTH U-BOAT FLOTILLA
NINE DAYS LATER
29 SEPTEMBER 1943

WATER DRIPPED FROM MAX AS HE STEPPED OUT OF THE TUB IN HIS room at Hotel Beau Séjour, which had been requisitioned from its French owners for use by the officers of the U-boat force. Four hours in the bath had soaked away the dirt and stink of the patrol. As the water drained out, it left behind a brown ring of grease inside the tub. Let the French clean it up.

While he soaked, his trunk had been placed on the bed by a headquarters orderly and Max opened it to find his uniforms and some of the few possessions that mattered to him—his sextant, books Mareth had given him, a picture of her, a rosary from his father. Also his last will and testament, dutifully made out and notarized. U-Boat Command required a valid will from all crewmen before sailing, a practicality that did little to inspire confidence among the men. It was a sensible precaution, Max knew— Germanic, thorough, and he liked thoroughness. With casualties in the UBootwaffe over fifty percent, sailors no longer joked about making a will. Before going on a war patrol, you packed your belongings, careful to omit French postcards and indiscreet letters. One hardly wished for one's family to discover that your most treasured correspondence was with a local fille de joie named Enchanté. Then you put your will on top, closed the lid, handed the tin trunk over to the orderly, and tried not to wonder who would open it next—you or the deceased property officer.

Max put his will aside to save it for next time. No need to write a new one—he left everything to his father. All two thousand marks. That's all he had in the Dresdner Bank, all he'd been able to put away, despite the raise that came with his last promotion. Since *Meteor*, he'd been spending every mark he earned. Why save money for a future he would never live to see?

There was a letter to Mareth tucked into Max's will, telling her to be brave, to go on with life, find someone else to love, have children. Noble sentiments but hard to feel with conviction. As the war went on what he mostly felt was his courage trickling down his legs like the urine he'd let go when the destroyer appeared out of the night. He was terrified of dying, of losing Mareth, of losing the small dreams they had for a life together—a house in Kiel overlooking the harbor so he could watch the ships, a gaggle of children, a dog. He clung to this fantasy all the more strongly as it receded amid the chaos of war. As for death, his acceptance of its mounting certainty did not bring a sense of peace. He only feared it more.

Max put on a clean pair of underwear for the first time in eight weeks, then slipped into a pair of clean uniform pants. The pants were old; he'd brought them from home. He'd paid one hundred marks plus twenty clothing coupons for them before the war at Stechbarth's in Berlin, official tailor to the forces. After pouring himself a glass of wine from the bottle on the nightstand, he took up the thick packet of letters Mareth had sent while he was at sea. She wrote him every day. There must have been fifty envelopes in the stack. He smiled as he flipped through them. The field post was free but Mareth had stamped the envelopes anyway—with stamps that showed a U-boat commander, white cap reversed, peering into a periscope. She'd written Max's name below each one.

He lay down on the bed and began to go through the letters, starting with the oldest. Maybe it was his naval training, or simply the Prussian blood in his veins, but he liked to do everything in its proper order. "Prussia is proud of you," Mareth sometimes teased him.

She prayed for him every morning in the Kaiser Wilhelm Gedächtniskirche near the Zoo Tower now, with St. Matthäus off the Tiergartenstrasse having been destroyed. All the stained glass at the Gedächtniskirche had been taken down and stored after the first bombing raids and it was dark in the church with the windows boarded up, but hundreds of candles burned, their reflections dancing on the polished wooden pews and altar. She lit a new candle for him every day. Maybe it was good that he wasn't in Berlin now, because everyone smelled musty and damp—bathing was no longer permitted on weekdays. When he visited they could take baths together, patriotically conserving water. But he should bring the soap, preferably something French and perfumed. She'd run out of the supply she bought in Paris and all you could get in Berlin was a synthetic soap substitute that smelled terrible, left a thick scum behind on the water, and was strictly rationed besides: each person received just two ounces per month. The allotment of detergent was hardly more generous, and it was fortunate under these circumstances that the Sergeant Major had been able to send along several boxes of Persil washing powder he'd "just happened to come across in one of his storerooms." (Max could only shake his head at that. His father probably had an entire storeroom full of the stuff.) He downed another glass of wine and felt the warmth spread through his belly. U-Boat Command provided unlimited amounts of alcohol for its sailors between war patrols, a small consolation to men living under a sentence of death.

Max knew he couldn't get too drunk in the room—within the

hour he had to attend a dinner being laid on by the flotilla commander for the officers and crew of *U-114*.

He worked his way through the pile of envelopes. Soot fell out of one. She had passed a chimney sweep on the Hohenzollernstrasse—renamed the GrafSpeestrasse now—and he let her break two small bits off his brush. She'd kept one and sent the other to Max in the hope that it might bring them luck. On the U-Bahn last month she saw a new poster showing women how to examine their breasts for lumps every week, part of the party's anti-cancer campaign. She would teach him to do this for her. But only if he promised to do it regularly. The twelfth letter now. He smiled at Mareth's news and gossip: how she had stuffed her purse with rolls at a banquet given by the Spanish ambassador so she'd have something to eat later; how she was feeding ten stray cats outside her apartment building; how her father was furious with her for wasting food on the strays. She accompanied Herr von Woller to diplomatic receptions at least twice a week. Mostly they were boring but sometimes there was dancing, and Mareth loved to dance. One could only do so now at diplomatic receptions because Goebbels had banned dancing in public after the defeat at Stalingrad. At the receptions she never took any partners under the age of sixty, so Max should not be jealous, though it was true that most of the older men were lechers. His Excellency, the Swedish ambassador, had let his hand wander over her derriere during a slow waltz. She ground her heel into his foot without saying a word and the hand returned quickly to its proper position. The Croatian ambassador was even worse: he went so far as to pinch her on the bottom. She kicked him in the shin and he didn't do it again.

The bombing had not been so bad in recent weeks. Perhaps the British were being worn down. Perhaps they were feeling the pinch because of brave men like Max who were doing everything they could for Germany. She hoped so. She prayed so. Meanwhile, she was volunteering three nights a week for the NSV, the National Socialist People's Welfare Organization, providing assistance to those displaced by the bombings, many of whom had lost everything and become desperate—women with small children to look after and a husband at the front. Mareth had given away most of her wardrobe so he shouldn't expect her to be so well dressed the next time he returned on leave (though she promised she'd kept the lingerie he bought for her in Paris). She and Loremarie played Ping-Pong at least twice a week to unwind and Mareth was getting quite good. Max should be prepared for defeat next time they played.

He stopped reading and stood to put on his shirt, tie, and blue naval tunic, now heavy with the Iron Cross First Class, black wound badge, auxiliary cruiser badge, and the U-Boat Service Medal, all pinned to the left breast of his coat The headquarters orderly had polished his knee-high black riding boots. Max knew the boots were an affectation but enjoyed wearing them all the same; most U-boat officers did, even though they were non-regulation.

Max took the last letter off the bottom of the stack and opened it. Mareth's writing seemed unsteady. She had used an unusual black ink. The letter began, *My mother was killed last night in a bombing raid. She agreed to come to Berlin for the Foreign Minister's birthday party at the Adlon. We were to fetch her at the apartment at 8:00. The British came over early, about 7:30, just as Papa and I were leaving his office. Just as Daniel brought Papa's automobile, the sirens went off and the police ordered us back inside. Papa was terribly upset and we rushed to his office to telephone Mother. He said to go immediately to the bomb shelter in the far end of the cellar—that it was very safe. I spoke to her and said please not to worry, that I loved her and soon we would all be together. The police told us later that most residents of the building had properly gone to the cellar but a heavy bomb hit the back of the building and it collapsed on top of the shelter and killed everyone. Our flat had no damage except for some window panes blown in. Mother could simply have stayed in her room and would not have been harmed in the least. Max, please, please come to Berlin as soon as you can.*

He put down the letter and stared at the wall for a moment. He couldn't remember his own mother and didn't know what he should be feeling. He hardly knew what to feel about anything anymore. At least Mareth hadn't been hurt, thank God. He crossed himself. It was selfish to think this way when her mother was dead, he knew, but that's the way he felt. Besides, he had never even met Countess von Woller. He quickly piled his belongings into the suitcase and summoned the orderly, a sailor too old for sea duty who still remembered how to take orders. "When does the U-boat train leave for Kiel?"

"At 0200, Herr Kaleu."

"You can get me a berth on it, yes?"

"At once, Herr Kaleu."

Admiral Dönitz kept a special train that ran between the U-boat bases in France and the main base in Kiel, so Max didn't have to be at the mercy of the Reichsbahn, grown increasingly unreliable now that the Americans were bombing every major rail yard in the Reich. Mail, supplies, torpedoes, and spare parts for the submarines were carried to and from Germany aboard the shuttling U-boat trains, along with the men of the service. Max handed the suitcase over and asked the orderly to make certain it got on the U-boat train.

After polishing his medals in the bathroom with a damp washcloth and pocketing the soap for Mareth, Max made his way to the first-floor banquet room. The windows of the big room had just been replaced after the British blew them out in a nuisance raid a week ago; he could still smell the putty and paint. The tables had been positioned in a horseshoe, their starched white tablecloths hanging to the polished floor. Already his men had assembled and begun to make use of the bar.

Heinz, the torpedo chief petty officer, saw Max first. "Achtung!" he called. Immediately the men came to rigid attention, a few of them overbalancing, already unsteady from drink. Max smiled at his crew. They weren't such a bad lot. Clean-shaven now in their regular blue naval uniforms, they looked trim and shipshape—far better than they had looked seven hours ago when the boat had finally docked. The prewar sailors were especially trim in their short monkey jackets with double rows of brass buttons; such jackets hadn't been issued since the war broke out. Still, everyone's eyes were bruised from lack of sleep, faces white as chalk from being locked away in their narrow tube, only the bridge crew ever seeing the sun. To an outsider the men might appear feverish and stricken but to Max they looked good considering what they had endured. In any event, he was proud.

"As you were," he said.

Immediately the drinking resumed. Most would be puking in a few hours, but they had earned it. After their first patrol Max had drunk two bottles of brandy the first night back and passed out in the officers' club. Tonight he would spare himself because of the banquet and the train ride. A cigar was what he wanted most after five weeks without enough tobacco. Fortunately, the flotilla commander had sent a fresh tin over to him after they docked. Max pulled one from his pocket and lit it, the rich smoke filling his mouth. Damn it was good. Ferret was already sitting at the officers' table and Max joined him. Lehmann was mingling with the men. He'd probably have them all out the next morning collecting for Winter Relief.

Max gave Ferret a cigar. "A good patrol, Leutnant."

"Thank you, Herr Kaleu."

"Plans for your leave?"

"Nein, Herr Kaleu."

Ferret never said much, a blessing on the boat but awkward on land. Was he married? Max couldn't remember. "You will see your girlfriend soon, yes?"

Ferret shrugged. "I just go to the officers' rest house and have the women there, Herr Kaleu. No involvements."

"But the involvements make it more interesting."

Ferret nodded. "It's hard to get close to a girl when you know you're going to dic soon."

Max puffed on the cigar to steady his features. "Well now, Leutnant, you know we have an excellent chance of surviving until the war ends."

"Do we, sir?" Ferret pointed to the wall at their backs. "Like them, Herr Kaleu?"

Max turned around. The wall was lined with black-bordered portraits of the flotilla's captains who had died in action since the war began. There wasn't much space left. My God, Würdemann was dead? They had picked up a radio transmission from him not five days ago.

Max thought for a moment, puffing again on his cigar. Now he knew why Langsdorff had smoked them: they gave one a few moments to think. "Ferret," he said, trying to speak with conviction, "you know we have a good crew. We've made it through two patrols now. That's the hardest part, getting past the first two, you know that. From now on our experience will give us the edge we need to survive." He could hear the hollow ring in his own voice.

Ferret looked down into his beer. "I don't want to die, Herr Kaleu," he said quietly.

Was Ferret drunk? Max didn't know how sympathetic he ought to be. At the Marineschule Mürwik, it would have been a cuff around the ears and no more gloomy talk. But that was in 1936. Ferret had never even wanted to be a naval officer—he'd been a junior officer on the Norddeutscher Lloyd Line before the war, before he was "volunteered" into military service like the chief, like any merchant navy officer who could manage to hold a sextant. Max said, "I don't want to die either, Ferret, but we will if we don't keep our wits about us. That much I can guarantee you. I don't know what chance we have, but if we don't keep our heads up before the men, then we have no chance at all. They must have faith in their officers."

"Achtung!" someone shouted.

The flotilla commander. Thank God. Max sprang up and

came to attention. Eckhardt entered, also wearing knee-high cavalry boots, and made his way slowly to the front table, detouring to shake hands with the men. Smiling when he finally reached Max, he said, "A fine-looking crew, Brekendorf."

"Thank you, Herr Kapitän."

"At ease," Eckhardt called. "We're here to enjoy ourselves."

That brought a cheer from the men. Eckhardt grinned, teeth shining white beneath his bushy gray mustache. Everyone liked the flotilla commander, but more, they respected his nine war patrols and the one hundred twenty thousand tons of enemy shipping he'd sunk. His Knight's Cross had been personally awarded by the Führer himself, but Eckhardt wore the great honor lightly. Of all his accomplishments, it was the magnificent Kaiser Wilhelm mustache with which he claimed to be most satisfied. "The pride of the fleet," he'd once told Max with a laugh.

Now he motioned for Max to sit. Taking a seat himself, Eckhardt leaned in and lowered his voice: "I say, old man, the flotilla engineer assures me that you were damned lucky to make it back alive. Another half meter out of the water and the Brits would have opened you up."

Max shrugged. He'd been trying not to think about this very fact for nine days now. "I'd prefer to never see a British destroyer that close again, sir."

"I expect not, Brekendorf, I expect not. But you're back here in one piece and that's what counts. I've sent your report on to Admiral Dönitz and I know he'll be pleased with what you and your men have done."

Max puffed the cigar and blew out a cloud of thick gray smoke. "And helping the British sailors?"

Eckhardt held out his open hands. "Who can say what the admiral will think of that? You'll have a chance to ask him yourself."

"Sir?"

"You are to report to him in Berlin as soon as your leave is up.

The 'Lion' wants to see you in person." Dönitz had moved U-Boat
Command back to Berlin from France in February after his promotion by the Führer to commander in chief of the Kriegsmarine,
replacing Grand Admiral Raeder.

Max felt his stomach tense. A reprimand? Court-martial? "For
what, sir? Do you know?"

The French waiter placed a glass of wine before Eckhardt, and
he took a swallow, wiping his mustache and smacking his lips.
"Good, that."

"Herr Kapitän?"

He looked at Max. "Don't worry, Brekendorf—he's not going to
hang you from the yardarm. He's sending you and a few others
to operate off Florida. Think of it as a government-paid vacation
to America—a 'Strength Through Joy' cruise, yes?" Max laughed.
But America was something else altogether. Max couldn't keep a
smile from his face. No more of the damned North Atlantic. He'd
heard stories about how good the hunting was off the American
coast, how their shoreline was not blacked out. Ships silhouetted
against the lights made perfect targets. To be sent on such an assignment meant the High Command had tremendous faith in his
abilities. He said, "I am honored, Herr Kapitän."

"The admiral said he wanted a few young bucks, so naturally you came to mind. I'm certain you won't disappoint me,
Brekendorf."

"No, sir."

America. Many on the Naval War Staff had regarded the U.S.
Navy with contempt since Pearl Harbor. "They're inept," one of
the bureaucrats in the Torpedo Directorate had said to Max. "No
one could ever have surprised our fleet like that." Max had been
tempted to point out that Germany barely had a surface fleet left
to surprise. He did not think the Americans were so inept. He had
met U.S. Navy officers on his training cruise when *Emden* called
at the port of San Diego. Max and his crewkameraden were invited
aboard the aircraft carrier U.S.S. *Saratoga*; they watched *Saratoga*

launch and recover aircraft. The Amis didn't look inept that day. It would be a very long crossing. So much to think about.

Eckhardt put a hand on his shoulder. "Don't plan it out tonight, old boy; tonight is to enjoy." He signaled the headwaiter to begin serving before the sailors became too drunk to eat. Lehmann took his cue and shepherded the men to their seats. Eckhardt stood, Knight's Cross gleaming about his neck. The collar of his shirt almost obscured the shoelace he and most other recipients used to keep the heavy medal around their necks. He twirled the waxed ends of his mustache, then took his glass up from the table and raised it in the air. "To my comrades, the gallant crew of *U-114*." Everyone drank.

Lehmann stood, too. Max raised his eyebrows, hoping this wouldn't embarrass him. "To the Führer," Lehmann said.

Everyone got to their feet, lifted their glasses, and drank.

"Ein Reich," Lehmann shouted, "ein Volk, ein Führer!" Was he drunk already?

Eckhardt looked angry. Party slogans weren't to be repeated at naval gatherings. He put his hand on Lehmann's arm to quiet him. "Men of *U-114*, under your Kommandant, KapitänLeutnant Brekendorf, you are in the front line of our struggle against the Allies. All Germany speaks of the courage of her U-boat men. Everyone in the Fatherland follows your exploits with pride. For the achievements of your last patrol, for the courage with which you faced exceptional danger and persevered, the admiral commanding Unterseeboote West has directed me to award each of you the Iron Cross Second Class."

The crew applauded wildly.

"And now, men, to your victory dinner. All of you have earned it."

The appetizer was a dozen raw oysters for each man with real Spanish lemons for seasoning. Max forked the oysters down. Damn, they tasted good. And the lemons—he hadn't seen a lemon in years. He sucked the pulp out, even swallowed the seeds. No sooner had he finished than the waiter dropped another dozen oysters in front of him, then filled his glass with champagne. Easy, Max told himself, go easy.

"Will you go on leave tonight, Brekendorf?"

"I will, sir. To Berlin. My fiancée's mother was just killed in a bombing attack last week."

Eckhardt put his fork down. "I'm truly sorry to hear that, truly sorry. These damn terror bombers." He shook his head. "The Allies are so high and mighty about the Reich violating a few rules of war, but they've simply torn the rules up. They make war on our women and children—Goebbels is right for a change, they are murderers." He brought his fist down on the table. "My wife is from Hamburg. She lost both her sisters this summer, most of her cousins. The scene there . . . I can't even begin to fathom it."

Neither could Max. Two hundred thousand people had died in a single night in the inferno that followed a British raid on Hamburg at the end of July. The number simply could not be real. No one could fathom it. The climatic conditions had been perfect over the city that night for the bombers: warm and extremely dry. The Tommies attacked with seven hundred planes and their incendiaries created a firestorm, literally a tornado of flame that tore through the center of Hamburg with winds of better than two hundred kilometers per hour—sucking people into the cyclone, cremating them in the shelters, setting the asphalt afire. The Fire Protection Police could do nothing to stop it. And the next day, the Americans came over and bombed what little remained.

"Where is the Luftwaffe?" Eckhardt said. "I ask myself that every day. I ask Marinegruppenkommando West every day: 'Where is the Luftwaffe?' No one knows. If only the navy had some planes of its own, instead of that swine Göring having them all. You know he doesn't ever fly? He has his own train. Can you imagine? The commander of the air force won't get in an aeroplane. The damn

Tommies are everywhere in the air, the sky is full of them. They're sinking half our boats as we run out through the Bay of Biscay before we even get to the Atlantic. Half of them! I don't know how their air force is so strong and ours doesn't even seem to exist. And now their American cousins have joined in with gusto. The damn Amis." He shook his head again. "The Führer always says, 'There is more culture in one Beethoven symphony than in all of America.' And he's right, Brekendorf. The Führer is right. But a Beethoven symphony won't stop a bomber and the Americans aren't writing symphonies to drop on us. They're making bombers and bullets and bombs and ships, and they're damn good at it."

Max took a gulp of wine to hide his surprise. Half their boats were being sunk from the air in the Bay of Biscay? Eckhardt picked his fork back up and resumed eating. "Don't worry. We're tearing out that popgun you have now and putting in some real anti-aircraft firepower while you're on leave: two twin-mounted twenty-millimeters and one quadruple twenty-millimeter. Herr Tommy will have a bear by the ass if he comes after you."

More armament would be welcome but it would mean a change in tactics. Max would have to run out in broad daylight so they could see the British planes; crossing the bay surfaced at night would be too risky now. And what if more than one plane came at him? What if two or three came at once from different directions? He could submerge and creep out underwater. But he would have to proceed at just two knots. Even at two knots, he could keep moving underwater for no more than sixteen hours; after that he would need to come back up and run on the surface for six hours so the diesel engines could recharge the batteries. It would take a week to reach the Atlantic that way and Max knew he wouldn't have a week to spare. Every boat had to make for the front as quickly as possible to stop the Allied ships pouring men and supplies into Britain. Well, he would have his whole leave to consider all the options. For now there were more oysters and fresh boiled lobster with real Normandy butter, and fresh brown bread—not the green mold-covered lumps they'd been reduced to eating on the U-boat by the middle of their patrol.

The waiter brought real coffee and real cream once Max had demolished his lobster. There was cheese and fruit, fresh apples. Max felt bloated. He belched. The champagne went down so easily, like cool water on a hot day. Pray God they had a wheelbarrow on hand to get him to the train.

"A cigar?" Eckhardt said, opening a new tin.

"Thank you, sir."

He lit Max's cigar, then offered them around to the other officers. "A woman is only a woman," he said, "but a good cigar is a smoke. Rudyard Kipling."

Max grinned. Eckhardt must be drunk as well if he was quoting an Englishman. In front of Max, the relentless waiter placed a brandy snifter half-filled with amber liquid. As he raised his glass, Lehmann stood again. "Comrades! A song!"

The men banged their fists on the tables in approval.

"*We are sailing against England,*" Lehmann bellowed, starting them off:

> *Today we want to sing a song,*
> *We want to drink the cool wine,*
> *And clink the glasses together,*
> *Because we must, we must part.*

Soon everyone joined in, waving mugs and glasses as they sang, their pale faces now flushed and red.

> *Give me your hand, your white hand,*
> *Live well, my sweetheart,*
> *Live well, my sweetheart,*
> *Live well, live well.*
> *Because we sail, because we sail*
> *Because we sail against England, England.*

The songs and toasts went on for hours:

"To our cook, the best in the fleet!"

"To the brave men of the second watch!"

"To the joy girls of Lorient!"

"Three cheers for the Kommandant!"

"To the joy girls of the world!"

Finally Max stood to leave, bracing himself against the table. Around him, the room had gone blurry at the edges. At least he hadn't puked. Yet. "God bless you, sir," he said to Eckhardt. His salute was off-center and then he remembered that he wasn't supposed to salute without his cap on anyway. To hell with it. "Thank you most kindly for the new anti-aircraft guns, sir. A thousand thanks. Thank you." Turning to his men, he shouted, "Auf wiedersehen, comrades! May you always have a hand's breadth of water under your keel!"

Those who heard him answered with drunken salutes. A few already lay facedown in their plates. Others went on singing, pausing between verses to drink from magnums of French champagne. One young sailor stood to salute Max properly but toppled over, clipping a table, sending a half dozen dishes to the floor with a tremendous crash.

When he woke at dawn on the U-boat train, Max felt like there were coal miners at work in his head. His body swayed to the rhythm of the train and the motion put him back to sleep. An hour outside Kiel, Josef, the steward, woke him with a jug of hot water and clean towels. Max shaved and wiped himself down. Josef had also pressed his uniform and even spit-shined his riding boots. "Can't have you front-line officers looking like a lot of Italians, Herr Kaleu," he explained. Josef didn't think very highly of their former Italian allies. Of course, Josef had spent his first ten years at sea in the old Imperial Navy, where every brass bolt sparkled, every deckboard gleamed, and every crease was razor sharp. But Max had a certain fondness for the Italians. He'd been aboard an Italian submarine once. It was much larger than a German boat, and

even had a small officers' lounge with a bar. God bless them—that
was the way to go to war. But the Italians were no longer fighting
alongside the Reich. The Allied invasion had broken them; they
surrendered three weeks ago and were now reportedly preparing
to switch sides.

Max smiled and shook Josef's hand. "Thank you for making
me presentable."

Josef snapped off a parade-ground salute. "Good luck and good
hunting, Herr Kaleu."

Max tried to phone his father from the station in Kiel but no
one answered at the shop, which was strange. The Berlin train left
in four hours. Max felt guilty for not seeing his father when he was
so close, but Mareth needed him now.

Hanging up the phone, he gathered his greatcoat around him.
Even in October, the afternoon air had a bitter edge to it. Soon
there would be snow, winter would come again to the North Atlantic: unrelenting cold, freezing spray driven so hard by the wind
that it split your lips. No dry clothes. The Florida assignment was
a miracle, almost a vacation, as far as the weather was concerned.
If they drowned off Miami, at least the water would be warm.

Around him the rail station was totally shattered, windows
blown out, ceiling beams lying across the floor. No one even used
the old main station, its roof now completely gone. Passengers simply congregated on the stone platforms. Max bought a copy of *Signal* from one of the news vendors and flipped through the pictures
of German soldiers and sailors in action. There was a color section
about an artillery unit in the East. The men looked so strong with
chiseled jaws and fierce eyes. There had been reverses on the Eastern Front, terrible reverses, everyone knew it. And Stalingrad was
more than a reverse—it was a calamity, the worst defeat in German military history. But maybe they could still win the war. Max's
father had told him at the beginning of the war that victory was
most uncertain, and once they attacked the Soviet Union it was
impossible. After the Amis came in, he had written Max and said

that his cousin Heinrich was coming to visit very soon. Heinrich had immigrated to America before the First War.

Max knew of America's strength. He had seen it. And as each weary day of the war passed into the next, everyone could see with their own eyes that it wasn't German bombers dropping incendiaries on Washington, or New York, or Los Angeles; it was American planes bombing Berlin, the Ruhr, and whatever remained of Hamburg. But maybe they could still win the war if they just kept pushing. It would take longer than anyone had thought, but still — in another year or two they might be able to win, or at least fight the Allies to a stalemate. He just had to keep going, stay alive until then. Could he stay alive for two more years? He tried to put the question out of his mind because the answer was plain: he could not. Living two more months would be an accomplishment.

He tried his father's shop again a half hour before the train left for Berlin. Still no answer. Six in the evening was his busiest time of day, with people stopping by for groceries on their way home from work. Buhl, the party Kreisleiter, would know where Johann was — Buhl was forever keeping tabs on everyone, writing things down in a little tan notebook embossed with a swastika. Max took another fifty-pfennig coin out of his pocket and dropped it into the phone. The operator put him through directly.

"Buhl?"

"Ja?"

"Maximilian Brekendorf."

"Max, our brave warrior of the deep. A pleasure to hear from you. You are well?"

There was static over the line, and Max had to raise his voice. "Very well, thank you, Buhl. I'm trying to get through to my father but can't find him. I thought perhaps you—"

"I did everything I could for him, Max, you know that I would."

Max felt a chill race through his body. "What are you talking about?"

"You don't know?"

"Know what, dammit?" Max yelled so loud that two old women on a nearby bench startled and stared up at him in fear.

"Your father was arrested by the Gestapo."

He should have never helped those English swine in their lifeboat. "For what, Buhl? Surely not for anything I—"

"For sleeping with the Polish girl."

Max came up short. "Buhl, the Gestapo arrested my father for sleeping with his maid?"

Again the static. It crackled over the line and then cleared: ". . . against the racial laws of the Third Reich."

Max bellowed into the phone with his best quarterdeck voice: "Are you out of your mind! My father is a decorated veteran of the Prussian army! He's been arrested for screwing his maid?"

The two old women got up from the bench and shuffled away as fast as they could on worn house slippers stuffed with newspaper.

"I did everything I could, Max, everything. I had warned your father about this. Someone reported him—a customer perhaps, I don't know. The Gestapo office in Kiel received an anonymous call. I even wrote a letter on his behalf to the Gauleiter detailing your gallant service to the Reich. There was nothing more I could do. But it's only a four-month sentence and he's been in for one month already. Three more and he'll be out."

Had the world gone mad? His father obviously bribed half the party officials in the district to overlook his activities on the black market, but disobeying the racial policies of the Nazi Party was apparently unforgivable. Something you couldn't bribe your way out of even with an entire storeroom of Persil. "May I see him, Buhl?"

"I—I don't know. Perhaps I can arrange it. They're holding him at the city jail in Kiel. Max, I'll try to see if I can arrange it. For old times' sake. Can you phone me in three days?"

"Yes, yes, of course. I'm on my way to Berlin now. And Buhl, thank you—I'm sure you did what you could."

"Heil Hitler!" Buhl shouted.

"Heil Hitler," Max said quietly.

He replaced the phone on its hook.

Max stood on the platform in stunned silence until it was time to board the train, a sloppy mixture of banged-up Reichsbahn rail cars and cars confiscated from France and Belgium, with the occasional Dutch car sandwiched in. WHEELS MUST TURN FOR VICTORY had been chalked in prominent letters on the side of each rail car. That was a great slogan. What was it supposed to mean? Don't be late for the train?

The Reichsbahn didn't offer private compartments with hot water and clean linen like the U-boat train. He couldn't even find a seat. Soldiers bound for the Eastern Front were jammed aboard, their backpacks piled everywhere, cigarette smoke hanging in a dense cloud above their heads. A few civilian families sat scattered among them, their children staring wide-eyed at the soldiers. Most of the windows had been blown out by bomb concussions and replaced by sheets of wood that blocked all ventilation and most of the light. The cars were hot and stuffy and stank of unwashed men.

He stepped out onto the small platform between two cars and set his suitcase down, dropping his tired body down beside it and leaning back against the metal wall. An army captain had done the same and the two of them sat facing each other. It would be a cold and drafty ride out here but at least they would have room to stretch out. "Guten Abend, Herr Hauptmann," Max said to the captain.

The man nodded. "U-boat?"

"Ja," Max said. The captain wore the Eastern Front Medal, awarded to those who had taken part in the initial Russian campaign. Soldiers called it the Frozen Meat Order. He also had a silver wound badge on his left tunic pocket, just below his Iron Cross First Class.

Max pulled a pack of Murattis from inside his coat. U-boat men could still get them but no one else. "Zigarette?" he asked, extending the pack.

The captain took one, sniffed it. "Danke."

"Ost Front?"

"Ja."

"How is it out there with the Russians?"

"Cold," the captain said. "Damned cold. And you, in the ocean?"

Max shrugged. "Cold."

The train got under way and as it rumbled through the dark country they talked about the war—about the Russians in their endless numbers, inexhaustible and relentless, ready to keep dying forever, and the Americans, who the captain had heard were poor soldiers but could supply anything and everything the Allies needed, including the six-wheel-drive Studebaker trucks of which the Soviets seemed to have so many. And Jeeps, which the captain especially liked. His unit had five of them, captured from the Soviets. A coat of feld grau paint and the small vehicles were ready to play their part in the struggle against Bolshevism. Max had to laugh. What next? Capture Benny Goodman and force him to play for the U-boat men in Lorient? The captain produced a bottle of schnapps and offered it up. Max smiled, accepted the bottle. He took a long pull and the two of them fell silent for a time, passing the schnapps back and forth as the train rolled on toward Berlin.

The captain gazed at the passing countryside as if watching for a Russian ambush. Without shifting his eyes, he asked if Max had ever been to America in his travels with the navy. Yes, during his training cruise. And was it as big and powerful as everyone said? No, it was much bigger, much more powerful. And where had Max gone? Where in America? California first, for twelve days. He saw the sights, met some pretty American girls, even took a tour of Hollywood. They laughed at that. Hollywood, the captain said, smiling. Hollywood. As if such a place could even exist on the same planet as them. What had the Führer said: "What is America but millionaires, beauty queens, stupid records, and Hollywood?" Max shook his head. All of Germany could fit into the state of California with room to spare, and there were forty-seven other states besides. Americans had no culture, they worshipped money like a god, but they had energy, and no one ever need tell an American what to do. They just did it, unlike the Germans, who were always waiting for a word from the man in charge. And what about New York? Yes, Max had been to New York. And what had he done there? Gone to the top of the Empire State Building and drunk a Coca-Cola. The captain laughed again. He looked down at the bottle in his hands, took a sip.

"And to think," he said, "we declared war on America."

Max leaned his head back against the metal wall of the platform. "Just as we did on the Soviet Union, Kamerad."

They talked through the night. Max didn't introduce himself. Names weren't important. The captain knew what it meant to order men into battle, to see them die, to live with that responsibility. He had seen friends die and die horribly—one set afire in his Kübelwagen, stumbling out to stagger a few steps in a ball of flame before he dropped; another run down by a Soviet tank, ground into the mud by the forty-ton monster.

Toward 0200 the train came to a halt in a wheatfield ten kilometers outside Berlin. Max had fallen asleep but was wakened by the jarring of the cars banging against their couplings as the air brakes exhaled. A roar sounded as the engineers blew the steam pressure from the engine. The train and all aboard her fell silent. Max heard the droning of the aeroplanes. He got up, unlatched the heavy metal exit door, and leaned out. Others did the same up and down the line of cars, their faces visible in the bright moonlight.

On the horizon, the searchlights ringing Berlin sent up white columns that swept the night sky. Sometimes one of them would catch a bomber in its cone and hold it there, illuminating the aeroplane so one of the German night fighters could home in and attack—or, if the bomber was at low altitude, so the anti-aircraft batteries could take it under fire. Max could hear the staccato beat

of the flak artillery pouring shells into the darkness. The projec-
tiles were fired in specific patterns set to explode at a designated
height and spew metal fragments at the British planes, which had
to fly in strict formation on their bomb runs, practically wingtip to
wingtip, to minimize their time over the target. The flak reached a
crescendo—every barrel in every battery firing—as each formation
swept down on its run. But more prominent was the heavier sound
of the falling bombs destroying Berlin. Fires burned all over the
city, lighting the horizon with an orange glow.

The RAF had a method for this, the murder of a city, a method
so terrible it was worthy only of Gog and Magog. They began with
blockbuster high-explosive bombs to blow the roofs off buildings
and blow the windows in, exposing wooden beams and interiors,
giving fire endless pathways along which to spread and providing
through-drafts of air to rush it along. Then came the small incendiary bombs, falling in their hundreds of thousands into buildings;
and then the fires began. Fires medieval in their terror; fires that
could not be extinguished because they were composed of burning phosphorus; liquid fire that flowed in burning streams down
gutters and into the basements where women and children took
shelter; fire so terrible, fire so merciless, there was nothing to do
but run from it with all the strength God had given you; fire spreading so fast that running with all your strength was never enough.
Fire so hot it set the very asphalt in the street ablaze and if your
feet became stuck in the liquid tar, you burned like a torch, your
screams unheard over the roaring of the firestorm. This was the
hell brought down on Hamburg by the Tommies, and now they
were bringing it to Berlin. And Mareth was somewhere in that
godforsaken pyre, its columns of poisonous yellow smoke twisting
slowly into the heavens.

Max dug his fists into his eyes. He couldn't look anymore. Was
she safe in the flak tower? Safer than the Führer bunker, they said,
but was this one of her nights on duty? His whole body was tense
and trembling. He pulled his hands from his face and watched

again. Damn the English and the Americans, damn them all to bloody hell. This terror bombing—just dumping bombs blindly on women and children, on a defenseless city. It was a crime. It was murder—against the laws of war, the laws of humanity, against the Hague Convention. After the war the Allies would be made to pay for this. He should have shot the English sailors in that lifeboat, payback for what was being done to Berlin. Wave after wave of aircraft came over the city loosing their bombs, the muffled explosions shaking the earth until the entire horizon seemed to be burning. If a British pilot parachuted from his bomber and came down close by the train, Max would take out his pistol and shoot the man on the spot like a dog. It happened all the time now, all across Germany: mobs of enraged citizens beating downed pilots to death before the Feldgendarmerie could arrive.

Max stood and watched the firestorm, the night still and soft once the aeroplanes had finally gone. Could anyone in Berlin still be alive? It seemed impossible. Occasional towers of fire exploded into the night air where a building had collapsed, or a delayed-fuse bomb had gone off. And Mareth was there. He pictured her unconscious, half buried by fallen beams. He pictured her gasping, screaming as fire consumed her. Finally he looked away, pulled himself back into the train, sat down again with the wall at his back. His army friend hadn't moved a muscle through the whole attack. He just stared, his eyes passing through Max to someplace else.

Without focusing his vacant stare the captain asked, "You have someone there, in Berlin?"

"My fiancée," Max said, trying to say more, but he couldn't even speak for long moments. Finally he said, "I went through a raid myself, but not like this . . . there are more planes now. I don't know how we'll ever . . ." He stopped. Hands still shaking, he drew out a cigarette and offered one to the captain. "Have you seen this? What the Allies do to us?"

The captain accepted the cigarette, lit it, took a long inhale. "My family was killed in a raid in Berlin five months ago." He finished his cigarette before speaking again. "They send a thousand planes from England—from England! And Dr. Goebbels told us the English were through. They send a thousand planes over Berlin whenever they like, while the few bombers we have left are trying to stop the Russians. My wife and children were killed by the incendiaries, burned to death, in the capital of the Thousand Year Reich."

Max met the captain's stare until he finished talking and then Max looked away. That kind of talk could put a man in the hands of the security police, but the captain could have cared less. What was left for the Gestapo to do to him? Arrest his dead family? Kill him? He would die soon enough in Russia anyway. Max closed his eyes. Mareth could just as easily be burning as they spoke.

Toward dawn, the train began to creep forward again, the screeching and banging of the cars loud in the morning stillness. Most of the passengers had slept after the raid. The few who didn't sat quietly, shocked into silence by the fury of the attack. They came awake now and so did Max, who had been passing in and out of a restless sleep from pure exhaustion. He smoked, the tobacco bitter in his dry mouth. In the daylight he saw the notice that the rail car to his right was a no-smoking car. Yet another rule made laughable by the war.

No one had bothered to close the metal exit doors. The trains were short on crews, every available man having been drafted into the army, so railwaymen long retired had been pressed back into service. Closing and latching the exit doors was too much for them, or maybe they just didn't care. Who could blame them? Max rose and stood in the open doorway, watching Berlin as they approached. A smoky red haze hung over the city, eerie in the breaking dawn. As they crept through the outskirts of town, buildings shot up flames in the distance—toward the center of the city, where Mareth lived and worked.

A year ago when they were training in the Baltic, a young sailor on Max's boat got his arm caught in a mooring wire as they were coming in to dock. A sudden jerk caused the wire to tighten and it cut the sailor's hand clean off. The lad stared in disbelief at the bleeding stump for the longest time, shocked into numbness. Now Max felt much the same looking out over Berlin as the train rolled in. Ahead, a Reichsbahn worker signaled with a lantern, directed them onto a new track, heading them north, skirting the city, making for one of the rail stations on the far eastern edge of Berlin.

In the residential neighborhoods they passed through, most of the houses seemed to have suffered little damage except for missing windows that had been replaced by cardboard or wood. Maybe one in five had burned, blackened timbers and smashed brickwork lying abandoned in a scorched yard, often with a sturdy brick chimney standing sentinel over the devastation. As they creaked along an overpass, Max looked down. A bright red post office van lay on its side. The rear doors had burst open and letters lay scattered on the street, mixed in with the glass and bricks from a toppled home on the corner. A postal worker picked through the debris, gathering the letters, occasionally glancing at passersby working their way to their offices in the middle of all this chaos.

In the distance, a thick tower of smoke rose from the city center, which had been the target of the raid. The bombs had shattered the water mains; fires would burn for days. Berlin's Fire Protection Police could rarely access water after severe raids, excepting small amounts they could pump from the Havel or the Spree or the Landwehrkanal. All they could really do was dynamite buildings to make firebreaks and try to keep the flames from spreading.

The army captain gave Max a salute when they finally got off the train an hour later. "Good luck and good hunting, Kamerad."

Max saluted in return. "Keep your eyes open and your ears stiff, old fox." They would never meet again on this earth.

Max checked his suitcase at the station, went outside, and flagged down a member of the Orpo, the uniformed police, distinctive in his shako. "How do I get to the Zoo Tower?"

The policeman saluted him. "The 122 tram will take you

there, sir, but it is not recommended. Not recommended at all, sir. They were hit hard last night. The Fire Protection Police are still calling for help—we've sent every spare man from this precinct, and two of the Luftwaffe's heavy rescue units are being brought in as well. Todt Organization crews, army men, too. It's hell down there. Headquarters says it was one of the worst."

"Doesn't matter," Max said. "I have to go."

The Orpo man pointed to a tram coming down the middle of the street. "That's the one, sir. It will take you as close as you can get."

He was surprised to see a female conductor collecting fares aboard the tram. Were they this short of men? Or were these women just pushing their way into these jobs to get out of working in a munitions factory? That was the new decree: any woman not already working was to be sent off to make ammunition. The tram waddled down the tracks, stopping every other block to take on passengers, the driver slowing where debris was strewn across the pavement, letting the wheels of the streetcar gently push the flotsam aside. Max wanted to seize the tram at gunpoint and make them go faster.

Closer to the center, the roar of flames became audible. It sounded like seawater rushing into the ballast tanks of the U-boat. Thin strips of aluminum lay everywhere: in the street, on the sidewalks, scattered over roofs and lawns, caught in the branches of trees, hanging from the few phone lines that remained. RAF bombers dropped the strips to make false images on German radar and confound the Luftwaffe controllers who vectored in German night fighters.

Rounding a corner, the driver slammed on the tram's brakes, throwing up a shower of white sparks. The shells of burnt-out buses and trams blocked the way ahead. Several buildings had collapsed into mounds of rubble in the street. Policemen armed with military rifles stood atop the smoking piles to guard them from looters, who now faced summary execution. A typewriter from one of the toppled office buildings sat upright on the sidewalk as if waiting for a secretary. A row of bodies, mainly women and children, lay on the opposite sidewalk.

The tram wasn't going any farther. Max jumped off and began to run, guided by the smoke that spiraled into the sky up ahead. If he could find the Unter den Linden, he could follow it to the Tiergarten.

The devastation mounted as he ran, forcing him to dodge around heaps of wreckage where offices and homes had stood — splintered boards, burnt black, broken brick and stone, a bicycle bent and crumpled on the curb. Survivors poked through the wreckage, cloths knotted around their noses and mouths to protect them from the smoky air. One woman held a lamp she'd found, tears pouring down her face. Max stopped for a moment to catch his breath, gulping in air and coughing from the smoke. Two men dug frantically in the remains of a building. Looking for what, he wondered. Their families? Friends? Money? A squad of soldiers appeared from a side street and their sergeant approached him, went rigid as a lamppost and snapped a salute. "Orders, Herr Kapitän?"

Max shook his head. "I'm not in command here. Ask him." He pointed vaguely to a policeman across the road. No army sergeant would like taking orders from a policeman, but what did it matter? The two of them conferred briefly, without exchanging salutes, and the sergeant quickly set his men to digging.

Max moved on, walking now, picking his way over the rubble. Everything had been flattened here. Only the odd section of wall remained standing, whether as a testament to skillful masonry or the vagaries of a bomb blast. The heavy smell of charred wood was strong in his nose, and beneath it he could make out the rotten-egg stench of natural gas.

He walked and climbed for another hour, twice having to produce his identity papers for the police, before reaching the Unter den Linden, its broad boulevards littered with overturned automobiles and buses. A Mercedes-Benz had been hurled upside down against the snapped trunk of a tree. Trams lay crossways on their tracks, windows blown out, advertising posters hanging in colorful strips that fluttered in the breeze. Occasional explosions sounded in the distance as delayed-fuse bombs went off—designed to take out the rescuers and onlookers who gathered after a raid.

As he made his way to the Tiergarten, Max recognized the side street he'd used to reach von Woller's office in January, and he could see from the corner that the building had been obliterated, reduced to a smoking pile of stone. A group of Luftwaffe men from one of the special rescue battalions pushed past him and Max followed them down the street. As they approached the place where the building had been, he realized that the hatless man waving his arms and shouting on the sidewalk was Herr von Woller.

"Hurry!" he yelled at the Luftwaffe crew. "Hurry! For God's sake, there are people trapped down there." He was pointing feverishly at the ruins of his collapsed office. "Right here, come quickly, quickly, I insist!"

Max seized him by the shoulders. "Is she in there?"

Von Woller stared at him dumbly for a moment. Max wasn't easy to recognize with his face covered in soot, uniform torn, boots cut in a dozen places by shards of glass. "The U-boat captain. Brekendorf."

"Is she in there?" Max was shaking the old Nazi.

Von Woller nodded. "Yes. Under the rubble. The basement was fortified six months ago at the foreign minister's insistence: steel, concrete, wooden beams. We received everything we needed, everything because of his priority order. They may have survived the hit. No incendiaries, just high explosives. But we have to get them out—they might be hurt, or running out of air."

Max eased his grip on von Woller's thin shoulders. He looked over at the mass of debris.

"We're trying to dig a tunnel to the shelter. That's why I sent for the Luftwaffe rescue men—they're trained for this."

Already the air force crew had relieved the office workers and

passersby who'd begun the digging. Several of the men pulled long
boards from the rubble and set about cutting them into tunnel
supports. Others started in with pickaxes to uncover larger beams.
Four men had long iron poles to pry the beams up so the supports
could be placed underneath. In this way a small tunnel was gradually opened to the building's first floor. Max fell in line and hauled
out chunks of wood and stone being passed back from the face
of the tunnel. He could hear the tunnel leader, flat on his belly,
calling out to the people trapped below. "Hold on, we're coming,
we're coming."

For half an hour, then an hour, he called into the silence. No
response. But finally a small voice answered. It said, "Vasser."

"What?" The tunnel leader quieted the men at his back and
listened.

"The water is up to our chests!"

The tunnel leader looked around at his crew. A main must
have been shattered and begun pouring water into the bomb shelter through a crack. It happened—happened often. People survived an air raid but rubble blocked the shelter door and everyone
inside drowned. Not in the ocean, not in the lake at Wannsee, but
in the basement of their office building, in the middle of Berlin.
"Hold fast," the tunnel leader said, turning back around, shouting
to whoever could hear him. "Just hold fast."

They had to dig. "Raus! Raus!" The men fell in, moving twice
as fast now, the blows of pickaxe blades ringing out against stone.
They worked in a rotation, taking turns at the face of the tunnel,
the lead man attacking the debris with all his strength until he was
exhausted and the next man stepped in. Max waited in the queue,
seizing the rubble as it was passed back down the line, flinging it
between his legs, his hands bloody and torn, cut to ribbons by the
chipped bricks and splintered boards.

"Mareth!" he shouted, moving into the tunnel face for his
turn, hefting the leader's small rock axe. "Mareth! Mareth!" Nothing. He swung the axe as hard as he could in the tight space,

shattering a mass of bricks, part of an interior wall still covered with taped notices, one of them reading: FIGHT THE COAL THIEF!—an exhortation to save electricity. He hammered the wall again and again, the men behind raking out the shards of brick Max knocked loose. How fast was the water rising?

"Mareth!" he shouted again. "Mareth!"

"Max? Max!"

It was her. He swung with all his strength, breaking through the wall, pushing away some broken boards. Another blow and this time the axe hit wood—thin wood—and he felt the blade go clean through.

"Hurry, Max—the water's coming in faster!"

He pried the axe free, pushed bricks between his legs to get more room to swing, then with a fury buried the axe into the wood again.

"Max! Hurry, please Max, hurry!"

The rock axe split the wood panel—opened a small hole—he wedged it larger, then swung again and then again with the power of desperation. An entire section of the door gave way and Max almost fell into the cellar. A hand came through—he grabbed it. Mareth. He yanked her out. She sobbed and clung to his tattered shirt. "Go!" he shouted, pushing her back.

There were four more women after her, young secretaries in the building. Max pulled them out one at a time, soaked and shivering, and they clawed past him into the daylight. As he pulled the last one of them out, his thighs were seized by such stabbing cramps that the Luftwaffe men had to drag him out of the tunnel and knead his legs before he could stand.

Wrapped in a thick blanket, Mareth leaned against her father, hugging him tightly, but she kissed von Woller and broke his embrace as Max limped over. They kissed, her lips so cold. Folding her in his arms, he rocked her gently as she shivered and wept against his chest. Through her crying and shivering she looked up and said, "Well, Max, here's another nice mess you've gotten me into." And he laughed with her, tears now streaming down his face as well.

Daniel, von Woller's chauffeur, touched Max on the shoulder. "Herr KapitänLeutnant, I have the automobile three blocks from here. Shall I carry her?"

Max shook his head. He slid an arm under Mareth's legs and lifted her like a child. Her clothes were entirely soaked through and still dripping cold water. Daniel led them away with von Woller following. Through careful maneuvering he'd managed to get the big Horch convertible within three short blocks before his path was barred by a pair of fallen lampposts sheared from their pedestals.

Herr von Woller held the car door and Max slid onto the large backseat with Mareth on his lap. Her arms were still tight around his neck but her tears had slowed. She wiped her cheeks, pulled back to look at him, then reached out with one of her small hands and wiped the grime from his nose. "Thank you," she whispered.

Von Woller sat in front with Daniel as they wound through the devastated streets, detouring left and right until they finally reached the apartment building on the Tiergartenstrasse. Before the war it had been one of Berlin's finest addresses, with porters and maids in regimental strength, a starched doorman saluting at the curb, and three men in the garage to wash and park cars. It was different now. Most of the servants were gone, the men drafted into the army and killed on the Russian Front, the women drafted into munitions factories. Several guest workers from Belgium had replaced a handful of the prewar staff, and a few elderly house-maids from the old days were still about, Herr von Woller's among them. But the doorman was gone—blown to the next world by a mortar shell at Stalingrad. His wife had taken over his duties, opening and closing the big doors—filled now with wood since the glass had been blown out—and reporting on the tenants to the Gestapo, just like her husband before her.

Max surveyed the outside of the building. Most of the windows were gone, though in the von Woller flat the missing panes had been replaced with new ones crafted from broken glass and glued together with industrial adhesive, a process fast becoming a cottage industry in Berlin. From Mareth's letter he knew the back of the structure had collapsed, leaving only the front apartments habitable. He carried her to the fifth floor—the elevators had snapped their cables when the building was hit—and laid her on a couch in the drawing room. But after a moment she sat up on her own strength and patted the cushion beside her. Max dropped onto the couch, turned to her—and they simply looked at each other. There was nothing to say. This was something else the war did to you. Loved ones killed, drowned, blown to bits, burned to death: after a time, what could you say?

Herr von Woller went across the hall and returned with an old and feeble army doctor, who gave Mareth a shot of morphine—a hard item to come by in wartime Berlin. She hardly needed the morphine, she thought, but took it anyway, then snuggled herself in Max's arms and nodded off. He could feel her stiff body going soft as she relaxed into sleep. Her warmth and slow breathing against him made him feel safe and warm and his muscles unknotted. His head fell slowly back on the couch cushions and he drifted away into his first calm sleep in months.

———

Herr von Woller left them alone that week and Max barely left Mareth's room, barely left the bed. They made love constantly, desperately, as if it were laughable to think that either of them might live to see 1944. The old man made no objection—what could he say? That they were ruining her reputation? That it was scandalous? With thousands of Germans dying every day, scandal had become quaint, like a postcard of the Kaiser. Von Woller could rarely be found in the flat anyway—he spent long hours in a temporary office at the Foreign Ministry. Each time Max saw him he looked even more pale and more drawn. Everything was going poorly. General Dittmar admitted in one of his nightly Wehrmacht communiqués that the situation on the Eastern Front was deteriorating, that the Volk should prepare themselves for very heavy losses. As if the losses hadn't been heavy enough already. The government could prohibit public expressions of mourning—it was an honor for a son to give his life for the Führer, so mourning was unpatriotic—but the casualty lists spoke for themselves.

Max shut the war out for those few precious days with Mareth. With the drapes drawn, the gramophone playing, it was almost possible to pretend there was no war at all. The maid was a good cook and they dined well. Given his rank, von Woller had access to food and delicacies that had vanished years ago for everyone else. So they drank his whiskey and coffee and sherry and Max smoked his cigars. Von Woller even had some Coca-Cola from before the war, which Mareth drank, and something Max had rarely seen before: a television set. Max had been to public television parlors in Kiel and Berlin, but private sets were rare—only a few thousand could be found in all of Germany, reserved for the highest-ranking members of the government and the party, though it seemed a pointless curiosity. It broadcast only a few hours a day and the only time Max and Mareth turned it on, they discovered a program of buxom fräuleins exercising on a rooftop garden. They couldn't stop laughing for the longest time and finally turned it off and went back to bed.

Because the city outside was in ruins, they didn't go outside. They didn't talk about Mareth's dead mother or Max's father sitting in the jailhouse in Kiel. Their agreement to ignore reality was unspoken, a mutual fantasy, and it bound them together more strongly than ever. Their vacation ended when the British aeroplanes returned.

German radar stations in Holland picked up the RAF bomber stream and Deutschlandsender began their running commentary on its direction. Max listened to the big Philco in the living room: "Enemy bomber formations at a high altitude now reported to be approaching Denmark in an easterly direction. Target unknown. Luftwaffe High Command predicts Berlin. Achtung! Achtung! Enemy bomber formations approaching Denmark in an easterly direction."

Forty-five minutes later the early-warning siren went off, signaling the possibility of an air raid, cautioning everyone to take cover. By 2300 the British target had been established clearly enough and the earsplitting warble of the "immediate danger" siren pierced the darkness: "Achtung! Achtung! For Berlin. Danger fifteen! For Berlin. Danger fifteen!" Fifteen meant a raid of maximum severity. Already Max could hear the flak artillery on the far western outskirts of the city opening up. Herr von Woller came into the drawing room when the distant flak guns began to fire, holding an army helmet in one hand. "We must go across the street to the shelter."

Mareth shook her head. She sat on the couch with her legs crossed. "I refuse to go anywhere."

Von Woller tugged at her sleeve and pleaded. "Child, we must go! We must!"

Mareth kept shaking her head. "I will not climb into my own grave again. If they want to blow me up, they can blow me up here."

Max took her arm and tried to smile. "Mareth, we'll all go together. Come."

"No."

"We will all be killed!" von Woller shouted. Beads of sweat stood out on his creased forehead, his hands trembled as if he had palsy.

"So go, Father," Mareth snapped. "Go then. I'm staying here."

"I will go!" he shouted.

Mareth rose and pulled Max with her into the narrow archway leading to the kitchen. She sat on the floor and yanked him down. It was the safest place in the flat, but it would hardly protect them if the building suffered a direct hit. Von Woller was frantic. "I insist!" he screamed. "I demand that you both come to the shelter with me at once!"

Mareth looked up and stared at him, her face rigid but tears dripping down her cheeks. Max, holding her, felt her muscles trembling. Or perhaps it was his muscles trembling. He used to think of Mareth as fearless—then again, he had once thought himself fearless. Von Woller sat down beside them. He looked up when the first bombs hit somewhere out to the west, then put on his army helmet.

The explosions moved closer: five kilometers, then two, then one, the low roar of the detonations mixing with the bark of hundreds of anti-aircraft guns. The Kinderflak were hard at work, the faint patter of shrapnel from the flak shells raining down on the building.

Herr von Woller lit a cigar, stoic now, while Mareth shook violently. The bombs marched toward them. She squeezed Max's arm until he thought she might rip it off. Her nails dug into his skin. The explosions sounded like someone throwing sticks of dynamite down a well. Plaster dust sifted onto them from the ceiling as the building rocked in the concussion waves of the exploding bombs. No one said a word. Max felt his knees getting weak, just as they did on the U-boat when he waited for the depth charges to explode.

It lasted fifteen minutes. As the bombs came closer the building shook as if in an earthquake. No more plaster dust falling but plaster chunks now, bombs going off all over the neighborhood, the drone of the aeroplanes audible above the falling shrapnel when the anti-aircraft guns fell into a quick lull. The gradual easing of the banging guns told Max the raid was ending. Von Woller stood and brushed himself off. Max stood, too, unsteadily. He tried to help Mareth up, but she collapsed back to the floor and he carried her to bed. She smiled when he laid her head on the pillow, but tears still slipped down the sides of her face as the long steady wail of the all-clear siren began to sound.

He kissed her softly and left the room. Von Woller was on the drawing room couch, vacantly puffing his cigar. "This cannot go on," Max told him. "You must get her out of Berlin. You must use your influence to move her somewhere safe. Anywhere but here. If she stays, she'll lose her mind unless she is killed first."

Von Woller nodded. "I know."

"You're a golden pheasant, Herr von Woller. You can get to the Führer himself! You must use your influence now. Pull whatever strings you have to pull."

The old man looked up. "I've already pulled the best strings I know."

"I don't believe you."

"You should. My old friend Heinrich Schrempf has agreed to take her in. He lives in Mexico. We came into the Foreign Ministry at the same time and were in the Turkish Legation together years ago, but he left for private enterprise and made his fortune arranging for the importation of Mexican oil. He's sitting out the war with his family in Mexico. I condemned him for it. I thought he was being a coward and I wrote him personally when the war began and told him so. But Heinrich is a gentleman. He has been gracious enough to forgive me. He has a compound in Mexico City with twenty servants—a hacienda, he calls it." Von Woller drew on his cigar, creating a cloud of smoke around him.

"Mexico is against us now," Max said. They had joined the Allied cause the summer before last after the Americans had put a pistol to their heads and suggested that joining was a good idea. "How will she get into the country?"

"That is not a concern," said von Woller. "She may go there whenever she wishes. I have obtained a Finnish passport for her."

"How . . . ?"

"How? I am a diplomat, Herr KapitänLeutnant. Could you have done it? I think not. I have been received at the very highest levels in Finland, the very highest levels, and I have influential friends there willing to help me."

Max was impressed. Finland was fighting alongside Germany on the Eastern Front, but none of the Allied powers except Russia had declared war on the Finns, who were widely admired for their independent resistance to the Soviets in the Winter War of '39 and '40. "Then she will go to Mexico at once."

"I fear that is impossible, young man."

Max stared at him. "I don't believe you. You must get her the bloody hell out of here. She cannot go on this way."

Von Woller shook his head. He rolled the cigar around on his fingers, examining its flaking ash. "She refuses to leave."

"That's ridiculous."

"Of course, I agree, Herr KapitänLeutnant, but perhaps you should tell her so. She refuses to leave because of you. She's afraid that if she leaves Germany, the two of you will never see each other again."

Now it was Max who shook his head in dismay. "If she's dead, Herr von Woller, then I'm quite certain we won't see each other again."

"Indeed."

"You will ensure she stays in Mexico for the remainder of the war, yes? You will promise this to me on your honor as a German?"

"Yes. If you can prevail upon her to go, Herr KapitänLeutnant, I will do everything in my power to ensure she remains in Mexico City until Final Victory."

They looked at each other in silence for a long moment while outside Berlin burned in the night like a vast beacon fire. "Yes," Max said, "until Final Victory."

"Then I shall persuade her to go. I will insist. And I will insist she do so immediately. She will fly, yes?" It was hard to imagine such a thing.

Von Woller nodded. "Swedish Air to Lisbon. It's perfectly safe, I assure you. They fly in bright orange planes, in specially marked air corridors negotiated for neutral airliners before the war. I negotiated them myself. If you're able to convince her, she can leave in two days."

Two days, then he would be left to face the war alone. And Mareth was right: they would never see each other again. Knowing he could come home to her after a war patrol was all that had kept him going. And now it was over. She would be safe in Mexico. And she would survive. And if she survived, then a small part of him might survive as well. At least he could try to think of it that way.

Von Woller rose, crossed the room, and touched Max on the shoulder. "Thank you," he said. "She's all I have left, all that remains of my family. After the war, I hope the two of you will give me many grandchildren."

"I would like that very much, Herr von Woller. Thank you. But I think it most unlikely." They fell quiet, staring for a moment at the bookshelf, the polished leather bindings gleaming in the dim light.

"And what will become of you then, Maximilian?" von Woller said, turning to Max.

Max looked directly back at the old man, whose Nazi friends had worked so hard to bring the war about. "I will be killed," he said.

CHAPTER TWELVE

THE BAY OF BISCAY
ABOARD *U-114*
TWO MONTHS LATER
DECEMBER 1943
1400 HOURS

THE PLANE CAME OUT OF THE SUN, FIRING ON THEM BEFORE THE
forward lookout ever saw it, machine guns already rattling by the
time he yelled, "Fliegeralarm! Aircraft bearing green zero nine
zero!"

"Emergency full ahead!" Max shouted. Behind him the U-
boat's anti-aircraft guns returned fire with a loud burping sound.
Belts of ammunition streamed through the open hatch, replacing
the brass cartridges that fell in a bright river to the deck. Beneath
him, the U-boat jumped in the water as the engineers cut in the
second diesel and the electric motors.

The plane was a four-engine Liberator from RAF Coastal
Command coming at them abeam. Its machine guns raked the
water ahead of them, and then bullets tore into the boat itself,
walking down the foredeck, splintering the deckboards. Max
dropped below the combing of the armored bridge, jerking one of
the openmouthed lookouts with him, and tried to meld his body

to the heavy bridge armor. Bullets whined around him, some ricocheting off the armor plate.

"Medic! Medic!"

One of the gunners had been hit. With a roar like an express train, the Liberator came over them, black canisters falling from its open belly.

"Emergency right rudder!" Max yelled into the control tower. The depth charges struck the water fifty meters aft and blew towers of spray into the air, some of the foam washing over the bridge. When the shock wave hit, the force heeled the boat over. Max had to grab the bridge railing to keep from being swept over the side.

"Where is he?" Max asked, hoping someone would know.

"Coming over again, Herr Kaleu!"

"Fire, dammit, fire!"

Again the staccato beat of the anti-aircraft guns, but only six barrels this time. A brace of dual twenty-millimeters didn't fire, the gunner down and bleeding on the deck. Machine-gun bullets from the Liberator churned up the water around them, leaving white trails in the sea.

"Got him! Got the swine!" one of the remaining gunners yelled. Smoke streamed from one of the aeroplane's engines, then it was over the boat again—dropping another pattern. The aircraft banked away as the charges exploded in U-114's wake, the shock wave jolting the boat.

Max felt his whole body shaking. He clung to the periscope housing and gulped for air. Since they sailed from France just two days ago, his body had been betraying him at odd moments, spasms of fear seizing his muscles. He was skittish as a cat. Just getting used to it again, he tried to tell himself, like breaking in an overhauled engine. "Aircraft position!" he called out finally.

"Disappeared over the horizon making southeast, Herr Kaleu."

"Get Gerhard below," Max ordered. "Easy now."

Two of the gunners climbed down slowly into the control room, taking their wounded man with them, leaving their petty officer behind to discharge the ammo belts and drop them below.

"Quickly," Max said.

The petty officer dropped through, followed by the lookouts.

"Prepare to dive!" Max called down after them.

The boat had held up well so far, but he still didn't trust the French dockworkers who had repaired her. Too many skippers sailing from Lorient had found false welds that burst when they submerged and allowed water to flood in—and Max knew only of the lucky ones who'd managed to make an emergency surface and struggle back to base. Others had just gone to the bottom.

"Reporting all outboard vents closed, Herr Kaleu," the control room petty officer shouted up through the hatch. "E-motors engaged, diesels disengaged and secured."

The crew understood why Max was being so cautious. He scanned the sky once more to make sure a plane wouldn't pounce on them as they submerged. "Flood!" he shouted, then dropped through the main hatch into the conning tower. He dogged the hatch shut against its rubber gasket and then they were under, buried in a silence that seemed deafening after the roar of the plane and chattering guns topside. Max slid down the ladder to the control room.

"Both slow ahead. Chief, take us to thirty meters and trim the boat."

The bow angled forward, then the boat leveled off as the chief juggled the amount of water in the trim tanks fore and aft to put the boat on an even keel—something of an art since even one man could throw the trim off by moving suddenly. For this reason, the sailors were forbidden to leave their stations without permission when the boat was submerged.

"Thirty meters, Herr Kaleu. All stations reporting watertight integrity."

So far, so good.

"Forty meters."

"Jawohl, Herr Kaleu."

They went slowly to one hundred thirty meters, their operational depth, dropping ten meters at a time, until Max was satisfied the flotilla engineers had missed nothing in their inspection of the boat. "Chief, take us up to sixty meters." Max examined the plotting chart in the control room. "Helmsman, come port ten degrees and steady up on two four zero degrees. Half ahead, both engines."

He was so damned slow underwater. In an emergency, he could go to eight knots, but that speed drained the batteries in four hours, forcing him to surface and recharge whether it was safe or not.

He ran at depth for two hours; when he surfaced again it was dark and they encountered no more planes. By dawn of the next day, they were in the Atlantic proper, the U-boat taking the long swells in a gentle rise and fall, like a rocking horse moving in slow motion. Max could feel how sluggish she was, packed to the gills with extra diesel oil for the long voyage to America, cans of the filthy stuff stacked in the passageway so the entire boat reeked of diesel. The smell brought him back to the sinking of *Meteor*, his body covered in oil and Dieter burning to death in a pool of blazing fuel. Max realized that he didn't think about Dieter much anymore.

He checked his speed again on the dial in the control room. Seven knots—their most economical speed on the surface—running on one engine at seven bloody knots, slow as a damned tugboat. A clipper under sail could go twice as fast. They switched engines with each turn of the watch to even out the wear. It was going to be a monotonous crossing, poking over to Florida at seven knots. They were supposed to arrive in three weeks, maybe four if the weather kicked up, but now Max would have to pause for a mid-ocean rendezvous with a homebound boat to take Gerhard off so he could be treated back on shore. That would cost them a day, maybe two or three. Few boats in the force still carried a doctor on board. Too many boats sunk. Too many doctors killed.

Max looked up through the open hatchway. "Bridge!"

"Bridge, aye-aye." Ferret came to the hatch and looked down at him.

"Watch for aircraft."

"Jawohl, Herr Kaleu."

Max picked his way through the narrow corridor to his small bunk and drew the green curtain behind him. Two months, maybe three lay ahead, confined in this steel tube. Already the boat was heavy with the stink of men on top of the putrid diesel oil. And his damned hands were shaking again. He was like an old woman now. All he wanted was to get off the damned boat and go home, but nothing was the same at home either—Mareth had gone to Mexico, and his father was still locked in the jail at Kiel for another month.

Buhl had arranged for Max to see the old man, and Max knew it hadn't been easy. He'd given Buhl a bottle of schnapps to thank him. The two of them took an early train from Bad Wilhelm, not bothering to buy tickets. Buhl's Nazi Party uniform was enough. People cleared out of his way when they saw it, some smiling obsequiously, others just scowling.

Ordinarily a robust man, barrel-chested with the strength of an artillery horse, Johann appeared pale, his blood seemingly drained from him. Max tried not to betray his surprise when the old man shuffled into the visiting room, twenty pounds lighter and moving uncertainly in his shapeless prison uniform. The jailer had the decency to leave them alone. They embraced. Max said, "Papa, you are well, yes?"

"As well as anyone in this shithole."

They talked about life back in Bad Wilhelm, about the store, which Albert, the deliveryman, had taken over for the time being—"I'll be lucky if there's any beer left when I get back,"

Max's father said—and finally about the arrest. "Gestapo sent that fool Cajus to come get me. Can you imagine? Cajus? He would have died twenty different times on the Western Front if I hadn't been there to save his fat ass, and now they send him to arrest me. Cajus. I don't even think he had bullets in his pistol. I should have let the French shoot him. He couldn't even put the cuffs on right. I had to show him how."

Max smiled at his father's telling. "Cigarette, Papa?"

"Yes, but you smoke too much, Maximilian, I've been meaning to tell you. But I guess you earn it, trapped in that damned U-boat of yours."

Max shrugged. He slid the pack across the table. "Keep it," he said. "Maybe you can barter them for better food."

His father nodded, looking down at the package.

"And the girl, Papa?"

The old man didn't answer. He went on gazing down at the table and a silence developed.

"Papa?"

A single tear fell from his eye and landed on the paper wrapper of the cigarette pack. Max tried to remember if he'd ever seen his father cry.

"Papa." He reached out and touched his father's shoulder. "Tell me."

His father brushed Max's hand away and began to weep openly.

"Papa, what happened to her?"

"It doesn't matter."

Max stared. "Were you in love with her?"

His father shook his head. "Yes, maybe. I don't know. I don't even know what that means anymore—at my age, in the middle of this war. It doesn't mean anything." He sat up ramrod straight, bracing his shoulders back like the Prussian sergeant major he had once been, and looked up at Max. "It doesn't mean anything."

Max didn't know what to say. He took hold of his father's rough hands and said nothing—Johann's grip was forceful and he didn't let go for a long time. Finally they nodded at each other and Max stood, turned to leave. At the door he turned to salute but his father had buried his head in his arms, his body trembling with quiet sobs. On the train home, Buhl told Max that the Polish girl had been shot.

Back in Lorient, Max spent his days supervising the extensive repairs on *U-114* and returned each night to his small room at the Hotel Beau Séjour. Armed naval sentries now stood guard outside the hotel and patrolled the inside halls as well, so Max didn't have to worry about French assassins. Every evening, after luxuriating in the bath, he drank himself off to sleep—not a good idea, he knew, but the only way he could ever sleep. Hopefully he wouldn't become like the three town drunks in Bad Wilhelm. All three had served under Johann at Verdun and he often gave them money. "Why do you do that? They just use it to buy more schnapps," Max had asked his father. "Because they saw such terrible things in the war they cannot face life sober." Locked away in his room at the Beau Séjour with its sparse personal effects for company—his sextant, his books, his rosary and photo of Mareth—he could relax after a bottle or two of wine. After a bottle or two of wine, the room felt like the last safe place in the world.

Only that was an illusion. Max had been back in Lorient for just ten days when the whistle of a falling bomb sent him sprawling to the ground, his body reacting from instinct before his mind had registered the threat. He'd been walking from the hotel to the giant concrete bunkers, their ceilings seven meters thick, that protected the U-boats from Allied bombers. This bomb hit no more than five hundred meters away, its shock wave washing over him, knocking his breath out and almost bursting his eardrums.

He saw a slit trench ten meters away, scrambled up, ran for it, rolled in just as the next bomb exploded. Behind him the Beau Séjour disintegrated, its wooden splinters cutting down the sentries and anyone else close by. There had been no air raid siren, no warning whatsoever, but this was hardly remarkable anymore. The RAF's high-altitude Mosquito bombers were made entirely of wood and German radar often failed to pick them up. Max watched from the trench as fire spread through the Beau Séjour's collapsing frame. If the Tommies had come two minutes earlier, he would have been killed.

This seemed, however, like a trifling stroke of luck since he was sailing off to his death, while his father, racked by bitterness and heartbreak, waited for word of Max's death to arrive at the jail in Kiel. How had all this happened? Barely four years ago, Max had been a promising young naval officer with a beautiful fiancée and the world at his feet. He put a cloth over his nose to block the stench of the diesel fuel, closed his eyes, and finally dropped off to sleep. It seemed no more than five minutes before Bekker was shaking him gently awake. "Herr Kaleu?"

Bekker was the oldest man on the boat, a paper-pushing personnel clerk down to his wire-rimmed glasses. He still had the habit of slicking his hair down with lime-scented brilliantine, as men had before the First War. Max smelled the lime before his eyes were open. "Ja?"

"Message to captain, Herr Kaleu: 'Convoy in sight U-480.' "

Max came bolt upright at the news. "How long did I sleep?"

"Eight hours, Herr Kaleu. First watch officer reports U-Boat Command is forming a battle line and instructed me to wake the Kommandant."

When a U-boat sighted a large convoy, it kept in contact with the convoy at a distance but refrained from attacking while U-Boat Command summoned other boats to form a wolfpack that could attack in force. Dönitz had developed this tactic in the twenties after his run as a decorated U-boat skipper in the First War. "Anything for us?"

"Nein, Herr Kaleu."

Please God that it stayed that way. Loss rates in convoy battles could be as high as four boats in five—so many had gone to the bottom in the last months that Dönitz had briefly pulled all U-boats from the North Atlantic. Now he'd sent them back although nothing had changed. British escort ships were becoming more numerous and better equipped every week, with more effective radar, more highly trained crews, and now continuous air support from Allied planes based in Greenland and Iceland. The swine flew so high you didn't even know they were there until an escort charged out of nowhere, guided onto you by the patrol plane. Everything had changed since 1939, when U-boat skippers owned the seas. Prien sank a British battleship at anchor in Scapa Flow in the first week of the war, for God's sake, but now he was just as dead as all the other old bulls who turned down Dönitz's offer to become flotilla commanders or staff officers. Going after a convoy at this point was close to suicide. Max felt shame admitting this to himself, but he wanted to be left alone to complete his mission to America.

He pulled on his white cap and went to the radio station. Bekker worked from a small niche on the starboard side and he handed Max copies of the messages being sent to other boats from U-Boat Command, ordering them to the scene. Max took the typed messages and plotted them on his tracking chart. The convoy was four hundred kilometers away. Please God, let that be far enough. Maybe the little wooden marker that represented his boat on the huge green baize plotting table in Berlin would be overlooked. Maybe even now someone at U-Boat Command was saying, "What about U-Max?" and the operations officer was replying that they were too far away, or on a special mission.

Taking up the dividers every half hour, he marked their progress on the chart, trying to will the boat to go faster. He began to relax when they were five hundred kilometers from the convoy. For the first time that day, he climbed to the bridge and smoked, leaning against the stern anti-aircraft gun, watching their wake disappear into the twilight, the December wind strong and cold, tugging at his hat and bridge coat. Whitecaps were everywhere, raised by the wind, and waves slapped against the boat. The view seemed peaceful to his eyes—the gray-green waves, the clean blue of the sky, the ozone smell of the air, the sun fading from yellow to orange as it dropped down toward the horizon—but Max didn't relax. He knew this was an ocean at war. Lehmann had the watch. He'd been looking on all day as Max marked off their distance from the convoy. Had he seen that Max was afraid? Had he been afraid himself? Not even the most ardent National Socialist could be immune to the effects of so many depth charge attacks—not even one like Lehmann, who had attended one of the Adolf Hitler schools designed to groom young men for future leadership in the party and the nation. Whatever he thought, Lehmann had said nothing to Max about the convoy. None of the officers had. Everyone wanted to make Florida, to be done with the Brits and winter in the North Atlantic, where clothes froze to your body on the bridge, where you could never get warm, and where the constant rolling of the boat left you listless and constipated, your belly full of rotten food. When Max descended into the boat for the evening meal, he noticed a certain lightness among the men, and he knew they had all been praying along with him not to be summoned to the convoy attack. They understood the casualty rates as well as he did, and Bekker kept them informed of the four-digit coded messages he copied and deciphered for Max to read: "Message for captain, signal just received, 'Liberator. Attacked. Sinking. U-604'"; "Message for captain, signal just received, 'Attacked by aircraft. Sinking. U-89'"; "Message for captain, signal just received, 'Attacked by destroyers. Sinking. U-844.'"

The fare wasn't so bad yet, this early in the voyage: the bread wasn't green, the butter hadn't gone rancid, the vegetables and meat were still fresh. Tonight they had potato pancakes, applesauce, roast pork with beans, and cake to finish it off, but Max's appetite was weak; it had been weak since they left Lorient.

Actually, he hadn't had an appetite for several months—he'd lost ten pounds off his thin frame since the end of their last patrol. He sat at the head of the small fold-down table that served as the officers' mess and forced the meal down anyway. The men were watching, and word that the captain was too tense to eat would spread quickly through the boat. He tried to keep his face impassive, wondering as he plowed through the pork whether his poise would ever return—and whether, more immediately, he might puke.

While the food still had a decent taste, the utensils were already greasy. No freshwater could be spared for washing dishes on the U-boat, so the plates and dinnerware were washed in seawater with a special saltwater soap that didn't work very well. Max wiped his fork with a napkin as Uwe, the officers' steward, set a piece of cake in front of him. He took a bite and willed himself to smile. "Better than any cake I've had at home," he said.

The other officers nodded politely. Max sensed they were relieved, but the meal had still been a quiet one, like every meal since they returned to the boat. They had all lost their starch. Had the events of their last patrol not been enough to do it, the others had returned from leave to find Lorient in ruins, the dockyard leveled, the Beau Séjour reduced to a charred foundation. Of course the staff officers maintained their empty bravado—"All they did was kill some cows and burn up a few trucks that we took from the French anyway"—but everyone knew the Luftwaffe didn't have the strength to assault Allied naval bases, while the Allied air forces acted with impunity. It wasn't fair to the navy, having to deal with additional enemies from the sky. Every officer in the U-boat force kept saying to whoever would listen, "Where is the Luftwaffe? Can they do something, anything, to help?" Why did the Führer not get rid of Göring? Was it that the Führer didn't know? Were these facts being kept from him?

RAF Bomber Command and the U.S. Eighth Air Force were paving over rural Britain with new runways and covering those new runways with the countless bombers churned out by factories in the United States. *America produces a new bomber every five minutes!* the Allies claimed in the propaganda leaflets dropped all over the coast of Brittany. Max believed it. He read through the leaflets whenever he sat on the can, and propaganda or no, he was prepared to accept every grim boast they made—the evidence plain to see in the wreckage throughout Berlin. But he was glad to have the leaflets all the same, since their constant supply ensured the UBootwaffe would never run out of loo paper again.

Despite this windfall, the hotel's destruction brought a marked decline in living conditions at Lorient. New quarters for the crew were buried in the shelters underneath the giant concrete U-boat pens—sunless rooms full of stale air, dampness, and the reek of petroleum. They barely offered any more comfort than the boat itself, and the men were often stuck in the barracks at night. They could go into what remained of the town of Lorient only in armed groups; the French Resistance grew stronger each week and killed German sailors with regularity.

———

For the next three weeks the boat plowed through the Atlantic swells, taking green water over the bridge more than once. One night it got so rough that Max submerged for six hours to let the crew sleep and have a meal. Trying to eat with any kind of sea running was impossible; most of the food ended up on the deck. Not that this represented any great loss; by the time they were halfway to America, the smell of petroleum had permeated even the canned food.

But there was something new in the air those three weeks later when Carls woke Max one morning—a heavy warmth that carried with it a breath of seaweed. Florida. The temperature of the water around them had risen perceptibly during the night; Max could even feel it when he touched the steel plating to which his bunk was fastened. "Where does the navigator have us?" he asked Carls.

"Seventy-five kilometers east of Miami, Herr Kaleu."

"Very good. Very good indeed. The crew?"

"Glad to be warm, Herr Kaleu. But nervous as whores in church. Never been up against the Amis before and they wonder what it'll be like."

"So do I, Carls."

"Can't say as I know, sir, but I did meet some American sailors in Shanghai ten, maybe fifteen years ago. We was on a training cruise aboard old *Emden,* Herr Kaleu, and ended up by accident in a bar with some American sailormen who were three sheets to the wind."

"Perhaps you made a wrong turn on your way to divine service."

"I believe that was it, sir. After a time I got to speaking in a way with one of the Amis. I don't speak any of the English, but he had a little German and proceeds to tell me that he didn't think much of our Kaiser Wilhelm, and I'm not one for letting any man say a word against the All Highest, so I punched him as hard as I could."

"What happened?"

"Nothing, Herr Kaleu. Absolutely nothing. I had knocked him one on the jaw as hard as I could, but he didn't move a muscle. So I raised my hands up in surrender and said, 'Beer?' and he didn't say nothing, but I get us two Tsingtaos and give him one."

"And?"

"He drunk his beer in one swig and broke the bottle over my head, Herr Kaleu."

"Most Americans are more polite than that."

"Do you think they'll be as rough as the Tommies?"

Max put on his white captain's hat. "Nothing could be as bad as the Tommies."

"I'll remind the Kommandant of that when the Americans begin dropping depth charges on our heads."

Max shook his head and smiled. Thank providence for Carls—it would have been hard for him to manage without the big man's deft handling of the crew. Senior noncommissioned officers were worth a pocket full of gold, and the Kriegsmarine didn't have very many left. "We're rare birds," Carls had told Max on their last patrol. "Almost extinct. They'll have us in the Berlin Zoo soon."

"Most of the birds in the zoo have been eaten."

"Even more reason to put us somewhere safe, Herr Kaleu."

He got off his bunk and went up to the bridge with Carls following behind.

"Dolphins, Herr Kaleu." Max looked to the starboard and saw them racing the boat, arching clear of the water with their little sidelong grins. They seemed to be having a good time.

"Look to your sectors!" Carls yelled at the lookouts. "This isn't a pleasure cruise."

Already the sun was hot on Max's neck, the bridge armor warm to the touch. Was it safe to venture closer to shore in broad daylight, or should he submerge and wait for nightfall? Maybe twenty-five more kilometers. "Stay alert," he told the men. "Stay alert."

Around them the green water was marked by brown patches of seaweed floating on the surface. Max swept his binoculars in a slow arc to stern, then to starboard, then past the bow to port, but saw nothing. Everything was quiet except for the rumbling of the diesels as they turned over at full speed.

Max dropped below for thirty minutes to look over the charts with the navigator. When he returned to the bridge seagulls flocked in the sky above them. He peered at the birds through his binoculars as they soared up, drifted down, wheeled in tight turns, chasing one another in slow circles, diving occasionally for fish. In the far distance one of the gulls glided, wings fixed like a plane.

"Alarm!"

"Go, go," Carls yelled to the lookouts, almost tossing them below. Max landed on top of him in the control room, water already hissing into the ballast tanks. Above them, in the conning tower, the helmsman shut and dogged the hatch.

"Hatch secure!" he shouted.

"All hands forward!" Max bellowed. "Get us down, Chief, down!" Red lights blinked up and down the passageway as the crew stampeded for the bow, piling onto one another, the boat now pitching forward at an angle of fifty degrees.

The first depth charges detonated far in the distance. Max listened intently as he clung to the periscope housing, trying to gauge their position relative to the explosions. "Right full rudder! All ahead full. Go to one hundred meters." No use holding the same course with the wake pointing at them like an arrow.

Another explosion, also well off the mark, but the sound unnerving all the same. The control room crew stared upward as if they would be able to see the depth charges falling.

"Look to your stations," Max snapped. Like a damned bunch of conscripts gawking at the Eiffel Tower. He resisted the impulse to look up himself. How did the Americans attack? Were they dogged like the British, or did they get impatient and go charging off in every direction? Certainly they couldn't drop depth charges with any accuracy.

The next two explosions were even farther away and Max knew they were out of danger. Carls looked at him and Max put his palms out as if to say, I told you so. They smiled at each other. These Americans didn't have the Tommies' experience—soon enough they would. "Both engines ahead one-quarter," Max ordered. "Resume base course."

They sank the first freighter at dusk, three torpedoes hitting her broadside. She was gone in less than ten minutes. Two lifeboats were launched as the ship went down, and Max was happy to see it. At least he hadn't killed everyone aboard—save for a handful in the engine room. A twenty-five-kilometer sail to land was all the survivors would have to manage, then a hot dinner and tall tales. If ships had to be sunk, he supposed sinking them inshore, where most of the crew could get away, was the humane way to do it—if launching torpedoes at a vessel with no warning could be called humane.

The second freighter, two hours later, was more difficult. She saw the U-boat in the moonlight just before Max launched his torpedoes, and the ship's auxiliary gun crew took him under fire with an antique deck gun from the First War. Shells came over the boat with the high whistle he remembered from battles aboard *Meteor* and *Graf Spee*.

"Dammit!" He pounded the bridge railing with his fist. "All ahead full. Lehmann, shoot, shoot, shoot!"

Another shell from the freighter. This one plowed into the sea about two hundred meters abaft the starboard beam. At least they were no more accurate than the American patrol plane had been.

"Herr Kaleu," Bekker called from below, "she's sending a distress signal."

Suddenly the freighter's searchlight fell directly on the bridge, illuminating them for any aircraft or destroyer to see. Max threw a hand up to shield his eyes.

"Tube one, fire!" Lehmann yelled. "Tube two, fire! Tube three, fire! Tube four, fire!"

"Helmsman! Right full rudder," Max ordered, shouting through the open hatch to the helmsman just below. "Emergency full ahead."

Another whoosh overhead, followed by another explosion in the sea as a shell hit the water, closer this time. They were finding the range, even with their old gun that belonged in a museum.

"Thirty seconds," Lehmann called as the U-boat turned away, propellers roiling the green water as the diesels breathed a throaty rumble, blowing exhaust across the bridge.

"Twenty seconds!"

Max fixed his binoculars on the ship, seeing nothing, blinded by the searchlight.

"Ten seconds!" Lehmann shouted. "Five, four, three, two, one."

Nothing. The first torpedo had missed and still they were fixed in the searchlight's glare as the ship's gunners fired another shell. Max wanted to submerge but it would take too long. He kept going hard starboard, bringing the boat stern to so she would show her smallest silhouette.

"Number two missed," Lehmann shouted above the growling diesels.

Number three did not.

It struck the freighter square in the stern and ignited with a terrible blast that threw the sailors manning the deck gun into the air. Max breathed a grateful sigh of relief and watched the ship begin to list. Boats dropped over the side and men did the same, too panicked even to climb down the rope ladders. A high-pitched whine pierced the night like a long banshee wail as the engineers blew the steam remaining in the boilers. The searchlight went out as the ship lost power, and by the time Max's eyes readjusted fully to the darkness there was nothing left to see: the freighter had vanished beneath the waves.

The distress call was sure to bring American warships to the scene, so Max decided to take the U-boat a hundred kilometers out, to lie there on the bottom for a day until the search for him had died down.

His men welcomed the respite when they finally submerged; they always seemed exhausted after an attack, and certainly Max was exhausted himself. Leaving only essential crew in the control room, he dismissed both watches and soon the sailors were sleeping everywhere—in bunks, beside the spare torpedoes, in the galley, one beneath the chart table—all of them slack-jawed from fatigue. Max hadn't heard snoring so intense since his cadet days aboard the sailing ships, where they'd all slept together in hammocks on the mess deck.

At 2100 he surfaced to recharge his batteries and ran south through the night, maintaining a distance of one hundred kilometers from land, until he reached a spot that seemed right for picking up Caribbean-bound traffic. Then he submerged to wait for morning; he could see nothing in the dark and did not want to be surprised at dawn, when patrolling planes or ships were hardest to see.

While the crew ate their lunch of blood sausage, canned brown bread, and fruit juice, Max worked over the chart table in the crowded control room to fix his position as best he could. When they surfaced again, he and the navigator would use their sextants to take a sun sight. A glance at the almanac told him that sunrise would be at 0618. Twenty minutes, then. That gave him time for some lunch of his own, though he had no stomach for blood sausage in this heat. Powdered eggs would've been better but the U-boat always stayed on German War Time—Berlin time—during combat operations, and that made it the lunch hour, even though Max and his crew lay on the seabed a hundred kilometers off Miami with twenty minutes to sunrise.

When Max sat down at the officers' table, he found Lehmann up to his old tricks again, providing the National Socialist perspective on the latest war news. Bekker took down the late-night Wehrmacht communiqué whenever he could and passed it along to the officers. Lehmann usually tried to intercept it so he could put a good face on the latest grim reports from Russia. Now he was saying, "Of course, the Russians are taking fearful casualties and our retrograde movement is only meant to straighten out our lines."

Max listened without comment. He was a sailor, not a soldier, but he doubted that a retrograde movement was good, especially since it was the only type of movement the Wehrmacht had been making since the Battle of Kursk in July—an immense struggle that had gone on for days. In Lorient the flotilla commander had told him that at one point, over three thousand tanks had engaged, firing into enemy tanks at point-blank range. The news from Russia was an endless source of discouragement. All through last year and the first half of this one, Max had gone on praying that the Führer still had some trick up his sleeve, a secret plan that would turn the tide on the Eastern Front, a mighty blow he was holding back until the time was right to strike. But Hitler had nothing. Maybe Lehmann had the right idea; perhaps the war news needed a little dressing up, not that intercepting the communiqué before the men saw it did much good. Ferret tuned in the BBC for news reports every hour when he didn't have the watch. He put it on the speaker for everyone to hear and usually left it on, so the men could listen to jazz and American big band music—all strictly verboten in Germany. Lehmann protested, of course, reminding him that listening to the BBC was a capital offense in the Third Reich, but Max doubted any of them would live long enough to be shot by the Gestapo. The British newsmen, in any case, did not describe the Wehrmacht retreat as a "retrograde movement," and never speculated that the German army was simply attempting to straighten its lines.

Max looked at his watch: 0630. He pushed the plate of sausage away. What he really wanted was a cigarette, but for that they would need to surface.

Entering the control room, he straddled the small seat of the sky periscope. Like all boats of its class, *U-114* had two periscopes. The sky periscope was used to reconnoiter the sea and air before surfacing, while the attack scope in the conning tower above was fitted with special lenses to register angles and range.

"Periscope depth," Max ordered.

Muttering to his planesmen, the chief brought the boat up. "Sixteen meters, Herr Kaleu. Scope clear."

Peering through the lens, Max slowly turned the right handle, manipulating a small mirror that allowed him to look upward of seventy degrees above the horizon. His left hand operated the control that moved the scope up and down to compensate for the action of the waves and motion of the boat. Because it was heated to prevent its delicate lenses from frosting, the periscope was warm against Max's body, like Mareth sleeping against him in bed. He used the foot pedals to rotate the scope through the compass. Nothing but the empty Atlantic. The sea was covered by gray mist, a fine rain falling. Then he saw it in the last ten degrees of his circle.

"Down scope!"

Who knew how alert their lookouts might be? It seemed impossible to Max that a periscope would ever be spotted in the water, but Dönitz had personally assured him that it happened.

"Action stations!" he shouted. "All tubes stand by!"

Lunch was forgotten as the sailors bolted for their posts, dishes breaking as they fell to the deck. Red lights blinked but the men needed no prodding. Everyone knew they could go home as soon as their torpedoes were expended. In ninety seconds the boat was quiet again, all stations manned. Max took up the P.A. microphone. "Achtung! We have sighted a large enemy ship. I can't make her out in the mist but she looks to be a freighter of fifteen thousand tons. The ship is coming directly over us, so we will execute a submerged attack. Stand by." He climbed into the conning tower and took up the handles of the attack scope, then called down to the chief. "Up scope."

Below him the men were silent but alert. He could feel their tension as he put his eyes to the attack periscope's rubber sockets, like looking into a cine camera. There she was. "Range, four thousand meters. Angle on the bow green one five zero.

"All ahead two-thirds."

Had to keep his speed up and not lose her in the mist. In the dim light it was difficult to identify the type of ship, but it must be a freighter—no other ship would be steaming on this route. Unfortunately, she was not a tanker. Tankers were the biggest prizes of all because they took longer to build than other ships and were in short supply to the Allies.

"Down scope."

"Escorts, Herr Kaleu?" Lehmann asked.

So, our National Socialist hero was worried about depth charges. Max shook his head. "Just a fat freighter sailing along by herself," he said, and the news went through the boat faster than the crab lice the men all suffered from. Apparently this really was the perfect hunting ground—the Americans weren't nearly so cautious as the British. But why should they be? They had more ships than any nation in the world.

"Tubes standing by, Herr Kaleu," Carls said.

Max smiled to himself. This would be no more difficult than hitting practice convoys in the Baltic. Those days of endless drills seemed very far away now. He looked down into the control room. "Ferret, firing data in?"

"Jawohl, Herr Kaleu."

Max nodded and looked down at the control room crew, their eyes fixed on him. "Stand by then. Up scope."

The chief pushed his controls and the scope rose again. The rain was falling more heavily now, and at first Max couldn't see the ship at all. He cursed under his breath, but then she was there again, a shadow in the fog. But damn it all to hell, the visibility was almost zero. He could barely make his calculations, but he had to take the risk and fire now or lose his prey. "Angle on the bow green one five zero. Range three thousand meters. Set depth at four meters. Stand by, stand by . . . Tube one, fire! Tube two, fire! Tube three, fire! Tube four, fire!"

Ferret had the stopwatch out. Forty-five seconds on the first one.

"Down scope. Helmsman, right full rudder, steady up on two eight zero. All ahead full."

"Thirty seconds."

Max dropped down into the control room, folded his arms, and stared at the deck.

"Fifteen seconds."

The boat was swinging to starboard, turning away from the target.

"Ten," Ferret began to chant, eyes fixed on the stopwatch, "nine, eight, seven, six, five, four, three, two, one!"

Silence. Then the roar of an explosion carried through the water. His sailors cheered. Carls even thumped Max on the back. Another explosion, then another. Good shooting. The chief even said it: "Good shooting, Herr Kaleu."

Deep-throated cheers now, deafening in the U-boat's cramped space—whistles, hands clapping, men stomping their feet. "Beck's! Beck's! Beck's!" they chanted. There were several cases of it on hand for just such an occasion. A fist punched Max's shoulder. He turned to see Lehmann grinning at him. Max threw him a salute.

"Form a line and everyone can take a look," Max called as the cheering died down. He straddled the seat of the smaller sky periscope in the control room. "Up scope." He caught the periscope as it moved up and peered through the eyepiece. Raindrops and spray splashed against the lens. Damn but it was hard to see. Then he made her out, listing sharply now, just a few boats manned. Some of the boats on the low side had been destroyed by the torpedo blast. On the high side, opposite the list, none of them had launched because the ship had heeled over too fast. She was going quickly, too, tipping heavily to port and down by the bow. People crowded the few lifeboats that had made it into the water—far too many people.

A slow chill spread through Max's body as he watched them struggle in the falling rain. Pulling his eyes away from the scope, he wiped them with the back of his hand and then looked into the eyepiece again. A throng gathered on the ship's deck, bodies rushing up from below, some clinging to the stanchions now. Braver or more desperate souls leapt into the sea as the slant of the deck increased. People in bright orange lifejackets spread out like a terrible stain from the side of the stricken vessel. The chill flooded him completely as he realized what he'd done.

He had sunk a passenger ship.

Lehmann touched Max on the shoulder and Max stood back, mouth hanging open in shock. His crew had stopped buzzing and fallen dead silent, aware from his expression that something was amiss. Lehmann looked through the periscope briefly and then stepped back. "We cannot help them," he said. "Strictly verboten."

Max ignored him, staring through the eyepiece again. In the water, women clutched children to keep them from drifting away. The three lifeboats that had been launched were packed to capacity.

"We cannot help them!" Lehmann repeated, almost shouting, his voice shrill in the cramped control room.

"Back to your posts!" Carls ordered the men, and even the officers obeyed.

Max continued to stare. How many were there? Two hundred? The steamer was on her beam ends now, stern rising, propeller still turning, her bottom dirty red. Then she was gone, leaving nothing but a whirlpool of boiling foam behind.

They were over one hundred kilometers from land with a storm kicking up. Max knew all the people in the water would die unless he rescued them.

He backed away from the periscope and tried to collect his thoughts. They would never fit two hundred passengers aboard the U-boat. He banged his head against the scope. He couldn't call out for aid, but neither could he leave so many innocent people in the water to drown. It was impossible to say which shame would be greater.

Turning around, he saw Carls and Ferret staring at him along with the rest of the control room crew. Lehmann had disappeared. The lifeboats drifted farther away with every minute he stalled. Perhaps he should just allow that, allow them to drift off until he could no longer see the people struggling in their lifejackets in the swell, coughing up seawater. When the storm set in, mothers would be separated from their children, who would float along on the endless ocean until they died gasping for breath, seawater filling their lungs—the same way Max would die when *U-114* finally met her destiny.

He looked through the scope again, he couldn't say how long. No one in the control room seemed to be breathing. Max knew what was required of him, but he would rather die than do it. He wanted just to stand there silently in the limbo of indecision forever. He wanted to have nothing required of him anymore, but that was not one of the available choices. "Stand by to surface," he said. He scanned the sky for planes and, seeing none, stepped away from the periscope. "Chief, take us up."

"Halt!" Lehmann cried, reappearing with a Luger in his hand.

"Leutnant Lehmann, achtung!"

Lehmann didn't move. He had the pistol trained squarely on Max's chest. "We will not surface. I am taking command of this U-boat now, you traitor. Our orders expressly forbid us from offering aid to the enemy."

"Leutnant," Max said, "you are under arrest."

Lehmann took a step forward and raised the pistol to Max's face. He was just beginning to say something when the chief brought a heavy steel flashlight down on the back of his head. "Bloody hell," the chief grumbled, stepping over Lehmann's crumpled body to retrieve the Luger.

"Tie his hands and put him in my cabin," Max ordered Carls. "Chief, take us up."

Compressed air hissed into the diving tanks, pushing the water out, and the U-boat broke the surface in a welter of spray, like a whale coming up for air. Max climbed to the bridge, followed by the lookouts. They were no more than a kilometer from the lifeboats and the bobbing mass of people in the water. "Left full rudder," Max ordered. "Ahead dead slow."

The eyes of the passengers fixed on the U-boat as she approached. Everyone in the lifeboats stopped talking to look, those in the water stopped their flailing around, terror on every face. Slowly the boat came on. Max reduced power till he lay still in the water just meters downwind from the lifeboats. Except for the slapping of the waves against his flanks, the silence was complete. A light rain came down, dark clouds on the horizon threatening more. A warm, damp wind played over Max. The storm would be on them soon. Time was critical but something still held him back, though he knew the choice had already been made. This would be the end of his reputation and career; he would become infamous throughout the Kriegsmarine as the man who scuttled his U-boat to rescue some enemy civilians. What would Eckhardt say? Max's father? Mareth? Surely she would understand that he was a warrior, not a murderer. Certainly there was a difference. There had to be.

Carls cleared his throat at Max's side. "Shall I rig lifelines on the deck, Herr Kaleu? With so many people . . ."

"Very well. And bring up pistols for the bridge crew. No enemy men below, only women and children. Understand?"

"Jawohl, Herr Kaleu."

Carls shouted orders down the hatchway and coils of bright manila rope were soon coming up through the hatch. Then the Lugers were handed up and Max passed them out to the lookouts along with his instructions. Never give any man a gun without instructions on when to fire it, they'd always told him at the Marineschule.

The people in the water and those in the lifeboats continued to stare at the U-boat with uncertain faces, less terrified now because Max hadn't machine-gunned them yet. He wiped the rainwater from his brow and cupped his hands around his mouth, feeling the roughness of his patchy whiskers. "What ship?" he yelled.

Nothing. He could hardly believe what he was doing. He didn't want to die, but at least death would be over quickly enough. This was a shame that would follow him forever. "What ship?" he yelled again.

A man stood in one of the lifeboats, showing the blue tunic and gold rings of an officer. "R.M.S. *Dundee*, Red Star Line in passengers and mail for Kingston."

They were British. Of course they would be. These same damned people were obliterating Berlin with their bombs, massacring women and children, and now Max was wrecking his own life to save a few hundred of them.

The officer continued to stand, looking up at Max. The rain was coming thicker now and if he didn't get the passengers aboard soon they would all be lost. Nothing reduced visibility at sea like rain. He had to do it now—there was no going back. "Are you in command?" Max asked the officer.

"I am. First Officer Wilkes, sir. Cap'n's wounded, unconscious, sir."

"I want these people in the water to swim to the U-boat. Understand?"

"To the U-boat, sir?"

"That's right."

"You—you're rescuing them, sir?"

"Correct."

The officer nodded slowly but said nothing, seemingly shocked into silence.

Max called for the megaphone to be sent up. "Attention those in the water," he shouted into the mouthpiece. "Swim for the U-boat. I repeat, swim for the submarine."

At first no one reacted, but Carls and his men were stringing lifelines from the bridge to the bow and throwing rope ladders down the side, and gradually some of the passengers began to move. The first man reached the boat and climbed one of the ladders, two crewmen pulling him up onto the deck. Carls pointed to the foot of the bridge tower and the man walked there and sat like an obedient schoolboy.

Max wondered how many people he could fit along the foredeck. Maybe a hundred, and another hundred on the aft deck. He just might be able to get everyone aboard if he put some of the women below.

Seeing that the man who'd come aboard had not been shot by

the German sailors, the other passengers in the water approached the boat en masse. Waves knocked some against her battered hull and they were cut by the rough metal. One small boy bashed his head and Max had to summon the medic, who sewed the lad up as he wailed from the pain.

Carls hung from a ladder, pulling other children from the water with one hand and setting them on the deck. Adults climbed the rope ladders themselves and sailors posted along the deck helped them up. More and more people crowded onto the foredeck in their orange lifejackets, creating a solid block of color. No one seemed hysterical, Max noted, though many were shivering, soaked and crowding together in the rain as the storm moved in, the waves growing larger, slapping the boat and rolling her in the seaway. Without the rope, some of the Brits would have been pitched off the deck.

The foredeck filled and Carls began leading people aft, passing down the side of the bridge. Many of the faces turned up to Max as they went by. Some nodded. An RAF man gave him a stiff salute; a woman with a child in her arms held his eyes with no expression; a man in a brown suit gave him a toothy smile and two thumbs up. Max just stared down from his place on the bridge, unsure of how to feel. He could see that the passengers were still tense. To them he was the Hun, the devil incarnate, one of the sea wolves. No doubt these same people cheered when they heard that some German city had been pounded flat by British planes. He wondered what any of them would do in his place, if they were in command of an Allied sub and the water were full of German civilians.

It was time for Bekker to send out the signal, but again Max hesitated. The rain felt good on his face. He thought about his days at the Academy, about standing rigid in formation in the quadrangle for inspection in rain just like this, but much colder; about the many times he'd fallen asleep in geometry class; about the night he and his crewkameraden had silently carried the Kommandant's small BMW down to the waterfront and left it. He thought of going aloft with Dieter on their training barque in the Baltic to reef the sails, and of those days aboard *Graf Spee,* the great ship buffed and gleaming. The impending order cast a shadow across these memories. When he was first admitted to the Marineschule, his father had been required to post a bond of eight hundred marks, subject to forfeit if Max didn't perform to the required standard. He hoped the old man had gotten the money back because, if not, he'd certainly not see it now. Finally Max called down the hatchway: "Radio."

"Ja, Herr Kaleu?"

"Send on the six-hundred-meter band: 'Have torpedoed British liner R.M.S. *Dundee.* Many passengers in water.' Give our position. 'Commencing rescue operations. Require immediate assistance. Will not attack provided I am not attacked. German U-boat *114.*' Keep sending."

"Jawohl, Herr Kaleu."

He got them all aboard in the next hour, most squatting on the deck now, jammed together like spectators at a soccer match. Room had been made below for a handful of the women and children, strange visitors aboard a U-boat, and they stared quietly around, eyes wide with fear. Cigarettes had been distributed on deck, by whom Max didn't know, and some people huddled together smoking under their sodden coats. It seemed that once he'd made the terrible decision, the sailors had taken over. Certainly they had performed the whole operation with few orders from him. Blankets appeared on deck, along with hot coffee. Iodine came up from below. Towels were brought up, too, so the people covered with fuel oil could begin to scrub it off. Fortunately the oil slick had been on the far side of the ship and most of the passengers had avoided it. The rain was steady now. They clung to the lifelines to keep from sliding off the rolling deck.

And so the long wait began. Max held his place on the bridge and tried to think through their surrender. The Americans would get him and they would get his men, but he would see them all in hell before they got his boat. But he knew it would be difficult to prevent. Scuttling charges would have to be set in the engine room to blow the packings out from around the propeller shafts. A massive jet of water would then pour in and the boat would go quickly by the stern: four minutes or less. The timing would be critical. First the passengers would have to be taken off, then most of the crew. Then, under the guns of a U.S. Navy warship, he would have to hold off a boarding party and blow the charges. Whoever was left on the boat would have to jump for it. He would have to quickly make his way from the stern to the main hatch of the sinking U-boat, or he'd never get out.

Max smoked as he considered these variables. They had scuttling charges on board and had practiced the procedure, but the Naval War Staff had never planned for anyone to scuttle a boat under these circumstances, so there were no contingency measures for him to look up in any manual. In war, despite training, improvisation proved to be the most crucial skill. Nothing could actually prepare you for the absurdity of war. In any event, none of his men betrayed any hostility toward Max. They probably realized he was saving their lives. The arithmetic of the U-boat force's current loss rates was a secret to no one. The crew understood that, if they weren't killed on this patrol, they'd almost definitely be killed on the next one. Life as a POW would be no holiday, but neither would it be a watery grave.

Four hours passed. The rain fell off, finally, and the cloud cover moved away, but the sea still pounded them, passengers clutching the ropes for dear life. Max felt his heart jump as usual when the port lookout shouted, "Aircraft bearing green zero nine zero!" His pulse raced, adrenaline shot through him, his knees went to jelly. But all he could do this time was watch the plane through his binoculars as it came in. He just hoped the pilot wasn't bent on blowing them up.

Sunlight gleamed on the fuselage as it began circling at a distance, drawing slightly closer when the U-boat did not fire. The plane must be guiding the rescue ships to them. Its bomb bay doors remained shut. Before long the first destroyer appeared on the horizon, smoke billowing from her stacks as she raced toward Max at full speed.

Carls stood beside him, watching the destroyer carefully. "Charging like she found us on her bloody own," he said. Max nodded. No doubt the ship's captain would get a medal the size of a pie tin for this. Another destroyer appeared on the heels of the first, and both bore down on *U-114*, guns trained, bow waves foaming as they tore through the heavy seas. Behind them, a third vessel came into view—another destroyer, this one new, flying a command pennant. This would be the squadron commander.

"Bring me the signal light," Max ordered.

Carls dropped below, reappearing a moment later with the portable light and handing it over to Max. Bracing himself against the roll of the U-boat in the swell, Max turned the light to the American ships and blinked out his message: "Stand off from me one kilometer and send boats." No need to let them get too close.

Two of the destroyers began to circle at a kilometer's distance while the other destroyer stopped dead in the water parallel to Max and dropped a large whaleboat into the sea, careful to stay wide of the U-boat's venomous snout. Obviously they had no idea he could fire a torpedo ninety degrees off the bow. "Ready machine guns," he said to Carls, who signaled the men on the guns. They swiveled their weapons toward the whaleboat as it plowed toward them through the waves. Max counted six men in the boat—five sailors and an officer, all of them armed. Sometime during the evacuation they would rush him and try to seize the U-boat. It was only natural. He would do exactly the same.

Each of the three warships had every weapon that would bear trained on Max's submarine to cover the men in the whaleboat. Bekker reported that they were ranging with their sonar, too, just in case there was another U-boat around, perhaps also to let Max know how quickly they would be on him if he attempted to dive.

Carls handed him a holstered Luger, which Max took and buckled around his waist. It just might come to that in the end.

"Ahoy, German submarine!" the American officer in the whaleboat called through a megaphone.

Max looked him over. A youngster, maybe twenty or twenty-one. Each man in the whaleboat had a lifejacket on. The officer wore his khaki uniform and the crewmen looked sloppy in blue jeans and work shirts. "Throw your rope to the sailor on the bow," Max shouted back. "Load the passengers from there." He could see the young officer's surprise at being addressed in fluent English. Max's father had been right about the language coming in handy, although he hardly could have ever foreseen the present situation.

Dietrich, one of the deckhands, caught the rope and held it. Others reached down and grabbed the whaleboat's gunwales, keeping it still and helping the British passengers in. Or throwing them in, really—it was the best they could do in this sea.

Boats had been dropped from the other American ships and now two more headed in, but from different directions. Conniving, these Amis, worse than the damned Tommies. Max took the light back up. "All boats come in on my starboard bow or I fire," he signaled. He couldn't have boats of armed men coming at him from all angles.

"Carls!"

"Herr Kaleu?"

"Cover those other two boats!"

The gun crew swiveled their machine guns to face the approaching boats and they stopped, bobbing up and down in the swell. After a minute or two they relented, circling around to come in on the starboard bow.

When those two boats began to load, Max knew it was time to send off some of his crew. The English passengers would provide the best cover for his men. Five went in the second boat, the Americans eyeing them suspiciously, the Brits saying nothing. The engine room crew and the e-motor men went in the third boat, their beards and filthy clothes singling them out from the civilians When the first boat returned for a second run, he put the torpedo men aboard, along with the cook and the men who operated the diving planes. Heinz gave Max a big salute. Ferret went off, then the chief, then Lehmann, hands tied but still unconscious. Let the Americans deal with him.

In two hours, only a small knot of British men remained on the foredeck, perhaps ten in all, hands raw from clinging to the lifelines for so long. Max had exchanged no words with the Americans throughout the slow rescue. They just went about their work, occasionally staring up at him as if he were a man from outer space. Max met their eyes from time to time but said nothing. They all seemed incredibly young—faces so fresh, so innocent. Max felt empty and much too old for his years.

Carls had gone below to set the scuttling charges, leaving Max above with two men on the machine guns. Everyone else in the crew had gone off. The first shot surprised Max because of the Englishmen still on the deck. Where had it come from? Another bullet clanged off the bridge armor, then two more shots and one of the sailors dropped at his machine-gun post. Max drew his pistol. On the bow, the crew of the two remaining whaleboats kicked the terrified Brits into the water and opened fire on the bridge, charging down the foredeck. Max squeezed off a shot and brought one man down as another of the U-boat's machine guns began to chatter, stitching two Americans across the chest. Then the remaining gunner slumped forward over his weapon. The bastards. Max fired off a clip, dropping another two men, then ducked behind the bridge armor to reload, bullets ricocheting off the thick plating. Crawling on his stomach to the open hatch, he dropped below into the conning tower, pausing to shut the hatch behind him and dog it home. That wouldn't stop the Americans for long but it might hold them up a little. Carls stood waiting for him in the control room.

"Charges set?"

"Jawohl, Herr Kaleu. They're wired together. Just push the detonator and they'll blow in fifteen seconds."

"Hold them off as long as you can."

"Jawohl, Herr Kaleu." Carls saluted and drew his Luger.

Max ducked down the narrow passageway to the stern. The signs of the quick evacuation were everywhere: drawers opened and rifled, a deck of cards spilled across the deck, clothes strewn about. Behind him, he heard the Americans pounding on the hatch as they struggled with its metal wheel. He had to blow the charges now but didn't know if he'd be able to get out in time. No matter.

Carls had placed the charges in the engine room around the packings where the propeller shafts left the boat. Max went down on his hands and knees, grease staining his pants, and crawled behind the massive diesels, both engines quiet now, the lights running on battery power. He would have only fifteen seconds to get clear of the space once he pushed the detonators. Gunshots sounded toward the bow. He had to do it now but the charges were hard to reach. More shots—the Americans were in the boat. Stretching as far as he could, his shoulder straining at the joint, he touched the detonator, feeling for the switch. A bullet ricocheted off one of the diesels. Max pulled the switch and scrambled out from behind the engine.

Another shot, the bullet shattering the glass of the engine telegraph at his back. Max dropped to the deck, crawling along the cold steel plates, slick with grease beneath him. The explosion blew the breath from his body, its shock wave compressing him to the deck plating. His ears rang so badly that he couldn't even hear the water jetting in, but he felt the boat beginning to incline.

More gunshots. They sounded far away. Carls was firing steadily at the Americans. Good for him. Kill the bastards trying to take his boat.

Max crawled forward down the passageway, struggling over

the hatch combing, feeling the boat sink beneath him like a slow-moving elevator. She was down five degrees by the stern now. When he reached the control room he found Carls, shirt soaked with blood, taking cover on one side of the half-open hatch that could seal off the aft compartments from the control room.

"They're in the boat, Herr Kaleu. Hit me in the arm, the dirty swine. Couldn't stop them."

"I want you to surrender, Carls."

"Herr Kaleu?"

"Surrender now. Get out. She'll go any moment. Get out."

Carls tossed his Luger through the hatch and it clattered across the control room floor. "Kameraden!" he called.

"Come out, you no-good son of a bitch!" one of the Americans called back.

Max would be damned if he was going to leave the boat with enemy sailors on board. Kriegsmarine tradition dictated that a captain had to be the last one off a sinking ship. He knew the Americans must be searching for codes, but Bekker had thrown them all overboard hours ago at Max's direction. A ten-degree slope now and listing to port. The green sea was sluicing into the stern like water through a millrace.

Carls crawled into the control room and was helped up by two American sailors in their strange white hats. "She's going, Lieutenant!" one of them yelled.

"Okay, you guys, beat it and take this Kraut with you."

The list increased. Seawater reached the batteries and blew the lights as the Americans escaped. Only the emergency lanterns in the control room stayed on, casting a dim glow. The boat lurched and Max jumped for the ladder. She started her final plunge, stern dropping rapidly, bow rising out of the sea. A trickle of water streamed into the boat from the open main hatch. He removed his white U-boat captain's hat and threw it to the deck, then grasped the rungs of the ladder, pulling himself up, fighting against the water. A torrent of brine cascaded over him, clawing at his fingers, trying to tear them loose, then forcing itself into his mouth. Only a few more rungs to the top but the water held him down. Maybe it was for the best. He began to relax his grip but a hand came down and grabbed his collar. Carls. The big man used his good arm and his massive strength to jerk Max up through the hatch. They rolled off the bridge into the sea and *U-114* sank beneath them with a final sigh.

CHAPTER THIRTEEN

CAMP TAYLOR
PRISONER-OF-WAR STOCKADE
NEAR JACKSON, MISSISSIPPI
SIX MONTHS LATER
7 JULY 1944
0300 HOURS

THE GUNFIRE JOLTED MAX FROM HIS SLEEP—TWO SHOTS, THEN A machine-gun burst. Lights snapped on throughout the camp. Four of the Afrika Korps men had gone over the wire.

The desert veterans had been in the camp only two weeks. Prior to their arrival, Camp Taylor had been home to just Max and Carls, who were lying low, and a few hundred men from one of the Wehrmacht's stomach battalions who didn't want to escape since each of them suffered from chronic digestive problems that had made them ineligible for military service at the start of the war. As losses on the Eastern Front mounted into the millions, the German army called up every man who could hold a rifle. Those with stomach ailments were mustered into their own units where they could receive a specialized diet and were assigned to work in support capacities such as field post, which is what the stomach battalion had been doing when captured in February 1943 by the Allies during their campaign in North Africa.

At first they were as deeply apprehensive as any captured soldiers, but after a few weeks at Camp Taylor they felt themselves living in Elysian Fields. Not only was there more food available than they had ever had before, but the stomach battalion mess sergeants finally had the proper ingredients—such as butter and cream and milk—to turn out dish after dish of very bland, highly digestible food. Many of the men began to gain weight, some for the first time in years.

"Out, out, you guys! Move it, you Nazi pricks," the guards yelled. "Line up, line up, move, move."

Max slipped on his pants and boots and followed the other officers into the assembly area in the middle of the floodlit yard, which was covered with a thick pad of pine straw. Lieutenant Colonel Stoddard, the camp commander, stood in the square, face grim, hands holding a riding crop behind his back. Stoddard was a reserve officer from the First War who had been recalled to the colors and given command of this backwater POW stockade—hardly a distinguished assignment.

He was rarely on post anyway since he spent most of his time at a barbeque restaurant he owned in Jackson. "Best goddamn barbeque in six counties," he'd told Max defensively, as if Max might have heard otherwise. "Whites lined up in front, and niggers lined up in the back." Max had nodded, not sure of what to say.

Gunshots continued to sound in the deep pine woods that surrounded the camp. These American troops had no fire discipline. Once they opened up, they didn't stop till they'd shot away all their ammunition. They were ill-disciplined and disorganized in everything they did. It galled Max to take orders from such men, to be a prisoner under their watch, to be losing the war to them.

Max stood with his hut mates, all army officers, while to his left the three hundred men from the Afrika Korps formed up under their sergeants, the Americans having sent their officers to a separate camp fearing they would make mischief if confined with their men. But Max had been separated from his crew for a different reason. The Americans sent him to Mississippi after just a week in the transit camp in Virginia, because Lehmann was working to bring Max before a secret Court of Honor for rescuing the enemy and scuttling his U-boat. No one else from *U-114* was involved in the plot, but Lehmann found friends among other Nazi fanatics in the camp. The situation had grown very dangerous for Max by the time he received the transfer orders.

"Achtung!" the Oberfeldwebel called.

Max came to attention with the others. Major Hessler, senior German officer at the camp, smoothed his Wehrmacht tunic into place, looked around, then came to attention and saluted Stoddard.

"I'm surprised at you, Major Hessler," Stoddard said. "No escape attempts for six months and now a few of your boys decide to up and go over tonight."

Hessler straightened up; he had a tendency to droop. "It is the duty of every POW to escape, Colonel. Those men are veterans of Rommel's Afrika Korps and tough as leather."

Stoddard laughed. "So tough, they surrendered. Listen up, Major, I appreciate their heroic resolve, but it's a bunch of bullshit and you know it. Your duty is to convince these men not to get themselves killed for no reason, because they got no chance to get away nohow. The only thing any of you will accomplish by trying to escape is making me look bad, and I won't have that. It's bad enough I gotta spend the war babysitting you Krauts. I will *not* let y'all make a fool out of me, understand? I'll do whatever I have to."

One of the American officers handed Colonel Stoddard a clipboard. "Four unaccounted for, sir."

The colonel looked at Major Hessler for a long moment without speaking. Finally he said, "You may dismiss from parade, Major, but remember what I said."

Max woke early the next day—Sunday, a day he enjoyed because of the Lutheran service offered in German at the camp by a
minister from Jackson. He loved to sing the old hymns, to hear the
Bible readings in High German, but most important were the quiet
moments of contemplation when he prayed for the comrades he
had lost, for his father, for Mareth, for Germany, for himself. As he
stepped into the yard after the service, Max saw a corporal's guard
of American soldiers leading the four escaped soldiers through the
camp gate. Two had black eyes and swollen faces, another held his
arm at an unnatural angle. The fourth had blood all over the front
of his shirt, a split lip, a broken nose.

"Doktor!" Major Hessler shouted.

Stoddard came in behind his men and ordered them to let the
four Germans loose.

Hessler advanced on him. "These men are prisoners of war
and must be treated as such under the terms of the Geneva
Convention!"

Stoddard nodded. "Now listen here, Major, these boys got a
little bruised up running through the woods, that's all. My men
didn't lay a finger on them."

A mass of Afrika Korps men, still lean and hard from their
months of desert fighting, formed up in back of Major Hessler.
The American soldiers in the guard towers swiveled their machine
guns toward the yard.

"Colonel Stoddard, I shall make a full report of this reprehensible behavior to the Swiss government."

"Major," Stoddard said, "your men fell down while they were
running through the woods. I think that's plain as day." Without
waiting for a response, he turned and left through the front gate, a
flimsy structure of two-by-fours and chicken wire. The Americans
hadn't wasted a lot of effort building an escape-proof camp. Why
should they? Where were the Germans going to go?

Hessler was angry, but the Afrika Korps men were seething. They had learned to hate the Americans in combat at Tunis, and they didn't think much better of their comrades from the stomach battalion, whom they regarded as slackers. Still, Major Hessler had been a regular infantry officer in the Prussian army before ulcerative colitis had forced him into the premature retirement from which he'd been recalled; he was not a man to stand for insubordination, and he could hear the desert troops grumbling all around him. "Oberfeldwebel!" he called.

The senior noncom of the Afrika Korps detachment stepped forward and snapped a salute. "Ja, Herr Major?"

"Dismiss these men at once!"

"Jawohl, Herr Major." The sergeant spun on his heel with parade-ground precision. "Achtung!" he bellowed, the three hundred soldiers of the Afrika Korps coming immediately to rigid attention. Damn but their discipline was impressive, Max thought. "Dismissed!"

Max returned to his tin-roofed hut.

Besides reading books and newspapers from the camp library and teaching a course in English, Max had little to do but think of Mareth. He had already gone nine months without seeing her, and the pain of her absence seemed only to sharpen as the days and weeks piled up behind the camp wire. It had been bad enough when he was at war, but he'd been preoccupied then with his own survival. Now there was nothing to take his mind off the lines of her body he was unable to touch, the sound of her voice he was unable to hear, her sly humor, the comfort of how well she knew him.

A knock on his door.

"Permission to enter, Herr Kaleu?"

"Carls, of course—come in."

Max looked at the big man. Carls had been very loyal to him—too loyal, perhaps.

"News from home? About the others? The crew?"

"Yes, sir. I has a letter from my mother here," he said, clutching a small envelope. POWs were not allowed to write each other directly but sent news to one another through their families back home. "Most are still in Maine, cutting timber same as us, Herr Kaleu, only it's cold there and the men like it better. My mother didn't want to put no details down on paper, but she says Leutnant Lehmann and Bekker got into some sort of trouble. They got sent to a special camp out west. A place called New Mexico. A camp for troublemakers, she said."

"Well, they've got that right. Who did she hear this from?"

"Heinz, Herr Kaleu. He got sent there himself because he knocked down two American guards when they snatched the U-boat medal off his uniform." *U-114*'s torpedo chief petty officer had been Carls's closest friend on the boat. Max smiled. Captivity had not changed Heinz.

"Your mother is well, yes?"

"She finally took my advice and got out of Hamburg, Herr Kaleu. Brought herself to my cousin's farm in Schleswig-Holstein. Get as close to the Allies as you can, I told her. Don't go nowhere near the East."

"The Afrika Korps men, how are they?"

"Restless, Herr Kaleu. Very restless. Seeing their comrades beat up, it's got their venom up. They're tough men, almost as tough as U-boat men. They fought under Rommel for almost two years."

"Problems?"

"Perhaps, Herr Kaleu."

Max liked the Afrika Korps men. They were tough and proud and disciplined like the navy he had known in the early years of the war. Last week Major Hessler had given him a squad from the Afrika Korps to supervise and the desert soldiers went at the pines like they meant to cut down the whole forest before sunset. Certainly the Americans were getting their money's worth for the eighty cents a day they paid these men to cut timber.

That night he sat up late and smoked. It stayed hot now even at night and Max's sheets were damp from the humidity. How many nights had he lain awake in this hut, replaying in his mind the events that led to the surrender of his U-boat? Remembering the sighting of the ship through the mist, the adrenaline pumping through him, the jolt of the torpedoes as they shot from the boat, the rumble of the explosions, then the shock of seeing all those people scrambling over the top deck of the steamer, of realizing what he'd done. He'd been right to save the passengers, but he felt such guilt over scuttling the U-boat, and it hung heavy on him like the thick night air. Carls had told him that he had worried off twenty pounds, and he was right. Max's uniform hung loose on his body—the appetite he had lost in France had never returned.

Mareth's letters arrived once a week, all he was allowed under camp regulations. She was grateful to be in Mexico City and did her best to sound cheerful. But Max knew it was a front. She yearned for him as he did for her and when not worrying about him she worried about her father.

Max smoked till dawn, burning through half a pack of Lucky Strikes. He bought the cigarettes with the scrip the Americans paid him; the scrip was worthless outside the camp but it was easy enough to purchase things at the canteen and sell them cheap to the American guards for hard currency. Not that hard currency was much good to a POW, but at least it was real. He had accumulated eleven dollars this way.

After breakfast he found Carls with the ten men of their woodcutting detail formed up by the main gate. An American sergeant counted out their axes, all of which Max had to sign for.

"All is in order?" Max asked Carls.

"Jawohl, Herr Kaleu."

"Carry on."

Carls gave a parade-ground salute, then wheeled around to the Afrika Korps men, wiry youngsters with bright eyes. "Achtung!"

They came to attention as one, like a machine, as the American sergeant looked on. Max had watched the American troops on the rare occasions when they drilled, and they always looked like a pack of conscripts on their first day in the army. Some seemed not to know the difference between left and right. No one had the discipline of the German fighting man. No one. Then again, the Wehrmacht hardly assigned its finest soldiers to guard POWs, and Max didn't suppose the Americans did either. But the men of the Afrika Korps were damned impressive all the same, and Max wondered what they would think of his surrender if they knew.

Outside the gate the bus waited for them—an old school bus, Max thought it was, painted olive green, the peculiar color with which the Americans covered everything associated with their army. The bus driver, a Negro named Malachi, a veteran of the American Expeditionary Force in the First War, sat quietly behind the wheel. Malachi had been wounded in France in 1918, even walked with a limp as a result, but the young American soldiers didn't treat him with any more respect than they displayed for other Negroes.

"Two minutes late, boy," the corporal of the guard said, leading his men onto the bus.

Malachi nodded at him.

"Two minutes late, I said."

"Had to put gas in the bus," Malachi said. Max noted the omission of "sir" or "cap'n." Most Negroes around the camp tacked one or the other onto the end of their sentences when addressing the white guards.

Max had struck up an acquaintance with Malachi. The colored man spoke passable German from the eight years he'd spent working as a trumpet player in a Negro jazz band in Berlin after the war. "Where did you play?" Max had asked a few days back.

"Place called Johny's on the Kurfürstendamm."

"Johny's? The cabaret? I've been there. Next to the Café Wien?"

"That's the one. 'Authentic American Negro Jazz Band' was the sign they put up on the nights we played. Paid us good. Your people treated me a damn sight better than what I'm used to around here," Malachi had told him, "and your women . . ."—he winked at Max—"let's just say a colored man in Berlin drew powerful attention from your women back then."

The Afrika Korps men followed the guards onto the bus, Carls and Max the last to board.

"Okay, boy," the corporal said, "let's move it."

Malachi nodded, then spoke in German to Max: "That white boy ain't got the sense God gave a cow."

"If he was in my unit," Max replied, "I would have him sent to the Russian Front."

The corporal eyed them suspiciously. "Hey, you boys talk American for me. None of that Hun language. Bad enough you Krauts using it, but I can't have niggers talkin' Hun." Max fell silent. The only thing these Americans had over Germany was their inexhaustible resources. They could manufacture anything in unheard-of quantities and ship it all over the world. What had the leader of the Hitler Youth said? "Every German boy who dies at the front is dying for Mozart." Americans didn't even know who Mozart was. They listened to Benny Goodman and Cab Calloway and the Andrews Sisters, and when Max's young sailors were able, that's who they listened to as well. Whenever Ferret had played American music from the BBC over the U-boat's loudspeaker, almost everyone started bobbing their heads to the music. Georg, the control room petty officer, even acted like he was playing the drums. None of Max's men had shown the least bit of interest in dying for Mozart.

The bus went down one dirt road for several miles, turned and turned again, stopping at their worksite from Friday last. "You ever get lost out here?" he asked Malachi, still in German.

"Came up in these woods till we got in the first war with you people and I went to France with the army, and then to Berlin, but I come back home in '28 because my folks was getting on, and I been here ever since. Still live over the store my daddy ran. Guess you just know the territory once you been around it so long."

"Is it far from here?"

"'Bout six miles north. Place called Poole's Crossroads. Just a bump in the road. Ain't even a stop sign."

In another few minutes they reached the clearing and they divided into two groups. Carls took five men and led them into the woods to start a new worksite one kilometer north. They were followed by the corporal and another American soldier, rifles slung upside down across their backs. The other two guards stayed with Max and his five men at the original site. Malachi came down off the bus and limped to a spot in the shade. He settled down in the dirt, produced a book, and began to read.

"A nigger readin'," one of the guards said, "now don't that beat all."

Taking up one of the axes, Max marked a row of tall pines for his men to fell. He handed the axes out to the young soldiers and motioned them forward. The rhythmic percussion of axe blades biting into wood rang through the forest. Working methodically, like the disciplined Germans they were, the men went down the long row of trees, pausing from time to time to stand back when one of them tilted and pitched over, tearing limbs from other trees as it crashed down, the final thump sending birds to wing.

Later in the day, after a truck had brought lunch to them, Max went to check the progress of the other detail. Because he was the officer in charge, Max could move between the two groups without an escort. "Guard," he called to one of the young Americans. The man sat in the shade, smoking, rifle propped against a tree.

"I'm going to inspect the work of the other group."

"Okee dokee, sir."

"What?"

"Okay, sir. That's fine."

Max started down the trail Carls and his men had taken, stamping his feet hard like the American guards did to scare the snakes, two of which slithered away during his walk. Ordinarily he marched double-time on such an errand; it was the military way

and he had a desire to show the Americans how real soldiers be-
haved. The sloppier they were, the more military he became. But
the forest was quiet today and the heat wasn't so bad in the shade
and Max took his time, breathing in the bitter earth smell of the
rotting pine needles. He began to run only when he heard the first
gunshot.

When he reached the clearing two of the Afrika Korps men
were sprinting hell for leather in the opposite direction, making
for the cover of the forest. The corporal was sighting them down
the barrel of his rifle when Carls knocked him cold with a pine
branch thick as his arm. Blood spurted from the corporal's skull.
Carls dropped the club and started after the two fleeing men and
without pause the other three Afrika Korps men followed him.

The second sentry was scrambling to his feet five meters to
Max's right. Must have been napping. The youngster bobbled his
rifle awkwardly and Max plowed into him on a dead run, both of
them crashing into the bed of dust and straw. A bayonet flashed
in the morning sun as the young sentry rolled into a crouch and
drew the long knife from its scabbard. He lunged at Max, who
sidestepped and hit the boy on his backside, sprawling him out on
the ground. But the lad rolled and came up, moving damned fast,
passing the bayonet from hand to hand as he and Max circled each
other. The sentry lunged again, faking with his right, and almost
drove the blade through Max's ribs, but Max spun and delivered
a kick to the youngster's kidneys. He stumbled and Max dived for
the branch Carls had used on the corporal. The sentry dived after
him and Max rolled onto his back, bringing the branch around to
catch the boy aside the head. The American somersaulted, crashed
into the trunk of a pine, and pulled himself up again—pausing
only to draw another knife from a sheath in his boot. Now he had
one in each hand. He smiled at Max and spit out a tooth. Blood
dripped from his mouth and nose onto his starched khaki shirt.
Max gripped the branch halfway up, feeling the sticky pinesap on
his palms. He feinted forward, taking a short swing at the sentry's

head, then drew back. With a war whoop the boy jumped forward. Max reversed his grip and drove the butt end of the branch into the boy's forehead, just above the nose. The sentry dropped to his knees, unconscious, and pitched forward into the soft straw.

Max dropped the branch, then darted through the trees, following the others, fearing he'd lost them. Move, he told himself, faster. The trees grew dense, he could see the broken tree branches that marked the passage of his men. In the far distance a rifle shot, followed by a dozen more. Were these Americans shooting into the woods at random?

After another ten minutes of hard running, a sharp pain stabbed his side like a poker in the gut. Had to stop for a moment. Head down, clutching his knees, sweat poured from his face as he gulped in great lungfuls of air. The hand that touched his shoulder caught him completely off guard and he jerked upright in fear.

"Herr Kaleu!"

"Shit! Carls, for God's sake, man!"

Gasping for air, Carls said, "Those lads run like ponies."

Max didn't speak, just continued to gulp air, chest heaving, as Carls did the same. Finally Max said, "Report?"

"I heard the guard give a shout and looked up. Seen two of our boys running. That swine of a corporal went to shoot and I clubbed him."

Max ran a hand through his greasy hair. Shit. They could still give themselves up, but he'd already been through the shame of surrendering once. He didn't want to do it again. Ever. But what to do? He knelt and put his head down with his hands over his face. Had to think for a moment. Carls was silent. Perhaps two minutes went by before he heard the rifle fire. He jerked his head up. More shooting now. A fusillade of rifle fire broke out, but it was far in the distance. Southeast of them, he felt sure.

But he knew what they had to do. A freighter. They had to get aboard a neutral freighter. It was the only alternative. They weren't that far from New Orleans. He'd been there during his training cruise on *Emden*, had roamed the city for several days. But how in the name of Saint Peter and Paul were they going to get there?

"If we want to try and escape, we need to get to New Orleans and find a neutral freighter," Max said to Carls, who nodded. "Maybe one that would take us to Mexico. I can't think of anything else." Carls still worked at catching his breath. Finally he said, "What about the nigger bus driver you talk to, Herr Kaleu?"

"Malachi?"

"Yes, sir."

Max thought about this. Would the colored man help them? They would hardly be welcomed guests. Could they even find Poole's Crossroads? Was there an alternative? No, there wasn't.

"He said he lives about six miles north of here, town called Poole's Crossroads."

Carls looked up at the sun, then pointed to his left. "North would be that way, Herr Kaleu."

"Then let's carry on." They forced-marched through the woods for another hour, following the sun north, then stopped, put their heads down, hands on knees, and gulped air like blown horses. They were drenched in sweat and Max knew they had sweated out all their body fluids. They had to find water. Soon. Carls seemed to be suffering badly. "I'm not the youngster I was on *Kronprinz Wilhelm*," he said between gasps.

They moved on, much slower. Max saw spots in front of his eyes and knew they were approaching heatstroke. He could shoot someone for a canteen of water. Dusk now—they came to a dirt road and dropped to their knees. Carls saw it first, across the road, a large cow pasture with a water trough big enough to bathe in. There were no cows. They had been led back to the barn by then and the pasture was deserted. Covered by the falling night, they slipped across the dirt road, stopped and listened. Quiet. Max cut himself going over the barbed-wire fence but stifled a yelp. Carls got over without cutting himself and helped Max down. On all fours they both crawled to the water trough. Max motioned for

Carls to go first and the big man plunged his head in and drank, came up breathing hard. Max followed, Carls keeping watch.

Max finished drinking then whispered to Carls that they must take their shirts off, rinse them out, and then put them on inside out to hide the white PW letters painted on the back of each shirt. For the next fifteen minutes they alternately drank water and rinsed and wrung out their shirts. They both took one last drink of water, then retraced their steps across the road till they were back in the trees about fifty meters from the dirt road. Neither of them could go on without sleep, so they made themselves as comfortable as they could on a mat of pine straw and slept.

Three hours, four hours went by, Max wasn't sure. The sound of a truck in the far distance woke him and he was up and in a crouch before he was barely awake. But the sound receded into the distance. Dark now with just a hint of light from a half moon. They had to be close to Poole's Crossroads. No more than a kilometer at this point. Time to move. Max could not get Carls to wake up no matter what he did. Finally, he leaned close to his ear and whistled the bosun's call for "Rise, rise, get up," the signal for the sailors to get up and stow their hammocks. That woke him. They crept to the dirt road and walked north, staying on the down moon side so they wouldn't cast a silhouette. A dog barked. Now two. They dropped. But this was it—Poole's Crossroads. In the dim moonlight he could make out four or five tin-roofed clapboard shacks scattered around the intersection, their windows dark. The small grocery was unmistakable with its weathered Coca-Cola sign and the single rusted gas pump in the dirt driveway outside. An open staircase on the side of the building climbed to the second-story apartment.

"The bus driver lives up there," Max whispered.

Carls nodded, too exhausted to speak. Max led the way to the staircase and they made their way up very slowly, the weathered steps creaking faintly.

On the landing at the top of the stairs, Max paused, listened. Nothing. He waited. A dog in one of the other houses started to bark. He looked around. This had to be the place. Now what? Knock on the door? He rapped gently. Rapped again. Nothing. Two more dogs added to the flurry of barking, which trailed off after a few minutes. Max went to rap again, but as he did so the door opened slowly. It was Malachi, holding a kerosene lantern in one hand and a sawed-off shotgun in the other, both barrels pointed at Max's gut. With great care, palms outward to show he was unarmed, Max slowly raised his arms into the air. No one spoke for a long moment. Then Malachi, suddenly aware of the lantern light, hissed, "Get in here 'fore somebody sees you, you goddamn sons of bitches. You trying to get me lynched?"

Malachi set the lantern on a table in the main room. It cast a dim light that sparkled on a spiked Prussian helmet from the First War mounted over the fireplace. Malachi spoke quietly, still pointing the shotgun at Max. "Took that helmet from one of your fellows I bayoneted in the Argonne. He didn't have no more use for it. Your people thought fighting colored soldiers was going to be easy, reckon they thought we could only sing and dance." He tightened his grip on the shotgun. "And we can sing and dance. You know what else we can do—at least those of us who was in the 370th Colored Infantry? We can fire six aimed rounds a minute of .303 caliber from a Lee-Enfield and bring down a whole line of you. Did it more than a few times."

"We want nothing from you, Malachi. We ask only how one must journey to New Orleans. For a ship. That's all we want. To learn how we may travel to New Orleans for a ship. That's all."

Not wanting to challenge him by staring, Max flicked his eyes to a photograph on the mantel—a younger Malachi in his doughboy uniform with the silver bars of a lieutenant. "Yes, that's me," Malachi said. "I was a lieutenant. An officer. You know what they called that war, the first one? The 'war to end all wars.' And here it is ain't twenty-five years later and you people has started it up again. As far as Malachi is concerned, we should just shoot every damn one of you German sons of bitches."

Max looked down.

Silence now, the faint hissing of the lantern the only sound. Malachi still gripped the sawed-off shotgun but slowly pointed it in the air and set the hammers to half cock so it wouldn't go off accidentally. "I didn't plan this," Max said. "We didn't plan to escape. We never would have involved you. It just happened and . . . I thought . . . I thought you may help us."

"Help you? Help you? Why in the name of Jesus would I help you? You ain't the one who's in danger. Don't you understand nothing? All they gonna do is beat up on you two. But they'll hang me from the nearest tree. Didn't think of that, did you?"

Holding his arms down with his palms out, Max looked up and said, "No, Malachi, I'm sorry. I never thought of that. I just never . . . I don't even understand it. We're the enemy."

Malachi looked at both of them for a moment, then shook his head. "'Cause you're white and I'm colored and it don't matter that you're Krauts. You're white Krauts. I'd just as soon shoot both of you as look at you but then I'd be in hell's own trouble for killing two white Germans." He stared at them.

Max looked away, trying to think of something to say. They had to get Malachi to help them. He slowly moved his hands up in surrender. "We just need to get to New Orleans. For a ship. That's all I'm asking. Will you tell us how to get there?"

Malachi gripped the shotgun with both hands, brought it down from his shoulder to his waist, pointed it directly at Max and Carls. "Get out."

Max bit his lower lip. "Can you at least tell us what direction New Orleans is in?"

"Get out," Malachi said, pulling both hammers back to full cock; a pull of the two triggers and both barrels would fire. Max kept his hands up, palms out. "We're leaving. We wish you no harm." They backed away slowly. Carls turned to open the door.

"Stop!" Malachi said. They froze.

"Shit. Someone could have seen you headed this way. If you're caught anywhere near here, they're gonna come for me next." He shook his head violently. "Damn you. God damn you."

Malachi walked backward to a large dresser at side of the room. "Y'all take off them stinking clothes." Holding the shotgun on Max with one hand, he rummaged in a drawer and pulled out a worn pair of bibb overalls, threw them at Carls. Then he balled up an old black suit of clothes and threw them at Max along with a white shirt. "Used to wear this suit when I played in Berlin. It should come close to fitting you." He reached again into the drawer and flung a tie at Max.

While Max and Carls stripped to their skivvies and put on their new clothes, Malachi moved to the small kitchen area.

"You," Malachi said to Max, "tell the big man to pick up one of those watermelons by the door. Hurry up." Malachi reached under a counter and pulled out an Adluh flour sack, which he threw at Max. "Fold up your old clothes and puts them in the sack then puts the watermelon in on top."

Carls held the sack open while Max quickly folded their filthy uniforms and stuffed them in, followed by the watermelon. "Now you look like some dumb ass rednecks on the way to visit some of your redneck kinfolk."

Max straightened his suit. "New Orleans?"

"Take the Panama Limited from Jackson—it's ten miles due east of here. Follow the road you come in on till it cross Highway 22, then turn east. Get as far away from here as you can. You hear me? As far as you can. You got money for tickets? It's three dollars to New Orleans."

"I have eleven dollars," Max said.

"That'll do."

Using both hands, Malachi brought the shotgun to his shoulder and took steady aim at Max's face. "Now get your goddamn selves out of here."

———

Their strategy was simple. Max spoke English well enough to pass as an American from another part of the country. "Just tell 'em you're from Brooklyn if they ask about the accent. Them buckras is so stupid they won't know the difference," Malachi had said. "And don't keep looking around like you got the nerves. Just walk straight and steady like you own the place. That's how white folks do."

At the station Carls was to stay at a distance from Max, find a seat, and pretend to sleep. With his bib overalls, dirty shirt, and the smell of sweat all over him, he looked the picture of a Mississippi dirt farmer. They reached the rail station in the late afternoon, 4:15 by the gilt clock on the King Edward Hotel across the street from the station.

Max bought the tickets without trouble, spreading his six dollars on the smooth wooden counter and telling the clerk, "Two coach for New Orleans." He felt a strange fear she was going to look up and say, "Ausweiss, bitte," but the woman behind the barred window didn't even look up as she passed the tickets through. So different from the Reich, where identification papers and leave papers and permits were required to travel anywhere on a train.

"Luggage, sir?"

Max spun around and saw a colored man smiling at him from beneath a red leather cap. A police check?

"Do you have any luggage you need carried, sir?"

"No. No, thank you. I don't have any luggage."

Couldn't he see that Max had no luggage? Was it suspicious not to have any? But the colored man was just a porter, Max realized, not a police officer. Still, his heart raced. There were plenty of real policemen stationed around the terminal, and he had to keep steady. Get hold of yourself. Where was Carls? Max scanned the crowd, but he knew that standing in the middle of the huge waiting room staring about made him stick out. He needed a newspaper to hide behind. A newsstand stood on the far side of the cavernous room, he could see the sign: NEWSPAPERS, MAGAZINES, CIGARETTES, CIGARS, CANDY, ICE COLD COCA-COLA.

He walked across the terminal, eyes straight ahead. American soldiers were everywhere in the station in their strange-looking khaki uniforms. It felt odd to move through them unnoticed, but they all seemed to be sleeping or playing cards.

At the newsstand he took a paper from the stack by the register and saw his own picture staring up at him. *NAZI SUB CAPTAIN AT LARGE,* the headline shouted, and, below that: *Top U-Boat Ace Escapes from Work Detail.* Luckily, the photograph was from his identity card issued at the transit camp in Virginia months back. It was grainy and didn't look much like him since he had lost more weight in the time since the picture was taken. Nor was he in uniform now like he was in the picture. Instead he wore the ill-fitting black suit Malachi had given him that made him look like an undertaker. He dropped the paper and ducked into the coffee shop next door, finding a stool at the counter.

"What'll it be, hon?"

"Coffee."

The waitress stared at him over half-moon glasses and smiled. "You ain't from around here. You a Yankee?"

"Ship captain. From New York."

"Honey, you're a long way from New York, but I reckon with the war on, we got more Yankees down here in Jackson than any time since y'all burned the place down."

Max smiled. He had no idea what she was talking about. "It's the war. Changes everything."

"You got that right, hon." She walked away to a large urn and returned with the coffee. "Two bits, hon, pay the cashier."

How much was two bits? Damn these Americans and their stupid slang for everything. He sipped the coffee. It was hot and strong; real cream, too. People over here had no idea how good they had it. The light tap on his shoulder made his whole body go tense, and he spilled coffee on his hand. He turned slowly around on his stool to see a soldier standing with a cigarette in his mouth.

"Say, bud, got a match?"

"A match?"

"A match, pal, a light."

"No." Max turned back to the counter, wiped his hand off with a napkin. His heart was thudding against his chest. Would the Americans be looking for them even here, at the train station in the middle of Jackson? They would certainly be beating the swamps and combing the pine forests, but would they imagine that Max and Carls would have the guts—or the stupidity—to walk right into the state capital and catch a train?

He finished his coffee and paid the cashier without speaking, dropping two quarters on the register and stepping back out into the crowded terminal. Two uniformed policemen walked toward him and both saluted. Max's arm began to jerk up by reflex but he stopped, looked over his shoulder and saw an American army colonel behind him, returning the policemen's salutes.

Max crossed to the far end of the terminal and there was Carls, sitting quietly as he was told but fast asleep. Max dropped heavily onto the wooden bench across from Carls, then closed his eyes and tried to sleep. How long before the train came? Thirty minutes, maybe. Longer? Were American trains on time like German trains? Or like German trains had been before the war. He put his head back and thought for a while that he might actually drop off, but the tension was too much. It didn't matter how tired he was. It seemed a week before the announcement came over the loudspeaker: "Panama Limited 5:45 to Brookhaven, Macomb City, Hammond, and New Orleans now boarding gate seven. All aboard."

Max blinked, felt for the tickets, found them. He stood and nudged Carls, leaving one ticket on the bench. Carls was to follow him at thirty paces—just close enough to keep him in sight. Max walked slowly across the terminal and through the two large doors leading to the cement platform of track seven. As he walked down the platform toward the train he glanced around and saw Carls hanging back, watching him. Max went to the nearest car, the last one on the train, standing aside at the metal steps to let a Negro woman board in front of him. She gave him a skeptical look. He ignored her and climbed into the rail car.

Fortunately it was almost deserted, only a few Negroes scattered about, so Max knew he wouldn't have to talk with anyone. He settled into one of the plush seats. If they could get to New Orleans unnoticed, maybe they could get aboard a ship—even a ship to Mexico. It wasn't totally out of the question. Neutral ships called in New Orleans all the time. It was one of the biggest ports in America, with ships from all over the world. The very activity around the port would serve to disguise them.

Max closed his eyes again and kept them closed for five minutes before he felt the cold steel of a pistol barrel pressed against his left temple.

"Hands up," said a voice. "Real slow."

Max put his hands in the air.

The two policemen he had almost saluted were standing over him in the aisle. One held the pistol to his head while his partner did the talking. "Pretty ballsy, you Krauts coming here to get a train," he said. "And you almost got away with it, didn't you? Almost. But I gotta tell you, son, down here white never goes with colored. Even a Yankee would know not to sit in the nigger car."

CHAPTER FOURTEEN

ABOARD A TRAIN BOUND FOR NEW MEXICO
ONE WEEK LATER
14 JULY 1944

NIGHT. THROUGH HIS RIGHT EYE MAX SAW THE STARS, BRILLIANT
and seemingly so near in the clear air of the desert. His left eye
ached and wasn't working very well, still swollen from the beating Stoddard's guards had delivered when Max and Carls were
returned to Camp Taylor by the police. Sitting in the rail car with
the Negroes had been a foolish mistake. Max had seen the separate restaurants and bathrooms for Negroes, and he should have
guessed that colored people would be forced to ride in separate
railway coaches as well.

Carls sat beside him in the closed compartment, both of them
handcuffed like convicts—a strict violation of the Geneva Convention, but Max could see how much that meant in the American
wilderness. Stoddard's men had made that clear as day in a back
room in the camp warehouse. Both of Max's eyes had been blackened, lips split, a tooth chipped, balls kicked till they swelled, the
bottoms of his feet strapped. A week later he was still sore every time
he moved, waking each morning stiff as a board before his bruised
muscles gradually loosened up. The guards had been even harder

on Carls because he struggled with them, tossing one across the room and breaking the noses of two others. Besides beating him all over, they shattered his nose in return and the big man was in terrible pain until an escort aboard the train became concerned enough to summon a doctor during a thirty-minute stop in Baton Rouge. The doctor set Carls's nose, gave tetanus injections and pain pills to both men. "This is a disgrace," he told the young escort officer.

It was a disgrace, but the doctor didn't know the half of it. Colonel Stoddard had come in after the beating and forced Max to watch as the special protection orders were ripped from his file. Stoddard put a match to the orders and dropped them into a metal wastebasket, watching the papers burn as if they were his promotion orders. "I'll let your own people do for me what I'm not allowed to do myself," he said. "I warned you boys not to make me look the fool, but you don't care a thing for old Colonel Stoddard and he's never gonna make full colonel now."

So now Max and Carls were headed to New Mexico, probably to the very same camp Lehmann and Heinz had been shipped to—the camp for Nazi troublemakers. Leutnant Lehmann would no doubt be very pleased to see Max arrive. True, Max could write an angry letter to the Swiss Red Cross, but it hardly seemed worth the effort: he'd be dead at the hands of his own countrymen before the complaint ever reached Geneva.

He leaned his head against the train window, the glass cool against his cheek. Max had never imagined that the desert would be this flat or this immense or this cold. It went on forever, big as the sea itself, and seeing it made him ache for the bridge of a ship with the salt wind in his face and spray breaking over the prow. Instead he was handcuffed in a rail car filled with unwashed men smelling of a U-boat.

At least Carls was doing better. Max had tried to focus on worrying about him since they boarded the train in Jackson two days before, escorted in shackles through the same station where they'd been captured on the way to New Orleans. The painkillers seemed to have done Carls some good. But the big man had paid dearly for standing by Max. Just as Malachi had paid dearly for even letting them into his home. He had been dealt with the way troublesome Negroes had been dealt with for centuries in the American South: dragged from his jail cell by an angry white mob and lynched. Max felt sick, he tried not to think about it. But that didn't work. When he learned of Malachi's fate, Max had wondered if he should kill himself, as Captain Langsdorff had done. How else could an honorable man atone for causing the death of another? But what had Langsdorff's suicide accomplished? It left his crew stranded in a foreign country without a leader and left a sorrowful mother, a grieving widow, and two fatherless children back in Germany. Max thought of his father in Bad Wilhelm, of Mareth in Mexico City, of Carls. Killing himself would not bring someone back from the dead. There was nothing he could do for Malachi but grieve for him as he had already grieved for so many in this war.

As he watched from the train, a fire flared in the distance and was gone. It might have been a campfire, like the old days in the far west—sleeping beneath a star-spangled sky, tracking wild beasts across the plain, living simply off the bounty of the land.

At dawn, a guard—a new man Max had not seen before—came on duty with coffee for them. Max held the tin cup in his shackled hands, swaying to the rhythm of the train as he drank.

"Smoke?" the guard asked.

"Yes," Max said, including Carls with a nod of his head. "Thank you."

The young guard reached out and placed the cigarettes directly into their mouths, then lit them. Even so, it was no simple trick to smoke and drink coffee at the same time while wearing handcuffs.

"You guys don't look so tough, for Nazis," the American said pleasantly. "I seen some other Nazis and they looked tougher."

Max looked at the youngster. "We are not Nazis. We are German navy men."

"Well, I guess you boys ran up against somebody who ain't too fond of German navy men."

"Yes."

The guard smiled. "Camp you're going to's full up with Nazis. That's what it's for: Nazis and rabble-rousers. They're always running around yelling, 'Heil Hitler' this and 'Heil Hitler' that."

Max drew on his cigarette and turned again to look out the window. The pink light of sunrise washed over the scrub of the desert and shone bright on the sandstone hills.

"You the U-boat skipper? The other fella told me you were a Nazi U-boat captain. Killed hundreds of people."

"I was on active duty in the German navy when I was captured," Max said. "I am not a member of the Nazi Party, nor have I ever been."

"Kill anybody?"

"Perhaps."

"What's it like?"

Max looked at the guard. Were the Americans raiding grammar schools for soldiers? But then, why not? Everyone else was doing it: the Germans, filling out their divisions with sixteen-year-old boys press-ganged from a dozen countries; the British, handing out commissions in the infantry to nineteen-year-olds, so terrible was the attrition of junior officers in the front lines; in Russia, six-year-old boys served as scouts and toothless grandmothers planted bombs on the rail lines. Sooner or later the world would run out of people to kill. He faced the dusty eternity of the desert again without answering, and the guard didn't ask a second time. But Max knew the answer and it troubled him for the rest of the journey: killing men hadn't felt like much at all.

The train came to a tired halt around 1000 in a mere slip of a town. Max could see two saloons along the main street, a bank, and a small hotel that probably had a few girls available. Two olive green army trucks waited behind the station.

The guards helped Max and Carls off the train. They stood on the rough cement platform, already baking in the sun; six other Germans were brought down as well. The eight of them lined up as if on dress parade, all shackled in handcuffs.

A lean sergeant missing his two front teeth addressed them. He wore the broad-brimmed campaign hat favored by U.S. troops in the First War. "Listen up, boys—I know you can savvy American when you want to. You fucking scumbags have been sent here to the remotest corner of God's green earth because you are no-good, low-down, troublemaking Nazi shitheads," the sergeant barked.

Max let the thin desert air fill his lungs. It was hot but dry and clean. So much better than the brutal humidity of Mississippi, but, looking around, he didn't see much else to commend this place. The heat, even with no humidity, was powerful and it enveloped him, as if he had just been put in a dry sauna. The sergeant went on yelling at them but Max stopped listening to the words. He had a boastful swagger but Max could see that the sergeant's brass uniform accoutrements had not been polished and his boots were badly scuffed.

It was no better at the prison camp. Two of the six guards at the main gate had rust on their rifles, and even the officers in charge of the place looked slovenly, moving slowly around the office as they processed Max. One had a soup stain on his shirt. Another hadn't shaved in several days. But with the big push under way in France, why would the American army send good men to the desert of New Mexico to guard POWs? During the train ride Max had been thinking of explaining his situation to the camp officers: the circumstances of his surrender, the conspiracy plot in Virginia, what Colonel Stoddard had done. But something about the sloppy manner of the officers kept him from doing so. Even if they understood, Max doubted the Americans would go out of their way to help him now, and asking for a private interview in front of the other men would only draw attention. So he stayed quiet. The unshaven officer stamped his papers and issued him a blanket and sheets. "Dismissed."

Max came to attention. "Heil Hitler," he said, giving the Nazi salute. Maybe it would help him blend in and survive.

The unshaven officer came to rumpled attention. "Fuck you," he said, giving the Nazi salute in return.

Max stepped out into the dusty yard. The camp sat on a slight declivity, surrounded by patches of rock with nothing else around but the desert, stretching to the horizon, shimmering like water in the sun. A double barbed-wire fence surrounded the compound at a height of four or five meters, broken by three guard towers. Each tower mounted a fifty-caliber machine gun. There looked to be twelve or maybe fifteen huts for the men, with other buildings scattered around inside the wire, all cheaply constructed of plywood and two-by-fours, white paint flaking from the boards. A hand clapped him on the shoulder.

"Name?"

Max turned and found himself facing a German enlisted man.

"Name?" the man said again.

"You may address me as Herr KapitänLeutnant and let me remind you that you may not touch an officer."

"In this camp, Kamerad, a committee of noncommissioned officers runs affairs because of the lack of commitment to the National Socialist cause among officers. Distinctions of rank have been abolished."

Max lifted his eyebrows. This was worse than he'd imagined. There was a radical wing of the Nazi Party that favored the abolition of class and rank, a return to the egalitarian days of the German tribal past—or so they said. Many of the military's young noncoms had been exposed to this kind of foolishness in the Hitler Youth before the war. Men like Lehmann. But to have them in charge—it was like the Kiel mutiny all over again.

"Name!" the sailor said again, louder this time.

"Brekendorf, Maximilian, KapitänLeutnant."

The man wrote it down. "Hut nine. Heil Hitler."

Max came to attention. "Heil Hitler," he said, jutting his arm out. A ridiculous gesture, like hailing a taxi.

He walked to hut nine, which was nothing more than a large rectangular room with twenty bunks along the walls. He stowed his gear: a bundle of letters, including one from Mareth he hadn't opened yet, a razor, some toothpaste, a bar of soap, a book. That was all he had aside from the fresh bedding and towels provided by the Amis.

Wandering back outside, he stood by the caution line behind his hut, five meters short of the wire, and stared out across the bare land.

"One hundred and twenty kilometers," said a friendly voice.

Max turned to see his old torpedo chief petty officer smiling in the sun. "Heinz!"

"Herr Kaleu. Carls said I would find you here."

Max smiled, too. "So you're a troublemaker, eh, Heinz?"

"And apparently so are you, Herr Kaleu."

"It certainly looks that way. One hundred and twenty kilometers, you said. To where? Hell?"

"Mexico, Herr Kaleu. The border is one hundred and twenty kilometers due south."

"Has anyone gone over the wire?"

Heinz laughed. "Why, Herr Kaleu, you'd have to be a madman. One hundred and twenty kilometers of open desert is as dangerous as running through the Bay of Biscay on the surface, and then what would a blue-eyed German sailor do in Mexico anyway?"

Max nodded. "That must be what the Americans think."

"That's why they sent all us troublemakers out here, Herr Kaleu."

"But you've got a plan, Heinz, yes?"

"I have several, Herr Kaleu," Heinz said, "but the getting out isn't very difficult—these Americans are careless enough to give us opportunities. It's the staying out that makes the challenge. Perhaps the Amis feel they can afford to be careless for good reason."

"Yes, Carls and I found out all about that in Mississippi."

"So I can see. You both look like hell, Herr Kaleu, if I may beg your pardon for saying so, sir."

"I know. They knocked us around some. Carls worse than me."

Both men turned back to the fence, to the expanse of bleak desert stretching south.

"When will you make your break?" Max asked.

Heinz shrugged. "I don't really know, Herr Kaleu. We're gathering supplies right now, some of the men and I. We're collecting food, cereal mostly—we pound it into bits and add dried fruit. Makes a good mixture. We have a tailor from Stuttgart working on civilian clothes. I scavenge all the useful things the Americans leave lying around: maps, canteens. Weapons. Found two compasses on the front seat of a jeep last week."

"Sehr gut, Heinz, very good."

"Thank you, Herr Kaleu. Not sure what good it'll come to"—he gestured vaguely toward the enormous nothing beyond the wire—"but it keeps me occupied, at least. That can be a challenge here."

"There is a camp university, yes?"

"In a manner of speaking, sir, but the only classes it offers are in National Socialist thought."

"A contradiction, in my experience. I'm surprised the Americans allow it."

"They don't seem to care, Herr Kaleu. Why should they? They didn't bring the fanatics out here for a cure. The Allies are pushing through France and they'll go all the way to Berlin by Christmas, and the Soviets are closing in from the East. They've broken through Army Group Center—the High Command has admitted it in the communiqués."

Max shook his head. None of it was news to him. The Soviets had torn a one-hundred-kilometer hole in the German line in June and pushed the Germans back three hundred kilometers in less than a month. "There are others here from the boat?"

"Just myself and Lehmann and Bekker. That's what I've come to warn you about, Herr Kaleu. Since the . . ." Heinz paused. He did not want to use the word *surrender*. "Since the incident, Lehmann has vowed to take vengeance against you. You knew about the plot in Virginia, didn't you, sir?"

"I did. Perhaps I've been hoping his anger might have faded."

"I'm afraid not, Herr Kaleu. He hasn't stopped talking about it all across the damned country. He is certain that he would have received command of his own boat on our return if we had not been captured, and that he would have proven himself a great Kommandant, a hero of the Reich, and the Führer himself would have hung the Ritterkreuz around his neck."

He should have shot Lehmann for insubordination before they ever left the U-boat, Max thought. He drew a pack of Lucky Strikes from his pocket and offered one to Heinz, who declined. "Then I must be very watchful here."

"Yes, sir, but it would have been much better had you not come at all. The men in this camp, many of them are very committed to the party. None of them are March violets, Herr Kaleu," Heinz said, a reference to the opportunists who had joined the Nazi Party only after Hitler seized power. "They are true believers. When Lehmann tells them what you did in the Atlantic, they will not understand. They will not be sympathetic. Bekker is already on his side. You must be on guard, Herr Kaleu. Carls and I will do everything we can to protect you, but it won't be easy."

Max drew on his cigarette. He felt a headache building in the brutal sun. This was worse than Kiel: it was like Munich after the First War, when Communists took control of the city and shot every military officer, policeman, and industrialist they could find and drove the King from the throne. "I do not wish for you or Carls to risk your life for me, Heinz. It is not required."

The torpedo chief petty officer nodded and looked away. "Perhaps not, but you saved us all, Herr Kaleu, and more than once. That surely is the truth, sir. It was a miracle we ever come home from our second patrol. One engine, every piece of equipment in the boat shattered—no crew has ever made it back to Lorient in worse shape, sir. And losses in the U-boat fleet have grown to almost one hundred percent these last months, Herr Kaleu. Worse than ever, worse than when we left on patrol. That's what I hear. For every Allied merchant ship we sink, they sink a U-boat. All of our boats have been withdrawn from the North Atlantic again—all of them. You know what that means, sir."

Max nodded. It meant the same thing it had the last time they did it: the Anglo-American convoy defenses were so formidable they were on the verge of destroying the entire U-boat force.

"If you had not surrendered the boat," Heinz said, "all of us would be dead."

"Nonetheless, Heinz, I order you and Carls not to risk yourselves for me."

Heinz smiled. "Herr Kaleu, don't you know that officers are not permitted to give orders in this camp? Here, sir." He produced a knife and offered it to Max. "Use it if you have to."

Max accepted the knife, bone-handled with a six-inch blade. He felt its solid weight in his hand. He hadn't made use of a knife in years, not since his days on the sail training ship. But how much was there to know? If someone comes for you, bury the knife in his guts. "Thank you, Heinz."

Heinz said nothing, simply giving a quick nod to acknowledge Max's rank—saluting officers was forbidden—and walked away, leaving Max alone at the caution line. A hot wind came down from the north, ruffling the edges of his hair as he stared into the ocean of sand.

Life at the camp quickly became a mix of boredom and fear for Max. There was nothing to do: no trees to cut or courses to teach. Max spent much of his time in his hut. It was unbearably hot, but the roof protected him from the scorching and unrelenting sun. He lay on his bunk all day, smoking Lucky Strikes, drinking Coca-Cola, and reading movie magazines passed on by one of the guards in return for cigarettes. In Mississippi the prisoners had to buy their tobacco with credits earned on work detail, but in New Mexico there was no work detail and the cigarettes were free.

The guards would trade for anything—they viewed their job as a business. Tallulah Bankhead was having romance troubles again. Clark Gable had gone off to make a propaganda film for the American Bomber Command. Incredibly, Max thought, Gable was actually trained as a waist gunner and flew half a dozen bombing missions over Germany, his plane coming back full of holes on several occasions. Only men who had never been shot at wanted to be shot at.

Men stared at him like a cripple in the yard, whispering to one another, no doubt spreading some wildly exaggerated story of what Max had done off Florida. Carls and Heinz stayed with him as often as they could, but few others approached. Lehmann certainly didn't. He strutted around like a peacock, surrounded by Nazi friends, moving around the compound in a pack like a squad of bully-boy storm troopers in Berlin, Bekker among them. Occasionally they looked over at Max and gave him condescending smiles.

Returning to his hut alone after breakfast one morning, Max found three of Lehmann's toadies waiting at the door, blocking his way. The three men stood blinking into the sun, saying nothing. Max stopped in front of them.

"Excuse me," he said.

"Yes, excuse you," said the man in the middle—hardly a man, even: tall and burly, but still young enough to have a tight cluster of acne on each cheek.

"You're in my way," Max said.

"Oh—oh, excuse *me*, then. I hadn't realized." The young man grinned and stepped aside.

Max felt for the handle of the knife tucked into his belt but didn't draw it yet. He moved forward, up the two steps to the doorway. A blow struck the back of his head, and a hand caught his ankle, sprawling him face first into the hut. He flipped over in a panic and yanked the knife out—muscles taut, pulse racing—but Lehmann's men were already walking away. Max could hear them laughing.

"Careful there," the tall one called back over his shoulder. "Watch that last step up."

Max sat on the floor with the knife in his hand, watching the three men amble across the yard. Finally he stood, brushing himself off, wiping the sweat from his eyes. They were just trying to scare him. And he was scared.

He thought again about writing Admiral Dönitz in Code Irland, the secret code all U-boat crews learned so they might communicate useful information if captured, explaining Lehmann's insubordination, the circumstances of his surrender of *U-114*, of asking the admiral to issue a coded command for his protection. But Lehmann was unlikely to obey orders from anyone. And truth be told, Dönitz would agree that Max should die for surrendering his boat. Max buried his face in his hands. His mind was fixed on hopeless alternatives out of bare desperation, but the truth was that nobody could help him.

Certainly not Mareth, though he badly wanted to unburden himself to her. But the American censors would read whatever he wrote, and if they began questioning the other prisoners it would only make matters worse for him. He was convinced of that. Besides, why send Mareth into a panic when there was nothing she could do?

He took the bundle of her letters out from under his mattress and unfolded the latest one to read through the first line again, as he did four or five times a day.

July 27

Dearest Max,

How can I complain? How can I complain when you are safe and I am safe and when this war finally ends we will be together.

Max pictured Mareth crying as she wrote these letters on the veranda of her temporary home in Mexico City, taking refuge from the merciless sun. She would be tan now, her blond hair gone almost to platinum. He would never see her again.

Max sat alone in his room for the rest of the day, sometimes smoking, mostly staring at nothing. The next day was more of the same, as was the day after that. He skipped most meals and appeared only for mandatory roll call in the morning. Carls smuggled food out of the mess hall—apples once, bread another time, and then a few of the miniature cereal boxes that served as breakfast for the prisoners. Max liked Kellogg's Corn Flakes the best. Luckily, he found that sitting all day on his bunk without moving reduced his appetite even more: he was never hungry, he ate only because Carls told him to.

Nights were the worst. He tried to sleep but was too anxious, lying there gripping his knife, waiting to be set upon in the dark, listening to the men snoring around him, his body going tense at the slightest sound. It seemed impossible to control his nerves once the sun went down. But after three such nights, nobody had come for him, and Max knew he couldn't keep living this way. In the morning he went to the mess hall with Carls and Heinz and bolted three boxes of Corn Flakes.

Coming out of the latrine after the meal, Max found Lehmann waiting in the hall. He was alone, smoking, his back against the wall. He smiled and said, "Guten Morgen, Maximilian. I haven't seen you in these last few days. Thought maybe something had happened to you."

Max fixed his best parade-ground stare on Lehmann. "Thank you, Leutnant. I find such sentiment on your part heartwarming."

Lehmann scowled, pointed the end of his cigarette at Max. "You're a traitor, Maximilian. You ruined my navy career and betrayed me — me and the crew and the Führer as well. You're a traitor to the Fatherland, you swine, and the men in this camp know it."

"The men in this camp have no respect for the proper discipline of the Wehrmacht. You are a traitor to the German navy, Leutnant Lehmann. You and your friends should all be court-martialed for insubordination."

Max had the knife secured beneath his uniform. He could slit Lehmann's throat right now and maybe it would be better that way. He stared at the young man without saying anything.

"You should be more at ease," Lehmann said. "When we want you, we shall come for you. There is little you can do to stop us, so don't lose your rest over it." He dropped the cigarette butt and crushed it with his shoe, smiled again, then walked away.

"Worst of it is," Heinz said over a cigarette later that night, "the filthy pig might be right. We'll do our best to keep you safe, Herr Kaleu, but there's nowhere to hide in this camp."

Max nodded. What Heinz said was true. And because it was true, he let Carls and Heinz convince him to go with them to the movie being shown that night. "We'll be on either side of you, Herr Kaleu," Carls assured him. "There will be American guards everywhere, Lehmann won't go for you there."

"What are they showing?"

"*The Thin Man*."

Max smiled. Myrna Loy. She would be worth seeing again. And *The Thin Man* was a favorite. He'd seen it twice with Mareth in Berlin before the war. He smiled, something Carls and Heinz hadn't seen in a while. "Then let us go, gentlemen."

"Jawohl," said Carls, "all ahead full."

Smoke filled the brightly lit mess hall. Everyone seemed to be smoking; it was almost like a hobby in the camp. The Americans gave the men as many cigarettes as they wanted. Max, Heinz, and Carls sat on the floor at the back of the hall, not far from the door. Hardly anyone seemed to have noticed them come in. Even if they had, it would take a brave soul to jump him with Heinz and Carls on either side.

The men began to stomp their feet around 2000 hours. They did it in unison, like participants at a Nazi rally, and the American guards took the cue. They cut the lights and started the projector, beginning the show with a newsreel about the war. Allied progress in France was steady, unstoppable. Caen had indeed fallen; the newsreel showed Allied tanks rolling through the burnt-out city. The men booed vociferously, throwing cigarette butts at the screen. They went on booing as the footage shifted to Italy, to the American troops now in Rome, and the Pacific, where the first American bombs had begun raining down on Tokyo.

Finally the movie itself began, the prisoners shouting and catcalling at any woman who walked through the frame. They erupted when Myrna Loy finally came on screen, one man in front jumping up to rub his crotch in her direction as the others howled. The Americans hadn't added German subtitles but this hardly seemed to bother the men, who followed along as best as they could.

Max was able to lose himself in the laughter for a few minutes. American movies were the best in the world. Max whispered translations of the dialogue to Heinz and Carls at crucial moments. The men went on smoking, laughing loudly when they sensed the slightest joke; they were eager to laugh. Max had noticed this in the movies at Camp Taylor, too. It was as if they were all trying to prove to themselves that they hadn't lost the ability.

Halfway through the movie, the screen went dark. The men hooted but the lights did not come back on. Max realized the building's electricity had been cut. No one moved because it was too dark to see and they wanted to watch the rest of the movie. But Max's battle instincts had him rising to his feet before his mind had even consciously registered the danger. A hand clapped over his mouth. He drew the knife and plunged it blindly at whoever was behind him. The knife cut into flesh but something metal slammed against the back of Max's head, staggering him, and he dropped the blade. A burlap sack dropped over his face and he heard Carls and Heinz struggling beside him. Bodies hit the floor but he couldn't tell whose. Men in the audience were getting to their feet, some of them beginning to shout for the movie to come back on. Max had gone groggy from the blow to the head. His joints went loose as they dragged him to the door.

Outside now. Max felt the cool night air on his skin. He was being carried by three men, maybe four, walking quickly across the dark compound. Nobody said anything. They passed through another door, dropped Max into a hard wooden chair. Someone yanked the bag off his head.

They were in one of the outbuildings. Max couldn't tell which. The room was not large, just a small hut made of thin plywood. Six men were seated at a rectangular table in front of him—Lehmann, Bekker, and four of their comrades, all noncommissioned Nazi extremists. A soldier stood at parade rest on either side of Max; he recognized one of them as the burly young acne sufferer who had harassed him the week before. The man's uniform was torn and blood dripped from a shallow knife wound below his ribcage, but he seemed unfazed.

Lehmann presided. He sat at the center of the table, holding a ceremonial Nazi dagger. Max wondered how he'd gotten his hands on one of those—it was among the first items American soldiers looked for to take as a souvenir. The British fought for empire it was said, the French for glory, the Americans for souvenirs. The table was draped with a homemade banner: a mildly warped swastika in a white circle on a field of red that looked more like burnt orange. The room was lit with candles stuck in empty Coke bottles. All the men at the table stared directly, severely at Max, with the exception of Bekker, who seemed to have his eyes fixed on a point on the wall above Max's head.

Lehmann cleared his throat. "This Kriegsmarine Court of Honor is convened to hear evidence and pronounce judgment on the conduct of a certain Maximilian Brekendorf, who is charged with disloyalty to the Führer and German Reich and cowardice in the face of the enemy."

Max raised his voice. "You will address me as Herr Kapitän-Leutnant," he announced, but none of the men paid him any attention. His head was still ringing but he felt calm—the suspense was over. War was an endless series of absurdities, any one of which might prove fatal. "And for which of these do you suppose I was awarded the Iron Cross First and Second Class, Leutnant?" he said. "Did I receive those for my disloyalty, or for my cowardice? And the black wound badge, and the auxiliary cruiser badge? And the German Cross in gold for bringing my U-boat safely back to port after being rammed by a British destroyer? Was that awarded to me in the name of the Führer for betraying the Führer, Leutnant? Are you mad?"

Lehmann frowned. "You will have an opportunity to defend yourself once the evidence has been heard, Herr Brekendorf."

"And you will have an opportunity to be court-martialed for violating the Military Law of the German Wehrmacht with these illegal and irregular proceedings if I ever get out of here, Leutnant."

"If, Herr Brekendorf. Shall we begin?" He turned to Bekker. "Our first witness is Rudolph Bekker, former radioman aboard *U-114* under the command of Herr Brekendorf."

The man to Lehmann's right began writing dutifully in a small black notebook, as if this might lend the trial some official flair.

"Herr Bekker," Lehmann started in, "please tell the court your position before posting to the fleet."

Bekker was the oldest man in the room. Gray streaks ran through his hair. He glanced briefly at Max before looking up again at his chosen point on the wall. "I served as a personnel clerk in the Naval Records Office in Kiel."

"I see. And did this position allow you access to any pertinent information regarding Herr Brekendorf's background?"

"Yes. When I was posted to *U-114*, I read the file on the Kommandant so I might know something about the man under whom I would serve. Naturally I was curious." Several of the other men at the table nodded in understanding. "To my dismay, I discovered that the Kommandant had been taken in for questioning by the Gestapo in Paris after helping an Allied spy escape capture."

Lehmann lifted his eyebrows and swept the room with a significant look.

"That is a specious allegation," Max said. "It was a misunderstanding. They never would have given me my own boat if there was anything to it."

"Silence," Lehmann ordered. "You will be allowed to present your case in due time, Herr Brekendorf, but the court will look on your behavior with severe disapproval if you continue to speak out of turn."

"Enough," Max said. He began to rise from his chair but the two soldiers forced him back down.

"Continue, Herr Bekker. You said he had been arrested by the Gestapo on suspicion of assisting an Allied spy ring?"

"That is correct, Herr Lehmann."

Max shook his head.

Lehmann looked to the other members of his kangaroo court. "Questions?"

The man with the notebook leaned forward. "So you are telling us that Herr Brekendorf's treasonous activity against the Reich predates the surrender of *U-114*?"

"Jawohl."

Max stared at Bekker, and now Bekker stared back. His eyes had a hollow look in them. Looking through classified personnel records was illegal, a court-martial offense in its own right, and

Bekker must have known as much. If Max ever got back to Germany . . . but that was a moot point.

Lehmann picked up the ceremonial dagger and began twirling it in his right hand. "Our second charge is cowardice in the face of the enemy. Herr Bekker, did *U-114* in fact torpedo and sink the Royal Mail Ship *Dundee* while that ship was sailing alone and unescorted off the southern coast of Florida?"

"She did, Herr Lehmann."

"And did Herr Brekendorf then make any effort to leave the scene of the sinking in order to avoid enemy patrols?"

"Quite to the contrary, Herr Lehmann—Herr Brekendorf forced me to radio the enemy patrols myself."

Lehmann animated his face with false surprise. "And what did Herr Brekendorf do when the enemy patrol vessels arrived?"

"He immediately surrendered the U-boat."

The men at the table now stared at Max in unison with mock disbelief. Max just shook his head slowly. He'd seen more combat than all six of them combined.

"Now, Herr Brekendorf," Lehmann said, "do you have any response to these charges before the court presents its findings?"

Max looked steadily into the hostile faces before him. "This trial is a sham," he said quietly, "and all of you know it. If I am a traitor, then Germany has no heroes. I have given my life to the navy, done all that I was asked, killed more men than I wish to recall, and watched my friends die around me, just as my father did in the trenches at Verdun. Although it was within my orders to do so, I would never have sunk the *Dundee* had I known it was a passenger vessel. Nor would it have befitted the honor of the German navy, the navy of Admiral Graf von Spee, the navy of Count von Luckner and Captain Langsdorff, to stand by and watch women and children drown when it was in my power to save them. If we have lost our humanity to this war, then we are fighting for nothing. If Germany gives her honor for Final Victory, she will still have lost."

"Stirring." Lehmann smiled, then turned solemnly to his panel. "How say you?" he asked the first man.

"Guilty."

"How say you?" he asked the second.

"Guilty."

They went down the line like that—the verdict unanimous.

Standing now, boyish in his wrinkled khaki uniform, Lehmann said, "Of course there is only one punishment for treason against our Führer, Adolf Hitler, and cowardice in the face of the enemy. That punishment is death."

Max swung with all his strength and hit the soldier on his right in the kidneys. As the man doubled over in pain, Max swung the other way and hit the big soldier to his left in the balls.

"Stop him!" Lehmann bellowed, scrambling over the table, dagger in hand.

Max leapt up from the chair, seized it, and broke it over Lehmann's head. The other jurors rushed forward, one of them catching Max full in the face with a roundhouse punch. The guards recovered, pulled at his arms, and Max struggled free before more punches knocked him to the ground. Three men piled on top of him. He squirmed like an eel, flailed wildly with his fists, smelled the sour breath of the men as they pinned his body to the wooden floorboards. Then a loud crack sounded as the building's flimsy door flew from its hinges.

Carls leapt forward with a lead pipe. It landed heavily on somebody's head, then again, and suddenly everyone was shouting until a new voice froze the room.

"Hände hoch! Hands up or I shoot!"

Heinz. He stood in the doorway pointing a pistol. Carls helped Max up from the floor. Massaging his face, Max could feel the blood pouring out of his nose. "I thought you men would never get here."

"We wanted to watch the end of the movie, Herr Kaleu," said Heinz.

Lehmann seethed, his face also bloodied, knuckles white on

the hilt of his dagger. He glared at Max, then Carls, then finally at Heinz. "I will kill you all," he hissed.

Heinz smiled. "Not if we kill you first. Hand over that dagger."

Lehmann didn't move.

"Hand it over," Heinz repeated, twitching the barrel of the pistol for emphasis.

Lehmann tried to twist his lips into an ironic grin of his own. He held the dagger out in his open hand and Carls snatched it away. "Go," the big man said to Max, who turned and ducked out the door into the darkness, followed closely by his rescuers.

The compound teemed with men just out from the movie and they mixed in with the crowd, Carls pushing Max toward the camp's southern end, Heinz trailing just behind in case someone gave them the jump. They cut between two of the narrow wooden huts. Carls looked around. "Under," he ordered. Max dropped to the sandy ground and rolled underneath the hut, which sat about a meter up on cinderblocks. The big man and Heinz did the same and the three of them stretched out behind the cement pedestal that supported the water pipes. They lay there panting for air in the dark without speaking for several minutes. Finally Max caught his breath and said, "Where in the name of Saint Peter did you get a pistol, Heinz?"

Heinz smiled and whispered, "Keep your eyes open, Herr Kaleu, and you can find anything around here. When I find some bullets for this it will be even more useful."

Now Max shook his head in amazement. "You have the courage of a lion, Heinz. The two of you have done more for me than I deserve. Thank you."

"You should be holding off them thanks for a while, sir, since we ain't out of the jungle yet. We have to get you out of this camp, sir. It's much too dangerous for you here now."

Around them men tramped across the yard, heading to their huts for the night. Footsteps echoed through the floor above Max's head as well. Lehmann and his dupes might be out searching for them right now, moving from building to building, sweeping the camp. Or maybe they felt there would be time enough for that. After all, Max would be around the next day, and the next day, and the day after that.

"We have to get you out of this camp," Heinz said again.

"Ja, you are correct, Heinz. You are correct. But it would be easier to smuggle a crate of schnapps onto a U-boat than to get me out of here."

"Not at all, sir. Me and Carls smuggled a case of schnapps onto the boat before every patrol, if you must know, Herr Kaleu."

Max looked from one of them to the other. "How? Where did you put it?"

"Begging your pardon, Herr Kaleu, it would be best for us not to be getting into all that. You go out tomorrow. Tomorrow morning, sir. On the garbage truck."

The garbage truck entered the camp each Monday morning near the time of roll call and backed up to the garbage shed on the western edge of the main yard. Two civilian workers in beige coveralls then emptied the garbage cans into the back of the truck. Each can required both men to lift, and they usually worked at a measured clip, so the process took perhaps fifteen minutes. After the cans had all been emptied, the garbage workers would share a smoke with a few of the guards. Then back in the truck and out through the main gate. The truck was usually inside the camp fence for twenty minutes.

Max had seen it but he hadn't taken much notice. Heinz had taken notice and had carefully timed it out over weeks. Of his many escape plans, the garbage truck was the best, he said.

"You want me to hide in one of those garbage cans, yes?" Max asked. That would be unpleasant, though it could hardly smell worse than the inside of a U-boat after a few weeks on patrol.

"No, Herr Kaleu," said Heinz, "that's a bad idea. The truck is a new American model with a compactor built right in. It would crush you into a bouillon cube, even if the workers somehow missed you when they emptied the can. You go underneath, Herr Kaleu."

"Underneath? Underneath the truck? You are certain of this?"

"The truck is quite large, Herr Kaleu. It has plenty of clearance and I think there are pipes and grips you can hold on the undercarriage. I took a quick look several weeks ago—seems to me that a man could wedge himself in between the rear axle and the drive shaft."

"How long will I have to hold on?"

"That I don't know, Herr Kaleu. I don't know where the truck goes when it leaves here."

Max bit the inside of his lip. Underneath a garbage truck? A bugle call sounded, reminding the POWs that it was almost 2230—five minutes until all prisoners were confined to their huts for the night.

Heinz said, "Stay here until morning, Herr Kaleu. Just to be safe, stay here until roll call begins. I'll bring you some supplies at roll call, and then you can make your break. Do you understand, sir?"

"Ja, ja. And what of you, comrades?"

"They won't be looking for us—not tonight. Perhaps for you, but not for us."

"Thank you, Heinz. Thank you both."

"Take this," said Carls, pressing the hilt of Lehmann's dagger into Max's hand. "We will see you tomorrow morning, Herr Kaleu."

"Carls, Heinz," Max whispered.

"Sir?"

He shook each by the hand. "May you always have a hand's breadth of water under your keel," Max said quietly.

Heinz whispered: "Good luck and good hunting, Herr Kaleu."

Carls nodded, too overcome to speak. Then they were gone. Max lay alone beneath the hut, the dagger clutched to his chest. Quiet came with the men in bed. Max knew he wouldn't sleep a wink on the hard ground with nothing for a pillow. He hadn't worn his jacket to the movie and shivered now, though it had been almost a hundred degrees at noon.

Mexico. Heinz's plan sounded simple enough, and if Max could get out of the camp, Mexico would be only a hundred and twenty kilometers away. How far then to Mexico City? He wasn't sure, but he might be able to make it if he got across the border somehow. He closed his eyes and tried to picture how it would be when he walked into the courtyard of Schrempf's house: Mareth with a glass of cold gin and a parasol in the heat, leaning in the portico with a flower behind her ear. A carnation, a rose. But this was just a fantasy. It would never happen. He hadn't been able to stay on the outside for more than a day in Mississippi; this time, if the Americans didn't just shoot him, Lehmann and the Nazis would finish him off when he was returned to the camp.

Lying there in the dirt, Max thought of the night he had proposed to her. They were in a small boarding house in Flensburg, the gasthaus where Mareth always stayed when she came to visit him at the Marineschule, because it was easy for Max to steal up the back stairs into her room. Of course, no men were allowed in the building, nor were Seekadetten supposed to be off base at night. But the boarding houses in Flensburg were often full of young women, and they hadn't come for the scenery. The Marineschule was just three kilometers away.

Max had bought the ring that week without settling on when to ask her—he wanted something spectacular: a mountaintop, a sailboat on the Baltic, an intimate table at the Germania. But the ring seemed to burn a hole in his pocket once he had it, and it was all he could do to get through their first dinner together without showing her. That night, after she let him in and latched the door behind them, he dropped immediately to one knee and opened the velvet box in the lamplight for her to see. She wore a crafty smile as he stumbled through the question.

"Are you certain of this, Seekadett Brekendorf?"

"Of course I'm certain."

"And have I been approved by the Kriegsmarine to be your wife?" The navy had to approve an officer's choice of bride before he could marry her.

"You have, Fräulein Countess von Woller, although the request had to go to the very top of the Kriegsmarine, because of the year you spent as a showgirl at the Wintergarten."

"Forever is a long time," she warned him, "and that's how long you will have me."

"Good." He put the ring on her finger. It was much too big—he'd never even thought of rings having sizes before the jeweler asked him. It wouldn't stay on her finger. "Did you buy this for another girl?" Mareth said.

"Yes, I did. A fat girl I was seeing in France."

They both began to laugh.

Max stood and put his arms around her. "Well, we have the rest of our lives to improve on it."

"Yes, we will, Max," she whispered in his ear, pulling his body tightly against hers. "We have the rest of our lives."

When Max awoke from his dream it was morning. He was surprised to find that he'd slept. For how long he wasn't sure, but when he opened his eyes, the sun was already bright and men in the hut above were filing out for the morning roll. He waited until they had all gone out and formed up in the middle of the yard. The American sergeant began calling names. Then Max scrambled out, stiff all over from sleeping on the packed earth, and joined the rear of the formation.

Over to his left he saw Carls and Heinz, caught their eyes, then looked away. When Max answered to his own name, Lehmann turned full around from where he stood, several rows ahead. He had a gash above his right eye that would need stitches. That was from the chair. Max fixed him with a hard stare. Lehmann faced forward again just as the main gate opened to admit the lumbering garbage truck.

After the men were dismissed Heinz approached Max with a haversack in his hand. "Sleep well, Herr Kaleu?"

"Well enough." Max eyed Lehmann as the lieutenant crossed the yard to his group of Nazi toadies. They shot sidelong glances in Max's direction, talking briefly among themselves before slinking off.

Heinz handed the haversack over. "I wish I had more to give you, Herr Kaleu, but this is a start: a suit, some food, twenty-five dollars of American money, an Esso map of Mexico, a compass, one canteen of water. The suit won't fit you very well, but it'll be better than your uniform."

Max looked into the bag. "I can't take all this, Heinz. You've been scavenging these things for months—it's bad enough that I'm stealing your escape plan."

"Take it, Herr Kaleu, take it." Heinz smiled, not without a little sadness. "It's like I said: scheming gives me something to do, but I can't make it out there. I don't speak English, and even if I could, why take the risk? You don't got much to lose. They'll kill you if you stay."

"They'll try to get you, too, you know. You and Carls both."

Heinz shook his head. "No, sir. They won't. I've been here longer than Lehmann, Herr Kaleu. I have friends among the men, and among the Americans, too. I may have helped you, but I didn't surrender U-114. There are some other prewar petty officers in the camp. We stick together. And we know how to use our knives and the youngsters don't. If I may beg your pardon, Herr Kaleu, it will be easier for us once you aren't here."

Max looked down at the ground. Pray God that was true.

"Stay near the garbage truck, Herr Kaleu. Watch me and Carls and be ready. When we make our diversion, go." Heinz turned, strolling back to where Carls stood alone in the sun.

Max strapped on the haversack and walked briskly over to hut five, which stood beside the garbage shed in the shadow of the truck. The garbage workers dumped a can into the back of the truck, then took it back empty to the shed. Max leaned against the wall of the hut and watched them make another trip, then another, keeping his eyes also on Carls and Heinz loitering by the flagpole out in the yard.

The trash men returned the last can to the shed and came out with their hands empty. Heinz had still done nothing. Two guards approached the workers. Just as Heinz had predicted, the four of them all lit cigarettes. One of the guards said something that made the others laugh. Max's heart pounded. He glanced up at the guard towers, their mounted guns pointing down into the compound. In the nearest tower, a soldier leaned on the rail reading a comic book. Suddenly, Carls pushed Heinz with both hands and Heinz stumbled backward. He shouted something unintelligible, recovered his balance, and punched Carls in the face. Now Carls was shouting, too, in his deep voice that could wake the dead. "She wasn't a whore, you swine! She was a proper young woman!" He punched Heinz in the stomach and cursed him again. "Call her a whore again and I will punch your mouth out of your asshole!" The guards dropped their cigarettes, ran toward the flagpole. Max dropped to the ground, rolled underneath the truck.

He wedged his feet above the rear axle, reached up to wrap his arms around the thick pipe running down the center of the undercarriage, then locked his hands around smaller pipes on either side until his grip felt solid. Heinz and Carls were still cursing at each other but he couldn't see them anymore. What he could see were the boots of the two garbage men. They stood with their backs to the truck, watching the fight. They went on watching for another minute or two, then let their cigarettes fall into the dust and crushed them out before separating to board the cab from opposite sides. Max heard the truck drop into first gear, and the pitch of the engine rose as they began to roll forward.

His hands sweated against the greasy pipes. He pulled himself up, closer to the undercarriage, and braced his arms for the truck to pick up speed. It eased to a stop instead. Max felt his stomach drop. He couldn't hear over the noise of the engine, couldn't see what was happening at the front of the truck. It was like being trapped in the U-boat, waiting for the depth charges to explode. He closed his eyes. Dear God and the Virgin Mother and all the Saints, just get me outside the fence. A minute passed. Heinz had said nothing about this part of the procedure, it wasn't normal, someone had seen him — but then they lurched forward and were moving again. Max turned his head and saw the little guardhouse pass by, along with the boots of the sentry on duty.

They were on the outside.

Now the truck began to speed up. The road was dirt and Max heard pebbles turned up by the wheels striking the undercarriage, but he was far enough behind the front axle to avoid being hit. The vibration of the engine rattled his body, though, and he wondered how long he would have to hold on.

They drove for five minutes, then turned left onto asphalt. The ride was smoother now and Max's muscles hadn't yet begun to burn. Moving faster, they rolled down the highway for ten minutes, then fifteen. His fingers started to ache. Should have worn gloves. If his grip gave out, his feet would remain locked in place and he would be dragged into a bloody corpse on the pavement. Don't think about that. How long now? Thirty minutes? His muscles burned like fire from holding on. Suddenly the truck slowed and turned back onto dirt and a heavy smell hit Max in his nostrils: trash.

The land itself smelled like trash.

The truck growled up a hill and turned again, paused, dropped into reverse, then backed to a stop. Max pulled his feet free, slowly unwound his hands and fingers from the chassis, eased himself to the ground, drew the Nazi dagger from his boot. He lay still, breathing hard, flat on his back with the haversack on top of him, flexing his cramped fingers. He could see piles of trash off to either side. One of the workmen jumped down from the cab, walked to the back of the truck, and then the truck itself began to rise into the air over Max's head. A hydraulic motor had been engaged and whined loudly above the rumble of the engine idling beneath the hood.

Sunlight poured in on Max as the body of the truck tilted upward, away from the cab. He was totally exposed but the view of the man at the back of the vehicle was blocked by the tipping trash compartment, and his partner remained behind the wheel in the cab. No one else was there—just garbage, stinking heaps of garbage. Max stayed flat to the ground, holding the dagger down at his side, ready to use. The compartment reached its apex and began dumping its contents. Blood pounded in Max's ears. One of these days his heart would just give out, explode from the strain of beating so hard. Could that happen? The hydraulic motor kicked in again, lowering the empty compartment back down. It seemed to take an age. It locked into place and the motor cut out. The workman's boots walked past Max and disappeared upward as he returned to the cab. Max waited.

There was no end to it, really. Survive a sea battle off the Rio Plata, cross the Argentine pampas on foot, and the next thing you knew, they were sinking a glorified cruise ship out from under you in the Indian Ocean. Survive eleven days in a lifeboat full of corpses. Get stuffed into a U-boat with a bunch of greenhorn virgins for a crew. Make it through that and your own German brothers vow to kill you in a nameless POW camp, and if you get away from them you end up sprawled in the foul-smelling dust of some godforsaken American nowhere, waiting to be run over by a garbage truck.

The truck dropped into gear. Max realized one of the back tires might roll him flat if the driver moved forward at an angle. He didn't. The truck moved away and left Max blinking up into the white desert sun. Don't look back in the mirror, he thought. Don't look back in the mirror. He waited to hear the truck pause, hear it turn around and head back in his direction. Nothing. The sound faded away, leaving only the noise of scattered birdcalls carried on the hot, dry breeze.

He stood, body exhausted, hanging loose at the joints; his primal will to survive was nearly spent and he knew it. Trash surrounded him on all sides, the smell powerful—much worse than the inside of a U-boat that had been a month at sea.

Max reached into the haversack and pulled out the new suit of clothes. He stripped down to his underwear and stuffed his tattered uniform, stained with blood from the fighting the night before, into a soggy cardboard box lying amid the refuse. The suit must have been made for Heinz—the pants were too short but loose in the waist, and the jacket fit loosely as well. But it would do. Max wondered where Heinz had even gotten the material. He wondered if it was right to leave Heinz and Carls behind to deal with the Nazis in the camp. He wondered where in the name of God he was.

Climbing a pile of trash, Max saw that he stood at the center of a vast landscape of garbage. The dump stretched out for hundreds of meters on either side of him, occupying the top of a rocky plateau, and the birds he'd heard screeching were black-winged turkey buzzards. They gathered in packs here and there, squawking at one another, fluttering their long dark wings, pecking at their unearthed treasures with their horrible beaks.

In front of Max a broad valley of scrub brush and white sand stretched out to another line of hills far in the distance. Taking out his compass, he saw that he was looking south: toward Mexico. There was no sign of life in the valley, save for a single thread of empty blacktop running down the center of the empty land. It must have been the highway on which the garbage truck had come, though it could have been any highway at all. The sun was searing now, the distant ridgeline wavering in the heat. Max could feel sweat on his brow, a scratchy dryness in his throat. He turned and saw one of the vultures staring him down. The Americans would not know he was gone until the next morning, but then they would know. He looked down at his feet in their camp-issue cardboard shoes. He was standing on the headless body of a child's doll, on the disembodied back of a kitchen chair, on broken milk bottles and cereal boxes and an old cabinet radio, one hundred and twenty kilometers from Mexico. He'd come halfway around the world and survived five years of war to stand on this trash heap in the desert summer, surrounded by ugly scavenger birds that might soon be picking the flesh from his bones. Soon enough: he would finally be picked clean.

EPILOGUE

BAD WILHELM, GERMANY
SIX WEEKS LATER
10 SEPTEMBER 1944

BUHL FELT A LUMP RISE IN HIS THROAT AS HE LOOKED DOWN AT THE telegram for Johann Brekendorf. It had come from Berlin and bore the official party seal on the outside of the envelope. How many had he delivered this year? Several dozen, maybe more; as Kreisleiter, the duty fell to him. "Volk and Führer," he would say as he presented the envelopes, or "died for Greater Germany." These were suggested phrases of condolence sent down from Party District Headquarters in Kiel, but the words never provided comfort. The tears were rarely immediate now—people seemed to expect the news; anger came first. They would take the telegram from his hand and stare icily at Buhl, setting their jaws, saying nothing. Of course the only reason he had not gone off to fight was the important party business he had to attend to. It was no secret. Seeing him at their door with the telegram, hearing his hollow words of sympathy, he wondered if the parents of the dead resented him for not having been killed along with all the rest. Resnau, the farmer east of town, had lost both his boys. He never left the house anymore, his farm going to ruin. Then Bruno, the tavern keeper, his son killed at Stalingrad, and Maus, who worked in the bakery, his youngest dead in Sicily. Juergen Kraus had been lost on the Volga, and August Faslem near Voronezh; Friedrich Fuge, shot down over France; Walter Guggenberger, blown up in Libya; Otto Drescher at Stalingrad; Fritz Zundorf and Kurt Hoferichter in the retreat from Rostov; Reinhard Drescher in Minsk. It seemed as if all of Buhl's schoolmates were dead. And now Max was gone.

Buhl stood and straightened his tan party uniform, pinching the blood red swastika armband into place. He walked outside and mounted his bicycle. Even within the party, only the most senior officials could get petrol anymore. With a push he was off, pedaling slowly toward the large home where Johann Brekendorf now lived alone. The sky was cloudless, something normally welcomed, but no longer. A cloudless sky meant American bombers. Nonetheless, the air was warm and pleasantly dense. It was a good day for walking in the woods, swimming in a lake, or taking the sun.

Buhl parked his bicycle outside Johann's two-story home and paused. What should he say to the old man, whose wife was twenty-five years in the grave and whose lover had been shot by men in the same uniform Buhl now wore? Best to say nothing at all. He took a deep breath, then stepped up to the door. Before he could even reach up to knock it swung open very slowly. Johann stood silently in the door frame. His weight had fallen off badly; the skin hung slack from his face. Even the ones who lived were hardly living anymore. Drawing himself up, Buhl gave the stiff-armed Nazi salute and thrust the telegram forward. The old man refused to take it. He opened his mouth to speak, then closed it again, no words forthcoming. Finally he reached out and accepted the yellow envelope.

His hands shook so badly that he could hardly get it open. Buhl thought to help him, then thought: I should leave. But he didn't. Instead he stood very still on the doorstep, arms hanging loose at his sides, and simply turned his face away. Wildflowers bloomed among the weeds in front of the house in a patch of dirt that had once been carefully tended by Johann's gardener, killed three years ago in Crete. Lazy bees wandered from flower to flower. Their buzzing filled the heavy air. When Buhl looked up again, Johann was holding the telegram out to him. The old man was weeping, but light burned in his eyes. Buhl took the paper and read:

Herr Brekendorf,
Your son is alive in Mexico City. My daughter is with him. Both are healthy. More news soon. Heil Hitler, Helmuth von Woller.

Acknowledgments

In the early 1980s I corresponded with the late Jürgen Wattenberg, Kapitän zur See a.D.(Captain, ret.), former senior navigation officer of *Admiral Graf Spee*. I wish to acknowledge the information he shared with me.

I wish to thank Mr. Joseph Gilbey of Ontario, Canada, who sent me a copy of his book, *Langsdorff of the* Graf Spee: *Prince of Honor*. This excellent biography deserves a wider circulation. Mr. Gilbey answered a number of questions and kindly gave his permission to use several quotes of Captain Langsdorff's cited in the book.

I wish to thank Mr. Jak P. Mallmann Showell, the foremost authority on the German UBoatwaffe in World War Two, for answering my questions about U-boats and daily life in the Third Reich. I recommend any and all of his many books, all of which are excellent. Two were particularly helpful: *U-Boats under the Swastika* and *U-Boat Commanders and Crews*.

I wish to thank the many people, including former U-boat crewmen, who shared their experiences with me, responded to my letters or e-mails, or answered my questions on various Kriegsmarine forums.

Details of the historical events that underpin the novel, along with suggestions for further reading, can be found on my Web site: www.charlesmccain.com

I can say without reservation that *An Honorable German* would never have been written and published without the encouragement, enthusiasm, and constant support of my friend the distinguished historian and author Derek Leebaert. He not only made time to listen and empathize with my frustrations over writing, he introduced me to my agent. Thank you, Derek, for everything you did for me. Without you, it never would have happened.

There is a proverb that I have found to be true throughout my life: "When the student is willing, the teacher appears." And so it was that I met one of the best teachers I have ever had: Jürgen Meyer-Brenkhof (Crew X/71M), Fregattenkapitän a.D., Deutsche Marine (Commander, retired, German Navy). I offer my heartfelt thanks and sincere gratitude to Jürgen, who shared with me his encyclopedic knowledge of the German navy, German history, and all subjects nautical. Jürgen read the entire manuscript, made numerous corrections, offered many suggestions, and answered hundreds of questions. Further, he entrusted me with the private memoirs of his late father, who served with great bravery in the Kriegsmarine, and whose memoirs are rich in the kind of detail I was seeking. All of this greatly improved the accuracy of the narrative. Thank you, Jürgen, for all you taught me, your friendship, and your support of this endeavor.

My literary agent, Deborah Grosvenor, who, among her many accomplishments discovered the novelist Tom Clancy, put her considerable reputation on the line to sell my novel. Both her decision to represent me and her constant encouragement during the year and a half I spent rewriting my novel were critical in keeping up my morale. Her enthusiasm and passion for *An Honorable German* resulted in a letter to publishers so strong as to be the equivalent of a broadside from *Graf Spee*. Thank you, Deborah, for all you did. No author could have asked more from an agent.

I offer my most sincere thanks and gratitude to my editor, Mitch Hoffman. His uncompromising vision of what the novel could be, his sharp pencil, and his gentle requests for me to re-work (and re-work) certain scenes in the novel not only challenged me to do my very best writing but made the book so much better than it otherwise would have been. Further, Mitch always knew just the right words with which to reassure me during the many times I became so stressed out I wanted to throw my laptop out the window.

I want to thank Tom Rancich, Lt. Commander (ret.), U.S. Navy SEALS, who kindly answered a number of my questions about ships and other subjects nautical.

I want to thank my friend Captain William D. Messer, Palm Beach Pilots Association, who carefully reviewed the manuscript for any errors or omissions.

I owe special thanks to my friend Stuart Brodsky, who spent so much time listening to me talk about the novel that he became an expert on the German navy, even though he did not want to be.

I want to thank the following fraternity brothers, who have been listening to this story off and on since we first graduated from Tulane: Larry Comiskey, Nelson Gibson, Scott Katzmann, and Bob Warren. I am grateful for their support over these many years but, far more important, I am grateful for the bonds of brotherhood and friendship we formed in college, which have stayed with us to this day.

I would like to thank the following for their friendship and support over many years: my brother Will McCain and my sister-in-law Jeanelle, Hugh Auchincloss, Greg Barnard and Roman Terleckyj, Dana and Stan Day, Scott Guenther, Glenn Hennessey, Jon Low, Isaac Lustgarten and Edward Flannigan, Anne Messer, Tom O'Rourke, Dana Pickard and Joyce Elden, Robin Rance, Joy Ryan, David Sperling, Stacey Jarrett Wagner, Eleanor Weinstock, and Matt Weissman. To this list I add, in memoriam, my late friend and one of the finest men I have ever known, Sander B. Weinstock.

* * *

In the book of sorrow that is the Second World War, there exists a chapter seldom read, the words now so faded as to be indecipherable. These are the names of the countless Germans who gave their lives resisting the tyranny of the Third Reich. They deserve to be remembered.

In the process of publishing *An Honorable German*, many people put their mark on the manuscript with suggestions, corrections, edits, queries, advice, et al. However, as the author, I had the last word on all the changes, and the manuscript did not go to press until I had given my final approval. Therefore, I am solely responsible for all errors, mistakes of omission or commission, or any other inaccuracies—which is as it should be. After all, it's my name on the cover.

Writing *An Honorable German* has been a journey of its own, one that has lasted much of my adult life. Like all such journeys, it taught me lessons I never expected and took me places I never imagined.

Charles L. McCain
Washington, D.C. 2008
New Orleans, LA